dirty deeds

jamie buchanan

www.fredbird-publishing.com

Published by Fredbird Publishing

Fredbird Publishing
Suite 34, New House
67-68 Hatton Garden
London
EC1N 8JY
England

www.fredbird-publishing.com

This edition first published by Fredbird Publishing 2015

Paperback edition: ISBN 978-1-910668-00-9

Kindle edition: ISBN 978-1-910668-01-6

To my fantastic family who
have been helpful, patient and
understanding while I remained
buried in the project to the
exclusion of pretty much
everything else.

CHAPTER 1

What value do you place on chance? As far as Martin Minchin, Certified Accountant, was concerned, there was no such thing as chance. Two and two always made four, not three, not five, only four. Chance was for dreamers and lottery losers; professional accountants dealt in tangible amounts, certainties, hard facts, assets. To Martin, chance had no value.

It certainly wasn't chance that had led him up the aisle to his disastrous marriage to Beverley: it was an idiotic combination of misunderstandings. He understood exactly how it had happened and accepted that his own gullibility had contributed to one of the twentieth century's most egregious mismatches. The errors were easily identified and filed neatly in his head, readily accessible in the event of another stumble into dangerous territory.

Yet chance had now wrenched Martin from his auditor's comfort zone and plunged him into an alien world of villainy, adventure and real peril. He had done nothing – consciously at least – to influence these events. So, contrary to the principles he had held throughout his adult life, he couldn't deny that his massively changed circumstances were down to nothing more nor less than pure, outrageous luck.

And that was what convinced him that he had taken a huge leap from accountancy to an altogether higher calling: adventurer, entrepreneur, lover, father? Chancer!

~

Wednesday morning

'Socks, hmm... better get about six pairs. Pants, same.' Martin composed the list mumbling aloud, partly because he thought it might lessen the risk of his omitting something crucial and partly because there was nobody else around to hear. Since being compelled to move out of the marital home, occasions when he talked to himself had increased markedly in their frequency. More disturbingly, he had become a compulsive list maker; not just making proper, useful lists, like this shopping list, but also compiling lists in his head of anything at all, usually focused on a random subject. In alphabetical order.

Alone, Bisected, Cast-off, Divorcé-to-be, Estranged, Forlorn, Gutted... Martin Gordon Minchin, the certified accountant, was thirty-three years old and six feet six inches tall. He had become aware of his excessive height at the age of thirteen when the teasing switched emphasis from his initials ('Oi, MGM! Where's yer lion?') to his stature ('Oi, beanpole wanker! What's the weather like up there?'). To disguise his uncommon loftiness during his teens he had affected a round-shouldered stoop that became his natural stance. As a result his jackets and jumpers tended to ride up his back, exacerbating an ungainly bearing.

This Wednesday morning in May 1995, Martin was trying hard to look forward with enthusiasm, but the lack of clean socks had come as a bit of a blow. He stood, his bare feet striking a discordant note in his neat and tidy office, and gazed through the window at the High Street. Shimbley is a typical small market town in the south of England. In its centre is an imposing church of Norman origin, a timbered, sixteenth century coaching inn, a small river, various shops, a disenfranchised garage, a doctors' surgery, an estate agency, an Italian restaurant, a couple of solicitors' and accountants' practices and a takeaway food outlet named Kebabbaburger. Perhaps with the exception of Kebabbaburger the town is easy on the eye. It's an agreeable place to live and work, for those who enjoy a quiet life. And a quiet life was what Martin, Shimbley's tallest accountancy professional, was enjoying. Or, more accurately, would be, as soon as he moved into the cottage he was buying in a neighbouring village. In the meantime he was sleeping at his office; or rather trying to but, as it occupied two-and-a-bit first floor rooms over Kebabbaburger, it failed to provide any peace at all between the hours of noon and midnight.

The question exercising Martin right now was whether retrieving a previous day's socks from one of the plastic carriers that now served as his 'smelly bags' would be a bigger social gaffe than going out correctly dressed but sockless. The latter might be interpreted as worse than eccentric by Shimbley's conservative citizens, many of whom were his clients. On the other hand, he did like to maintain certain standards, despite the shortcomings of his temporary accommodation. He was due to see his solicitor and, on the basis that he would have to walk there completely naked in order to compete in the eccentricity stakes with the town's senior lawyer, he decided that sockless but sweet-smelling was the way to go.

Ten minutes later, Martin sat in the ancient and heavily beamed front office of Filkington Parver Thrupp, Solicitors and Commissioners of Oaths, sipping from a cup of tea and making pleasant small talk with the solicitor's faithful assistant, Dora Simkins. Mrs Simkins, a septuagenarian widow, was receptionist, bookkeeper, secretary, tea lady and, since the death of Freddie Filkington some fifteen years ago, sole colleague of Peter Parver-Thrupp. Employed by the practice since the mid-sixties, she had been responsible for its efficient running ever since, a role that was vital in balancing the surviving partner's notorious vagueness.

'I'm so sorry, Mr Minchin. Mr Parver-Thrupp must have been delayed. I did remind him of your appointment so I'm sure he'll be here any minute.' She smiled apologetically at him and gave a slight shrug of her shoulders to suggest that she knew that he knew that Petey P-T, as he was known behind his back, could be absolutely anywhere, following an agenda entirely his own.

'Please don't worry, Mrs Simkins. I've nothing on this morning.' Martin noticed her looking at his feet and toyed with the idea of explaining why nothing covered the bare flesh between his black leather lace-ups and the hems of his trousers. He was about to utter when a twenty year old Mercedes-Benz saloon wheezed its way into the cobbled yard outside, its matted, dusty bodywork bouncing rather too freely on well-worn suspension. Martin watched its arrival through a tiny casement window, which had been forced open, sweeping to one side the ivy that normally obscured the view. The car door's hinges emitted a distressed groan and a hand stubbed out the damp remains of a thin hand-rolled cigarette on the sill. Petey P-T swung a leg out of the car, his lurid yellow and green trainer providing a startling contrast to the rest of his ensemble of rumpled corduroy and tweed.

Petey P-T was sixty-three but looked ten years older. His thick, grey hair had grown beyond his collar, more by accident than design, and was matched by generous eyebrows that sprang out in every direction, as though an explosion had occurred in the middle of each. His face was puffy, florid and inclined to wear an expression of puzzlement. With a deep sigh he swung the door shut and entered the small office that bore his and his late partner's names.

'Morning Dora, anything new? Car problem. Wouldn't start again. What d'you reckon, eh? Damn mice in the loom. Tcha! Going to have to use poison. Too small to shoot. What's the matter?' He followed her gaze across the room to where Martin was now standing, the low ceiling forcing him to adopt an even more pronounced crouch than usual. He frowned, then smiled.

'Martin, dear boy. Young Mr Minchin! What brings you here?'

'We are assisting with Mr Minchin's house purchase,' Dora prompted, rather frostily.

'Ah, yes!' Enlightenment lifted Petey P-T's face into a jovial grin. 'Come, come, come.' He beckoned Martin to follow him through a door bearing the nameplate F.J.J.Filkington. It led into a large, dark, stuffy room in which every surface – tables, chairs, a leather covered chesterfield and most of the floor – was littered with heaps of papers and files, many tied with thin red ribbon. The nicotine yellow plaster between the black beams hadn't been touched by a paint brush for decades. 'Do sit, won't you', he said as he made his way carefully to the other side of a massive oak table that served as his desk. Martin looked around and spotted an insubstantial antique dining chair, which had only one file on it. He picked the file up and lowered himself onto the seat.

'How's your father?' Petey P-T turned to face Martin. 'No! Don't sit on that!'

Martin sprang to his feet, driving the top of his skull hard into an unyielding beam with a loud thud. Crashing back down, he just managed to make eye contact with Petey P-T before the chair collapsed underneath him with a crack like a gunshot.

'Ooh! Ow! Oh, good grief, sorry about your chair.' Martin scrambled upright again, rubbing the buttock which had taken the brunt of his fall and casting a wary eye at the ceiling. 'Father's fine. Well, he's in hospital actually, in Norwich. Waterworks. How are you? Wow. Took a bit of a biff there. I really am sorry about the chair; I'm afraid it looks like a write-off.'

He gently shook his head from side to side, winced, then fingered the top of it where a swelling lump was already making itself felt, cartoon-like, under his fine, sandy hair.

'Oh dear. What a shambles.'

'Don't worry about it, you poor chap. Tried to warn you – it was a bit dicky. Plenty more chairs. Hope you're not concussed; it was a mighty blow, that. Needed some kindling anyway.'

'Well you'll certainly be able to light a few fires with that,' said Martin, nodding towards the pile of broken wood. 'I think I'll live.' He looked for an alternative perch; Petey P-T pointed at a stronger looking carver.

'Tip all that stuff on the floor. That's the way. Surprised you don't wear a helmet; head needs all the protection it can get at that altitude. Hope you weren't waiting too long. Mrs Simkins fusses so. Makes bloody awful tea. Bags. Never get the proper taste. Cigarette? Damn newsagent's been taken over by some life-sucking conglomerate. Used to sell what you wanted. Now lucky to find papers anywhere. It's not what I call progress.'

Martin squinted through a dirt encrusted window at a pigeon sitting on a fence and tried to ignore the throbbing pain in his head. He had embarked on another mental list, starting once more at A. Advocate, Beam, Crushed skull, Daily Telegraph. Papers? He recalled buying The Times without difficulty less than three hours earlier.

'I thought Top News was something of an improvement; they seem to have most titles...'

'I mean cigarette papers. Ask for them now and they think you're a bloody hippy.' Petey P-T leaned back in his chair and concentrated on constructing a miserly smoke. 'Tried cannabis once. Niece grew some. Had a session with her university chums. Didn't do a thing for me but it got the others giggling. I'll stick to claret. Know where you are with claret. Until half way through the second bottle. Your parents alright then? Except your father? Remind me where they're living now.'

'Malding Castle; it's a little village on the Norfolk Broads. They've got a bungalow with estuary views.'

'Sounds delightful. And how is the divine Mrs Minchin?'

Martin sat up and stared at Petey P-T. Divine?

'Er, mum's fine.'

'No, I mean good! Yes, splendid. I mean young Mrs Minchin, your lovely wi... your ex, er, Beverley.'

Beverley! For Martin, the very name had an awful, lurking menace, which made his spirits nosedive. The merest thought of her was guaranteed to plunge him into a deep gloom, no matter how good his prevailing mood. It stirred up in him the same sort of unease that an impoverished pensioner might feel at the sight of an electricity bill dropping onto the doormat.

Beverley was the overindulged only child of Frank Waverley, a surprisingly wealthy councillor from Yorkshire who had taken sudden and early retirement and moved south to Shimbley, following the collapse of a police investigation into town hall corruption. His personal mantra was If You Want It Badly Enough Beat All The Other Buggers To It, and he rarely missed an opportunity to boast of its efficacy. His daughter had been an early convert to this philosophy and had spent most of her life beating all the other buggers to a succession of expensive toys of which she quickly tired: dolls' house, Wendy house, kitten, puppy, pony, pretty cars and a time-share in the Caribbean. Tall, with a thick mane of fiery red hair, Beverley was a striking young woman with undeniable sex appeal. She carried herself with an aristocratic authority and was used to commanding the complete attention of anyone within shouting distance. When she arrived at the mistaken understanding that Martin was heir to a vast Scottish estate, she dispensed with her then current boyfriend with an award-worthy display of anguish and set about her acquisition of Martin with the subtlety of a heat-seeking missile.

Being on the receiving end of more-than-friendly overtures had been quite a novelty for Martin, particularly when the pursuer was a handsome and well-to-do woman whose usual partners were dashing young men who made the Friday evening trip from London to Shimbley in Porsches. It wasn't that Martin was unattractive; on the contrary, he was bright, personable, had a lively sense of humour and a gift for listening. His height had done him few favours when it came to romance, and he had tended to date similarly lanky girls. Since immoderate length was the only thing he had in common with most of them, the relationships had been short-lived. There had been one exception, a girlfriend with whom he had drifted in and out of love for eight years from his late teens. There had been a special bond between them that allowed their close friendship to endure, even during periods when they were seeing others. She finally found a soul mate, a poet from Amsterdam, and Martin had attended their joyous and predictably unconventional wedding. The newlyweds left to try their luck in Australia where they hitched a ride with a psychopath who murdered them. It was a shocking way for such gentle lives to end and Martin still missed her. His grief, however, had been offset by the attention he began to receive from Beverley. When he accepted her proposal of marriage, he was flattered, proud and ecstatically happy. He had even been amused that she styled herself Beverley Minchin-Waverley so that she could brandish one of her favourite initialisms. 'You'll never get a better ride my love,' she had promised.

After barely two years of wedded togetherness, with her Scottish home just a castle in the air and wearied by girlfriends teasing her about her sky-scraping accountant, disillusioned Beverley met a married property developer with a convertible Mercedes and an unsatisfied libido. From that moment her adoring husband was superfluous and under her feet. Beverley and her new beau needed privacy for their trysts, so she made the unilateral decision that Martin should quit the marital home with all possible speed. 'Time waits for no man,' she said to him, 'and nor will I, so I'd much appreciate it if you pissed off sooner rather than later, alright?'

It was entirely pointless to argue with Beverley. She would keep their house on Shimbley's outskirts and its principal contents, in return for which Martin would receive just sufficient cash for a deposit on a modest home and have the burden of alimony waived. After briefly flirting with and rejecting the idea of fighting her over the house, he caved in to her wishes.

'You really are pathetic, Martin,' Beverley pointed out after he had put his signature to the Deed of Separation. 'You'll never beat the other buggers to anything.'

~

'Please ignore me.' Martin's solicitor was embarrassed to have so carelessly raised a subject that clearly still pained his client. 'I'm becoming ever more stupid. Now then, about this house of yours. I've got the file here somewhere.'

Petey P-T was pushing various folders around his table as if shuffling dominos. Ash fell from the home-made cigarette drooping from the corner of his mouth and scattered in all directions. Martin leaned back, away from the table. He had never smoked and was always haunted by the lingering smell for hours after being in contact with tobacco and its by-products. A speck launched itself and Martin's eyes followed its teasing flight path this way and that until it crash-landed in his crotch. He weighed up the pros and cons of brushing it off. He didn't want Petey P-T to notice, in case it made him feel awkward for contaminating him. Petey P-T, however, now had his head under the table as he went through piles of paper on the floor. Martin swiped at the ash, smearing it into a grey splodge by his fly, and he set about rubbing it away.

'You'll be looking for this, Mr P.' Dora Simkins had materialised in the room and was holding out a folder. Her gaze, from under a slightly raised eyebrow, travelled from Martin's trouser cleaning efforts to his eyes and thence to the pile of broken wood on the floor. Martin felt himself blushing, prompting a continuation of the list in his head: Embarrassment, Fag ash, Gutted again.

'Thank you Dora. Thought you must have it. Know where everything belongs y'know. That's what matters.'

'Yes, Mr P.' Dora left the room as softly as she had entered.

'Right, let's see now, young man, here we are. Lockkeeper's Cottage, Shimbley Lane, West Vereham, Shimbley. No problems there – unless the Shimbley bypass goes through the kitchen of course. Wouldn't be surprised. Planners are idiots. All of them. Well, all seems to be in order.'

'I take it the bypass was a joke?'

'Bound to be. Aren't they all? Designed to free up traffic; just increase it, apparently. Oh, I see! Yes, take no notice. Talk first, think later – if I think at all! Mrs Simkins will tell you. No, you've nothing to fear – unless the ceilings are as low as this one! So, you're moving in on Friday.'

'Yes, at last. I've managed to organise a week off, so that should give me time to sort everything, get furniture and so forth.'

'Good! Well, I wish you well. I expect you could do with things going your way, eh?'

~

With his head and bottom both still feeling sore, Martin strolled back up the High Street towards its younger end where Minchin Associates resided. He had chosen a plural trading style to give the impression that his was a larger accountancy firm than the average one-man-band, but the fact that it was always he who answered the telephone rather gave the game away, not that it seemed to matter. His clients were mostly self-employed people and proprietors of small businesses and, while they were unlikely to make him his fortune, they enabled him to pay his bills on time and stay in the black, about which he was fastidious. His shoes feeling strange around his bare feet, he acknowledged to himself that Friday's move into Lockkeeper's Cottage couldn't come too soon. In the meantime, it was after midday and he needed something to eat. A doner kebab was too often the convenient thing to choose and he pushed open the door into the little shop beneath his office.

'Eh, Martin, 'ow you doin' up there?' Mehmet was Kebabbaburger's Turkish owner and chef. He had a wiry build, mischievous eyes and a highly belligerent attitude towards anything resembling authority, despite which, or maybe because of which, he made a very good living.

'Hello Mehmet.'

'You wanna doner?'

'Yes, I wanna doner. Plus ça change.'

'Eh?'

'How are you doing, Mehmet? Pretty well I think.'

'No way, Martin. I got trouble. Not your size trouble, ha ha, sleepin' 'ere. No, your majesty custom, 'e say I don't get back no V-A-bloody-T on petrol, on air fare, on the bloody shoppin' up Tesco. I tell 'im to go look up 'is books but 'e slap on the final demand an' say about penalty fines. I say I pay my national an' my bloody Tory tax on airports an' all but 'e not listen. 'Ow much you put 'im in 'is place? You wanna hot sauce?'

'I'm sorry, I can't. And no, mild, please. You've got to pay taxes like everyone else. What does your accountant say?'

''e say the same but I gonna fire 'im.'

'Don't shoot the messenger, Mehmet.'

'No, I only gonna fire 'im.'

'You know you can't beat the system. Death and taxes and all that.'

'Yeah, death to taxes an' the bloody system, that's what I say! You got no ambition!'

'You're sounding like my wife.'

'Oh no, not The Bimmer, dammit! I shut up now. That's two sixty-five. For you, two sixty.'

'You're all heart, Mehmet. It was two fifty-five yesterday.'

'You never 'ear of inflation, Martin? And you doin' bloody accounts an' all. Ha! Anyway, The Bimmer, she was lookin' for you earlier. You not bin upsettin' the ol' missis again?'

'Oh, probably; it's easily done. See you.' Martin trudged up the stairs with the ominous Beverley cloud once more hovering over his head. For someone who wanted him out of her life she had a funny way of leaving him alone. He unlocked the door and entered his office. There was a main room with three other doors leading off, one into a smaller room that he used for storage and sleeping, one into a tiny kitchen area and one into an even tinier lavatory. Martin's desk was arranged so that he sat with his back to the large window that overlooked the High Street, even though the resultant reflections made it difficult to read his PC's screen much of the time. He pulled a discarded newspaper out of the waste bin, put it on his desk as a mat and placed the paper bag containing his lunch on it. While he had been out, the fax machine in the corner had spewed a message onto the floor. He picked it up; it read: 'URGENT! To: Mr. M. G. Minchin. From: Mr. S. Essex. Re: Business Opportunity. I am travelling to Shimbley on Thursday morning and will call at your office to discuss a business opportunity. Please ensure that you are available.' Martin sniffed, scratched the back of his neck, frowned and read it again, stroking the lump on the top of his head. A little mysterious, he thought, pressing the messages button on the answering machine:

'Mithter Minchin, my name ith Ethicth,' lisped a man with a nasal, slightly high-pitched tone. 'I'm going to offer you a very lucrative deal. I'll call by your offith tomorrow morning. Thee you then.'

'Well, Mithter Ethicth,' Martin mocked aloud, 'that might not be convenient.' He erased the message, sat down and launched the diary on his PC, shifting his seat and cocking his head to make it easier to read the display. Everything was organised: closed for business from tomorrow, Thursday, evening until Friday morning next week, and he had all of what should be a quiet day tomorrow to prepare what he needed to take from the office. There was no reason why he couldn't give Mr Essex some of his time; it looked as though he would have plenty to spare. He turned his attention to his kebab. S for snake – a cousin had once kept a pet snake called Silas. Could be S for Slug, Terrible, Unctuous, Vile, Wretched. He ground to a halt, knowing that X would defeat him, as it always did. He had no idea why he had taken off along the 'slug' route while contemplating Mehmet's kebab. To be fair, whatever they contained, they were delicious and had yet to cause him any regret. It was clearly the fault of Eth Ethicth, whatever the Eth thtood for.

It was a curious name, Lockkeeper's Cottage, since there was no river, no canal and no lock anywhere in the vicinity. Martin had made one or two enquiries of long-standing local people but was no wiser. Petey P-T had suggested that it was named by a retired lock keeper for old times' sake, which seemed, in the absence of any other, to be a reasonable theory. The only hint of water of any kind was in the back garden, in the form of a 'wishing well', which Martin assumed was an ornate invention of relatively recent years, installed by an occupier with an unfortunate taste for quaintness. The cottage dated back in part to the eighteenth century; countless owners had created a mongrel that was not without charm, but unlikely to make the cover of a style magazine. It was presently owned by a bank which had repossessed it from some poor unfortunates who were victims of wider economic difficulties. The location was perfect for those who preferred their own company, in that it was on an unclassified road and separated from its neighbours on either side by fields. The bank was looking for a quick sale and had accepted Martin's first offer with alacrity.

'Oh God! You're not really going to put one of that greasy little man's things in your mouth, are you? You have no idea what he puts in them.' Beverley wasn't a kebab type of person. She was impeccably turned out in a green suit, sufficiently chic for a lunch with royalty. He had noticed her recent tendency always to be dressed as if for a formal engagement and wondered what she was up to. It was out of the question that she had landed a job: Beverley didn't do jobs. Perhaps she was angling for a mate even more moneyed than the property developer. Back to S: Smug, Snooty, Supercilious.

'Why don't you come in, Beverley? Off to a wedding?'

'Sarcasm is so lame, Martin.' Sarcasm? Strumpet! She stooped over his desk and picked up the fax message. 'Well, well, new business. Who's S. Essex? Anyway, about your clothes, Martin.' He instinctively looked down at his apparel and anticipated a comment about his lack of socks. 'I need more space.' She took a clean mug from a shelf and helped herself to coffee from the filter machine on top of a filing cabinet. 'Ugh! Do you really drink this? Your habits are repellent.' She poured the contents of the mug into a pot occupied by a cactus.

'I've no idea who S. Essex is. And that was yesterday's coffee to which you're quite welcome. I'm moving into my new home the day after tomorrow and I'll fetch the rest of my things at the weekend. I'm sure that your eight-square-metre, walk-in wardrobe will suffice until then.' He muttered this last bit through clenched teeth to no one in particular.

'What? Well it really isn't good enough, Martin. Try to improve on that – I don't want to have to mention it again. Oh, and the car must need a service or something because it keeps belching. I'll have the garage liaise with you about it, okay? Just look at this poxy little place; no wonder you don't have any decent clients. You really ought to get your act together. Bye.'

With that she turned on her statuesque, black stiletto heel and swept out as imperiously as she had entered, once more leaving him reviewing in his head what would have been stingingly appropriate last words. The car, a two-year-old BMW 325i, had been a gift from him to her and certainly shouldn't be belching or doing anything else untoward. She had probably put diesel into it, perhaps in an act of deliberate sabotage because she no longer liked the colour. Whatever, he had no intention of digging into his fast-diminishing funds to put that right.

Trying to rid his head of Beverley, he began to wonder who S. Essex was and what his 'lucrative deal' could be. Neither the fax nor the telephone message left any clues as to his location or how to contact him, not that Martin was keen on being approached in quite such a presumptuous manner by a prospective client or, more likely, a salesman in disguise. One of the things that infuriated Beverley was Martin's tendency to look on this sort of introduction as spurious instead of potentially profitable. While she would waste no time in beating all the buggers to it, he didn't really want anything to do with the buggers in the first place. Not for the first time, he felt resentment at her ability to insinuate herself into his thoughts, like some irresistible, malevolent force. The telephone rescued him from further introspection. 'Minchin Associates, Martin Minchin speaking.'

'Hello, Mr Minchin, it's Dora Simkins here calling on behalf of Mr Parver-Thrupp, just to confirm that we've spoken to the vendor's agent and you may collect the key from us at any time after nine thirty on Friday morning.'

'Oh, thanks very much Mrs Simkins. I'll see you on Friday, then.' He replaced the receiver and stared out of the window at people on the move. The usual mixture of traffic was stop-starting its way in both directions, most of it local citizens in four-wheel-drive vehicles investing fifteen minutes and half a gallon of fuel looking for the free space that would save them twenty pence and a five hundred yard walk from the pay-and-display car park. Most of them probably lived within a mile of the High Street. The sky was littered with vapour trails from airliners carrying passengers on longer journeys. A mixed group of kids, aged around twelve and shrieking with exaggerated laughter as they skived off school, did their best to look cool while breaking every rule in the Green Cross Code to get from Top News to Kebabbaburger. Some of them smoked cigarettes with theatrical ostentation. An unseen fan of techno music was driving somewhere nearby, the boom-boomticka-boom almost shaking the building. Martin stared at the sky and tried to remember which letter he had reached.

'Aeroplane,' he said, turning and sitting back at his desk. He opened up a computing magazine that had arrived, uninvited, in his mail. A CD fell from it into his lap. Aeroplane, Bumf, CD – that was clever: two for the price of one. He had a look at the free delights advertised on it and fed it into the front of his PC. A message came up on his screen, Welcome to BizROM 2.6. This CD-ROM has been tested for all known viruses but the publishers accept no liability for any loss or damage caused through or by its use. See the text file README on the root directory for full Conditions. Proceed entirely AT YOUR OWN RISK. Click OK for main menu or EXIT to exit. Escape clause, Fatuous, Garbage.

A dyed in the wool belt-and-braces man, Martin used both of the antivirus programs to which he subscribed to give the disk a third-degree interrogation. Satisfied that it wasn't going to pass to his hard drive a digital black death, he studied the contents and installed a graphics demonstration program named Kwik-Az-A-Krayon. He started it up and, faced with a blank drawing board, typed LOCKKEEPER'S COTTAGE. Aside from dealing with a few telephone calls of little importance, he spent most of the afternoon experimenting, putting the name into rustic looking typefaces and adding pretty borders. Finally satisfied with a version, he sat back, admiring his artwork. Attractive, Bold, Creative. He printed two copies, then carefully extracted every trace of Kwik-Az-A-Krayon from his machine, just in case it decided to assault his data when his back was turned. He began to feel really quite positive about the next phase of his life.

~

He locked the door into the office, went into the smaller room and removed his tie, shoes and the plain grey suit that he always wore on 'non-client' days. He carefully hung it up on the back of the door and pulled on some jeans, a jumper and a pair of trainers, which felt rather more natural on his bare feet. Returning to the main office, he switched on the answering machine, picked up his old transistor radio and the latest issue of Accountancy Age and retired into the lavatory. Ten minutes later, bladder and bowel emptied, hands washed, hair combed and lavatory bowl bleached, he was ready to face the evening. Of course, normally at this stage, he would be preparing to go home. Since, until Friday, this was his home, he had to come up with some other way to fill the time before dinner. He put on an old jacket, picked up his computerised sketch, folded it carefully, slipped it into an inside pocket and left, double locking the door behind him.

It was a warm, dry evening, an early treat of summery weather. As he stepped out onto the pavement, Mehmet's little shop was busy with customers picking up a lazy tea on their way home. Instead of heading down the High Street, he walked in the opposite direction, away from the town centre, then down a narrow footpath. The path ran between the end of a terrace of cottages and the back wall of a disused warehouse that occupied one side of the old cattle market, in which livestock was only a memory after the plethora of food scares in recent years. The alley soon opened out into a haven of well-kept public gardens running alongside the river. A young couple encouraged their two toddlers to throw bread to the excited ducks which were crowding at the low bank, bobbing up and down like the front rows at a rock concert. A pair of swans moved smoothly in and out of the group, claiming more than their fair share of the manna with effortless superiority. On the opposite side was the Shimbley Reaches Nursing Home, a rather austere looking Victorian building in a perfect setting, its close-cropped lawns sloping gently down to the water. Sadly, the owners had been obliged to erect a sturdy fence after one of their elderly charges had lost control of his wheelchair and sped to a watery end. The tragedy occurred on a slow news day and gave Shimbley at least fifteen minutes of fame in the national press.

Another aeroplane, Bread, Child, Duck, Evergreen, Fir tree, Grass. Martin followed the riverside path to the point just outside the town where it met the railway line. Steps led up the bank and a footbridge took him over the tracks to the main road. He walked back towards the town and into the open-air, long-stay car park. It was still early so he decided to drive out to West Vereham for another quick peek at the cottage.

Martin's Alfa Romeo, or, more correctly, Alfasud, which he had christened Alfredo, enjoyed a level of loyalty from its owner that was probably greater than it deserved. The 'sud' part of the name was important, because it signified that the car had not been lovingly created by proud Milanese artisans in Italy's northern industrial heartland; it had been thrown together in Naples by an unmotivated, untrained and underpaid workforce. In addition, the inhabitants of Italy's shin enjoyed a fine, dry climate and had few cares about what the rest of Europe's weather could do to unprotected, low grade steel. Alfasuds, therefore, were now something of a rarity in Britain but, unfortunately for their owners, no more valuable for that. Each annual MOT inspection became more nerve-racking than the last, not least because Alfredo shed bits of bodywork faster than a moulting dog. The accountant's knack of seeking out a tax-efficient little engine ensured that Martin achieved hair-raising fuel consumption, wringing every last ounce of power out of it to make any headway at all. The only hint of the great Latin passion for dramatic, blood red, blindingly quick cars was this Alfasud's strident note, the result of a failing exhaust system.

Martin fiddled around with various keys, trying to open the driver's door and starting, as he always did at this stage, back at A: Alfredo, Bella, C'mon baby. Replacement parts had left him with different keys for each door, the boot, the petrol cap and the ignition, on top of which each lock had its idiosyncrasies. Once in, it took half a minute of churning the starter motor, with the battery becoming weaker and weaker, to coax the little engine into life. Damn well start today you lump of Effluent, Forza, Geriatric Heap of Italian Junk. He gave up at the usual place, this having become almost a religious chant rather than a sincere attempt to reach the middle of the alphabet. At last, two cylinders, then another and, finally, all four burst into song with a spectacular show of oily smoke from the back of the car. As dusk was approaching, he twisted the knob to turn the lights on and it came away in his fingers. Knob. He put it in the ashtray with the other knobs and unidentified bits of plastic and selected a cassette tape from the glove box. He pushed it into the player which promptly disappeared from sight into the dashboard. 'Oh bugger,' he said, indicating right and unknowingly extinguishing his headlights. He pulled out onto the road that led from Shimbley to the Verehams.

On the grass verge in front of Lockkeeper's Cottage, the agent's board had a big 'SOLD' patch pasted onto it. Martin was going to have to hire a skip to remove all the rubbish – the garden had run riot, there were sundry building materials lying around and a rusty old electric cooker blocked the rudimentary drive. He heaved the cooker to one side and brought his car in off the road. A bit of spadework and pruning would soon allow vehicular access to the whole quarter-acre garden. I could build a garage for Alfredo, thought Martin, or dig a bloody great hole. The house appeared to be secure. Peering in through the windows, he could see that the ground floor had been left reasonably tidy, though he knew that he would have to tackle considerable redecorating throughout. He looked around at the garden and imagined lazy afternoons with Earl Grey tea in bone china cups, crustless sandwiches filled with cucumber and smoked salmon and the gentle thwack of a croquet mallet on a wooden ball. He smiled as he remembered that the last time he had played croquet was at university, an occasion which involved strong cider, chocolate biscuits and the distant clunk of a croquet mallet's detached head landing on the roof of a passing car.

He picked his way through some rampant roses to reach the 'well'. For an ornamental structure it had certainly been designed and constructed on a formidable scale: it had a retaining wall about three feet high and four feet or more in diameter, made of the same attractive stone from which many of the older houses were built locally. This was overshadowed by a pitched slate roof supported by two sturdy oak beams that were planted in concrete outside the wall. Between the beams was a winding mechanism with a length of thick rope coiled around it. Some chicken wire had been secured loosely over the well's opening through which the end of the rope descended. Slightly unsettled by its slimy touch, Martin pulled the rope up to find, instead of a bucket, just a frayed end. He didn't suppose that whoever had installed this folly had bothered to dig very deep; perhaps just ten feet or so, for the effect. The agent's description of the property had scrupulously pointed out that this was a decorative, not functional, feature.

As he climbed back into his car, the sun had gone down, leaving a thin line of red on the horizon under a sky that was turning from rich blue to navy. He started the engine and twisted the knobless shaft that operated the lights; his view remained unlit.

He twisted the shaft back and forth but the headlights refused to work. He stepped out and inspected both ends of the car; the side and taillights were working, but that was all. He returned to his seat and stared blankly through the windscreen for a half minute or so. It wasn't actually dark yet and it was only a few miles along quiet back roads to street lit sanctuary in Shimbley. 'To hell with it', he muttered and nosed the car through the gap in the hedge. He indicated left and the trees opposite were suddenly bathed in light. 'You're not for the crusher yet, then, 'Fredo,' he said, accelerating down the road with his reversing light shining brightly behind him.

~

Every market town in England has a George and Dragon – or King's Head, or Coach and Horses, or Red Lion. Shimbley's George and Dragon looked like a typical coaching inn which had enjoyed better times but had adapted to survive the rigours of boom and bust economics and the shifting sands of public tolerance of drinking, smoking, driving and lunching. It was certainly quaint, with plenty of exposed timbers, nooks and crannies, enormous fireplaces, crooked doors and windows with leaded lights. The bar, which dominated the lounge, was hung with pewter tankards, but that was where the stereotypical decor ended. Instead of pictures of hunting scenes or reproduction Speede maps or grainy group photographs of world war two airfield personnel, the walls were adorned unashamedly with illustrations from the landlord's life: a photograph of him aged three months, naked but for a bonnet and happily eating sand on a beach; a vast and rather frightening Victorian portrait of a stern great-great-grandfather; a set of psychedelic posters of the Beatles; several cuttings from local newspapers recording the triumphs of his daughters at gymkhanas and school stage productions; a complete set of Ten Years After gatefold album covers. Near the bar was a sizeable reproduction of a Breugel village scene, ornately framed and protected by glass. A felt-tip pen with water-based black ink made its home in the filigree of the gilt surround, a device to ensure that graffiti was applied where it could be monitored and removed with ease whenever necessary. On this day, the Flemish master's peasants were sporting improbably large codpieces while what might have been a 747 cruised across the sixteenth century sky; on the horizon a giant M looped its way across the vista, requiring three hills to support its overbearing corporate message.

The bar snack menu also held surprises at first glance: 'Shamblé', 'George's Dragon', 'Footloose', 'Fungicide' and 'Shimblaholic'. Regulations required the provision of accurate descriptions which were, respectively: ham-flecked cheese soufflé, chicken ('well it must have been'), pigs' trotters, an exotic, vegetarian-safe cocktail of wild mushrooms and, for pudding, crêpes drowned in extremely high-proof vodka.

'Evening, Martin. Can you hear me all the way up there? I said can you...' Kevin, the landlord's son-in-law, was manning the bar as usual. He was a bouncy, thirty-year old West Midlander, whose thick spectacles made his eyes look much too large for the rest of his cheery, moon-shaped face. Susan, his wife, was the elder of two sisters and managed the business, leaving her father, John Richards, to the cooking and Kevin to bar work and general skivvying which he tackled with unflinching and selfless enthusiasm. 'It comes to something when you money men have to slum it in a place like this.'

'Ha! Money man I'm not. On the contrary, I think I'm about to take on a bottomless pit, not to mention the well. I'll have a pint, please Kevin. And have something yourself.'

'Thanks very much, I'll have a half with you. Cheers.' Kevin hauled on the lever to splosh a local brewery's bitter into two glasses. 'So, what's this house like? Need a bit doing to it, does it?'

'More than a bit, I fear. Cheers.'

'You should have one of those paint parties. You know, lay on a bit of grub and everyone turns up with a brush and a can of vinyl silk emulsion. No guarantee that you get a sophisticated colour scheme, of course, but one man's mess is another man's Picasso.'

'Well, thanks very much for the offer, but I'm not at all sure I can live with cubist decor. I'll have to give it some thought. What's cooking tonight?' Martin had picked up the bar menu and was looking at a blackboard behind Kevin on which was chalked TODAYS SPECIALS, but was otherwise blank.

'No specials, I'm afraid. Molly turned up this afternoon and the guvnor's been too busy nattering to do any cooking. Stick to the frozen microwavables if I was you. Oh, hullo, gorgeous. I was just telling Martin how you've fouled up the catering tonight.' Kevin directed this to a petite woman approaching the bar. She was in her mid-twenties, with short blonde hair and a bright smile. Molly Richards was Susan's younger sister. Single, she lived, during term-time, in a flat in Exeter where she was a junior lecturer in History at the university, but her heart remained in Shimbley. She came home to the George and Dragon as often as her work allowed, to distract her father from his kitchen duties, coo over Kevin and Susan's toddler, Art, and lend some help. The main reason for her visits, however, was to ride the gallops and bridleways on Henry, her beloved hunter which she kept in stables a couple of miles from Lockkeeper's Cottage.

'Hello, Martin. How are you? Give us a kiss, then.' She craned her neck and Martin bent down to facilitate the exchange of pecks. 'My God, do you need extra oxygen up there?' Martin had heard it countless times before but he rewarded Molly with a laugh because her bubbly manner was infectious.

'Hi, Molly. How long are you up for? What are you drinking?'

'Oh, a G and T, please – thank you. I've got to go back on Friday morning for the weekend unfortunately, but I'm coming back on Sunday night or Monday morning for a few days. Get in a bit of quality time with Henry. And this lot, of course. But mostly Henry. Cheers. Anyway, how are you? I gather that cow's had you sleeping in your office, for God's sake! Sorry, I shouldn't call her that. But really!'

'Oh, it's okay. I'm moving into my cottage on Friday, so I can get myself sorted out. Have a bath, that sort of thing, ha ha. Actually, people have been really great; I could get away without a home for years. Mind you, I'm looking forward to cooking for myself again.'

'Well, no need tonight and, since I've messed up here and got some winnings from this afternoon's two-fifteen at Uttoxeter, I'm taking you out. Fancy dinner at Angelo's?'

'Gosh, well, there's no need for that. In any case, you probably want to spend the evening with your nearest and dearest...'

'What, Henry? Nah! He doesn't like pasta. No, dad reckons he's going down with the lurgy so he's taking Casablanca and a hot toddy upstairs for an early night, and Sue's got her head stuck in the books. Come on; I fancy some decent food and it's definitely my treat.'

'Well, it'll make a change from kebabs, but only if I buy the drinks.'

'Only if it's a decent Chianti.'

'Right, you're on,' said Martin, draining his glass.

'It's brilliant, isn't it?' asked Kevin of no one in particular. 'Just when you've got a starving customer lined up, ready to ply us with tips and free drinks, along comes a little blonde spanner in the works. Why don't you steal a few others? Hey, folks, it's spaghetti tonight and Moll's in the chair. Quick now! Last one out of here's a sissy!'

'They'd much rather stay here with you, Kev. Be good.'

Martin and Molly left the George and Dragon and crossed the High Street, their height differential making them look from a distance like adult and child.

'You've still got that bloody awful car, then,'

'What, do you mean faithful little Alfredo?' asked Martin.

'Yes. I saw you going through earlier this evening. Your, I mean Alfredo's reversing light was on.'

'He's Italian; he was designed like that,' explained Martin. 'It's in case you need to go backwards in a hurry.'

'Talking of Italian,' she responded, 'I'm famished. I know exactly what I want: that bunny they do, boiled up in Frascati with walnuts. God, I hope they've got some in.'

'How could you? Poor little bunnies.'

'With ease as it happens.'

'Hmm.' Martin had never known Molly to display any soppiness, except perhaps about Henry the horse.

Angelo's was an intimate restaurant that provided crowded eating conditions for a maximum of thirty. The service was cheerful, the food reliable and the prices reasonable. This prosaic formula was ideal for Shimbley and had enabled the restaurant to survive roller-coaster economics for well over two decades; now it played host to customers whose first visits had been as children.

The waiter sat them at a table in the bay window that looked out onto the best part of Shimbley. Here the street was bordered by wide, grassed verges, sheltered by the branches of horse chestnut trees. With the shops shut, the road was considerably quieter than it was during the day. Most of the passing traffic was now caused by the town's youths cruising around, being seen and going nowhere.

'I'm sorry I had a go about Beverley earlier,' said Molly, tucking into a bread roll. 'I never did like her but I suppose you must have loved her. They say at the stables that her pony was terribly neglected. People like her shouldn't be allowed to keep animals. The law should come down hard on them.'

'Ah, yes. A turkey is for Christmas – not just for life. All that sort of thing.'

'Don't take the piss, I mean it. Anyway, she hasn't treated you too well, either, has she?'

'No. I think I was a bit of a red herring for Beverley. And now she's thrown me back.'

'Is it true? That she thought you were some sort of millionaire or something?'

'Er, yes. Or something, I suppose.'

'Oh, go on, tell me about it.'

As they tucked into their dinner Martin recalled the misunderstanding that, unbeknown to him at the time, had led to his whirlwind engagement, marriage and separation.

'It started on one of those lazy, drunken, pubby days around Christmas four years ago. At your dad's, as I recall, as well as one or two other places. I don't think you were around for some reason.'

'Oh, that was probably the year I went skiing with that creep, Reggie Beam. Ugh.'

'Ah. Anyway, an old friend of mine, Donut Dave, was...'

'Doughnut Dave! Why Doughnut Dave?'

'Ha ha, two reasons: first, we used to go to a lot of race meetings – cars, I mean, not horses. Anyway, we went to the cheap events, clubbies, at Thruxton, Snetterton, Silverstone and so on. The crowds were small and largely hard up, so it wasn't worth their while for big caterers to bring their gear along. The wind blows across those old Second World War airfields and flaming June can feel like a Siberian winter; everyone had runny noses, including the unlovely mobile purveyors of what could only be described as snot dogs.'

'That's disgusting!'

'Oh yes. Well, the only edible stuff on offer was from the doughnut van, and Dave just couldn't get enough of them. I can remember the woman who ran the van; she was like a female Quasimodo, yelling "*Donuss! Donuss!*" as if calling for Esmerelda.'

'Why on earth did he like doughnuts so much?'

'He's American.'

'Ah.'

'Spell it D O N U T.'

'Right ho. You said there were two reasons.'

'Yes. The second reason is that he was quite fond of doing doughnuts in his car.'

'Do what?'

'It's basically getting giddy while wearing your tyres down to the canvas, a sort of car-based version of a fighter pilot's victory roll. He thought it would pull girls.'

'Can you do it?'

'Pull girls? No.'

'I mean do these doughnuts!'

'Oh no. You need rear wheel drive and a lot of grunt for that. Dave is a bit of a show-off and likes his cars to have a lot of grunt. American you see, a good ol' boy from Georgia.' Martin slipped into his best southern drawl.

'How exotic. What was he doing here?'

'As little as possible. No, I met him at uni; he was on some kind of exchange deal, studying geology.'

'Do you still see him?'

'Not much. He's in Scotland now. He bummed around the world for a year or two. Eventually he decided he liked it here, well, the British Isles, anyway. Now he's a landscape gardener, somewhere near Inverness. I really ought to go and see him. Anyway, where was I?'

'Having a pubby day with Donut Dave.'

'Oh yes. Well, no matter how broke we were, we always, always, always did the football pools. Week in, week out. Even in the summer, when we were reduced to betting on Australian matches – you know, will Geelong draw at home against St Kilda?

'The great thing about gambling when you're stony-broke is that it gives you such a buzz of anticipation right up to the moment when the results start to come in. For six days of the week, we would plan how we would spend our winnings. We would map it all out, calculate the income from hundreds of thousands stashed away, decide what cars would be sitting in our garages, which page three models could be bought and which ones were too cerebral, which countries we should look at for a bit of property investment, what we would name our yachts. Dave's was going to be the Donut Dame, after the woman in the van. My first purchase was always going to be a castle in Scotland – nothing too fancy, you understand, just a couple of dozen rooms and a few ramparts from which to survey my land. I was going to have deerhounds, too, and a massive, nineteen-twenties, ex-maharaja Rolls Royce from which to shoot grouse and chuck a bit of largesse about while touring the estate.

'So, whenever we came across a picture of a Scottish castle – any Scottish castle – it would be "my" Scottish castle. Likewise, any bloody great gin palace would be Dave's Donut Dame. Now, on this pubby day, we picked up on the old habits as if the intervening years had never happened. There was a whole crowd of us. I vaguely knew Beverley, having seen her around. Anyway, she had sort of latched on to us and Dave was looking through an old copy of Country Life he'd found in a rack at the Rose and Crown, or whichever pub we were in. Dave holds up a picture of this lovely old pile for sale and says, "Look, Marty, it's your castle." Beverley's ears apparently pricked up and she asked Dave what he meant. "When Marty lands the big one, he's going to live here," he says. So, a bit later, when we're all sozzled, including Beverley, she sidles up to me and says, "What's all this about you going to live in a Scottish castle?" So I said, "Yeah, my name's on it. Just got to wait now." That's all there was to it; Beverley drew her own conclusions about inheritances all by herself. In fact, I'm still staggered that she could even begin to believe it. You see, she can actually be rather dim sometimes, beneath the veneer.'

'You don't say.'

'Not to mention acquisitive.'

'I think you may have been the last person to spot that, Martin.'

'Yes, well, someone might have warned me.'

'I seem to remember several people warning you.'

'Well, I put that down to jealousy – of her money or something.'

'Hmm. It was Daddy Waverley's money, and it was bent by all accounts.'

'Ssssh! If it was, and I really don't know, he's probably untouchable, so it's best to let sleeping dogs lie, eh? Anyway, you know that piece of water that lies between the Outer and Inner Hebrides?'

'No.'

'Well, it's called The Minch. Beverley obviously started to do a bit of homework on Scotland and was soon reeling at the size of the Minchin estate. She also spotted that there was a place called Minch Moor near Selkirk; that was obviously coming my way too.'

'Lovely. And I suppose that place where Princess Anne lives was your Gloucestershire pied-à-terre.'

'Minchinhampton? Ha ha, yes, exactly! Then the clincher, I later learned, was when she heard me tell someone that my parents had moved to Malding Castle.'

'Aargh!' Molly nearly choked on a piece of rabbit and sat back, trying to stop laughing long enough to have a sip of wine. 'But that doesn't even begin to sound like Minchin! And it isn't even in Scotland.'

'No, of course not. But when someone like Beverley thinks she's heard what she wants to hear, greed takes over from any inclination to double-check.'

'Oh, what a classic! She never looked it up in her atlas, then?'

'Obviously not.'

'Boy, what a div. How come it's us blondes who get lumbered with the dumb label? It certainly served her right, though, didn't it?'

'Thanks a bunch.'

'Oh, God. Sorry Martin! I didn't mean it like that.'

'It's okay, I'm over the sad and tragic phase now. Being an embarrassing thorn in Bev's side is now one of the things that perks me up whenever she's spoilt my day.'

'Dad says she's dating some married bloke, twice her age.'

'Yes, a property developer. But I think she's keeping an open mind, you know? In case someone more, er, eligible comes along.'

'Don't pussyfoot, Martin. She's a gold-digging bitch and you're well off out of it.'

Molly told Martin about her life in Exeter, about her students and her teaching colleagues and how she was lacking an intimate partner, though one or two of her colleagues had made overtures when she would much rather it had been one or two of her students. The conversation made Martin feel distinctly middle aged and marooned on the shelf, but Molly was sparkling company. They lingered over puddings, then coffee and were the last to leave.

'Let's have a nightcap at home and you can sleep in a bed tonight,' suggested Molly.

'Mmm?'

'Room four is empty and Sue says the bed's made up and you're welcome to it.'

'Oh, right. Brilliant. Thanks!'

Molly slipped her arm through Martin's as they strolled back along the deserted street.

~

'Here you go: new toothbrush, towel.' Molly made sure that Martin had everything he needed in his borrowed room back at the George and Dragon. 'I'd offer you some clean knickers for the morning but the colour probably wouldn't suit you.'

'Thanks, I've still got some supplies at the office.' Martin held her hand and met her eyes. 'Thanks, Molly, for this evening, the meal and everything.'

'It's my pleasure, Martin. I'm sure things will start looking up for you now. It's Beverley's loss, believe me. You'll find someone much nicer. You deserve it. Night-night.' She stretched up to put a hand behind his neck and placed a quick kiss on his lips, then left, pulling the door closed behind her.

~

Martin was woken by a chirpy knocking on the bedroom door. Momentarily, he wondered where he was. Sunlight streamed through a chink in the curtains, casting a dazzling stripe up the length of his bed and he squinted as his eyes became accustomed to the brightness.

'Wakey-wakey, Martin!' called a cheerful Molly, 'Rise and shine. Are you decent?'

'Yes, come in, Molly.' Martin groped for his watch on the bedside table and peered at it. It was nearly eight. Molly was wearing muddy jodhpurs, tucked into bright red woolly socks, and a T-shirt bearing the slogan, I NEED HORSE POWER – GIMME MY OATS.

'Here's some proper tea.' She placed a tray on the chest of drawers and carefully poured a cup. 'Sugar?'

'No, thanks.'

She put the cup down on the bedside table. 'Take your time. Dad's got a temperature, so I'm cooking breakfast. You might be better off with one of Mehmet's kebabs. Did you sleep okay?'

'Like a log. I think that nightcap might have had something to do with it.'

'Yes,' she laughed. 'You weren't visited by Agnes, then?'

'Who's Agnes?'

'Some girl who met a grisly end here three hundred years ago. She pops up every now and then to give our guests a fright.'

'Oh well, if she did come to say hello I'm afraid I blanked her. You off to see Henry?'

'Already seen him. We've been a good few miles this morning. He's down in the yard, having his brekker. See you in a bit, then.' Molly left Martin to his tea and bath.

Thirty minutes later, feeling considerably refreshed, he skipped downstairs and followed the sounds of a lively family to the kitchen. Molly was standing at a cooker over a pan of sizzling bacon and Susan was sitting at a table, eating some cereal and reading the paper. Art sat next to her, in a highchair, playing with some fingers of toast. Her mouth full, Susan waved her spoon in acknowledgement of Martin's presence and hummed a greeting.

'Sit down, Martin,' said Molly, 'there's a new pair of socks for you there, on the house. Now, what's it to be, the full monty?'

'Gosh, yes. Thank you, that'll be fantastic. Hello Susan. Sorry to barge in on you all like this.'

'Hey, don't be silly, Martin.' She swallowed and wiped the corner of her mouth with a napkin. 'You're a good customer; there's no reason why you shouldn't enjoy a bit of payback. As long as you don't forget this place when you've moved into Minchin Mansions.'

'God, don't you start. I've had enough of people thinking I'm landed gentry.'

'Have you got any furniture for this cottage? I gather that you're coming out of your old place with little more than your clothes.'

'Well, I suppose that's true. I haven't actually organised much in the way of furniture yet. I thought I'd move in and do it bit by bit; see what fits, you know.'

'I suppose it's difficult finding a bed that fits. Or rather that you fit.'

'My feet are happy dangling over the end. They've been doing it for twenty-odd years.'

'Very odd. If it's not the laird himself.' Kevin had entered the kitchen from the yard. 'And what, milord, have you been up to all night with Good Golly Miss Molly?'

Martin felt his face turn a deep crimson as Molly hurled the crust of a loaf of bread at her brother-in-law. 'Sod off, you dirty-minded bastard', she laughed.

'Tch, tch. Not in front of Art, please,' Susan chided them, without raising her eyes from the paper, 'he's at a very impressionable age.'

'So am I,' added Kevin, retrieving the bread from the floor and sinking his teeth into it. 'Henry said he'd like two eggs, over easy, and a large black coffee. Didn't he, Arty, eh?' He tickled his son, whose plump face erupted into a big smile.

'Crow's feet, so young;' Molly observed, 'just like his mummy.'

'Cow.'

Martin spent the next twenty minutes enjoying the spectacle of a noisy, jolly family, trading insults and various pieces of food. He suddenly looked at his watch and remembered that he had another life.

'Good grief, I must fly. Get back into the old routine. Only a four-day week and all. Thanks ever so much everyone. Catch you later. Bye.'

Thursday was market day, the day when the older citizens gathered in Shimbley. They were up and about early, many of them bussed in from surrounding villages, others driving in and occupying every available kerb-side space, orange 'disabled' badges proudly displayed in their windscreens. They prodded the vegetables on market stalls, discussed grandchildren in small groups on street corners and loitered around Top News, waiting for its Post Office counter to open so that they could collect their pensions. Three elderly ladies were startled by six and a half feet of accountant emerging from the George and Dragon, new socks dangling from the breast pocket of his jacket, bare feet in trainers. 'Good morning', he said, as he accelerated past, bounding down the pavement as though he was wearing seven-league boots.

'Blimey, looks like he woke up in the wrong bed,' remarked the owner of a second-hand video and CD stall to his neighbour. 'Looks like it'll be another nice day,' he added.

It was nearly nine when Martin reached the door to the stairs up to his office. Strangely, it was ajar. His first thought was that he had forgotten to close and lock it the previous evening. His second thought, as soon as he realised that the first one was absurd, because he never forgot things like that, was that Mehmet, a key holder, had needed access for some reason. But Mehmet was never around this early, rarely seen before ten or later. His third thought, as he reached the landing and found the door into his office open, was that Beverley had decided to help herself to something. His fourth thought, as he noticed the broken locks on the door, then the completely ransacked office, was that someone had been doing some breaking and entering.

'Bloody hell,' he said, reaching for the telephone. The telephone's lead trailed loosely across the floor from its socket and he saw that the system's box of brains had been wrenched off the wall and smashed beyond repair. '*Bloody hell!*'

CHAPTER 2: Thursday morning

Martin was pounding back down the street, dodging between the closely spaced stalls. Ahead he saw a small, wiry man, aged at least eighty and wearing a smart trilby hat, walking unsteadily backwards into his path. 'Excuse me!' Martin yelled, but the warning fell on deaf ears. Then he realised, to his horror, that the old man's manoeuvre was a chivalrous act to let a woman of even greater years mount the pavement in her electric buggy. He reviewed his options: if he went to the left, he would certainly kill the gentleman and quite possibly break his own neck; if he went to the right, he would go straight through a stall's green canvas side awning which could conceal foam rubber off-cuts (good) or racks of clothes (less good) or crockery (bad) or assorted kitchen utensils, including knives and skewers and things (very bad); if he went straight on...

'Shiiit!' Martin somehow cleared the little car, even managing to give its stunned occupant an apologetic wave as he shot over her head. He hoped that the old woman hadn't collapsed from shock, but there wasn't a great deal that he could do about it; he was carrying such momentum that she would now be no more than a blur in his imaginary rear view mirror. He hurtled on towards the George and Dragon.

'Looks like his missus found out,' said the second-hand video and CD man, before turning to a group of dazed pensioners. 'Don't worry, folks. Now, look at this collectors' set: Marathon Man, Chariots of Fire and White Men Can't Jump. I'm not asking thirty quid; I'm not even asking twenty. No, luv! You're asking, "How can he do it?" Well, it's my birthday and, while I can't say it doesn't hurt, just for today and only while stocks last, they're yours for just fifteen quid. Hello? Have you lot got your wotsits switched on?' He gave one of his ears an explanatory flick but his audience was still staring down the pavement towards the inn.

Martin swung round through the archway into the yard and burst into the kitchen where he had been enjoying a terrific cooked breakfast only ten minutes earlier.

'Jesus, Martin,' said Kevin, who had been unloading the washer and was frozen to the spot with a pint glass in each hand, 'what's the matter?'

Martin struggled to regain his breath. 'Burglary... police... phone...'

'Right!' said Kevin, putting the glasses down, grabbing a handset from its cradle and stabbing the '9' with a chubby forefinger. 'Where? How many? Are they armed?'

Martin lunged across the table and managed to snatch the phone from Kevin's hand. He pressed the button to hang up. 'Not emergency,' he panted, 'Office. What's number... for police... station?'

'I've got it behind the bar. Come on.'

Martin, his heartbeat decelerating to a less excited rate, followed Kevin into the lounge and dialled the number for the local station. A recorded voice announced that he was in a queue.

'Nearly... killed... old lady,' Martin told Kevin, forcing the words out between gasps of breath.

'What? They put up a fight?'

'Not at... office. On way back... here.'

'They tried to stop you getting away?'

'No, she's... in car... thing.'

'Oh, I see,' said Kevin, his eyes narrowing and brow creasing into a riot of confused furrows. 'Ram raiders? Are the rest of them still in your office?'

'Rest... who?'

'The rest of the ram raiders.'

'No. Trashed the phone.' Martin was recovering from his exertions. 'Got no other phone. Came here... hello? Yes, I'd like to report a burglary. My name's Martin Minchin.'

He went through the details before hanging up and returning to the kitchen. He hadn't noticed when he had burst in a few minutes earlier, but Art was in a playpen in the corner, grinning from ear to ear, as if Martin was the current top man in toddler entertainment.

'You get back to your office, Martin,' said Kevin. 'I'll get some decent coffee and see you there in ten minutes, okay? Don't worry. You've got insurance?'

'Of course I've got insurance!' Martin was now very much on edge as he made for the back door.

'Hey, Martin!' Martin paused and Kevin motioned towards his breast pocket. 'Wipe your nose, eh?'

'Oh, right.' Martin pulled a sock from his breast pocket and wiped it across his nostrils, looking up in time to see Kevin doubling up with laughter. 'All I bloody need. Excuse my French, Art.'

~

When Martin arrived back at the door at the foot of his stairs, a policewoman had just emerged from her patrol car. She stepped into his path. 'Excuse me, sir. My, you're a bit tall. May I ask you where you're going?'

'It's okay. I'm Martin Minchin. I reported this. It's my office.'

'Right. I'm WPC Brown. Where did you call us from, Mr Minchin?'

'From the George and Dragon. Down there.' Martin pointed.

'When was the break-in?'

'I've no idea. I found it when I arrived this morning.'

'I hope you're going to arrest him. You'll need handcuffs, you will.'

Martin and the policewoman both turned towards the small crowd that had gathered, its average age around sixty-five, and only that low because it included some kids who were late for school.

'He's a lunatic!'

Their eyes descended, to meet those of the old woman in her electric buggy.

'Oh, shit,' said Martin.

'That's him!' she shouted, encouraging a murmur of agreement from the rapidly growing audience. 'That's what he said last time. Arrest him!'

'Would you like to come up?' Martin asked the policewoman. 'I can explain about her.' He led her up to his office, Hurdle Woman muttering disapprovingly at their departing backs.

Although he had now had a little time to become used to the idea that his private property had been violated, Martin was still shocked at the destruction that greeted him. He was taking in things that he had missed before: apart from paper strewn everywhere, over and under upturned drawers, there was a crunchy layer of concrete and polystyrene wherever he trod. What was it? It was as if a building site had marched through the place.

'You said that you discovered this when you arrived this morning, Mr Minchin?'

'Yes, that's right.'

'You didn't have any idea about it until then?'

'No.'

'It's just that, I couldn't help noticing that you don't really look completely ready for work; as if you had come here in a bit of a hurry.'

'Oh, I see! Yes, ha ha. No, I mean, I'm living here at the moment. Only I was at the George and Dragon last night. Er, for the night.'

'A lock-in, was it?'

'No, nothing like that, certainly not. Molly Richards let me stay there overnight.'

'Oh?'

'Oh, God. In a free room, right? Look, they're friends and they were kindly helping out. It was a spur of the moment thing. I move into my new house tomorrow, you see. And my clean clothes are here, in the other room. Or at least they were. I don't normally wear socks in my top pocket.'

'No problem, Mr Minchin. We'll need to have details of everything missing. Have you been able to check if anything's been taken?'

'Not really, but it's odd, isn't it? I mean, they haven't taken the PC, which must be the most valuable thing here'

'It's probably kids. If they can't convert it to cash instantly, they don't want it. They wouldn't know where to take a PC. Not until they're older, anyway. What about money?'

'Kids? Er, no, I don't have any money. I mean I don't have cash here, in the office. You think kids did all this?'

'Yup.'

Martin had gone through to the back office and his eyes settled on what remained of his magnificent old safe. Its door was hanging open and the whole thing looked as though it had been peeled like a banana. 'Call that kids?' he demanded. 'Kids with dynamite? This is where all this gritty stuff's coming from. That's fireproofing, that is. Oh, God, it's probably asbestos. Someone must have heard the blast.'

'I don't think it was explosives sir. Probably a hammer and chisel job.'

'Hammer and chisel job? Hammer and chisel job? Look at the bloody thing! Excuse my language.'

'I shouldn't worry sir. *Don't touch it!* Sorry, it's just that the scene of crime officer will want to see things as found.'

'The forensics man, eh?' Kevin had entered, stepping over the debris, with Art under one arm and a large cool box hanging from his free hand. 'I used to love The Bill, until the wife made me pack it in. Coffee?'

'The forensics woman,' WPC Brown corrected him. 'White with two sugars, please. And you are...?'

Martin intervened: 'This is the caterer, Constable Brown.' Art looked around, wide-eyed, and gurgled happily. 'And the caterer's dad. Can he use that table over there?'

'I don't suppose it matters.'

'That's a hell of a hole, Martin.' Kevin nodded towards the door to the back room as he decanted the contents of his box onto the table. Martin followed his gaze and wondered how he had missed it before; he had been concentrating on the mess strewn all over the floor of course, but all the same... it was a hole three feet square, knocked clean through the partition wall, directly above the connecting door.

'Why did they do that?' he squealed, scarcely believing his eyes and slightly surprised by the high pitch of his own voice.

'Standard practice, to get to the other side,' said Constable Brown. 'It's often quicker than trying to bash down reinforced, triple-locked doors; just go over the top. It's only plasterboard.'

'Only plasterboard? But that door's not even got a lock!' Martin protested, holding his arms up in despair. 'Jesus! Why didn't they try the door? What are they? Mad?' He appealed to Constable Brown to provide the answers.

'They're not brain surgeons,' she replied with well-practised patience, 'and it's obvious that your chap isn't the brightest.' She just succeeded in suppressing a giggle at the sight of the unnecessary hole and its owner's indignation. 'Look, Mr Minchin, I reckon that the kids must have come in, had a look around for the price of a few Es and scarpered, probably empty handed. If you reckon no money's missing, it's my guess that nothing else is. But leave things exactly as they are and the scene of crime officer will turn up anything of interest. Her name is Ms Hopkins and she should be here later this morning; she's got quite a bit on today.'

'Bloody kids,' muttered Martin, looking around again at the mess. 'I don't believe it, bloody *kids!*'

'Can we just go through a few forms now Mr Minchin. This is your case number, but you only need concern yourself with the two-four-one-three after the stroke; you'll need to quote that on your insurance claim. I take it you have insurance?'

'Yes, of course. Does this mean I'm the two thousand four hundred and thirteenth burglary this year?' he asked, pointing to the top of the form.

'Crime. This month.'

The more he looked around, and, for the moment, accepting WPC Brown's assertion about the capabilities of carpentry tool-equipped youths, the more he was inclined to go along with her theory that kids had simply conducted a frenzied search for cash. For a short while, he felt smug that the little oiks had wasted all their efforts and fled empty handed. Then he realised that it would have been a great deal better if he had just left a tenner on his desk, in an envelope marked 'Money for the burglars'. No, the little bastards probably couldn't read. '£4U' should get the message across.

Kevin was providing miraculous support, with a seemingly endless supply of excellent, strong coffee and an assortment of biscuits. Despite the big breakfast still sitting in his stomach,

Martin ate heartily, reckoning that a hefty intake of sugar might give him the energy to cope. As far as he could see, there was nothing missing; nothing of value, anyway. He had been concerned about client confidentiality but he didn't suppose that kids had much interest in balance sheets. Most of the files contained matter that was of public record in any case. All work in progress and vital archives were on his computer and on backup tapes in the wrecked safe, so it looked as though the integrity of his business, or rather that of his clients, remained intact. Having dealt with the police paperwork and drunk enough coffee to keep him awake for three years, he thanked Kevin, Art and Constable Brown in turn and showed them out to the landing. Before descending, WPC Brown turned back to him.

'As a matter of interest, Mr Minchin, what was that old lady in the buggy on about?'

'I haven't a clue Constable. She must be a bit, you know,' he rolled his eyes. 'Batty, that sort of thing.'

'Hmm. Goodbye Mr Minchin.'

In the back office, he pulled his suit out from under one of the pot plants and a pile of rubble and hung it again on the door; it would need to go to the cleaners. He went back into the main office and wedged the door closed with a chair, then retrieved some clean underwear and a shirt from a carrier bag he found under his desk. He shook the concrete and polystyrene crumbs from them and took them into his little WC. Ten minutes later, shaved and freshly dressed, he felt much more ready to face the mountain of a clean-up. He threw open all the windows, propped the broken door ajar and used the mobile phone, thoughtfully left by Kevin, to summon a telecom engineer to restore the phone and fax lines and a locksmith to return the premises to a secure condition.

'Mithter Minchin, I prethume.' A slim man of medium height, aged anywhere between early forties and mid-fifties, with short, dark brown, curly hair, flecked with grey, had entered. 'It lookth ath though you require the thervithith of a cleaner.' The accent was indeterminate English, the lisp unmistakable.

'Can I help you?' asked Martin, bristling.

'Yeth, you can. My name ith Ethicth, Thidney Ethicth. I left a methage. I have a thpot of bithineth for you. Thall we thit down?' His eyes, dark brown – almost black – looked, unblinking, up into Martin's. He wore a dark grey suit, jacket tightly buttoned, plain white shirt and grey tie. Immaculately polished black lace-up shoes completed the rather sombre ensemble. Martin was hardly a follower of fashion but his visitor struck him as being one who took care to avoid making any style statement. Perhaps he was an undertaker.

'Well, as you can see, it's not the best time.'

'Oh thith won't take long, Mithter Minchin.' Essex, with an assertiveness that Martin found deeply irritating, took a clean, white, neatly folded handkerchief from his trouser pocket and used it to flick some dirt off a chair before sitting on it. He motioned to Martin to sit as well. His face bore an expression that was a mix of annoyance, impatience and exasperation, his eyebrows raised at the inner ends, his forehead lightly creased. 'You reethently took pothethon of a property called Lockkeeperth Cottage in Wetht Vereham, yeth?'

'No. Actually I take possession tomorrow.'

'Cloath enough. Anyway, I with to buy Lockkeeperth Cottage, Mithter Minchin.'

'What?' Martin laughed. 'Too late, I'm afraid; it's not for sale. It isn't an investment purchase, it's to live in. For me to live in.'

'Quite tho, but I did thay that thith woth lucrative, Mithter Minchin. I'll pay you five thouthand poundth more than you paid. Even after your expentheth, thatth what I call a return on invethtment. Ath an accountant, I'm thor you agree.' Essex's manner was smooth and confident. He sounded entirely reasonable.

'As I said, Mr Essex, the cottage isn't for sale. I'm moving in tomorrow and I intend to stay there. I'm sure you can find somewhere else which will suit you just as well. If not better.' For the briefest moment the road in which Beverley lived flashed through his mind. No, perhaps not; Mr Essex was more likely to live hanging upside down in a bell tower.

A disappointed expression crossed Essex's face. 'You're a difficult man to pleath. Letth thay I make it theven thouthand five hundred poundth. I really do want it you thee, Mithter Minchin.'

'I'm sorry, there really is no point in pursuing this and I must get on. There's an excellent agent in the High Street who I'm sure will be delighted to show you some other houses.' Martin stood up and walked towards the door. Essex sighed and rose.

'Mithter Minchin, I really cannot recommend too thtrongly that you give thith thum theeriuth conthideraithon.' Martin thought he detected a trace of menace. 'I'll call you before the end of play, after you've reconthidered; theven and a half thouthand poundth for doing virtually nothing thoundth to me like an abtholute bargain; itth what I might call an offer you can't refewth. Good day to you.' He looked straight into Martin's eyes again. 'And pleath do take care.'

As he left, he passed a smartly dressed woman on the landing. 'Good morning,' he said to her, before skipping lightly down the stairs.

'Mr Minchin?' the woman stepped tentatively into the office. Her horn-rimmed spectacles made her look quite severe. She carried a bulky briefcase.

'Yes,' replied Martin.

'Jane Hopkins, scene of crime officer. I hope I'm not interrupting.' She nodded back towards the stairs.

'Hello, yes. Do come in. No, he was an unsolicited caller. Can I offer you a coffee?'

'No thank you. I shouldn't be long. What on earth are you, six-seven?'

'Not quite, only six-six.'

'It must be a rarefied atmosphere that you breathe. Oh, it's not our boy.' She was peering at a broken door lock and sounded disappointed.

'I beg your pardon?'

'Your intruder. It's not the lad we've got. I thought it would be.'

'You've got someone?'

Ms Hopkins took some items from her case and made up a silicon mixture on a piece of card. She applied this to the scars on the door lock. 'Yes. Fourteen-year-old boy, arrested red-handed a couple of hours ago. He'd been keeping one jump ahead of us all night. The junior school, the travel agent, the Rose and Crown, the railway station booking office, not to mention four houses. Used the same screwdriver for all of them. They leave their own distinctive marks, just like fingerprints. No, your boy's is, let's see, twelve millimetres; probably a chisel.'

'Well he must have had a crowbar too. Look at my safe.' Ms Hopkins followed Martin into the back office.

'Ooh, my,' she said, 'we'll have some of this.' She put some of the concrete and polystyrene grit into a small polythene bag, then took another silicon mould from one of the scars on the safe. 'No, it's your chisel again. This one's definitely new to me.'

'Do you need to take fingerprints?'

'To be honest with you, Mr Minchin, there isn't a great deal of point. If he'd hauled himself in through a window, it might have been useful, but whatever's been handled in here is going to be covered in a whole mess of prints. I think this is all I can get here. I don't envy you the clearing up. You should get yourself an alarm; I hardly attend any crimes on alarmed premises. Good day.'

The rest of the day went by in a blur, Martin hoovering, wiping, brushing and sorting, stopping only to explain to the phone engineer that he wouldn't leave alive unless a full service had been resumed, and to pay the locksmith. Kevin visited again during the afternoon with tea and cake and offered the use of room four at the George and Dragon. Martin declined, preferring to keep an eye on his belongings this time. He thought that it was quite possible that chisel-boy would return, perhaps this time having found a buyer for a PC. As promised, Sidney Essex telephoned at five.

'Are you ready to acthept my offer, Mithter Minchin? It really would be the right dethithon.'

'Look, Mr Essex, I told you before: I'm not selling. Now, with the greatest respect, please piss off.' Martin replaced the receiver, both alarmed and slightly thrilled by his own brusqueness. But still, he reasoned, some people need telling in no uncertain manner.

At around eleven, Mehmet produced an Extra-Mega-King-Size doner kebab, on the house. It was partly that, and partly the unsettling effect of the day's events, which prevented Martin from getting much sleep during the night. At last, as the dawn chorus was reaching its normal operating volume, he dozed off, only to dream of standing behind the counter of a market stall with an array of live doner kebabs on display, and Essex arrived wielding a huge chisel and cackled madly as he stabbed the doners, one after another, pushing them up the blade, to make one enormous skewered shish kebab. 'And now thumthing for pudding,' he said, advancing towards Martin.

Martin rose from his sleeping bag, carried out some rudimentary ablutions in the little sink and shaved. The previous evening he had arranged clothes and other essentials in neat piles in the main office. He checked his message on the answering machine, which still worked despite having taken a tumble, and left, carefully locking and double-checking the door. It was a little before eight.

He walked quickly through the town to the car park, sent a silent 'thank you' heavenwards as Alfredo started on the first attempt and took off to Shimbley's big, edge-of-town supermarket. Making sure that his list was to hand, he pushed a trolley across the store's threshold well before the end-of-week rush began. By nine-thirty he was parked on the double yellow lines outside his office. He had managed to relieve the shop of four large boxes, in addition to the one that held all of his groceries, and he took these up to his office and filled them from the piles on the floor. With the full boxes, plus two large suitcases and various loose items limiting the view out of the car except through the windscreen, Martin congratulated himself; he was ahead of schedule. He went back up the stairs to check, for the third time, that he had locked the office properly, and turned the car in the direction of Filkington Parver Thrupp.

'Good morning, Mr Minchin.' Dora Simkins smiled at him. 'Here we are; two keys for the front door. I'm afraid that there appears to be no spare set, but perhaps you will be changing the locks. I'm assured that the keys to all other doors and so on are inside the house. If you have any problems, do, please, give me a call and I'll help if I possibly can.'

'Thank you, Mrs Simkins. I'm sure that everything will be fine.'

'Now then, before you run off, Mr Parver-Thrupp thought that this might provide a bit of cheer on your first night in your new home.' She handed Martin a bottle of twelve-year-old single malt Scotch whisky.

'Wow! You bet it will! Thank you so much. Please thank Mr Parver-Thrupp for me too. Gosh, you certainly are spoiling me.'

'Do mind your head, Mr Minchin.'

'Yes. Thank you. Goodbye.'

He tenderly placed the bottle on a jumper in the top of one of the boxes on the back seat of his car and set off for West Vereham. He still hadn't retrieved the radio-cassette player from inside the dashboard, so he sang to himself. It was a beautiful day.

'I'll have to clear this drive a bit, create some turning space,' he thought to himself, as he carefully reversed in through the gap. 'Welcome to Lockkeeper's Cottage!' he shouted, springing from the car, then stopped in his tracks. 'Oh, bloody hell!'

The front door was hanging open, clinging to its frame by one hinge. He pulled it awkwardly to one side and ducked through into the hallway. Bright red paint had been splashed over the floor and up the walls. He went straight through to the kitchen. Water covered the floor and ran out under the back door. In one corner lay part of the ceiling, in a grey, soggy pile. A trickle of water ran steadily down the wall from the hole where the ceiling had been. The cupboard units had all been attacked with something heavy, not one of them escaping damage. The big picture window in front of the sink, looking out over the garden, was broken. A big slab of concrete sat on the steel drainer, which was dented and scratched. Shards of glass lay everywhere. The sitting room was worse; not one window pane was intact. The log burning stove in the fireplace was splashed with paint, its door bent backwards at the hinges and the steel flue dented and broken away where it met the top; the glass in its door was broken. All four pairs of wall light fittings had been pulled away, leaving wires trailing from big holes in the plaster. He went upstairs, stepping carefully over bits of smashed bannister. The bathroom suite was beyond repair, the smashed lavatory's cistern the source of all the water below. A chunk was missing from the washbasin; looking out through the hole in the window he spotted it lying in a flower bed below. The damage was much the same in all three bedrooms. In the main bedroom, in which he had been looking forward to sleeping that night, one of the walls was burnt, where wallpaper had been peeled away and ignited. Daubed on another wall in the red paint was the word DETH. The perpetrator had left a souvenir, an axe, the head of which had been embedded deeply in the wardrobe door, shattering the full length mirror on the inside.

'Seven years bad luck, you bastard, and not a year too many,' said Martin through clenched teeth, tears irritatingly escaping his eyes and rolling coldly down his cheeks.

He went out to his car and rummaged around in one of the boxes in the boot, emerging with a telephone in his hand. He took it into the house and looked around for a socket. One at the bottom of the stairs was in pieces. He found another in the sitting room; it didn't seem to be damaged, so he plugged in the phone and lifted the receiver. It was dead. He had been assured that the line would be connected by eight that morning. He ran up the stairs and into the main bedroom. There was a socket in the corner, close to where the paper had been burnt, and he pushed the plug home. To his relief, he heard a dialling tone. He went back downstairs to unload the car; his phone directories were buried in one of the boxes.

In eight trips he transferred everything from his car into the house, putting it all in the middle of the sitting room floor. He picked up the precious bottle of Scotch and looked around for somewhere safe to stash it until such time as he was going to be able to sit back and enjoy some. There was a recess in the fireplace, once used as an oven, and he placed it in that. The sound of someone pushing their way in through the broken front door made him jump. As he stood up, a large young man stepped into the room.

'Minchin is it? He said you were fucking tall.'

'Can I help you?' Martin's heart was thumping so vigorously that he was sure that his visitor could see and hear it. He was nearly as tall as Martin, but built like a heavyweight wrestler. Martin's gaze gradually climbed from his ornate, black, pointy-toed cowboy boots. His frame was barely contained by a shiny grey suit. Beneath it, he wore a black shirt, unbuttoned at his ample neck to reveal a forest of chest hair, jet black to match the hair on his head. The latter was tightly swept back into a ponytail. He had long sideburns and a neatly trimmed goatee beard.

'Vandals is it?' His voice was deep, with a strong Welsh lilt. 'No respect. What's that?' He had suddenly looked at something over Martin's shoulder and Martin turned around instinctively.

CHAPTER 3: Friday afternoon

The first thing that Martin was aware of was a terrible, throbbing headache. He raised his head and shouted in pain as it bumped into something. He recalled looking at the French window in the cottage's sitting room; what happened? He was puzzled. Now it was dark and he was lying on something very uncomfortable. He was also on the move. That Welsh man-mountain must have hit him – with something substantial, by the feel of his head, which felt a thousand times worse than it had after the blow it had suffered in Petey P-T's office. He realised that he was in the boot of a car and began to panic. Perhaps this was the person who had vandalised the cottage and he had surprised him in the act. Did this mean that the Welshman now intended to dispose of the only witness? No; people don't commit murder to cover up vandalism. If they're sane. What if he was mad? A mad axeman? Oh God! Had he retrieved his axe from the wardrobe door?

Thoughts raced through Martin's mind, most of them discomforting. He tried to concentrate on the sensations outside. Bump-thump, Axe, Bump-thump, Axe. Don't be ridiculous! This wasn't the time to play these intrusive mental games. The pitch of the engine was constant, as was the road-roar below, interspersed with the thud of expansion joints. They must be on a motorway. The nearest motorway to West Vereham was the M4 but then he realised that he didn't know how long he had been unconscious. He twisted around to free up his left arm and bring his watch within sight of his face. He found the little button on it and the display lit up: 1.35 pm. He started to do some mental calculations. Suppose they set off from the cottage by, say, eleven; two and a half hours at a conservative average of forty miles per hour – no, fifty, considering the motorway – that's one hundred and twenty miles, give or take twenty or so. That could take them to Cornwall, or the East coast, or Birmingham, or Wales... Wales! That was it! After all, the kidnapper was Welsh. But why would he want to take him to Wales? Axe, Bump-thump, Cardiff, Duw duw – wasn't that Welsh for Ohmigod?

He remembered the state of Lockkeeper's Cottage and wondered how he was going to tackle the clear-up. He worried that his insurance would not cover damage that had been caused deliberately. He really couldn't afford to have major repairs made, for instance to the kitchen and bathroom; the bare necessities in those rooms were going to cost at least a couple of thousand. Architect, Builder, Carpenter, Decorator, Explosives expert. Perhaps he should have accepted that extraordinary offer from Thidney Ethicth; then it would be his problem, not Martin's. But it was Martin's problem – and it was Beverley's fault! If that duplicitous bitch and her doting daddy had stayed put in Yorkshire, he would have settled with someone who valued him rather than his non-existent inheritance, he would probably never even have heard of Lockkeeper's Cottage and he wouldn't now be shut in the boot of a car rushing headlong into the heart of Wales with a deranged baritone at the wheel.

It was a practical joke. Probably one of Kevin's ideas. Soon, the car would stop, the boot would be thrown open and everyone would have a damn good laugh. No, his head reminded him that this wasn't in the least bit funny. His neck ached and his right arm had gone numb. He wriggled around, cursing the length of his legs; this was one circumstance in which small people definitely held an advantage over long ones. He pressed a knee against the metal above him. There simply wasn't sufficient room to try kicking it open, not that he fancied his chances of survival in the outer lane of the M4. He resigned himself to staying there until someone chose to let him out. What if cramp set in? On the occasions when he had suffered cramp in bed, nothing less than leaping up, yelling and doing a clumsy war dance around the room would relieve the symptoms. Was that twinge a warning of imminent cramp? He felt his head pressing painfully against something solid, then his whole body was pitched in the opposite direction. Either they were in the middle of a pile-up or they had left the motorway. For the next twenty minutes, he was thrown from side to side, the normal movements of everyday motoring accentuated in the darkness. Aargh, Bugger, Christ, Doh! He recalled his childhood journeys to holiday destinations, drifting in and out of sleep as his father's car sped through the dawn towards a fortnight of fun, except that his father had shown more consideration for his passengers than this. The car stopped. A door opened and slammed shut. He looked again at his watch: 2.29 pm.

'Out you get, boyo.' The fresh air hit Martin like a cold shower. He looked up and quickly closed his eyes again. Having been in darkness for two hours, he was unprepared for the assault on his retinas by the daylight shining around the towering silhouette of his pony-tailed abductor.

'Heeelp!' Martin shouted, with as much energy and volume as he could muster. Feeling rather pathetic, he opened his eyes in time for a fist to eclipse his view and his head banged back against the floor of the boot. He was still alive but his head was pounding and he needed a lavatory.

'You'll have to shout louder than that if you want your mammy. Come on now.'

'What the hell's going on? What do you want.'

'Questions is it? Come here.' A huge hand descended and Martin tried to shy away from it. It grasped his arm and hauled him to his knees.

'Alright!' said Martin, brushing away the assistance. He gingerly put one leg over the lip of the boot and felt for the ground with his foot. The other leg followed and he steadied himself on the wing of the car as he tried to stand up. His legs buckled under him and he was caught by a massive hand in each armpit.

'Careful now, Mr Minchin. You look a little unsteady.'

'Of course I'm bloody unsteady – I've been in there for bloody hours.' He pointed at the boot as the big man slammed the lid down. He looked around. They were in a yard outside a warehouse. The car that had brought him here was a fairly new Rover 600. On the far side, backed up to a loading bay, was an articulated lorry, its trailer bearing the words 'LM International Traders of Co. Kilkenny, Ireland'. His escort held tightly onto his arm and frogmarched him into the building through a small side door. They passed through a dingy lobby with men's and women's toilets leading from it and emerged in the main hall of the warehouse. Martin wondered why he hadn't taken the opportunity to demand access to the gents, but felt that the moment had passed. Half a dozen rows of racking occupied about a quarter of the floor space, the shelves holding nondescript brown boxes of various sizes. A battle-scarred forklift truck with uneven tines sat abandoned in one of the aisles. The roller doors at the loading bay were closed. Near them, stacked on the floor, were several large crates of potatoes. To one side was what appeared to be a refrigerated room over which was a mezzanine with an office, approached by a metal staircase. Martin was pushed towards this and he climbed wearily, his legs still feeling weak. As he ascended, he looked out across the warehouse; there didn't appear to be anyone else in it. At the top, the door to the office was open and, standing with his arms folded across his chest, was a neatly groomed Sidney Essex.

'Hello again, Mithter Minchin. I hope Evanth hath taken good care of you.'

'You!' said Martin. 'Where is this? What the hell's going on?'

Essex stood to one side, allowing Evans and Martin to pass into the room.

'Where's Mr Monan?' asked Evans, earning a reproachful glare from Essex, who chose not to answer either man's questions.

'Pleath thit down Mithter Minchin. Let go of our getht Evanth!' Essex had taken a seat behind a desk on which were some neatly placed folders, pens, a desktop calendar and a telephone. Martin sat down opposite him. Evans stood by the door with his hands loosely coupled in front of him, in the manner of an intimidating doorman.

'Have you been a little rough with Mithter Minchin, Evanth?' Essex posed the question without taking his eyes off Martin.

'He was winding me up,' the Welshman explained.

'I apolojithe for him,' said Essex, producing a box from a desk drawer and offering Martin a tissue. 'He can be a little unruly. Itth both an athet and a liability, to yooth language you'll underthtand.' Martin remained silent. 'You really ought to give your noath a wipe. Anyway, I'll not meth around. I intend to have thith houth of yourth, Lockkeeperth Cottage. I made you a very generuth offer which you dethided not to acthept. I think that woth the wrong dethithon and I thuthpect that you too might now be thinking it woth the wrong dethithon. Yeth?'

'No.' Martin studied the smear of fresh blood on the tissue with dismay.

'I thought you were going to be thmarter than thith,' Essex said softly. He picked up a paperknife and attended unnecessarily to his neat, clean fingernails. 'You could have been theven and a half thouthand poundth better off by now. You've got a degree?' Martin nodded. 'Of corth you have. You might not geth it, but I left thcool at fifteen with no qualificathonth. The only thkillth I had were thinking and lying. But I've alwayth been thmart, Mithter Minchin. Tho what duth that thay for a univerthity educathon? Thith countryth univerthitith have turned out thum of the thtupidetht people I've ever met. I could run ringth around them. I *do* run ringth around them. Pleath be in no doubt, Mithter Minchin, I thall eathily run ringth around you. I'm going to revithe my offer to you, only thith time itth revithed downwardth.' He gently stabbed the knife point-down on the desk. 'I'll pay you ten thouthand poundth leth than you've jutht paid. Call it an ecthpenthive lethon in property thpeculathon.'

'Don't be ridiculous!' Martin spluttered, astonished by Essex's unpleasant sales approach.

'Itth not ridiculuth, Mithter Minchin. For all I know, the plaith needth thum work doing on it. I might not have your degree but you won't find me paying over the oddth for thumthing in leth than perfect condithon.'

'It was you! You did that damage to my house?' Martin realised as he said it that he had been somewhat slow on the uptake, but he felt that it was excusable given the extreme circumstances of his day's experiences so far.

'You really don't know what damage ith, Mithter Minchin. And I promith you: you don't want to know. Where are the deedth?'

'What deeds?'

'The deedth to Lockkeeperth Cottage. Do try to keep up!'

'The bank's got the title-deed.'

'Mortgage, eh? The curth of the middle clartheth. You put all that effort into obtaining peetheth of paper which thay how thmart you are, then you thpend twenty five yerth bowing and thcwaping to moneylenderth. I don't bow and thcwape to anyone, Mithter Minchin. If I want thumthing, I'll have it, won't I, Evanth?'

'You bet,' replied Evans, grinning at Martin.

'It's all very well you and your pit-bull here threatening me, but you can't make me sell my house. A house isn't something you can take, you know, snatch and stuff in your pocket. To obtain a house you have to have the consent and cooperation of the owner, obviously something you're unused to. Anyway, why do you want it so badly? Do you think there's hidden treasure there or something?'

'Do you hear that, Evanth? Hidden trethur; heeth been reading too many fairy tailth.' Essex leaned back and clasped his hands together behind his head. 'You worry about your future, not about my motivathon. You're right, of corth, that itth a bit more complicated than, thay, redithtributing veerculth. But, thuppoath you meet an untimely end: I doubt that I'm in your will, but then again, I doubt that anyone elth in it will be minded to keep up your mortgage repaymentth. The houth would be back on the market in no time. Maybe the bank would repotheth it and thell it fartht and cheaply to the firtht buyer to come along with an actheptable amount of money. The trouble ith, that would be tirethum and take time, and I really don't want to have to wait. Ten thouthand leth than you paid and therth no more pain, thatth the deal.'

'You're not listening, are you? The house isn't for sale. Now, if you're not going tell me what it is about it that's so bloody important to you, I think I'm finished here.' Martin stood and turned towards the door where Evans blocked the way. 'Excuse me please, *Evans!*' he shouted the name, straight into Evans's face. 'I'm leaving.'

Evans attempted to deliver a backhanded punch to his head but Martin backed away in time to avoid it. Essex quickly stepped around the desk and stood between them, like a diminutive referee coming between two large pugilists. 'Hold it!' Martin was relieved; his head had taken enough of a battering and, beneath his bold veneer, he was very frightened.

'What are we going to do, boss?' Evans seemed to be agitated. 'Where's... you know?'

'Evanth, pleath!' said Essex sharply. 'You, my friend,' he placed a forefinger on Martin's chest and spoke softly but firmly, 'are going to do egthactly what I thay or Evanth here will be allowed to break thumthing, right? Now *thit!*' Martin sat. Essex returned to his seat. 'I'll come clean with you, Mithter Minchin. Itth not actually me who wontth your houth.' Essex threw the briefest of glances at Evans and continued, 'I'm a middleman. I do deelth. Thumbody elth wontth the property and ith paying me a commithon – a very generuth commithon, ath it happenth – to acquire it for him. Tho generuth, in fact, that I would thtill have made a healthy profit if you had acthepted the theven and a half thouthand, yeth?' He paused and looked at Martin as if waiting for him to concur. Martin remembered it as a sales technique that he had seen demonstrated at a dreadful seminar designed to instil the killer instinct in delegates from all kinds of professions and businesses. Embellished, with 'yeah?' tacked onto the end of each sentence, it was now a common conversational device, a kind of verbal slap in the face to ensure that the person you're addressing is still awake and holding onto every word. Martin found the practice offensive and had long ago learned to withhold the instinctive 'Yeah' response which the speaker sought. Instead, he stared silently back at Essex with what he hoped was a bored expression.

'Thith man,' Essex continued, 'my client, ith very wealthy and, well, thadly thentimental. He reethently lotht hith mother. He abtholutely wurthipped her and heeth grieving. In going through her belongingth he found her motherth – his granth – diary and dithcovered that hith dear old mother had been born in your Lockkeeperth Cottage. Well, thtraight away he thimply had to own it, a thort of thrine, if you like. Heeth a bithy man, tho he commithoned me. I couldn't believe my luck when I thaw the "For Thale" thine. But then you had already beaten me to it. Tho you thee, Mithter Minchin, therth no funny bithnith, no mythtery; jutht a man who can afford to indulge hith thentiment and a go-between hooth going to thwing it for him and pocket thum cath. I'm really thorry that itth all become a little unplethant. Letth bury the hatchet and get thith bithneth done. I'll give you ten thouthand to thell. Thatth half of my cut.' Essex's manner had changed from cool, frightening gangster to Mr Reasonable, extended arms, smiling eyes, raised eyebrows. 'What do you thay?'

'I thay that's the biggest pile of old bollocks I've heard since the Grimm brothers split up.' Martin was indignant at having his intelligence so very much underestimated. 'You don't go kidnapping people, beating them up, threatening them with death for God's sake, because some old fart's got an Oedipus complex. What the bloody hell do you take me for? And what's your so-called client going to say when he sees what you've done to his sainted mother's birthplace? Pull the other one.'

'Oh, fuck it.' Essex sighed and picked up the telephone, tapping out a number. 'Hello. Ethicth, yeth.' He paused. 'Yeth, but no. I know I did. Well thatth the problem. Yeth? Well, if thatth what you want.' He replaced the receiver and looked at Evans. 'We're going over tonight.' He sighed again and threw the paperknife into a drawer. 'We'll go to my plaith to eat.' He slammed the drawer shut. 'Thit! Get him out of here.'

Essex and Martin both rose. Martin shrugged his shoulders, looked at Evans and said, 'Okay, shit, get me out of here.' Evans frowned and looked at Essex with a pleading, hungry-puppy expression, as though requesting permission to retaliate. Essex slowly shook his head.

'Mithter Minchin, you're thuppoathed to be a clever man. Why the hell do you antagonithe thumwun who could hurt you? And enjoy it?' He waved his hand to indicate that he wanted Martin and Evans to leave, resumed his seat and picked up the phone again. Evans steered Martin through the door and back down the stairs. They went out through the same lobby, past the toilets.

'I need the lavatory,' said Martin.

'Tough.'

'Can I just...'

Evans pushed him up against a wall and placed a huge fist under Martin's chin. 'Just what? Just one more word out of you, you gangly English fairy, and I'll bite your fucking gonads off and spit them down the drain.' He relaxed his grip and twisted Martin's arm into a painful half-nelson. 'You're not so clever, are you? Eh? Now, we're going to get back in the car and you're not going to give us any more grief, okay?' Martin ignored the question, more concerned as he was by the discomfort Evans was causing. 'Okay, you bastard?' Evans slammed him forehead first into the wall.

'Okay!' Martin replied at last. 'Whatever you want. Dimwit!' Evans hauled him around to look him in the eye.

'Dimwit? Who the fuck are you calling a dimwit?' Evans was now hurt as well as angry, and intent on retrieving his reputation. 'Who's a fucking dimwit?' His nose was now pressing on Martin's, his eyes demanding answers that his fists could react to. Martin stared back into Evans's eyes, flinching from the pain in his damaged face.

'Me.'

'What?' Evans withdrew a few inches and relaxed his grip.

'Me. I'm calling me, I mean myself, a dimwit.' Evans frowned. 'Not you,' Martin added for safe measure.

'Why do you reckon you're a dimwit, then?' asked Evans brightening, obviously delighted that his prisoner was inferior after all. He marched him out of the building and across the yard towards the car.

'I must be a dimwit,' Martin said slowly and quietly, noticing Essex following them out of the building, 'for being hoodwinked by a brain-dead lump of lard like you.' Evans slammed Martin up against the side of the Rover. With his spare hand he fumbled for the key, plipped the locks, then threw open the boot. 'Oh, clever boyo; you can get back in the fucking tool box where poncy pricks like you belong.'

'Evanth!' Essex reached the car in time to save Martin from further indignity. 'I'll drive. You can look after him in the back.' Evans slammed the boot lid down, opened a rear door, bared his teeth at Martin and pushed him onto the rear seat, then slid in beside him. Essex sat in the driving seat, adjusted the rear view mirror and gave Martin another dose of his unblinking, cold, black-eyed stare. 'You're becoming a real aggravaithon,' he said. The tyres slipped on the broken tarmac as the car pulled angrily away from the yard, bits of gravel clattering their way around the inside of the wheel arches.

At last Martin could see where he was going, but the scenery gave him no clues as to where they were. It was an industrial area in which enclaves of modern units with bright plastic cladding and darkened glass were surrounded by unchecked decay. The potholed roads bore few nameplates, and these were no help. Essex drove with little respect for speed limits. He produced a cassette from his jacket pocket and put it in the player; it was

Abbey Road. Well, this wasn't Abbey Road for sure; Abominable Avenue, Bloodshed Bypass, Cat-food Cul-de-sac, Dead-meat Drive, Execution Expressway, Final Furlong. Martin's alphabet game took several turns for the worse. Just as Grand Guignol was knocking on his brain's door, they pulled into the forecourt of a sixties-built block of flats. Evans pulled Martin from the car and the three of them walked into the ground floor lobby. A group of boys, not yet in their teens, stood by the lifts, taking swigs from beer bottles and sucking hard on cigarettes. They wore a uniform of baggy jeans, drooping anoraks and centre-parted, heavily greased hair, reminiscent of styles seen in ancient silent movies.

'Alright, boys?' Evans growled the greeting in a menacing way, raising a fist in their direction. The surly youths shuffled away, trying not to display any haste and muttering various expletives amongst themselves. Martin thought he detected Liverpool accents.

'Nice children. Yours?' Martin caught Essex's eye.

'You're thertainly no comedian, Mithter Minchin.'

Martin wondered why he hadn't done anything to broadcast his predicament to the kids when he had the chance, but then he realised that they probably wouldn't have given a damn about him; they hadn't looked much like boy scouts. The lift arrived, opened its doors and unleashed the stench of urine. They stepped in and Evans prodded one of the buttons. The lift ascended to the second floor and they walked along a balcony overlooking the car park. Some seagulls flew past. The children from the lobby were jumping up and down on a car, but Martin could see that it wasn't the Rover. Perhaps they knew about Evans's fondness for meting out punishment. They stopped outside a solid looking front door with shabby red paint and a peep hole.

'Thith ith home,' said Essex, unlocking the door and standing aside to let Evans and Martin in. The contrast between the exterior image and the decor inside took Martin by surprise. The hall that ran from the front door through to the kitchen at the rear was like a narrow passage in a gallery or museum. Pinpricks of light illuminated sepia photographs of ships and dockyard scenes, probably taken at around the turn of the century. Their plain brass frames were spotless and reflected just enough light to reveal a polished parquet floor. Martin peered at one of the pictures and recognised the Liver Building.

'I need the lavatory,' said Martin, genuinely feeling quite desperate.

'Well you'd better thow him, Evanth, hadn't you?' Essex responded. 'Then you can join me in the kitchen. I'm going to put thum dinner on.'

'Great. I'm starving,' mumbled Evans, prodding Martin into a passage and indicating the door to the lavatory.

Having met the immediate urgency, Martin sat back on the seat and looked around. As in the hall, the decoration was immaculate. The fixtures and fittings looked expensive and everything shone as cleanly and proudly as in any five-star hotel. Illumination was provided by tiny downlighters mounted within the ceiling. There was a large mirror above the washbasin and another shipyard scene on the wall opposite it. On a shelf beneath the basin were some magazines on antiques. He wondered who the person at the other end of the phone had been back at the warehouse. Even if Essex's story had been a load of boloney, someone else seemed to be calling the shots. No, it must be Martin himself that they were after, not his cottage. People don't kidnap people because they've fallen for a house, at least not since the boom in the eighties. It must be something to do with his work, one of the people whose tax affairs he tended perhaps. In his head he started to sift through his client portfolio, coming up with no one whose financial details might cause the slightest interest in criminal circles. Accountant, Blackmail, Crime, Duplicity...

'What are you doing in there, boyo? Digging a tunnel?' Evidently Evans was becoming impatient. 'If you're not out in two minutes I'm coming in for you.'

Martin didn't answer at first. Evans was the first person ever to have punched him in the face. He was also the first person to have abducted him and the first person since Beverley to have shouted at him to hurry up in the loo.

'I'm only coming out if you let me go immediately. Then I might be persuaded to overlook the matter of your assault on me. Your two assaults on me.'

'Any second now I'm going to make it three, clever boyo.' Evans's retort was followed by some muffled words from Essex and then Martin was left in peace. Despite his bruises, cut lip and all-over aching, he was becoming less afraid of Evans; yes, he was a thug, but like a lumbering, leaf-eating, pea-brained dinosaur that could squash you, but not if you got out of its way first. Essex was potentially rather more dangerous, but it now seemed to Martin that his immediate future lay in the hands of somebody higher up the ladder. He found this mildly comforting, as though first Evans and now Essex could no longer hurt him.

He puzzled over his apparent sang-froid. He had a habit of adopting this kind of high-handed approach to anybody who had to answer to someone else, and it had not gone uncriticised. In performance assessments throughout his schooling and the early period of his career, he had repeatedly been told that he should make more of an effort to be a team player. At school the only team sport in which his services had been sought was basketball, and that wasn't for his agility. His successes had been in things like cross-country running, where his long legs could lollop gently along for mile after mile with just his own thoughts for company. Similarly, in the large accountancy firm that he joined after university, great emphasis was placed on teamwork. The senior partners insisted that their empire was a meritocracy but Martin's incisive mind and problem-solving skills were insufficient to impress people more concerned with exaggerated camaraderie, both during and after office hours. His no-nonsense view was that clients paid huge fees to be told that two and two make four, while his peers believed that it could make whatever the customer wants. That any of this should require either a three-hour meeting or a group of junior partners buying lunch for a client's accounts department he considered unnecessary and possibly unethical. What he regarded as economical use of his time and breath, his colleagues and superiors took to be stand-offishness. After some years of feeling like a misunderstood outcast, he decided that a loner's path was his preferred option. It might not lead to riches but it had to be better than brown-nosing people for whom he had little respect. As an individual he could deal one-to-one with decision makers; henceforth, his career was not going to rely on toadying.

He filled the basin with hot water, removed his watch and treated his hands and face to a thorough wash. Feeling as ready as he ever would to face whatever was coming next, he emerged into the hall. Evans was waiting for him and pointed towards the kitchen. Martin entered, with Evans following. Although it was a small room, a great deal of care and expense had gone into its furnishings. Designed and fitted out with impeccable taste, it was made for someone who liked to spend serious time in it. No space was wasted and an enormous variety of polished pots, pans and utensils were hanging from the ceiling. Sergeant Pepper was playing on a mini hi-fi system balanced on a swing-out bracket high on one wall. Essex, a crisp white apron protecting his clothes, was standing over a chopping board with a large knife in his hand. With the skill of a practised chef, he sliced three large carrots in a matter of seconds and scraped them off the board into a casserole that was steaming on the hob. Some diced bacon, garlic and shallots were gently frying in a pan beside it. Martin began to feel extremely hungry; it had been a long time since his Extra-Mega-King-Size doner kebab.

'Better?' asked Essex.

Martin looked at the pans on the hob and raised an eyebrow with what he hoped was a Roger Moore level of nonchalance. 'For the moment, thank you.' In fact, he could scarcely wait to tuck into some food, and the aromas coming from the cooker were practically making him drool. Essex waved the knife lazily in Martin's direction before dicing a dozen mushrooms with the same dexterity as before. 'Don't worry, Mithter Minchin, we'll all be eating the thame and I'm not ready to poithon mythelf jutht yet. You can arthk the big man here to taitht yourth for you if you like.' He laughed, while Evans appeared unsure as to whether to be pleased or worried.

'If that was an invitation to lunch, dinner, whatever you call this,' said Martin, 'I don't recall accepting. Do you mind telling me what you plan to do with me? We've established something of a stand-off on the question of my house which, as Jones the Lard here knows, is no longer exactly secure and which contains most of my worldly belongings.' Evans appeared once more to be straining at his imaginary leash.

'I promise you, boyo, I'm going to pull your fucking head inside-out.'

'Alright, Evanth, calm down. We're going on a journey. All three of uth. You're going to have another charnth, believe it or not. Tho, firtht we eat, then we go. And we thee if we can't change your mind.'

'I'm beginning to think that you're rather slow on the uptake, Mr Essex. I'm not going anywhere. I'm not selling my house and I'm not eating your idea of food.'

'You're a thtubborn man, aren't you, Minchin?' Martin had hit a nerve. 'Not, not, not! Can't, won't, tharn't! Didn't your poth thcool teach you to be broad-minded? Of corth it didn't. Thoath queer old men who took thuch very good care of you lovely boyth taught you to go through life with eight foot of broomthtick thtuck up your arthies. Twelve foot in your caith. I tell you, I can cook thingth you don't know how to pronounth. I've eaten in more deethent rethtauranth than you could add up with your moatht creative accounting. You'll go where you're fucking well told and eat what you're fucking well given.' Essex was now quite agitated as he looked to Martin for a reaction. 'Right?'

Martin refused to play, but pointed towards the cooker. 'You shouldn't burn garlic like that. It removes all the subtlety and leaves it bitter and disagreeable. Just like you.' Martin felt the presence of Evans immediately behind him and waited for his heavy hand. Instead, Essex laughed again.

'You don't want to find out how dithagreeable I can be. A degree? Evanth, get thith loother out of my thite until the foodth ready.'

Martin was relieved to have got away with another wisecrack and determined that he should escape from his new acquaintances at the earliest opportunity. They were presumably intending to take him to their leader, whoever and wherever that was, and he reckoned that it was one introduction he could quite happily do without, even though he couldn't help being intrigued to discover what it was all about. The way Essex spoke, it seemed that it really was the house at the centre of all this, but why?

Evans had steered him into the sitting room and Martin wondered how or why anyone had transformed a flat in an ugly, utilitarian, largely concrete structure into this cocoon of genteel living. A couple of good quality rugs lay on the gleaming floorboards and numerous houseplants and watercolour landscapes gave the room a sophisticated ambience that would sit equally comfortably in urban or rural surroundings. Bookshelves covered almost the whole of one wall, revealing a taste for military history, French philosophy, Britain's industrial revolution and cuisine from all parts of the world, from Escoffier to the Galloping Gourmet. Instead of a three-piece suite, there were three identical two-seater sofas, upholstered in loose covers with a wild flower motif. A flame-effect gas fire provided a focal point. He sank into one of the sofas and looked up at Evans, who looked preoccupied.

'What's the matter, Evans? You're looking even more lost than usual.' Evans's eyes darted momentarily to meet Martin's, but dived away just as quickly. 'I mean, have you any idea of what's going on? Because I certainly don't.'

'You smoke, boyo?'

'No. And for God's sake, please drop the "boyo" – you've convinced me that you're from the other side of Offa's Dyke.'

'Who are you calling a dyke?' Evans adopted a threatening stance again.

'Nobody. Good grief – it's what separates this country from yours, assuming we're still in England.'

'What the fuck are you on? Just shut it, okay?'

'Are you suffering from a nicotine shortage, by any chance?'

'Essex... Sidney... Mr Essex doesn't like the smoke.' Evans spoke without aggression for once.

'I don't blame him. Most normal people don't.'

'He says it damages the palate. Is that right?'

'I don't know, Evans. Does your palate feel damaged?'

'How do I know? I've always got a good appetite on me.'

'I can see that.'

'What he said – it's true, you know. He's a good cook. I love the stuff he does. Me mam cooks plain food. Nothing wrong with that you know, yeah? It's all my da' would eat, what they were brought up on. Me too, but now I've tasted other stuff. Foreign stuff, you know? Is it right, what you said about garlic, burning it?'

'Sort of.'

'I'm going to learn some cooking. Mr Essex is going to teach me. You know, garlic and all that. Can you cook?'

'I get by alright.'

'My favourite's salmon on croûte; that's salmon in pastry. I haven't done it yet but I'm going to learn.'

'Clever trick if you get it right.'

'But it's the business. I'm going to do it for me mam one day. She'll be amazed.'

'I bet she will. Look, what's the score here? Is it really all about my house? Who is it that wants it and why?'

'I don't know why they want it, do I? Grotty place if you ask me.'

'Thanks.'

'Well, it's in the middle of nowhere, isn't it? I prefer towns, places where there's a bit of life.'

'So, who's Essex working for?'

'Never you mind – you'll find out soon enough. I don't know why you're so fucking stupid about this, yeah? It was a simple deal, you'd have had some money and I'd have been paid by now, instead of pratting about like this. And I hate that bloody ferry.'

'Evanth!' Essex had entered the room.

'What ferry?' Martin asked, looking from one to the other.

'Ferry croth the Merthey, what do you think?' replied Essex. 'Don't arthk any more quethtonth. You've cauthed enough grief already. And now you're jutht going to have to thit back and enjoy the ride, okay? I trutht you don't have a problem with beef?'

'Pardon?' Martin was thrown by the question and momentarily wondered if Essex was inviting contributions to the food debate. Images of veal crates full of insane cattle swam before his eyes.

'Beef. Mad cow. You know, big thingth with hornth and udderth and bovine thpungiform encephalopathy.'

'Oh, er no, I don't think I have an opinion on that.'

'I couldn't give a damn about your opinion', Essex said wearily. 'Do you eat it?'

'Oh, er, yes!'

'Good. Becoth it wouldn't be much of a dith without the meat. You cook?'

'We've done that one. Yes, I do. Evans tells me you're going to teach him how to do saumon en croûte.'

Essex laughed. 'I think we'll get him thtarted on thumthing a little leth challenging.' He squatted down to inspect a small nick in a floorboard.

'It's a rather fine floor for this building,' Martin ventured, 'I mean unusual.'

'No, what you mean ith, you think thith building ith thit; and becoth the building ith thit, everyone and everything in it mutht be thit too. You know, millionth of people in thith country live in plaithith like thith and they're proud of them. Okay, thum people hate it and carp and complain, but they're people who would let their kidth pith in the liftth in Buckingham Pallith if they lived there. Jutht becoth theeth plaithith are concrete on the outthide, it duthent mean they have to be like prithenth inthide. Thith floor came from a big houth on the Wirral. Itth teak. The oak parquet out there,' he nodded towards the hall. 'I got that from a plaith down your way. The ownerth didn't know what they had under their wall-to-wall thag carpet.'

'And you relieved them of it.'

'Why not? They probably haven't mitht it yet.'

'I suppose your designer kitchen has a history too?'

'Ah, now that took thum finding. Either the colour wothn't quite right or the unitth were badly finithed. I finally hit the bull in a farmhouth belonging to the boyfriend of the Thecretary of Thtate for Coathtal Defentheth and Fithing.'

'I thought she was married.'

'Not her! The man who pretheeded her.'

Martin rather liked the idea of ripping off fixtures and fittings from MPs. It smacked of sweet revenge for all the taxpayers' money that had been poured into numerous black holes; he began to see Essex as a rather unusual crook. 'Well it makes a change from taking jewellery and the television,' he suggested.

'Oh, we would have had all that too but it woth crap; the old poof had hocked everything of value. Would've been bankrupt but for party fundth bailing out all the gamblerth, gayth, alcoholicth and therial adultererth whenever they thtarted to wobble. Nithe work. Letth have a bit of mewthic.'

Essex walked over to a floor-standing tower of CDs about four feet high. He stroked his chin as he perused the titles. 'Wotth your taitht, Mithter Minchin?'

'Pretty catholic, really', Martin replied.

'Church! What, hymns and stuff?' Evans frowned in disapproval.

'No, psalms! Good grief. No, I like, er,' he tried to picture the CDs he had bought during the past year, 'Paul Weller, the Manics, er, Oasis, that sort of thing.'

'Oaythith? Nobodith ever got cloath to the Beatalth,' said Essex, finally making his selection and loading it into a machine on a table in the corner. 'Lennon and McCartney were the betht tharngwriting team in the world. They'll never be bettered, not in my lifetime.' Evans was nodding in agreement; he had obviously been taught to appreciate the Fab Four. Essex looked at his watch. 'Tea will be in about an hour. Then we have to leave here by theven-thirty. Look, I'm thorry Mithter Minchin,' he anticipated Martin's protestation. 'You're coming with uth. Therth nothing you can thay or do now to change thith thituathon, tho, pleath, letth all try to make the betht of it, alright?'

Martin was too exhausted to be bothered to respond; his legs and arms ached as though he had fallen headlong into bad case of flu and, as long as he was in this flat with Evans the Thump standing by, ready to administer additional tender bruising care, he was unlikely to get away. What he really needed was a lie-down, a horizontal rest. Preferably voluntarily.

'Would it be too much to ask for a bed to lie on?' He stared at Essex, raising one eyebrow in a manner that he hoped conveyed irritation. 'I think I'm owed a bit of rest and recovery time.'

'Be my getht.' Essex's unhesitating agreement surprised Martin for a moment. 'You can thleep right there.' There was no trace of amusement in Essex's eyes, just a clear indication that the sofa was the best and only bed on offer.

'Yes, of course.' Martin shifted his bottom, rested his head on the arm of the sofa and threw his legs over the one opposite, leaving his feet dangling just a few inches above the floor. 'It's perfect.'

'Jeethuth.' Essex headed towards the door, shaking his head as though he had gone ten verbal rounds with a pointlessly obstructive public servant. 'If he moovth, hit him.'

'You're the boss,' Evans called after him, before turning towards Martin and shrugging his shoulders.

Martin rolled his eyes up and stared at the ceiling. It had been painted a rich claret, interrupted only by tiny, irregularly placed, deep holes, some of which emitted pinpricks of light aimed to bathe in white light selected pictures hanging on the walls. He wished that he could hate it, condemn it as thoroughly naff. The trouble was, he rather liked it. It was artistic. Bold, Colourful, Dulux, Emulsion, Fuck! Did this sort of thing require the attention of a shrink? Surely this isn't normal, playing obsessive mind games under these conditions? Under any conditions, come to that. Evans's fist in the face must have scrambled the head's content a bit more. Should try to sleep. Ha! Big laugh, that.

Evans was studying a newspaper, but remained sufficiently alert to meet Martin's casual glance. Martin gazed back at the ceiling. It was immaculate; not a crack, not a ripple, not a rustic bump in sight. Just smooth, perfectly painted surfaces. No Artex here. Artex, B&Q, Creosote. Going to need some creosote for those wishing well posts, if I ever see them again. Then put a match to them, tip the flaming bastards down the bloody hole. Only to come to rest a few feet below. Probably burn down what's left of the house instead. Yes, Mr Insurance Assessor, I did strike the match. No, I meant to burn the well. What do you mean null and void? Damnation, Evicted, Fucked. Should be so lucky. Lucky? Last time had been with Bev, who didn't exactly give us a standing ovation, petulant cow. What's worse than celibacy? A partner who despises you. Maybe some sprogs would have softened her. *Take that disgusting thing away!* Maybe not; she'd have probably eaten them.

Kids would be fun though. Nice kids, of course. Do that again and you'll go down the well! Seen too many little horrors, tyrants who really might benefit from a spell of introspection in some murky depths. 'Martin, my boy,' a senior partner had once offered when inebriated, 'the way to size up the fillies is to ask yourself one question: "Is this the gel I want to be the mother of my child?" In your case, the answer will almost certainly be "no".' Gosh, thanks. At least the pompous little arsehole couldn't look down at me, not unless he had an extendable ladder and a head for heights. Arsehole, Bastard... better abandon that list. Which is more deserving of the ultimate insult? A monocled, flatulent, dandy or Essex, printh of lithping thievth. Not much to choose between them really.

Smells drifting in from the kitchen, hunger beginning to hurt quite a lot. What price to be back in Angelo's? Warm company, one's face and cottage intact, nothing more frightening to look forward to than Mrs Booth-Tinderson's tax return. What's going to happen? She might have to find a replacement accountant. God help him. Or her. Oh, for the opportunity to warn them off, or just give them a helping hand, a friendly word in the ear. An explanation for the volumes of notes and correspondence. Dear God, it was precisely the sort of mess that could have one drummed out of the profession. Disciplinary panel or Essex and Evans? Tough call. No, the panel every time; just talk them through the client's fiscal history without provoking fisticuffs. Can't be too difficult; haven't been decked yet in the course of day-to-day professional duties.

How the hell does he change the bulbs? From above presumably, rip up the floor in the flat overhead, keep it for a rainy day. Probably fiddly little things. Holes surely aren't wide enough for the average adult digit. Maybe there's a widget, a bulb installer/extractor. Maybe there aren't any bulbs. Maybe the light comes from those optical things. Fibre optics. Single strands instead of bunches. How many villains does it take to change a bunch of optical fibres? Two: one to hold the victim and the other to punch his lights out. Change them for good.

~

Martin woke as his feet crashed to the floor; someone had pushed his legs off the arm of the sofa. He had been pounding the parquet, jogging along hostile streets paved with purloined surfaces, running from danger but struggling against the dragging quagmire of floor polish. His instant switch from dream to consciousness, without a momentary uncertainty about his location, suggested that his sleep had been brief and light, albeit one with a vivid dream.

'It's teatime.' Evans looked down at him expectantly. 'Well?'

Martin rose to his feet, all of his joints aching, and stretched. The inside of his mouth tasted like a gorilla's armpit, if that wasn't being too unkind to gorillas. Evans pushed him from the room, almost into Essex.

'Whoopth! Thteddy on.' He was holding a bottle of wine in each hand. 'Come and thit down.' Essex ushered Martin into a small room nearly filled by an elegant oblong dining table surrounded by six matching chairs. 'Take your pick.' He bustled out again. Martin focused his gaze on some bird shit streaking diagonally across the window, wondering if he possessed the right stuff, the stuff required to break windows and leap from great heights. No doubt his landing would flatten a gang of prepubescent mafiosi and have him up before the bench on a child molestation charge. Evans entered and placed a large bowl of rice in the middle of the table.

'Don't be starting without us, now.' He narrowed his eyes at Martin and left the room. Martin examined the rice; it looked light, white and fluffy, with no outward signs of lumpiness. Damn! The odious little man's cooking was as faultless as his taste in furnishings. Evans returned with some dinner plates and cutlery. Following him was Essex, his oven-gloved hands carrying a steaming casserole.

'Voilà, gentlemen,' he said. 'Another marthterpeeth.' He sat in a carver at the head of the table and motioned Martin to sit to one side, opposite Evans. The table mats bore facsimiles of Beatles album covers. Martin's was Rubber Soul. Although present as an unwilling guest, his hunger had the better of him and he attacked the excellent bourguignon with enthusiasm. The meal was punctuated with very little conversation as they concentrated on devouring the food. Even the choice of wine wasn't discussed. It was assumed that Martin and Evans would share the red, a robust Australian Shiraz, while Essex toyed moderately with a bottle of Bordeaux blanc. He kept everyone's plates topped up with rice and beef until the casserole was empty. Without a word, Evans collected the plates and took them out of the room.

'It hurts me to praise you,' said Martin, 'but that was very good.'

'Thank you,' Essex acknowledged graciously. 'Now we have to go.' He wiped his mouth daintily with a corner of his napkin and stood. 'If you want the toilet, go now; it'll be your lartht opportunity for a while.' Martin was beginning to feel the soporific effects of the food and wine and couldn't be bothered to voice once more his questions in the face of Essex's practised stonewalling. He decided to follow the advice.

When he returned from the lavatory, he found Essex and Evans in the hallway. Each of them held an overnight bag and Essex also carried a slim aluminium briefcase. Evans opened the front door and stepped out onto the balcony. Essex stood to one side.

'After you, Mithter Minchin.'

Martin joined Evans, who placed a vicelike grip on his upper arm. There was a bit of a chill in the air now and the dusk had brought dark clouds. Essex emerged from the flat, double-locked the door and activated an unseen alarm with an infrared device attached to his keys. As the three of them entered the lift, Martin could hear seagulls squawking in the distance. The lift descended to the ground floor and they climbed back into the Rover. Essex lowered the driver's window, pulled a wallet from inside his jacket, extracted a banknote and handed it to a girl, aged around ten, who had materialised beside the car and then vanished equally quickly.

'She looked a bit young to be running a protection racket,' Martin observed.

'Theeth kidth weren't born with your privilegeth,' Essex replied, 'but they're thmarter than moatht. They pitch their prythith well under the inthuranth manth increathed preemiumth – I tell you, replaithing your wheelth and tyerth every day getth to be a pain in the arth.' He started the car and sped out onto the road.

They retraced their previous route and, ten minutes later, pulled into the warehouse yard where the Irish truck was still sitting backed up to the loading bay. As he was led back into the building through the same door as before, Martin feigned disappointment.

'I was expecting a more interesting journey than that. I've been here already.'

'You'll get a more interethting journey than that, I promith you,' said Essex. He walked quickly over to the roller door, unclipped a latch at either side of it and prodded a switch on the wall. The door started a noisy ascent from the ground, rolling up and slowly revealing the rear doors of the trailer outside and the legend 'LM – Co. Kilkenny'. Essex jumped down to the ground outside, fiddled about with some keys, unlocked the driver's door and climbed into the cab. A few seconds later, he stepped back down, walked swiftly back to the rear of the trailer, lobbed a key up to Evans and hopped up onto the loading bay.

'Open it up,' he said to Evans, not taking his eyes off Martin. While Evans wrestled with a padlock on the trailer door Martin looked each way and over his shoulder, wondering vaguely whether this was a good moment to make a break for freedom. Essex placed a cautionary hand on his forearm. 'You're coming with uth,' he said softly. Evans threw back a couple of bolts and pulled one of the doors open. 'Come on.' Essex tugged Martin towards the door. Martin placed his feet firmly apart on the ground, determined to offer some resistance – having made one journey today in a car boot he wasn't about to enter this trailer without a struggle. Essex didn't wait even for a fraction of a second before kneeing him in his unprotected groin. 'Idiot', he added, as though the physical pain he had caused was insufficient.

Martin slowly looked up, the curious feeling of stomach ache, slightly at odds with the region struck, reminding him of the last time he had been knackered, as they had called it at school. Some light from the evening sky made its way through the translucent roof of the trailer to reveal a vast, mostly empty space. This time his feet staggered along as Essex guided him into the void.

'Now thtand perfectly thtill.' Essex's fingers pressed hard into Martin's flesh as Evans fiddled about at their feet.

'That'll slow you down boyo.' Evans stood up, brushing his hands together. Martin looked down and saw that Evans had used a pair of handcuffs to attach one of his ankles to an iron ring set firmly in the middle of the floor. The arrangement would ensure that he stayed well away from either side of his new, thin-walled prison.

'You bastard,' he said, looking from one to the other. 'Bastards. Why are you doing this to me?'

'To enthor that you behave yourthelf,' Essex replied. 'You had your charnth to make a bit of money but, no, not you. You had to fall back on your thtewpid pride and put uth all out. I have better thingth to do than thith. You've no one to blame ecthept yourthelf.'

'Oh be quiet.' Martin had been lectured to by more worthy people than this. 'And get this bloody thing off me,' he added, shaking his tethered foot.

'No,' Said Essex. 'I advithe you to thit down to avoid injuring yourthelf.'

'Oh yes, brilliant. You can't possibly leave me in here!' He shouted after Essex who was walking briskly back into the warehouse.

'Hush, man,' said Evans, looking a little confused. 'It's only for the ride like. You'll be fine. Make sure you're sat down when we're moving and you won't break anything. Don't bother trying to shout or kick or anything like that because you won't be heard. Here – there's a couple of blankets to keep warm, okay?' With that Evans threw a bundle onto the floor at Martin's feet and followed Essex out of the trailer. Shortly afterwards, heralded by the whine of its electric motor, the forklift appeared, preceded by a pallet piled high with boxes balanced on its outstretched arms. It deposited its load just inside the trailer's doors and reversed away. Evans reappeared and secured the boxes to the side of the trailer with some webbing straps. Satisfied that they were unlikely to break free, he closed first one door, then the other, wishing Martin an enjoyable journey before leaving him alone.

Martin looked around in the fast-fading light. He imagined that his only chance of being heard would be if he could kick the trailer walls, but, with one foot stuck exactly in the middle, he was barely able to reach either side, let alone deliver a hefty kick. It would be no use shouting, unless the truck was stationary and there was silence. He sat down on the floor and tried to arrange the blankets for comfort and warmth. He wondered what the time was and pulled his jacket sleeve up from his wrist. Damn! He had left his watch in Essex's bathroom, so now he was completely in limbo. What the hell was going to become of him? He lay down and stared up at his grey sky.

The engine started with the deep, guttural rattle of a large diesel. Although it was loud, the fact that it was in the tractor unit made the sound semidetached. Only the vibration running through the trailer's floor confirmed that they were in fact attached. There was a jolt and they were away, starting the next leg of his extraordinary journey.

The shuddering of chassis components, hissing of air-brakes and clunks and groans of the huge trailer were all unfamiliar to him and, for the first half hour or so, he was constantly surprised by them. Each time they moved off from a standstill, presumably at junctions and traffic lights, he strained to detect each change up through the gearbox. He counted at least eight forward gears; maybe more. Once they were going at a constant rate, possibly on a motorway, the ride smoothed and he was reasonably comfortable. Above him a flickering show of lights of various shades of yellow occasionally punctuated the darkness. He had lost all sense of time and found it impossible to estimate how far they could have travelled. He didn't even know how fast trucks like this could go on the open road. Fifty? Sixty? Probably more. He drifted off to sleep, lulled by the rumble of the road beneath.

~

He woke with a start and squinted into the light of a torch. He brought a hand up to shield his eyes as he tried to make out who was behind it.

'Thought you might want a drink or something,' said Evans, diverting the beam from Martin's face to the bottle of mineral water he was holding out towards him.

'Thanks.' Martin took the bottle. 'I need a leak too.'

'That's what the bucket's for.' Evans shone the light at a plastic bucket placed on the floor beside Martin.

'Great. Where are we?'

'In the land of my fathers, boyo.'

'Really?'

'Yup.'

'You know who your father was?'

'Of course I do! Eddie Evans.' Evans clearly thought that he was addressing a simpleton.

'And what are we doing in the land of your fathers?'

'Having a piss-stop.' Having all the answers had made him smug.

'And then where?'

Evans ignored the question. He took the bottle from Martin and shone the light again at the bucket. 'Come on now.'

'You mean I've got an audience?'

'Don't be shy, boyo. It's only a leak, isn't it? I'm sure I've seen bigger dicks than any you can wave at me.'

'You make a habit of watching big dicks then?'

'What do you mean by that? Are you calling me a queer? I'm not a bloody queer, man.'

'Just keep the light on the bucket, will you.' Martin relieved himself. 'How much longer do you plan to keep me in here?'

'I don't know; three or four more hours maybe. Wait and see. Do you want this?' Evans held out the bottle.

'Thanks.' Martin took it and sat back down. 'Can't you take this thing off?' He pointed at the handcuff on his ankle. 'I'm getting bloody cramp not being able to shift this leg.'

'No chance, boyo.'

'It's cold as well.'

'There's some more blankets here.' Evans walked towards the rear of the trailer and took a bundle off the boxes in the corner. He flung it towards Martin. 'There you go.' He pushed open the door, emptied the contents of the bucket into the darkness and hung it on a hook inside the door. 'See you later.' He jumped down into the night. There was a metallic clunk as the door was slammed shut, followed by the sound of latches being closed.

'Shit!' Martin cursed himself for not asking Evans what the time was. It was still dark, but that could indicate any time between nine and five. The fact that his bladder had needed emptying again suggested that they had been going for maybe two hours. They were obviously parked somewhere fairly deserted; somewhere in Wales if Evans was to be believed. Assuming that they had set off from Liverpool or its environs, they could now be in north or mid Wales. Of course, if Evans's father had been Scottish, they could have reached Glasgow. No, a Scot named Eddie Evans, with a very Welsh-accented son, was not terribly likely, even in this unlikeliest of situations. The engine started and they lurched off once again.

After perhaps twenty minutes, the frequency of street lights had changed from rare to constant. The truck had slowed and there was a marked increase in stopping, starting and turning. Martin reasoned that it must be a reasonably large town. He pictured a map of Wales in his head but the only places that identified themselves were Cardiff and Swansea and his attention kept on being dragged back to Shimbley and the miles of motorway that lay between his home and Liverpool. Of course, they might be returning him to Lockkeeper's Cottage, having realised that their plans had been foiled. No, that was ridiculously optimistic. Once more he began to speculate that he knew too much to be allowed to go free. He could identify Essex and Evans without any difficulty. Given a driver who knew his way around Merseyside, he might be able to find Essex's flat and warehouse. And, because Essex was a self-confessed crook, the police could probably find sufficient stolen property to bring a strong case. On top of that, there was the matter of kidnapping, assault, extortion, all of them surely even more serious than theft. On second thoughts, court cases regularly demonstrated that property was held in higher regard by the law than mere people. Except in cases of murder perhaps. Oh, bloody hell! If Essex was ever tried for murder, Martin's corpse would probably be Exhibit A. He tried to concentrate on something else and Beverley sprang to mind. From bad to worse, he thought.

They had been stationary for a while, with the engine idling gently and rhythmically, but now they were on the move again, under a great deal more light. Martin was puzzled by the sounds of machinery, industrial clunks and clangs all around them, what seemed to be the occasional raised voice. The truck traversed what felt like a series of speed humps and finally came to a halt, its engine now humming in unison with others. It must be some sort of truck park or freight depot. He considered yelling for help but decided that it would be pointless – there was too much noise around for him to be heard, or to hear any response, and he realised that any people who may be present could well be Essex's colleagues. Instead he sat still and concentrated on listening.

The myriad noises droned on without much change for half an hour or so. Their own engine had been shut down but others were running elsewhere. Martin wasn't sure, but he thought that he detected the truck moving again; there had been a slight sideways motion. Its engine wasn't running, yet it felt unsteady. He thought that perhaps a gust of wind had caught the trailer and made it sway. Then he began to doubt his senses; he was probably imagining it, his body taking its time settling after the constant motion during their time on the move, rather like the wobbly feeling experienced on dry land after a period bobbing about in a boat. Some machinery was emitting a constant drone somewhere outside but he could no longer detect the sound of other trucks. He stood up, wrapping a blanket tightly around himself; the night was becoming increasingly chilly. Suddenly the truck seemed to dip, as though the floor had momentarily gone from beneath his feet. He stumbled onto one knee and steadied himself with his hands – with one ankle attached so tightly to the floor, he imagined that breaking it would be easy during a lapse of concentration. He could feel a constant vibration through the floor but it was different from when they had been driving along. For a second he felt panic, unable to understand what was happening, before the cause of the sensation became apparent, as if through slowly clearing fog: they were on a ferry. Evans had mentioned a ferry in Essex's flat. The drone was from the boat's engines. The clunks, ramps, voices, other trucks... of course! Good grief! They were taking him out of the country. No chance now to expose his abductors to the long arm of the law; not the British law, anyway.

In no time they would be thundering across the European mainland. Oh God. He must have been asleep for hours; the nearest Channel port to Liverpool must be, what, five hours by truck? It had taken him nearly two hours to reach Portsmouth in Alfredo last time he went to France, and Shimbley was a damn sight nearer than Liverpool. Five hours? He couldn't possibly have been asleep for that long. No, they must be somewhere else. Scotland? Over the sea to Skye? That's daft; what possible business could they have on Skye? Land of Evans's fathers! They were on a bloody ferry to Ireland! Holyhead to Dun Laoghaire. Shit! That crossing must take hours! Martin cupped his hands around his mouth, megaphone-style. 'Heeeeelp!'

CHAPTER 4: Friday night/Saturday morning

Shouting for help proved to be a pointless exercise. All that Martin had to show for ten or so minutes of earnest yelling was a sore throat and a raging thirst. He took another swig of water and shivered. No wonder it was so cold; they were in the middle of the Irish Sea. He thought of the sign writing on the trailer and shook his head, as though censuring himself for being so slow to realise where they were going. Then, in self-defence, he allowed that the sensory deprivation that he had endured was a pretty powerful excuse for less than razor-sharp reasoning. He tried to remember exactly what was written on the truck. There had been both name and place, or was it just initials and a place? The place began with W. Waterford? Wexford? Wicklow? Kilkenny! Yes, it was Kilkenny, not W at all; County Kilkenny. The name seemed familiar to him, even though he had never been to Ireland. He knew what Ireland looked like on a map and he knew that the lump at top right held whatever the six counties were that represented Northern Ireland, but he had absolutely no idea whereabouts Kilkenny was. Not that it mattered a great deal to him where it was, of course. What mattered to him was what he was doing going to Ireland anyway. He had been given enough grief by an Englishman and a Welshman without an Irishman entering the frame.

The crossing seemed interminable. The pitch of the ferry's engines rarely changed, though occasionally they sounded laboured for a few seconds, as if straining against a strong surge of current. There were also moments of unsettling swaying; he assumed that trucks were carried deep in the bowels of the boat, in which case the sea must have been choppy. Unless it was a small ferry. He realised that he didn't really know anything about the ferries that crossed the Irish Sea. He presumed that they must be at least as large as the cross-channel ones, because he was sure that this piece of water was less hospitable than that separating England from France. What if it sank? He was fearful again. No one, except Essex and Evans, knew that he was on the ferry. Everyone would board the lifeboats, none the wiser that he was descending to a watery grave, chained to the floor of an Irish truck. What would his friends and relatives make of his disappearance? They would find Alfredo abandoned at Lockkeeper's Cottage, a few of Martin's modest belongings sitting on the floor in cardboard boxes, the cottage devastated. Would they think that he had been responsible for the damage? Gone berserk perhaps, the strain of parting from Beverley. Vanished off the face of the earth after a prolonged fit of vandalism. 'That was where Minchin the Mad Accountant lived', they would say in years to come. 'He smashed the place up and was never seen again, a tragedy for the beautiful young wife he left behind.' No, people would never sympathise with Beverley, surely. She was capable of eliciting many sentiments in people, but pity wasn't one of them; not in people who knew her, anyway. He wondered if anyone would ever find the whisky, resisting discovery in its hidey-hole in the fireplace. Perhaps some future owner of the house will light a roaring fire and lose his eyebrows to a ball of flame, as the bottle succumbs to the heat. Oh, how he could use a drop of that stuff at this moment.

He rearranged his makeshift bed and snuggled into it, one of the blankets serving as both pillow and ear muffler, damping the monotonous churning emanating from the ferry's engine room. When they docked he would have another attempt at raising the alarm. Even the slackest customs officer would wonder what a person was doing locked in a trailer. Apart from anything else, he was a stowaway; he didn't suppose that Essex had bought a valid ticket for his unwilling, unseen passenger. He wondered if there were laws against cross-border person-smuggling. Would he be regarded as an illegal immigrant? Or does it matter when both countries are members of the EU? What the hell? At least he would be returned home... wouldn't he? If not, a cell in an Irish police station would have to be an improvement over his current situation. He dozed fitfully, the events and conversations of the past twenty hours or so drifting in and out of his mind in bits and pieces and in no particular order. Each time his dreaming became surreal, he awoke to the same depressing reality.

There was a jolt and the engine note changed. They must have reached port. He heard a truck start and struggled to his feet, shouting so loudly that it hurt his throat. He felt a bit silly shouting 'help' but couldn't think of a more appropriate alternative. Before he had yelled half a dozen times, his voice was drowned by the noise of 'his' truck clattering into life and soon there was a cacophony – rattling diesels, slamming doors, groaning and clanking metalwork, screeching mechanisms. He thought that he might be better off waiting until they were off the ferry; perhaps there was some sort of customs shed they would have to drive through, in which he would have a better chance of being heard.

They waited, motor chugging, for around twenty minutes before moving. They were probably letting the cars off first. The last thing a car driver needs is a trundling line of forty articulated trucks impeding progress. Eventually they started off, bumping over the metal ramps, the trailer creaking as it twisted from corner to corner. He recommenced his shouting. He shouted at one wall, then at the doors, then the other wall, then back again, just in case the acoustics were better in one direction. They were going up through the gears; He shouted on, the grey sky of early morning growing steadily lighter above the grubby translucent roof. He estimated that they were now in seventh gear, and they seemed to be maintaining a regular speed. They had been off the ferry for several minutes now. He sat down, accepting that his ploy had been unsuccessful; no one had stopped them, no one had opened the trailer, no one except his captors knew that he was in Ireland. If, indeed, that was where he was.

For the next hour, as the daylight brightened his cell, he sat on the floor, bracing himself in vain attempts to anticipate each movement. There were frequent gear changes, bends, junctions, ascents and descents, bursts of acceleration and heavy braking – no motorway here. He envisaged the truck scaling mountain passes, snaking up and down twisty ribbons of road, putting mile upon mile between him and his much coveted home, the home he had yet to occupy. He wished that he could see out: apart from the fact that it would make it a great deal easier for him to pre-empt cornering forces, he had always wanted to see a bit of Ireland. Footage of breathtaking scenery glimpsed in TV commercials and sundry magazines had whetted his appetite. His mind was dwelling on an image of horse-drawn carts in an unspoilt land of green when a bulge, the diameter of a tennis ball, appeared on the trailer wall to his left with a bang that all but made his heart stop. It was followed by a crescendo of clunks on both sides, as though they were in the middle of a meteor storm. The air-brakes hissed and the tyres under the rear of the trailer howled as they slid along the tarmac beneath them. For some miles he had been holding the ring to which his leg was attached and now his grip on it instinctively tightened. His hunched body fell over onto one side, but his stretched arm succeeded in preventing damage to his ankle. He could hear some raised voices, possibly of children. He managed to right himself into a sitting position, muttering congratulations aloud for avoiding injury. Ankle, Bone, Connected, Disturbed! In a rare show of concern for his cargo, Essex opened one of the doors and climbed up into the back.

'Are you alright? That woth a thudden thtop I'm afraid.'

'No, I'm bloody not. What the hell's going on?'

'Thum children being naughty.'

'Are we in Ireland?'

'Congratulaithunth! You're not a complete ignoraimuth, then. Your fanthy educathon included baithic geography.' Essex was about to jump down out of the trailer again and Martin stood up, agitated.

'Let me out of here now!' Martin put such an effort into his shouted demand that his eyes were screwed tightly shut. When he opened them he could do nothing to prevent tears pouring down his face. So much had happened to him that he had bottled up most of his anxiety and fear. Now the dam had burst and he sobbed uncontrollably. Essex paused by the door, then walked slowly back to Martin.

'You poor man,' he said, without conviction.

'Poor nothing, you bastard, fucking bastard!' Martin was spluttering, his frustration and hurt and anger now bubbling to the surface in a barely coherent eruption. 'You bring me here to... I don't fucking know. You, you want my fucking house. Bollocks!' He was shouting now, like a child having a tantrum. 'Kidnapping, imprisonment, fucking people-smuggling. Who the hell do you think you are, you fucking bastard! Bastard!'

The punch took Martin completely by surprise. He stared at his stomach and then at Essex's fist as it retreated; he almost felt like a bystander, watching as the breath left his body and the pain spread through his abdomen. He sank to his knees and then on to his side. Essex's calm voice eventually penetrated the singing in his ears.

'Don't call me a barthterd, Mithter Minchin.'

Martin was shocked. He had misread the signals, mistakenly believed that Essex was pretty cool. Here was confirmation that he was worryingly unstable. The knee in the groin back in Liverpool had been provoked by his physical resistance but this – this was a violent reaction to an understandable and not entirely unreasonable taunt.

'Please don't do that.' Bracing himself on rigid arms, he stared at the floor between his hands and tried to regain his breath with some dignity. 'I need a lavatory now.'

'Ten minitth.' Essex jumped down from the trailer and slammed the door shut again. Martin had struggled back to his feet and now stood, throbbing with pain and wondering what 'ten minutes' meant. Did it mean that Essex was allowing him ten minutes of privacy, starting now? If that was the case, how the hell was he supposed to reach the bucket hanging up at least fifteen feet away? That would be a clever trick; a clever dick! A, Big, Clever, Dick's, Extraordinary, Firepower? Better than fountain! Best try to think of something else. He averted his gaze from the target and focused on the floor between his feet.

The brakes were released with a hiss; Essex must have meant that they had another ten minutes of travelling ahead of them, either to their destination or to a place where he would be permitted to meet a need that was now becoming urgent. He quickly sat down again and grasped the metal ring. After a few more miles of twisting and turning, the truck made a sharp turn and bumped along what must have been an unmade track.

At last they came to a halt and the doors were pulled open. Martin was pleased to see that Evans had been missing his sleep and creature comforts too. His ponytail was dishevelled, his shirt only partly tucked in to his trousers; his eyes peered out wearily from over capacious dark grey bags. He approached Martin without greeting him, or even meeting his gaze, bent down and released his leg. He took hold of Martin's arm and then, after looking him up and down, let go again, as if recognising that his prisoner was in no state to give him the slip.

'Come on, boyo. I expect you could use a bit of breakfast, eh?'

'I could use a lavatory. And then a policeman.'

'Yeah yeah.' Evans helped him down from the trailer. They were in a large, recently surfaced yard with new, white rendered farm buildings on three sides and a bright orange grain dryer standing guard in one corner. In the distance some green and dark grey mountains poked up into low cloud.

Martin looked at the side of the trailer, then gazed around. 'Is this County Kilkenny, then?'

Before Evans answered, Essex jumped down from the driver's side of the cab and approached them.

'Evanth!' He behaved as though the journey had barely dented his energy. 'Get the gear out – put it in that thed.' He pointed across the yard, then scowled at Martin.

'He wants the toilet,' said Evans.

'Itth in there.' He nodded towards the building nearest them. 'That green door, lartht but one.' He looked at Evans again. 'Are you thtill here?'

Martin walked in the direction indicated and found a newly furnished bathroom, incongruously installed within the farm buildings. He closed the door, noticed that there wasn't a key in the lock, opened it again to see if it was on the other side, which it wasn't, and decided that he didn't have time to be coy. He pushed down his trousers and underpants and sank onto the pan, not a moment too soon. Relieved and relaxing, he looked around. He saw a key hanging from a nail right by the door. Typical. On the back of the door was a calendar with a picture of a bikini-clad model, fondling a good looking heifer and grinning at the camera; a large plastic sack of something stood on the ground beside them. 'Fill em with Farson's,' said the caption. He wondered what Farson's was and whether it was for cows or women. Or both. The bathroom suite, in a surprisingly dated looking avocado green, had not been designed for the smaller home. A vast bath occupied one corner and the hand basin could clearly accommodate the largest hands – dirty hands too, judging by the grime on and around it. He was surprised; had he ever given it any thought, he would never have expected luxury bathrooms to be a must-have facility in the average farmyard, in Ireland or anywhere else. Perhaps this farmer's wife had tired of him bringing his work home, or rather bits of it. From outside came the electric whine of a forklift truck and a series of clunking sounds as it sought to gain a secure hold of the pallet in the trailer. It hadn't been much of a cargo for such a large trailer. He presumed that most of LM's international trade, as advertised on the trailer, was exporting, not importing, otherwise a Transit van would have sufficed. It certainly seemed to be a very extravagant way to transport one captive and a modest pile of boxes. Either Martin or the contents of the boxes must have made it worthwhile. Maybe the boxes contained some of the fruits of Essex's raids on country houses. The bathroom door flew open, banging against the wall, and Evans entered.

'Fuck me, you're a fruity boyo this morning,' he said, turning to the basin and washing his hands.

'I don't need an audience.'

'There's nothing you've got that I haven't seen.' Evans's face adopted a smug expression, as he took a towel from a rail.

'I shouldn't bet on it,' Martin mumbled, peering between his thighs into the pan.

'Eh?'

'Evans.'

'Yeah?'

'Go away will you, just while I do this.' Evans looked a little hurt but didn't make any immediate move towards the door. 'Piss off Evans!'

'Shy boy!' Evans replaced the towel and wandered out into the yard, closing the door behind him. Martin finished his business then lingered, curious to see more of his surroundings but apprehensive about his immediate safety. He grimaced at the mirror in only slightly mock panic as he dried his hands, then stepped back out into the yard. He looked around, taking in the newness of everything: pots of paint lay strewn around, the smell of freshly applied gloss lingering in the doorways; a window frame in the wall of a shed opposite was still wearing only grey primer; the roof slates were so immaculate that they looked as though they were made of plastic.

'Not bad, eh?' Evans was back at his side.

'What the hell's a bathroom doing in a farmyard?'

'Brilliant, isn't it? There's a jacuzzi in there, you know. Bubbles and everything.'

'I wouldn't have thought they were a novelty for a chap like you.'

'Eh? What?'

'Bubbles in the bath.'

'What's that?'

'Big tub, water.'

'I give up, you fucking weirdo.'

Martin sniggered, then Evans grunted before setting off at a brisk pace towards the gap through which their truck must have entered the yard. Martin eyed the fence bordering the field on the opposite side and wondered if this was the moment to make a dash for freedom.

'Don't even think about it.' Martin jumped. Essex appeared to be a mind reader. 'Letth go and thee the man with the money.'

They strolled out of the yard, following Evans's route. Just like Evans, Essex made no attempt to restrain Martin; this was their Colditz – Don't even think about it, Kapitän Minchin. Ethcape itht impothible. To attempt itht futile. And ve vill thoot on thite, ja? Martin saw a bicycle leaning up against one of the sheds and studied the meadow, looking for undulations sufficient to assist in a recreation of Steve McQueen's great escape. On a bicycle? Have to have a rocket strapped to one's bum. Or eat beans in industrial quantities. Around the corner were the remains of a large, old, stone-built house. Remnants of wallpaper and bits of painted timber suggested that it had been occupied during this century rather than the last, and probably quite recently. Martin guessed that it was the original farmhouse and thought its destruction was a shame; the dark stone suited this countryside. They reached a fork in the drive; one way led to the road and the other led to a newly built, whitewashed house. Were it not for the preposterous pillars supporting a portico over the extravagantly sized front door, it would have been an unremarkable detached family home.

'My God, it's the White House! Is the First Lady in?'

'Don't mock it. Itth a big improvement on the old plaith.' He nodded towards the ruin.

'That's a matter of opinion.'

'That woth an agricultural building, in dithrepair.' Essex continued, ignoring Martin's point of view. 'Get an EU development grant to replaith it, Mickth your Uncle. You've got a brand new houth and the only outlay you've had to make ith on hiring a J-thee-B to make the old plaith look thootably dithtrethed. Have a builder in the family and you can thee a profit in cath ath well ath on the perthonal balanth theet.'

'You've got to be kidding.'

'No. You're the accountant – I thought you people underthtood profit and loth, revaluathon rethervth, depreethiathon and tho on.'

'You can't depreciate real estate.'

'Thumbody depreethiated yourth, didn't they?' Essex gave Martin one of his long, unblinking stares. 'Anyway, take it from me, you thood feather your netht while you can.'

'So who's paying for it?'

'You and me. Well, maybe not me, but you and Fronthwah and Fabritthio and Jürgen and Juan, you get my drift? Thith unionth been the making of thivil thervantth and conmen in equal numberth.'

They walked around one side of the new house and Martin saw in a nearby double garage a black Mazda sports car and a big silver Mercedes-Benz saloon, neither looking particularly second-hand. He pointed towards them and said to Essex: 'Well, I can see that there's plenty of money here. Conman or civil servant?'

'Thatth a tractor,' Essex ignored the question.

'I'm talking about the Merc.'

'Tho am I.'

'You're calling it a tractor?'

'Not jutht me.'

'You mean – agricultural grant?'

'You're getting the picture now.' A back door was open and they entered a utility room that housed an immaculate suite of

German laundry and dishwashing appliances and a vast, American-style fridge. Essex stopped in front of the latter and stood admiring it. 'Now thith ith thumthing I would really like to have.'

'You don't have the room for it, do you?'

'Oh, I'd make room for thith. I applied for a grant.'

'For a fridge?'

'Yeth. A refrigerathon unit for my farm, actually.'

'Your farm at your flat, I suppose?'

'Thatth the one. How many farmth do you think I have?'

'Don't tell me you got turned down.'

'Thatth the trouble when the money hath to go around fifty-whatever million people inthted of three or four. "Fill in thith; thine that; how much hath your Auntie Flo got in the Poatht Offith?" Paint it every which way and itth thtill a pain to ecthtract money from our wonderful pen-pootherth.'

'But they didn't question your farm?'

'Yeth, they were a bit iffy about that too, ath it happenth. Thood have given my addreth ath a high-rithe in Dublin – you know they can obtain grarnth for thtabelth on the twelfth floor? People buy theeth poor old nagth and park them on every available peeth of communal grarth. The thilly thing ith, they'd get the grant without actually having to buy the bloody animalth in the firtht plaith.'

They entered the kitchen where Evans was studying a large frying pan.

'Wotth cooking, Evanth?'

Evans looked puzzled. 'Do you think we should use this one? It looks brand new.'

Essex took the pan from Evans. 'Martin,' he said, much to Martin's surprise, used now to being addressed as Mithter Minchin. 'Could you pleath thee what you can do about getting thum coffee on? Evanth, jutht keep an eye on him. Make thor he duthent find the knife drawer, yeth?' He went out to his dream fridge for a supply of bacon. Martin explored the cupboards, finding, bit by bit, coffee, mugs and a cafetière. He was in dire need of a hearty breakfast.

'Cor, real?' enthused Evans.

'I hope so.'

'Bee-jeezus!' Martin swung round in the direction of this loud, whiskey-soaked, Irish voice. 'You're one tall fecker, even for an Englishman. Liam Monan.' Martin examined the outstretched hand for a moment and pointedly kept his own hands to himself.

'Charmed,' he replied in a surly manner, though this didn't appear to faze his host.

'So! Yer Martin Minchin, Laird of Lockkeeper's Cottage and all-round stubborn son of a bitch.'

'And you must be the stupid bastard with the curious property buying technique and a nasty line in associates,' Martin countered, looking Monan up and down. Aged around sixty, he was completely bald, a condition that provided unnecessary emphasis to his wildly bushy eyebrows. He wore mechanic's overalls, bright blue and spotless, with precision-ironed creases. His feet were in black wellington boots, again without a speck of dirt on them.

'Ah, but yer've brought this upon yerself. Yer a man of numbers, but not a man of sense. Or you wouldn't feckin' be here!' Monan's grin might have been quite winning, were it not for his eyes, which were now bulging, as though straining to take a closer look at their visitor. 'Come, let these boys get the breakfast while you and I have a little chat.' Monan turned and led Martin out of the kitchen, through a spacious hall and into a small, informal sitting room. They sat in new-looking armchairs either side of a mock fire with plastic 'coal' and polished brass trim.

'What d'ya t'ink I do for a livin'?' asked Monan, sitting back, folding his hands together on his stomach and smiling at Martin.

'Oh, a bit of kidnapping, extortion, thieving, ripping off tax payers, that sort of thing?'

'Come, come now, Martin, play along wit' me, won't yer?'

'Alright. So you're a farmer with a sideline in road haulage and another in property speculation, sponsored by the European Union.'

'No, yer wrong, although I *am* a farmer in the sense that I keep some cattle here. Call me a hobby farmer!'

'What about all those new sheds? The grain dryer?'

'Oh, that's no grain dryer! Sure, it looks like a grain dryer, but yer couldn't dry feck all in that. No, that's what yer might call a folly. You wouldn't believe what a real grain dryer costs! Well, that fine monument is there solely to demonstrate to any inquisitive bureaucrat takin' a tour beyond the Pale that the money was indeed spent responsibly.'

'Right, so you live off fraudulent agricultural claims. What's with the truck? Drug running?'

'No, the freight business is perfectly legitimate. Well, relatively so, to be fair wit' yer. Ireland is busy knockin' out plenty of top class goods these days, you know. Not just beer, whiskey and spuds; we're makin' computers, clothes, car components, music, sane beef even! If yer've got the means, people will pay yer to shift as much as yer can. I've got two trucks, a depot in Liverpool and another near here and it makes me a punt or two. Also, if I can fetch back a few bits and pieces on the return journey, there's plenty of new money in Dublin chasin' a lump of furniture or an objet d'art.'

'So, you've got all that going, what the bloody hell do want with my house?'

'I'm the Lord of Drestbury.' Martin was confused. 'And Fitchin'hurst,' Monan continued, 'and half a dozen of yer other sad, unlamented and unwanted manors.' He waved a hand at some framed certificates hanging on the wall. 'Copies of course. The originals are in a bank vault. I'm also the Lord of the Manor of Vereham.'

Martin sat up. 'Am I supposed to be impressed? Buying those useless old titles is pretty silly, like having vanity plates on your car. I suppose you think that my house is your manor house – I'm afraid that's not the way it works.'

'Now then, Martin. Yer sittin' there sayin' I'm a thick Mick and wonderin' whether there ain't some truth in all yer tired old Irish jokes. Well, I'll tell you somet'in': this Irishman's got his feckin' head screwed on, and me manorial titles have repaid me a t'ousandfold. I've sold property access rights to eleven different companies: water, electric, gas, telecomms, cable TV, you name it. I've sold land regarded as wort'less to a car parkin' outfit for more money than ya'd make in five years. I've negotiated a remarkable deal wit' yer Department of Transport regardin' the widenin' of a section of yer M49 motorway. I've had yer County Councils beggin' me to take their ratepayers' money just to get me out of their hair. Ya see, yer useless, silly titles often come with shitty little strips of roadside verge, a hedge here, a godforsaken putrid bog there. These little bits of yer feckin' country, squalid square yards of crap that no self-respectin' Englishman would let sully his good name have made me a feckin' wealthy Irishman.'

'Yes, but even if you are Lord of my manor, what do you want with my house? I shouldn't think that it stands in the way of any other property developments. Unless the Shimbley bypass really is going to become a reality and plough through the kitchen, in which case I think I'm the one who would be talking compensation with the Department of Transport or whoever.'

'Well.'

'Well what?' Martin sensed that Monan was chuckling at an in-joke.

'Well. That's just it, isn't it?'

'What? What is?'

'The feckin' well.'

'What?'

'The well, Martin. Yer feckin' well at Lockkeeper's Cottage.'

'Oh, that well! Well, what about it?'

'The Lord of the Manor of Vereham has sole rights for mineral extraction t'roughout the Manor. But then, in 1796, along comes a codicil by government decree, givin' title of yer cottage to a Miss Mary McConnelly, includin' extraction rights to the mineral water that gurgles up in the garden, in yer pretty little wishin' well. This means that, in the absence of any descendant of Miss McConnelly comin' forward to claim the water, it belongs to whomever holds the deeds to the property. For the moment, then, the water's all yours. But I want it.'

'What on earth are you talking about? There's no water...'

'Oh, that's where yer so very wrong. Why else the alteration two hundred years ago? That was done very deliberately, for a very good reason. Water then was a valuable thing to own, you know, just as it is now. It took powerful people to use parliament to adjust the manorial rights. That feckin' obscenity in yer garden is clearly the route to a fortune, maybe even a global brand like Perrier. I tell ya, it's me retirement plan. Me pension. Lockkeeper's Cottage could be churnin' out half a million bottles a year for discernin' drinkers. And if Lockkeeper's Springwater or Monan Springwater or Vereham Springwater or whatever the feck I fancy callin' it fails to catch the public's imagination, I'm sure that Mr Tesco or Mr Safeway or Mr Sainsbury will be beatin' a path to me door.'

'There's a problem though,' Martin wanted to spoil the party.

'What?'

'There's no bloody well. No water. There is a rather unpleasant erection in the garden, but I fear it's unlikely to lead to hidden assets, liquid or otherwise.'

'Why so sceptical, Mr Accountant?'

'Because even the estate agents emphasised that the preposterous thing is for show. It's only a few feet deep, for God's sake. There is no water. The only way you'll get so much as a puddle in there is if you piss in it.'

'Well if yer so sure of that, why don't ya sell me the place?'

'Because I want to live there!'

'I heard that it's no longer very habitable, even for a not very bright Englishman.'

'It was until you set your arseholes loose on it, which must make you the dippy one.'

'Dippy is it now? Oh, Mr Minchin – Martin, Martin, Martin. Yer goin' to cooperate wit' me, because I intend to have that water. I intend to make some very serious money from that. And, let's face it, yer not exactly Mr Dynamic. Feck, it's so lucrative I'll probably pay some tax on me income. So,' he paused and met Martin's eye, a frown creasing his face, 'I have no feckin' intention of lettin' this slip through me fingers. That's why yer here. It ain't feckin' negotiable.'

Essex entered the room cautiously, anxious not to upset his paymaster. 'Breakfatht ith ready.' He gave Monan an inquisitive look.

'The workin' man's best meal,' Monan beamed as he rose from his chair. 'Come, Martin. Yer bones must be rattlin' with the hunger. Yer'll never accuse the Irish of being poor hosts.'

They returned to the kitchen where Essex had laid out a feast of bacon, sausages, grilled tomatoes, mushrooms, black pudding, poached eggs, fried bread, toast, a groaning cheese board, great slabs of soda bread and bowls of creamy white butter.

'How's yer heart, Mr Minchin?' asked Monan with a snigger. 'Tuck right in and kiss goodbye to tomorra!' The four men took their seats, all laughing except Martin, who seemed to be the subject of their mirth. They took turns spooning the contents of different serving bowls onto their plates. If a healthy diet was on the agenda of anyone present, it was well hidden for the duration of the meal.

'Them itinerants gone then?' Monan had speared an inch of sausage and waved it lazily in front of his face as he looked towards Essex for an answer.

'Yeth and no.'

'Tell.'

'I thought they'd gone; I mean, they've left the paddock but they theem to have taken root on the old Bellagh road. The children amboothed uth; threw thtoanth at the truck.'

'The gyppos?' Evans had woken up. 'Huge boulders it was! And they're hardly old enough to walk. I tell you, Mr Monan, those kids need a proper smacking. Their parents too.'

'If they know who their parentth are,' countered Essex.

'They've done some terrible damage to your trailer, Mr Monan.'

'Come on Evanth, don't exaggerate. I think we can deal eathily enough with a bunth of gypthith.'

Martin recalled the interruption on the last leg of their journey in the truck. 'That commotion on the way here? That was gypsies? Why?'

'They didn't like being removed from some land they t'ought they were entitled to. Am I ringin' any bells, Martin?' Monan raised a quizzical, shaggy eyebrow in Martin's direction.

'Ha ha. So they stoned your truck? Good for them! What happened, then? You fancied something you thought they had?'

Martin was looking at Monan and Essex in turn, enjoying their discomfort. 'A rich, subterranean seam of white heather perhaps?'

'Yeth, thatth very funny.'

'Yer don't want to be an apologist for t'em feckin' pikey bastards, so yer don't,' Monan was addressing Martin with clear sincerity. 'These feckin' itinerants are filt' – lyin', thievin', diseased didicois. They'd take the fillin's from yer teet' as soon as say "Hello", as God's my witness. Filt'!' His tone was contemptuous and the room remained silent as he refreshed his mug from the coffee pot.

'Good grief,' said Martin eventually, taken aback by Monan's tirade, 'you're not prejudiced at all, then.'

'I feckin' well am when it comes to feckin' itinerants!' Having made his position quite clear, Monan changed the subject. 'Yer have a mortgage on this property of yers?'

'Yes.'

'How much?'

'That's none of your business,' replied Martin indignantly.

'Okay, then. Wit' whom?'

'Wiltshire Bank, as it happens. But I don't...'

'Shimbley branch?' Monan interrupted.

'Why are you asking me all this? I don't think you can go over my head, you know, to the lender. I do have rights. Or maybe you plan to raid the bank, take the deeds from the vault.'

'Ah now, Martin, yer quite right there; yer do have rights. But if, let's say, yer left t'is mortal coil, God forbid, I do believe that the bank would have certain rights – to recoup their money, Martin.'

'Don't you think there are one or two people who might be suspicious? I mean, don't you think they'd be looking for a murderer?'

'Oh, please! I'm an Irish haulier and hobby farmer; I don't t'ink Dickhead of the Yard will be knockin' on *my* door any time soon. My God, Martin, I know they like to blame all sorts of shit on innocent Irish people, but the disappearance of a long streak of a nobody? Please do me a favour!'

'But if you show up at the Wiltshire Bank, expressing an interest in my property, I think that even the slowest policeman is going to prick up his ears and sniff promotion. And the bank manager will smell a rat. Literally in your case.'

'I've a feelin' that the bank would be more interested in seein' the colour of me money. We'll have to see, though, won't we?' Monan smiled and Martin felt distinctly uneasy. 'Anyway, while we decide our next move and yer think about yer future, yer may as well be comfortable. There's a fresh bed for yer, TV and so on.'

The meal continued, Monan and Essex quietly discussing their business in a verbal shorthand indecipherable to an outsider, and Evans eating like someone just released from a week's fast. Although Essex and Monan looked perfectly relaxed, each time Martin reached for his orange juice or a piece of bread they would throw him a wary look; only Evans seemed oblivious to everything except the contents of the plate in front of him. While becoming increasingly alarmed, Martin judged that a dash for freedom in the present circumstances would almost certainly end in tears – his own. It was unlikely that he could reach the back door without being brought down and he certainly didn't wish to accelerate what remained of his life. Taking them all on armed only with knife, fork and teaspoon would be equally foolish. While he didn't relish the idea of being put to death without putting up a fight, he rather reluctantly decided that a waiting game was still his best option.

'Come on then, boys.' Monan pushed his chair back and stood up. 'Sid, why don't yer show Martin here up to the guest room. Oh, and here's today's paper if yer interested.' He picked up a copy of the Irish Times from a sideboard and handed it to Martin.

Essex looked at Martin. 'Come on then, thith way.' He led him out into the hall and up the stairs. 'You'll find thith more comfortable than the truck. Evanth will keep an eye on you and will take great plethur in hurting you if you give him any trouble. And ath we won't be inclined to take you to any hothpital, that would be a very thilly opthon.'

'But your boss seems to be in favour of killing me anyway.'

'True.' Essex ushered Martin into a large bedroom. 'Here you are; not bad for a thell.'

Martin looked around. It was furnished in the manner of a million hotel rooms – comfortable but bland. He walked to the window that overlooked the drive in front of the house. They were modern plastic-framed, double-glazed units, locked shut. He tried one of the handles.

'Could I have the key to this? It's stuffy in here.'

'Nithe try.' Essex was on his knees, groping underneath the bed. For an idiotic moment Martin thought he might be praying, but then saw that he had unplugged a telephone, which he took with him. 'Bye then. Thweet dreamth.' He left the room, locking the door behind him.

Martin looked into the en-suite bathroom and opened and closed various wardrobe doors. He sat on the edge of the bed and bounced up and down a couple of times, then stopped, wondering why people always did that, as if bounciness was relevant to anything. He looked through the window again and examined the locks; if he was to escape this way he would have to smash the glass, which would require a hefty weapon. His eyes rested on the television and he smiled, envisaging himself emulating a wild rock star, sending TVs plummeting to destruction. Of course the noise of a TV passing through a large double-glazed window would not go unnoticed by Evans, or anybody else within a mile. On top of that, he guessed that to jump to the concrete drive, a considerable distance below, without a parachute, or several bouncy mattresses to land on, would be foolhardy. He heard the front door slam shut and watched Monan and Essex stroll over to the garage, climb into the Mercedes and drive away, Essex looking straight up at him from the passenger seat and giving him a casual, slightly regal wave. So, Evans remained as gaoler. Martin picked up the paper and settled down on the bed to catch up on the news – maybe there would be a little item about an English accountant running amok and vanishing.

After an hour or so, Martin's reading was interrupted by the sound of a key in the lock. Evans entered with a big white towelling robe, which he tossed onto the bed. 'Here you are, boyo. Mr Monan says you stink and I've got to put your stuff in the washer.' Martin saw that he had changed into a different shirt. He hesitated; his first inclination was not to give his clothes to anyone, but then he thought of having to wear them for another day, maybe longer.

'You know how to use a washing machine without wrecking everything?'

'Just give us your fucking clothes. You think I care? You think I want to do this?'

'Okay, hang on.' He took the robe into the bathroom and changed into it, re-emerging to hand Evans his shirt, underpants and socks. 'Now don't go mixing these with any exotic colours, and be sure to use an environmentally sound detergent.'

'Are you taking the piss?'

'Yes.'

Evans shook his head and left, clutching Martin's little bundle of laundry and muttering expletives about clever-dicks. Now that he had nothing but a robe to wear, Martin decided that he might as well have a bath. It was forty-eight hours since he had last had a decent wash. As in Essex's flat, the toiletries in this bathroom had been provided by a hotel group. He assumed that Monan had pocketed them during an overnight stay somewhere until he opened a cupboard to find dozens more of the same items; Monan must have robbed the factory, or hijacked a delivery truck. Perhaps there was a Mrs Monan who was a kleptomaniac. Or should that be Lady Monan of Vereham and other places? It was strange – there had been no signs of any female presence in this large family house, neither in person nor in photographs. Perhaps crazed villains didn't attract partners very easily.

He reclined in a foaming bath, his feet resting up on the end, either side of the taps. Perhaps this was the last wallow he would ever have. Encouraging thought. Why did he keep relaxing? He was in real danger here. But still, better to relax than to panic; think about one's sticky end and it takes the shine off the day. Oh, God, please tell me what to do. Wash hair, for starters.

He raised his legs in the air and slid his bottom towards the plug until there was room for him to tip his head back and immerse it. It wasn't the most graceful way to give the head a shampooing, but he couldn't be bothered to stand and fiddle about with the shower. As he kneaded his scalp, he considered his predicament. At the moment presumably Evans was the only other person present in the house, surely giving him his best opportunity to escape. Scenarios of him tackling Evans rushed through his head; how do you go about felling a man-mountain? A swift kick in the groin? It would be no good punching him, because he had no experience of punching people, and he had a feeling that landing a punch on any part of Evans would have no effect whatsoever, other than to irritate him. And an irritated Evans was not a desirable result. He could hit him with something sturdy, but what? He considered the television; not the handiest weapon. And the trouble with that route was judging it correctly; either it would bounce off, like a ping-pong ball off a rhinoceros, or it would kill him. Again, neither prospect thrilled him. In movies he had seen chairs being broken over the heads of people with no lasting damage done to the victims, but he had a sneaking suspicion that real life was more complicated. Of course his life had been threatened, in an oblique sort of way, so would the police look upon his slaying of Evans with tolerant eyes? Why should they? They might not believe him. Now, if he was to kill Evans, or at least slow him down to any reasonable extent, the only way that he could think of, short of using a bazooka, which he didn't have, was to stick a big knife into him. No, that would be a move too far for one so squeamish. In any case, he realised, with some relief, he didn't have a big knife.

Regretting his choice of the recumbent method of hair-washing, he completed the task in discomfort and with eyes stinging. He ran a hand around his face, the involuntarily grown designer-stubble softening as it lengthened. There wasn't a razor available, so he would just have to live with it. He climbed from the bath, soapy water slopping over the floor, and towelled himself dry, before using the shower attachment to rinse his hair. There wasn't a toothbrush either; he should have pocketed the one he used at Essex's flat. The mirror revealed a lightly damaged face: some bruising under one eye, a reddened but intact nose, and lines he was certain hadn't been there two days earlier. He pulled on the robe, padded damply into the bedroom and switched the TV on. Maybe there was something on to occupy his mind.

The day passed extremely slowly. Evans made an appearance at around one-o'-clock to deliver a glass of water and a massively constructed ham sandwich. Martin made no attempt to engage him in conversation, so he had only himself for company. He watched an American made-for-TV movie, a weepy about a young mother dying of cancer, followed by a cookery programme that sang the virtues of cooking pork with prunes, a recipe concept that he judged to be repulsive. Thoroughly depressed, he lay on the bed and tried to sleep. After tossing and turning, more than snoozing, for an hour, he turned the radio on. It was tuned into a local pop station that played the usual selection of old, overexposed, middle-of-the-road pap. He would have preferred Essex's single-minded diet of Beatles to this. He decided to tackle the crossword in the Irish Times, reasoning that it might help to keep his brain sharp, pending any getaway attempt. He was lost in concentration when Evans entered again, carrying a steaming mug in each hand.

'You want a cuppa?'

Martin looked at the clock on the bedside radio. It read 6.25. 'Yes please. I don't suppose you've got anything else to eat, have you?'

'No.' Evans sat down in an armchair by the window. 'Truth is, I'm supposed to be cooking our tea, but it's a bit difficult.'

'Why?'

'No instructions, like. You know, I've looked for books and everything but he hasn't got any. I'm not sure what to do.'

'What is it you're supposed to be cooking?'

'There's some mince. I'm supposed to use that.'

'Well, I'll give you a hand to make something with it, if you want.'

'Can't you just tell me, give me some instructions?'

'Well, it's a bit difficult when I don't know what other ingredients there are. Come on – I'm hardly likely to try anything on with you, am I? And I'm getting very bored with the Irish media.'

Evans rubbed his chin, shaking his head and occasionally glancing at Martin, then away again. 'I don't know.'

'Look, you can learn some basics from me, can't you? And I promise to be good!'

'Alright then. But you'd better behave or I'll fucking brain you. I can, you know.'

'I know.' Martin stood up and followed Evans out of the room, thinking wildly about what actions he could take. He was barefoot and naked under the towelling robe. He thought about tripping Evans at the top of the stairs. Jesus, this was frightening. Evans stood to one side on the landing, making him lead the way down the stairs. Right, what's plan two? He saw a walking stick in a stand in the corner of the hall, just inside the front door – too far away, and probably ineffective against this monstrous man, unless it contained a sword. They were now in the kitchen, the floor tiles cold under Martin's feet.

'How are my clothes?' asked Martin.

'They're in the dryer. You can have them later.' Evans pointed to a pack of minced beef on the table in the centre of the kitchen and said, 'There you go. That's the mince.'

'Yes, it is,' said Martin. 'Onions?'

'Yup.' Evans pointed at a vegetable rack.

'Two, please – no, make that three.'

'Do you want garlic? Are we going to have garlic?' Evans put the onions on the table and waved a little bowl of garlic cloves in front of Martin's face.

'Yes, we'll have some garlic. Tins of tomatoes? And a knife.' Martin eyed a wooden block from which protruded the handles of half a dozen knives of various sizes.

'Don't even think about it boyo.' Evans was looming over Martin.

'Suits me; you chop the onions.' Martin felt some relief; he really didn't want to play a game of bluff with lethal kitchen utensils. 'Mushrooms? Red wine?' Evans eagerly assembled ingredients. 'We need a big pan. That one will do.' Martin pointed at a huge, heavily built wok hanging from the ceiling. Evans lifted it down and placed it on the hob. 'Oil?' Evans bent down and picked up a bottle from the bottom of a cupboard. Martin looked at the ponytail on the back of Evans's head and wondered whether he would have the courage to hit it very hard if the opportunity arose again. Evans handed him the oil and he poured some into the wok. Evans chopped the onions, scattering bits on the floor and picking them up surreptitiously. He caught Martin looking as he put yet another stray back onto the chopping board.

'It's not dirty,' he said, defensively.

'I won't tell. How's the garlic?'

'I can't find a crusher.'

'You don't need one.' Martin joined Evans at the table. 'Flatten it with the blade and chop; it's quite simple.'

It seemed to Martin that Evans was becoming more relaxed and trusting, whereas his own brain was working at a frantic speed. With every passing minute the return of Essex and Monan grew nearer, so he had to make his move soon. He was frying the onions and garlic over a low heat, stirring them with a wooden spatula. Evans was standing to one side, transfixed by what was happening in the pan. Martin clumsily, rather too clumsily to his mind, flipped the spatula from his fingers in Evans's direction. Evans instinctively bent down to pick it up from where it landed, between his feet. Martin seized the wok with both hands and swung it down as hard as he could onto Evans's head, bits of oily onion and garlic flying in every direction. Evans keeled over forwards, banging his head on the floor, before coming to a peaceful rest on his side. Martin stood over the body, shaking violently as he held the nearly empty wok and gawped open mouthed at the result of his actions.

'Oh shit. What the hell am I doing?' He asked out aloud, before snapping out of his trance. He replaced the wok and turned off the hob. He wondered whether he ought to check Evans's pulse, but realised that it would make no difference to his current jeopardy one way or the other. And the further away he was when, and if, Evans awoke, the better. He ran into the rear lobby and pulled a bundle of clothes out of the dryer, stuffing them into a plastic carrier bag he found hanging on the back door. His jeans and jumper were upstairs but he didn't dare to waste time going back for them. He sprinted out through the back door, around the side of the house and up the drive towards the fork, wincing as the soft undersides of his pampered feet fell heavily onto thousands of sharp little stones.

He had already made up his mind not to go to the road; it might provide sanctuary in the form of passing good Samaritans, but he didn't want to risk running straight into the arms of Essex and Monan. He ran instead into the yard where he found the bicycle, still standing against the shed. He wheeled it between the buildings and threw it over the gate into the meadow. He scrambled over, a cool breeze suddenly making him aware of the vulnerability of his most personal possessions, and landed on the other side, cupping a protective hand between his legs. He picked the bike up and gently settled on the saddle, the bag of washing dangling from his left wrist. Fumbling with the gears, he set off across the field. He wondered what possible enjoyment could be had from mountain biking as he crashed through dips and over humps, occasionally risking a quick backward peek over his shoulder. The sight of Evans's body lying on the tiled floor alternated with visions of the wounded Welsh giant pounding across the fields, wok and huge knife held aloft, seeking bloody vengeance. He stood off the saddle and pushed down on the pedals with renewed urgency.

~

In the gathering dusk it was becoming difficult for him to distinguish ruts and boulders on the ground. While he wanted to put as much distance as possible between himself and the house, he was concerned about where he was going. Was he heading into some sort of wilderness, where his scant collection of clothes was little protection from the night's chill? Or was he heading straight for the main road and his captors? The thought was truly frightening: they were unlikely to treat his escape with much amusement. And what of Evans? Was he alright or not? Of course Monan and Essex would know exactly in which direction he had fled because they wouldn't have passed him on their return. He must assume that they were already on his tail, armed with guns, knuckle-dusters and dogs. His progress was halted by a high, dense hedge of overgrown shrubs, dark and intimidatingly deep. He looked along it right and left and was dismayed not to see a break in it. His heart was still thumping and he was shivering with cold. The excitement had failed to assuage his hunger and he cursed himself for not having had the presence of mind to grab something to nibble on; the scent of sautéed onion and garlic lingered to torment him. He took a guess at which direction was safest and continued cycling, with the hedge on his left. He was relieved that there was no moon; even without it, he felt rather too visible in Monan's bright white robe.

At last he arrived at a gap where a rickety wooden gate, tied shut with nylon twine, offered easy passage to the other side. He threw the bicycle over the top and clambered after it. He was now on a narrow track that ran between the hedge and a field of rape, the yellow flowers relieving a scene of darkening shades of grey. In one direction the path climbed towards distant mountains, which loomed black against the lighter sky. The other way led gently downhill, which at least required little in the way of physical effort. He climbed back onto the saddle and pedalled furiously, the slope allowing him to achieve an imprudent velocity, given the failing light and unpredictable surface rushing beneath the wheels. He threw another glance back, convinced that his pursuers would soon be on him and that he faced fighting for his life, an exercise in which he would certainly be doomed. Monan probably possessed an arsenal of blunderbusses with which to pepper his backside. He saw the dark shape move into his path almost too late to avoid it. He leant the bike sharply to the right and instinctively ducked. The front wheel plunged into a ditch and he sailed serenely over the handlebars into the rape, barbed wire tearing at the flapping extremities of the purloined towelling.

'What in God's name was that?' The voice betrayed bewilderment. 'Is that a person down there or what?'

Martin sat up and pulled the remains of the robe shut, rustling the bag of washing that was still attached to his wrist. His view was impaired by a cloud swimming before his eyes. Smoke? Oh God, fire! Don't be ridiculous; bicycles don't burst into flames. He sniffed. Pollen! Bloody rape dust. A sneeze exploded from deep in his throat, piercing the still evening like a gunshot.

'Well, bless you, sir, and that's a mighty relief. If I wasn't sober I'd have sworn that you were a flyin' banshee, so help me. Are you alright down there?'

'Yes, I think so, thank you.' He sneezed again.

'Bless you, sir. It's an allergy you have there, to the rape it is. You'd better come out before you sneeze yourself into an early grave.'

'Yes.' Martin remained seated, trying to regain his bearings and making sure that no bodily damage had been sustained during his short flight and graceless landing. For a few seconds, the only sound was that of his breathing. His eyes began to regain their focus and he took in the shape of a man peering over the fence at him.

'You were goin' at quite a speed there. I thought for a few seconds there that I was about to meet me maker.'

'Gosh, I'm sorry. Me too.'

'Don't you go sayin' you're sorry. If you didn't have the reactions of a champion jockey I think we'd both be in the rape with our necks snapped clean in two. Let me give you a hand up now.' The man held out a hand as Martin cautiously rose to his feet.

'Fuck me, you're a tall one and no mistake. You picked a curious time to be out on your bike; just out of the bath or somethin'?'

'I'm on the run. I mean I'm escaping from someone.' Martin was breathless and tongue-tied.

'Oh, I'm with you now. Her man came home early did he?' Martin's new acquaintance chuckled in a conspiratorial way. 'If I hold this wire up you can crawl straight under it, see? Here you come.' Martin wriggled through the fence, back onto the track, one hand cupping his testicles in case he sat on a barb in the gloom. He straightened up and belatedly noticed the shotgun hanging from the free hand of his helper.

'Whoa! Shit!' He took a couple of backward paces away from the man, his eyes fixed on the weapon.

'Oh, there's no need to be afraid of this here thing,' said the man, casually waving the gun around. 'I'm fucked if I can hit anythin' with it, unless I take both barrels in me hands and use it like a fuckin' club, ha ha. Hell, you're shiverin'. Is that the cold or your fear of firearms? Come along with you and catch some warmth in me van.' It was suddenly the man's turn to recoil and adopt a suspicious tone. 'You'll not be one of the bastard Monan's lot, will you?'

'No I won't!' Martin replied vehemently. 'He's the one I'm running from. I think he's planning to kill me.'

'Well that's alright then. Come on! You come with me. The name's Harry. Harry Keogh.'

'Martin Minchin,' said Martin, shaking Harry's hand.

Harry retrieved the bicycle from the ditch and together they walked on down the path, Martin limping on his sore feet.

'Do you live around here, Harry?'

'Yes and no, Martin. I'm a traveller. It's the likes of Monan that give us all the trouble. That fucker gets his boys to shite on anyone he can't make money out of. What did you do? Did you take somethin' of his?'

'Certainly not. I've got something he wants and he won't take no for an answer. They kidnapped me; dragged me here from England. I'm from England you see.'

'I'd never have guessed.' Harry laughed as he said it.

'Yes and I've got to get back home, tell the police. They've even got my clothes, apart from these.' Martin twirled the carrier bag around. 'Are you the people who ambushed his lorry this morning?'

'Oh, I think that would've been the kids. The little monkeys ain't afraid of anyone. What is it he's wantin' of yours so badly then?'

'My house.'

'Your *house?*'

'Yes.'

'He'll not be wantin' a great deal, then.'

'Ha ha, no. He's a bloody lunatic. He thinks he's Lord of my manor.'

'He's a dangerous bloody lunatic, Martin, that's for sure. He reckons he's Lord of every fucker's manor. You want to get as far from him as you can.'

'That's what I was doing.'

After about ten minutes they came to the end of the track, where it met a narrow country lane on a bend. Parked off the road was a large, battered van.

'You'll have to get in this side,' said Harry, indicating the driver's door. 'Other one's a bit stuck.' He opened the rear door and lifted the bicycle in. 'Might as well keep it. You don't want to be leavin' a trail for them.' He carefully placed the shotgun beside the bike.

Harry held the driver's door open and Martin slid across to the passenger seat. Harry settled beside him and groped under the steering column for some lose wires; the engine coughed into life.

'Goat ate the key,' he explained, turning on the headlights and setting off, the van rattling and groaning. Martin sat back and enjoyed the luxury of a moment's relaxation. To find an ally was a tremendous relief and he sensed, despite having met only minutes earlier, that in Harry he had found a valuable ally. Nevertheless, he fully realised that this new friend might draw the line at taking him to the nearest police station. There was also the very real possibility that the police would side with Monan if it came to one person's word against another's, that of a barely clothed Englishman against that of a local worthy. He determined that his best bet was to return to England before trying to do anything about Monan, Essex and whatever was left of Evans.

'It's extremely lucky for me that you were there,' said Martin, keen to acknowledge Harry as his saviour. 'Were you taking an evening walk?' As the words came out, he saw how rude they were; it was absolutely none of his business what had brought Harry so fortuitously to that place at that time, even if it was obvious that an innocent teatime stroll was unlikely, particularly when toting a gun.

'Tryin' to get some supper. Rabbits. I can't shoot the fuckin' things any more. Me girl will have been to the shops. You'll have supper with us.'

'Thank you. I'm starving.'

'How'd you get away?'

'I walloped one of them with a big wok and legged it.'

'That's the way, so it is! That's the only fuckin' language those arses understand. Break their fuckin' heads! I'll buy you a drink for that!'

CHAPTER 5: Saturday night

After a few miles Harry swung the van off the road onto some waste ground. Parked on it were three caravans, warm yellow light glowing behind ornate lace curtains hanging in the windows. Some children were kicking a barely visible ball around and two dogs barked halfheartedly at the new arrival.

'Home sweet home,' said Harry. They climbed out of the van and Harry led Martin into the smallest and smartest of the caravans. For the first time Martin could see his companion properly. He guessed he was in his forties, with thick, dark, curly hair on just about every visible part of him: head, face, neck and hands. He had been wearing a tatty tweed cap that he removed and placed on a hook on the back of the door. A young woman stood at a cooker. Her wild, raven hair flowed down almost to her slender waist. Her perfect bottom was tightly encased in skin-hugging blue jeans.

'Martin, this is me girl, Tara.' Harry beamed proudly. Lucky chap, thought Martin. Tara turned and slowly looked Martin up and down. Probably in her early twenties, she had a wide mouth, curling up at the edges in a hint of a smile, and green eyes that mesmerised him when they met his. Her firm breasts pushed against her close-fitting white tee-shirt as she breathed in.

'Are you lost?' she asked softly, her eyebrows arched and a note of surprise in her voice.

'No. Well yes, er, sort of.' Martin, acutely aware of his lack of clothing and feeling increasingly inadequate in the presence of this beautiful young woman, looked to Harry for support.

'He's English,' Harry said, laughing again.

'I see.' Tara turned back to her cooking. Her legs were long, with a becoming gap shaped by slightly curved thighs. Martin guessed that she was about five-foot-eight in her dainty bare feet. He realised that his eyes were boring rudely into her back and stared instead at the cream-painted hardboard ceiling, longing to look again at this goddess, but mindful that Harry's friendliness might evaporate if he suspected that Martin was falling head-over-heels for his partner.

'He's been havin' some difficulties with Monan,' Harry continued. 'Nearly ran me down on his bike in the dark so he did.

Took a mighty tumble into the rape. But he's done for one of Monan's men so he's earned a bite of supper.'

'Okay.' Tara seemed completely unmoved by Harry's brief tale, as though nothing would surprise her. Martin was staggered by her cool poise; he was being enveloped in wave of strange, wobbly emotions, which hadn't happened to him quite to this extent since he was a teenager.

'She's somethin' of a beauty, ain't she?' Harry had obviously noticed Martin's awestruck state.

'Don't, Dad. You'll embarrass us all.'

Dad! She was Harry's daughter! Martin looked from one to the other and wondered how he had failed to notice the likeness; the black, curling hair, the large, twinkly green eyes. 'She does you enormous credit,' he spluttered, immediately wishing that he had swallowed his tongue instead of spoken with such cheesiness. Tara sensed his unease and shot him a paralysing smile.

'Take no notice of Dad. He sometimes gets the devil in him and we all end up blushing.' She laughed; it was the musical laughter of a choir of angels.

'What have you got in your bag there, Martin?' Harry was pointing to the carrier bag that still dangled from Martin's wrist.

'Oh, er,' Martin began to poke around inside it, 'hopefully, some of my clothes. They were washed. They're a bit damp.'

'Give them here.' Tara took the package from his strangely uncoordinated hand, a light touch of one of her fingers sending a shivering charge up his arm. She arranged the laundry on a clotheshorse in front of a gas fire in the sitting area. To his horror he saw her pick up a huge, greying pair of Y-fronts.

'They're not mine,' he exclaimed, blushing. Tara laughed again and held them aloft.

'I should think not; they'd swamp you!' She placed them alongside the other items. With a terrible sinking feeling, Martin wondered if Evans had obtained a decent performance from Monan's washer; worse still, what if his smalls had been contaminated by somebody else's? No chance of her reciprocating his feelings for her if she thinks he's got smelly pants.

'I'll get you some other things,' said Harry, stepping out of the caravan.

'You're both very kind,' Martin said. 'I'm sorry to be such a nuisance.'

'It's no trouble.' She stood and faced him, smiling. Harry must occupy one of the other caravans, perhaps with the children.

'Whose are the children?'

'They're my cousins; some of many.' She was utterly charming, welcoming, open. The tension he had been experiencing in her presence began to ease, although the yearning feeling remained.

'Ah. A big family, then?'

'Oh yes! There's me and Dad, then there's my Uncle Brian, cousin Billy – those are his kids outside. We've got family everywhere; some in the north, some down in Cork, but me and Dad are kind of self-contained.'

'And you travel around?'

'On and off, you know. We try to make a living. I can sometimes find a bit of piecework. I sell some paintings. Dad does a bit on the farms. Then there's the benefit. It's not bad, apart from the trouble from those that won't abide us. "Itinerants": they spit the word out like it's poison. I should think it's the same all over.'

'Yes, sadly. I think, maybe, that people are inclined to be wary of others whose culture they don't understand.' He hoped desperately that he sounded wise, entirely without prejudice, a paragon of political correctness. Unsure of his ground, he turned his attention to a moody watercolour of a dark, ruined castle under a threatening sky, hanging in a simple frame on the wall.

'Gosh, this is a bit spooky.' He then noticed the simple signature, *Tara K*, in the corner. 'Oh Lord, it's one of yours! Gosh, sorry!'

'It's alright. It's from my dark period. I rather like it.'

'It's wonderful. Fantastic! You're so talented. Wow! I envy you. Marvellous.' With some difficulty, he brought his gushing praise to a halt.

'Thank you. And what do you do, when you're not running away from bullies?'

'Oh, I don't paint. Gosh, matchstick men are about my limit. Like Lowry, ha ha.' Now he worried that he had just compared himself to a master. 'But not as good. Not, er, nearly. Not, I mean, not at all.' He was digging an ever deeper hole.

'I mean, what do you do for a living?'

'God, sorry! Accountancy – I'm an accountant,' he said, wishing that he was a test pilot or theatrical impresario or designer of racing yachts. To his immense surprise, Tara's reaction was animated.

'Why, that's great! Look, Dad's got a problem with the Revenue Commissioners up in Dublin. I'm sure there's a way round it but it's so desperate it gets more and more difficult to try to work it out. And the worse it gets, the more he ducks away from it. Will you talk with him? Please?'

'Well, I'd love to help, of course, if I can. But I don't know anything about Irish tax. These things can be terribly complicated. Sorry, you obviously know that. Will Harry want to discuss it with a total stranger?'

'Of course not! He's as stubborn as a mule. He does what he thinks is right by me, but he doesn't realise that his problems are my problems too. But you being a professional, a real accountant, he'll take notice of what you say, even if he doesn't show it at first. He's very proud.'

'Well, good for him. I'll give it a go, of course.'

'Thanks.' Tara turned her attention back to the stove. Martin put his face up to a window and peered out into the night.

'How far are we from Monan's house?' he asked.

'I'm not too sure. Maybe about eight kilometres, five miles or so. Are you worried?' He was, now that he thought about it again. Very scared, in fact. But Harry's return removed the need to answer.

'Here you go, Martin!' He threw a bundle to him. 'I expect the trousies are a little short on account of you bein' ten feet tall, but the rest should fit. How are your smalls now?' Martin went over and felt his things on the clotheshorse.

'Hot!'

'Go through there.' Harry pointed at a door at the other end of the galley kitchen. 'You don't mind, sweetheart?'

'Of course not.' Tara stood aside to let Martin through. 'The light switch is on the left,' she added.

Martin closed the door behind him, conscious that he was now in Tara's room, the goddess's boudoir. He detected the sweet scent of pot-pourri, of perfume, of gorgeous, heavenly young woman. Feeling like a trespasser, he averted his gaze from anything not connected with the task at hand. He pulled his underpants on before removing the part-shredded, now filthy towelling robe and putting on his shirt and socks. Harry's bundle included a generously sized jumper and some corduroy trousers with plenty of slack in the waist but legs that ended a good way above his ankles. Beneath these flapping hems, he squashed his feet into a pair of grey, mock leather slip-on shoes, about two sizes too small. His reappearance from the bedroom was met with gales of laughter from Harry.

'Ah, you cut a fine dash in those, Martin. They'll see you back to your home, even though your ankles are feelin' the breeze.'

'Dad!' Tara scolded. 'I'm sorry, Martin, but those trousers are much too short for you. I do believe that you must be the tallest person I've ever set eyes on. The tailors must worship you.'

'It does make shopping something of a trial.' Martin sheepishly held up the robe. 'Er, what should I do with Monan's...'

'That'll make a fine fire in the incinerator,' interrupted Harry, taking the remnant from him. 'Perhaps we can use it to put a gypsy curse on the bastard.' His wink and cheeky grin didn't entirely dispel Martin's suspicion that he might be able to do exactly that.

'So, are you comfortable enough now?' Harry continued.

'Oh yes, thank you. Look, I'm terribly sorry, but I've no way of... I mean, is there an address or something?'

'Away with you now, don't you go worryin' yourself about that,' said Harry. 'Hittin' those bastards where it hurts is payment enough.'

'There is something, Dad.' Tara broached the subject hesitantly. 'Martin here is an accountant, Dad, please talk to him about the Revenue.'

'I will not. Martin is our guest and I'll not have talk of our problems get in the way of a celebration. Now, where's the whiskey?'

'Please, Harry.' Martin was determined to lend whatever help he could. 'Tell me what the problem is. I might be able to help and I want to; you've been so kind.'

Harry looked at Martin, then at Tara's pleading face, then back at Martin. 'Okay. The Revenue are after me for fifteen grand, Irish. Fifteen thousand. I'm afraid that even a bright man like you can't solve that one. Unless you are a rich and very generous, bright man, of course.'

'I wish. But that's a big liability. Are you sure it's correct?'

'I've a nasty feelin' that my liability is at least that, you know what I'm sayin'?'

'Crikey. How did you manage to get so behind?'

'I had a bit of luck a long while back, then liquidated, as they say, about ten years ago. Capital gains, that's the fucker.'

'Dad!' Tara threw him a disapproving look.

'Sorry, my darlin'.'

'And the proceeds are all gone?' Martin steered the conversation back on course.

'Yup. I didn't piss it all away though.'

'So, you've got some assets?'

Harry looked around the caravan in an exaggerated manner. 'Not many.'

'Dad!' Tara looked exasperated.

'Tara's got a little house.'

'I don't need it, Martin. Look, Dad, you know I love you for buying it, but I don't need it. Talk some sense into him, Martin. We could sell that, get the Revenue off our backs and still have enough left over to replace the 'vans.'

'There'd be more capital gains and you'd have nothin'. If I die tomorrow, you've got nothin' else to fall back on.'

'Nonsense! I'd still have the 'vans and I could sell your remains for medical science!'

'Er...' Martin stepped in. 'What's happening with this house at the moment?'

'There's a lovely couple rent it,' Tara explained. 'The rent's going into a deposit account; for a rainy day, you know. The thing is, these people really want to buy the place. They keep offering. They love it. It's perverse not to take their money.'

'You're not sellin', not while I'm still breathin', and there's an end to it! It's your inheritance. You're not gettin' rid or you'll regret it, so you will.'

'A lease.' The solution had come to Martin so instantly that he wondered what the catch was; in normal circumstances he would go away and study a problem from every angle before recommending any action, yet here he was breaking every rule in the handbook of prudent financial counselling by thinking aloud. Harry and Tara stared at him, united in puzzlement. 'Why don't you sell a lease to these people,' he continued. 'Ten, fifteen years, whatever it takes to meet the demand. That's the taxman happy, your tenants happy and you happy because you haven't burnt your bridges; you've just lent them to someone else for a few years.'

Harry and Tara exchanged pensive looks, then began to laugh. They turned to Martin.

'It sounds brilliant,' said Tara cautiously.

'Ah,' suggested Harry. 'But these people want to own the house, outright. Why should they want to hand over a pile of cash for this lease?'

'Well, it depends on how deep their love for the house really is,' Martin addressed Tara. 'Whether your house means more to them than the idea of owning a freehold. You see, a lease would put them on a much firmer footing for less than the cost of outright ownership; the house would be theirs to do with as they wish, within reason of course, for the term of the lease. Instead of paying rent, they'd be repaying a loan, which would be considerably less. You might have to sell the idea a bit.'

'You're a genius!' Tara squealed, to Martin's delight. 'You see, Dad?'

'Oh yes; an English genius! Now there's a rare thing,' laughed Harry. 'Where's the whiskey? You'll certainly take a drink with us now my friend.'

Tara produced a bottle and two tumblers from a cupboard. While Martin and Harry toasted accountants, travellers and tenants, Tara laid the table and served up a supper of boiled gammon, new potatoes and cauliflower, washed down with huge mugs of tea. Urged on by a rapt audience, Martin related his story. Despite the convivial company, however, he was unable to rid his mind of the nagging possibility that Monan and his unpleasant cohorts could still discover him; the sooner he was back on English soil, the better.

'I don't wish to spoil the party, but I really do need to get back home. I don't even know where I am! Is Dun Laoghaire much of a distance from here?'

'You'd be better off makin' for Rosslare from here. There's a night ferry, sails for Fishguard at midnight. Tara can run you down there; there's time enough and she's sober.'

'No, I can't possibly put you out any more than I have already.'

'Stop your talkin'! And I know you've no money so, as you've saved me and me girl from another twenty years of squabblin', I'll lend you the fare. Make it up next time you see us.' Harry reached into his back pocket and pulled out a wad of notes, which he thrust towards Martin.

'You'll get it straight back, Harry, I promise.'

'I know, Martin. I know. You're a decent fella and there's a little favour you can do me: if me girl tips up in England, will you keep an eye on her? She's a bright one true enough, but I'm uneasy about all the scoundrels you have over there, you know what I'm sayin'?'

'I'm not sure that I do, but I'd love to see you there.' Martin looked at Tara and realised that he had rarely spoken a truer word.

'Well, you never know,' she replied. 'I wouldn't mind seeing a bit of England. A change of scenery for my sketchbook.'

Harry rummaged around in a cupboard, eventually producing a Reader's Digest atlas of the British Isles, published in 1965. The absence of most of Britain's motorway system lent the maps a curious unfamiliarity, but Martin pinpointed Shimbley and the Verehams and wrote down the addresses of his office, of Lockkeeper's Cottage and of Petey P-T, suggesting that the solicitor might be a good person to contact should he vanish without trace.

'Come on now,' Harry stood up, took his cap from the peg and slapped it onto his head. 'I think it's time for you to get goin' if you're goin' to catch that boat.'

'Will you put some petrol in the car, Dad; I'll be with you in a minute.'

'Sure, sweetheart. Come on Martin.'

Martin followed Harry outside and watched as he fetched a jerrycan from the back of his van and poured the contents into the tank of a small pick-up.

'It's better than me van,' he explained. 'I don't like Tara to drive me van.'

'No,' Martin agreed.

'Truth is, Tara doesn't like to drive me van.'

Tara joined them. She had put on a thick jumper and an anorak.

'All topped up, me darlin'. You take care now.' He kissed her cheek. 'I'll be expectin' you when I see you, okay?'

'Okay Dad. See you later.'

Martin clasped Harry's hairy hand between both of his and shook it warmly.

'You'll hear from me. Somehow! I can't thank you enough.'

'Ah, you're alright, Martin. You mind how you go now.' Martin carefully folded himself into the pick-up's passenger seat and fumbled for the seat belt. 'And make sure you get that Monan bastard sorted out if he comes after you again!' Tara slid into the seat beside Martin, her hand brushing his knee as she pulled the gear lever back into neutral.

'I'll do my best. Bye!' Martin waved from the window as Tara steered out onto the road. 'He's one in a million, your dad.'

'He's that alright, crazy man that he is.'

Tara drove swiftly but carefully, the upright seating position giving her the deportment of a catwalk model. As they talked, Martin occasionally looked across to her, seeing her profile in the light of passing cars. She never returned his look, never averted her eyes from the windscreen or mirror, even when speaking to him. Martin was pleased; as a passenger, he was inclined to nervousness, something which had started a dozen years earlier and which had grown steadily worse, if not yet to the point of a phobia. Rain started to fall and the wipers squeaked a lazy arc back and forth across their field of vision.

'There we are, some real Irish weather for you,' said Tara. 'You know, last year there was talk of water shortages and hosepipe bans in some parts.'

'Oh we have that every year, practically all year round, now that all the water companies are owned by multinational corporations.'

'Yes, but in Ireland! Did you ever hear of anything so ridiculous? The landscape isn't Irish unless it's viewed through stair-rods of rain.'

'But beautiful nevertheless?'

'Oh it's certainly that. And oozing history. You can feel the past sometimes, sense it in the silence or hear it in the wind. You can stand on a hill quite alone but surrounded by your ancestors fighting, laughing, weeping – an awful many tears have been shed.' Her voice faded, leaving a moment inhabited only by ghosts, the splashing rain and Martin's awareness of the hairs on the back of his neck.

'Tara's a place isn't it? Where the kings were crowned or something? Harry must be something of a romantic.'

'Oh hell no! I was named after a TV heroine he fancied: Tara King in The Avengers. I've even got the same initials. Apparently, she was the one that nobody remembers. He always did like to be contrary.'

The edges of the road were now lined with puddles, every now and then one of them concealing a pothole across which the pick-up crashed and shuddered. As if the conditions were not sufficiently difficult, every other oncoming vehicle was lit up with headlights, foglights and, on the many lorries, additional orange lights like Christmas decorations, atop the cabs and along the flanks of the trailers, all creating dazzling starburst reflections on the windscreen.

'The ferry will have docked,' said Tara. 'All these trucks coming north. It'll be about twenty minutes now.'

As they neared Rosslare, Martin began to feel uneasy. The vision of Evans's unconscious bulk slumping onto Monan's kitchen floor replayed repeatedly in his mind. If he had done Evans any serious harm, the Irish police might already be after him. Even if Evans was undamaged, Monan could have woven a story to put Martin's name at the top of police wanted lists in every county. On the other hand, it was hard to see how involving the police would further Monan's cause; if Martin was in police custody, Monan would presumably find it difficult to do away with him. Until he was bailed, that is.

'There's the harbour,' said Tara.

'And there's Essex. Shit!' Martin crouched low in his seat as Tara pulled onto the verge and turned off the pick-up's lights.

'Where?' she asked. They were parked at the top of a hill leading down to an enormous, brightly lit expanse of tarmac, festooned with sheds, signs, stop and go lights, bollards and white road markings. Some cars were waiting by a small, single-storey building that Martin guessed was a booking office. Stretching beyond it were ranks of numbered lanes, anticipating greater queues than were likely to form on this inclement night. The floodlighting bounced up off the soaked asphalt, illuminating the silver streaks of relentless rain. A row of a dozen trailers had been parallel parked and abandoned, slouched forward over their trolley wheels. The tight precision with which they had been placed alongside each other – the gaps surely not wide enough for even a slim person to pass through – appeared ludicrous, given the acres of space all around them. In the distance, its white-painted superstructure looming commandingly over the dockside buildings, was the impressive ferry; Martin's means of escape, his lifeline to a place of safety and sanity.

Before reaching it, however, there was the not inconsiderable problem posed by Essex's presence. The black Mazda, which had shared garage space with Monan's Mercedes, was parked, two wheels on the pavement, alongside the only route to the ferry for passengers and vehicles. Essex was running towards it from the direction of the booking office, his leather jacket's collar turned up futilely against the weather. Martin pointed.

'Ah, yes, I've seen that car before and I'm sure I've seen him. So that's Essex, is it?'

'Yup. And there's no way I can get onto that boat as long as he's waiting there. Do you think that now's the time to tell my story to the police?'

'The big problem with that is there's unlikely to be a single guard on duty at this hour and, if there is, he's unlikely to take a shine to an Englishman waking him up with a tall story, begging your pardon, even if your bad man down there is English too.'

'Yes. And Monan might have already put me in the frame for attempted murder. Or murder, God forbid. It looks like I'm stuffed.'

'Nonsense.' She pulled a wallet from a pocket in her anorak and inspected its contents. 'I'll need another hundred or so.'

'What have you got in mind?' He offered her the wad that Harry had given to him.

'Well, it looks as though I'm going to see your country a little earlier than I anticipated. Or Wales, at least.'

'What do you mean? I mean, you can't. Oh, no! There's no way! Harry's expecting you...'

'Hush! Just look, will you, Martin? The only way to get you across the water without your friend there getting in the way is to smuggle you. You were smuggled in, so I'll smuggle you right back out.'

'But Harry's expecting you back at the 'van in the next couple of hours! And you've got no... I don't know!'

'Yeah, well that makes two of us with no spare knickers. There's a tarpaulin in the back. You'll have to hide under that.'

'But they'll find me!'

'Actually, I expect they couldn't give much of a care on a night like this. Come on, let's do it. Once we're on the boat I'll check that we've got no company and then come and fetch you, okay?'

Martin opened his door and adopted a crouch as he made his way along the side of the pick-up. Tara lifted the tarpaulin, causing a cascade of water to crash to the ground. She rearranged some tool boxes and spare wheels in the back and indicated to Martin where he should conceal himself. He slithered in, limb by limb, convinced that Essex would easily spot him silhouetted against the deep, dark void of the sky. At last, he was curled up on his side in a foetal position, his back against the back of the cab. Tara carefully placed some old plastic fertiliser sacks over him and then covered the whole pick-up bed again with the tarpaulin, tying it down tightly. In the black-out of his nest, outside sounds were muffled, despite his heightened aural awareness.

'Okay?' Tara's whisper must have been delivered close up to the tarpaulin.

'I think so.' He wriggled a bit, determined to make himself as small as possible, and practised breathing slowly and calmly. In the back of Monan's truck, he would have been delighted to have been discovered, but there had been no chance of that. Now, with very little between him and the authorities, the last thing that he needed was to be found. Well, officer, it's a long story, he rehearsed. The conditions were much worse than in the back of the truck, and worse even than in the boot of the Rover, what with a wet floor and somewhat less compliant springs. As he sensed progress down the hill towards Essex, he drew a deep breath and held it for what felt like a suicidal number of minutes.

The pick-up stopped and the engine was switched off. Tara's door opened and slammed shut. He waited, his every breath sounding in his confinement like a hurricane, each movement of the tarpaulin like some catastrophic seismic activity. Much more of this sort of travel, he imagined, and he would be unable to endure conventional modes. Long haul flights? You want to travel in a trunk in the hold? Certainly, sir. Caribbean cruises: the bilges, sir? No problem. If he ever got to live in Lockkeeper's Cottage he would have to excavate a cellar and live in that. And what of poor, faithful Alfredo? Blacked out windows were going to be the least requirement. Footsteps approached, squelched nearer and nearer, and stopped. He was certain that his heartbeat was making his hideaway shake; it sounded to him like the bass beat enjoyed by the trendiest of Shimbley's cruising youths.

'Hush, little baby, don't say a word,' Tara sang the lullaby as a surreptitious warning to Martin. 'Mama's gonna buy you a mockingbird,' Her voice was high and clear. Martin marvelled at her comprehensive cleverness. 'If that mockingbird stays down, mama's gonna get him right outta town.' So far so good then, he thought. Her door closed and the engine started, the tune remaining in Martin's head. Little baby? Was that how she just addressed him? Idiot! It was the song's lyric, intended to settle actual babies. She wouldn't call him 'baby', certainly not in a lovey-dovey way; he was way older than her, and there was absolutely no reason for her to be attracted to him, this long, coiled, rather pathetic fugitive in the back of her little truck.

Tara drove slowly, the chassis groaning over traffic calming humps every few seconds. Each time they stopped, Martin expected the tarpaulin to be yanked away by gun-toting policemen. Or Essex, perhaps backed up by a deranged Evans, his head wreathed in bandages. Soon the now familiar clanking of steel ramps below indicated that they were boarding. He was overcome by an awful sense of guilt; Tara had been expecting to drop him off at the port, yet here she was embarking on a three-to-four-hour voyage with no possessions other than a rather tired pick-up and a stowaway. They stopped and the engine died. Tara's door opened and a corner of the tarpaulin was lifted, allowing a chink of light in along with Tara's reassuring voice.

'He didn't even give me a second look. I expect that Monan's up at Dun Laoghaire keeping a similar watch. If I was them I'd reckon you were now trying to persuade a guard that you are indeed sober and requiring repatriation. Perhaps they'll go to this house of yours and wait for you.' She paused. Martin was considering this line of thought. 'Are you alright in there?'

'Yes, thanks. Er, I guess Essex might be getting on this ferry, then?'

'Well, he might. If you're alright, I'll do a few turns around the boat to see whether he's on it. Hey, sniff this!' Tara's arm dived under the tarpaulin, exuding a scent that seemed too sophisticated for his immediate surroundings. 'I got it in the duty free shop back there. Twenty pounds. What do you think?'

'It's beautiful,' he replied, breathing it in deeply and finding it deliciously intoxicating. He wanted to say how it made him feel: dopey, in love, randy, deeply in love. 'It suits you.'

'Good. I'll have a look around then. We'll be off in a minute. I'll be back. Beer?'

'Please.' She was a mind-reader too!

She re-tied the tarpaulin as he wriggled into a more comfortable position. Although visions of Evans, Essex and Monan were never far from his mind, Tara was now occupying centre stage. Despite his fear, he was actually enjoying every minute spent with her. He was ashamed and felt a hot blush spreading across his face. He should have refused to allow her to travel with him. On the other hand, she had a greater claim to Harry's bundle of cash than he ever would, and she was obviously an independent, free spirit. Yes, it was her choice. But what if he was leading her into danger? He despaired; every happy thought was tainted by ominous ones, hovering constantly at his shoulder. He started to dwell on what must be his selfish streak and determined that, at the first opportunity, he must release Tara from the burden of assisting him. Just as soon as he was home and dry, perhaps. Some hope; this was one big swell, assuming that they were still in the harbour.

CHAPTER 6: Saturday night/Sunday morning

Possessing a reasonably robust stomach, Martin rarely suffered from sickness, be it from illness, food, drink or motion. Now, however, lacking a horizon on which to focus, and forced to inhale a disagreeable cocktail of damp tarpaulin, oil, rubber and rusting steel, he began to worry that this might be one of those occasions when he might be reunited with his supper. How would he hide it from Tara? She might take it as pithy criticism of her cooking. Why on earth was he concerned about what she might think? After all, she was far too polite and considerate to show anything but sympathy. Even if he vomited in the back of her car? Why was he debating this at all? Committed to remaining where he was for the foreseeable future, succumbing to this creeping nausea was unacceptable. Very slowly he eased his fingers into the gap between the tarpaulin and the side of the pick-up, to create a little, visible air hole. He then slowed his breathing right down, swallowing frequently and burping as quietly as he could. A bead of sweat felt cold as it ran down his neck. Just a few more minutes, he kept promising himself, and the worst will be over.

Deep mechanical groans, vibrations and shudders marked the ferry's progress from its dock. He assured himself that a boat this huge, effortlessly accelerating to its cruising speed, could shrug off the excited sea with the ease and nonchalance of a cow flicking away flies with its tail. And he imagined that the voyage would grow calmer with every mile eastward. The corkscrewing motion that pitched him up and down, from side to side and backwards and forwards, all at once, therefore took him by considerable surprise. He hadn't fallen out of the pick-up, so he could rule out a capsizing.

'We're out of the harbour.' Tara's cheerful voice betrayed none of the fear of shipwreck that had suddenly crowded into his head. She pulled back a corner of the tarpaulin, allowing him to raise his head into the relative cool above, and handed him an open bottle of cold lager. 'It's a little wild, isn't it?'

'Wow, thank you. I feared we were going over. Can this thing handle these conditions?'

'I certainly hope so. Dad says that in the winter the waves break clean over the bows and you can't move for all the sick. It's not my idea of a luxury cruise.'

'Did you manage to have a good look around?' He shifted so that he was now sitting up. He looked around at all the empty cars. He and Tara appeared to be the only occupants of the deck. He drank gratefully from the bottle, quickly slaking his massive thirst.

'Yeah. I watched Essex drive away from the harbour as we set off. He'll be away back to Monan's. I don't think there are any nasty surprises aboard. But, just to make sure, and because I'm none too happy about this sea, I've got us tickets for the fillum. Come on.' She pulled the tarpaulin away some more to enable Martin to extricate his long limbs.

'A film?'

'Yeah. It's some sci-fi thing. One for the boys I expect. But it's right down there in the belly of the boat, so we won't feel any more of this sea than we have to.'

Martin followed her, snaking their way between the closely parked cars to a door in a bulkhead. They descended three flights of metal stairs and emerged in a small lobby. Martin took the opportunity to visit the gents, while Tara bought popcorn and Cokes from the little booth that served as the ticket office. The cinema was compact but by no means sold out. The screen was square, a bizarre change from the familiar wide-screen format and probably anathema to movie directors. It was framed by red curtains, just as he remembered the local fleapit, before it became a cut-price furniture emporium. They staggered to some seats in an empty row at the back, giggling as they steadied themselves. They sat down and looked at the screen.

'Oh, shit!'

'Oh, God!'

'Oh... ,' they said in unison, looking at each other, then back at the screen, where the red curtains were now hanging at a forty-five degree slant from the vertical. The curtains returned to the perpendicular, to a chorus of metallic noises from the bilges, before starting a swing in the opposite direction.

'I think this is going to be a lengthy ordeal,' said Martin. The film began with a spaceship exploding into a million pieces somewhere in the universe.

'And that's just the fillum,' she added.

~

In fact, for Martin, the time passed too quickly. Although the combination of the noises coming from deep in the ship's bowels and the dramatic movements of the stage curtains were enough to shake the confidence of the hardiest sailor, he was even more aware of the proximity of the person he liked more than any other; loved in fact. No! Talk of love was ridiculously premature, and he didn't wish to be presumptuous any more than make a fool of himself or push an extremely agreeable friendship too far. God, he loved everything about her. He felt as though he had known her for years. Occasionally his elbow brushed hers, causing in him the sort of frisson he hadn't experienced for many years, making the hairs in the nape of his neck stand up and his ears burn red. He could quite happily sit here, in this company, for days, providing they didn't sink of course. He imagined the Irish Sea to be deep, not just in normal sea terms, but seriously deep, in ocean terms. And cold. Perhaps he could rescue her and thus win her undying love; discover a rock and struggle onto it, give her the kiss of life, followed by passionate kissing, then adventurous groping, then wild, desperate, climactic, sweaty, shuddering sex. On a rock? Maybe they retrieved a pile of blankets or something from the wreckage. Or the rock has a sandy beach. No; that would make it an island and therefore unlikely to have remained undiscovered, to be named Minchin Isle and donated to him by a grateful nation. Because Tara was the long-lost, true heiress to the throne – hmm... British or Irish? Whatever, that would make Harry the dowager queen, or something.

'Martin.'

He sat up, startled.

'Were you in the land of nod there?'

'What, no. Well, a bit. Gosh, it's finished!' He looked around and saw that those members of the small audience, who had not already left the theatre, were in a deep sleep, legs resting over vacant seats in front. The curtains maintained their metronomic swaying.

'I reckon we've still around half an hour to go,' Tara ventured. 'How do you feel? I'm parched. I don't think we need worry about keeping you secret anymore; fancy finding another drink?'

'Absolutely! I don't care if Monan and all the forces of evil are on this thing; these must be British waters by now. I'll call for the captain, have them keelhauled, get them walking the plank.'

They walked out into the little lobby, bracing themselves against the wall when the ferry executed another vigorous roll.

'I think there's only one plank here.' Tara laughed and slipped her arm around his. 'Well, I was on the side of the slimy squiglidon,' she added.

'What?'

'That space beast, whatever it was called. Who gives American astronauts permission to go out there and waste anything in their path?'

'Hollywood, I suppose. Anyway, I'd rather pay my rates to a semi-competent district council than to a slimy squiggly-diddly. Oh, I don't know, though!'

There was a coffin-sized lift offering rides to the upper decks but, after exchanging worried glances, they started their way up the metal staircase. The higher they rose, the harder they needed to cling onto the rail, as the sideways motion became more pronounced.

'I wouldn't like to be the bloke in the crow's-nest,' joked Martin.

'The what?'

'Sorry, it's a nautical thing. Is it much further?' He aimed the question at her jeans-clad bottom, provocative globes swaying before his eyes as she led the way up. He wished that the climb could last forever, or at least until his legs gave up.

'I hope not.' Perhaps she could feel his lascivious gaze burning discourteously into her buttocks.

Reaching the main passenger deck, they were surrounded by signs advertising the attractions to be enjoyed: duty free shopping, self-service café, waitress service restaurant, blackjack tables, children's adventure romping room, TV lounge, bar with live music.

'There's a bit of a whiff up here, isn't there?' Martin looked at Tara to see if she was receiving the same signals.

'Yeah, sick and disinfectant. My favourite.'

'What do you reckon, try the loos or just wee over the side?'

'Well it's fine for you boys, isn't it? Anyhow, if you wee over the side in this weather it'll be coming straight back at you, yours or someone else's.'

'Got a peg then?'

'Pardon?'

'For by dose.' He pinched the bridge of his nose between thumb and forefinger.

'Oh be off with you.'

Martin gingerly pushed open the door into one of the men's lavatories, surprised by the strength of the return mechanism. Because it was a door in a bulkhead, he had to step over a substantial lip and winced when he heard his borrowed shoe splash in a pool of liquid. The smell of disinfectant was overpowering; he imagined that the staff simply lob in a Domestos bomb every quarter of an hour. The door slammed shut, confining him in a slippery cell, made more perilous by the pitching motions of the ferry. He tried to hold his breath as he emptied his bladder and he tiptoed across to the wash basins, in order to minimise his contact with whatever lurked on the floor. Back out in the corridor, he found Tara perusing the café menu.

'Fancy a spot of egg and chips, then?'

'Not until we're off this thing.' He put his face up to a window, staring through his reflection at the blackness beyond. 'How much longer do you think?'

She looked at her watch. 'By my calculations, we should be entering the harbour about now. But the lack of lights out there suggests to me that we're running a bit late. Perhaps they took a wrong turn and we're headed for New York.'

'That would explain the rough passage; we're in the north Atlantic, dodging icebergs. A lollipop for the first one to spot the Statue of Liberty!'

'I've got a cousin in New York, so I'm told.'

'I'd like to go to New York. But not dressed like this.'

'No! I think they'd arrest you for vagrancy.'

'How about that drink, then? Fancy risking the bar?'

'Yeah.'

They walked to the huge bar at the stern. Few tables were occupied, those around the perimeter the most popular, where passengers could doze on the brightly upholstered benches. On the stage to one side a chair propped up a blackboard on which was chalked the message, 'Tonites performance cancelled due to sickness'. A bored looking young barman, noticing the arrival of two more travellers not yet laid low by the length and excessive motion of the voyage, stubbed out a cigarette and returned to the working side of the bar.

'Yes, sir, miss?'

'Where'd you find your scarecrow, darlin'?' A small, drunk man, sitting alone at a table near the bar, laughed at his own wit before clamping a beer bottle to his mouth and lolling back in his seat.

'Sorry about him,' said the barman. 'He's been sucking on that bottle for two hours. It beats me how he's got into such a state. What can I get you?'

Martin and Tara perched on a pair of bar stools and ordered Cokes. They asked the barman whether he knew how much longer the journey was likely to last.

'About half an hour now,' he said. 'You see that light over there?' He pointed towards the starboard windows. They looked in the direction indicated. After a short pause a light shone at them and slowly disappeared again.

'That's Strumble light,' the barman continued. 'Fishguard's just around the headland.'

Martin was puzzled that the light seemed to be irregular. 'It's not very consistent,' he said.

'It's the roll of the ship, sir. The light is constant; it's our angle that isn't.'

'Now you see it, now you don't,' added Tara.

'Bloody hell. I suppose you're used to it?' Martin addressed the barman.

'Used to it, yes, sir, but that doesn't mean I like it any more than you do.'

'Oh come on!' Tara mocked them. 'Fancy being afraid of an ickle bit of bouncy sea!'

They took their drinks to a table in the centre of the room. Martin put his down and addressed Tara: 'I must say, I don't envy you the return trip in these conditions. Presumably you have a return ticket?'

'I don't, as it happens.'

'Oh. But there's enough of Harry's money left for you to get back?' It was going to be a terrible wrench. No sooner was he getting to know this wonderful person, than he would be waving a tearful adieu at a dockside. He would never see her again, and the thought was unbearable.

'I thought I might not go straight back.'

'What?'

'Well, I want to see this mysterious house that everyone seems to want to kill for. You be my guide and I'll be your wheels.' She grinned at him. 'I mean, there's not much point in coming all this way only to get right back on this heaving tub, is there?'

'What about Harry?'

'I'll call and leave a message at the pub. He won't be worried; he's used to me taking off now and again.'

'Well, if you're really sure, that's fantastic. Gosh.'

'Will we have to change this money?' She pulled what was left of Harry's cash from her pocket and counted it.

'Yes. There was a sign for a bureau back that way. I shouldn't think we'll find a bank open at five in the morning on a Sunday in deepest Wales.'

They finished their drinks and went in search of the bureau de change. The windows on the landward side were increasingly patterned with gaudy starbursts, pinpricks of light exploding across the clinging sheen of rain and sea spray. The labouring vessel would soon be embraced by the comforting breakwaters of Fishguard harbour. Ten minutes later, they had converted their

Irish punts into pounds sterling, the ship had entered calmer water and the lights from the dock grew larger and brighter.

'Let's go,' she said. They clattered down a staircase towards the car decks, swerving around passengers whose less confident progress betrayed old age, tiredness, drunkenness or illness. They arrived at Tara's pick-up well before the occupants of the surrounding cars and she pulled back the tarpaulin.

'Once more unto the bed, dear friend, once more.'

'Eh?' He gaped at her, not sure of what she had just suggested. She noticed his mouth hanging open, eyes staring.

'The pick-up bed, Martin, quick!' She flapped the tarpaulin and gestured frantically with her free hand.

'Oh, sorry! Right!' He jolted to his senses and launched himself into the space behind the cab. As he snuggled down, Tara securing the ties at the side, he could hear the approaching footsteps and conversation of other passengers.

'It's an 'orrible night to be travelling alone, gorgeous.' Martin tensed at the unseen Londoner's bludgeon-like chat-up line. He was ashamed that he remained in hiding while Tara was left alone to cope with whatever unpleasantness the great British moron could throw at her. She was an innocent abroad, a sensitive soul cast adrift in a sea of scum, a damsel in dist...

'Go fuck yourself, you inadequate arsehole!' she responded.

'Lesbian bitch!' the Londoner shouted back, retreating. Tara's door slammed shut and she started the engine. Blimey. This is definitely the sort of person you want on your side. No messing with Harry's girl. Martin took comfort from Tara's self-possession. Arsehole, ha ha, yes. Berk, Clown, Dunce, Eejit... nice one!

They disembarked within minutes, clanking over the steel ramps and bouncing over more speed humps. If there was a customs checkpoint, it was clearly manned in a relaxed fashion. This surprised Martin; with rising anxiety, he had assumed that people coming in on ships from Ireland would be strip-searched, their vehicles torn apart by men and dogs trained to detect bullets, fertiliser bombs, rabies and poteen. Perhaps the security forces were more subtle than that. Perhaps they would trail them instead, back to whatever remained of Lockkeeper's Cottage. And, jumping to conclusions at the sight of the wreckage, incarcerate him and Tara in some fortress police station, reserved for international terrorists and worse. Worse? Fugitives from the Garda. Murderers. Oh God! There were fertiliser sacks all around him! No prizes for guessing what forensic evidence the scientists could conjure up given these and his eccentric garb. What could be worse than being mistaken for an unscrupulous bomber? In Wales? Holy shit! He'd only murdered a Welshman. They would do away with a jury, just bring on some sheep – they bleat and you're guilty; you bleat and you've got scrapie. It's life in Caernarfon Castle either way.

The pick-up sped along, accelerating up through the gears and jumping, rather more than Martin would have liked, over bumps that felt like mountains. One moment he was prepared to be launched clean through the tarpaulin towards outer space, the next his spine was being flattened against the wall of the cab as Tara stamped on the brakes. Her door opened again.

'Hey, Martin, come and take a look at Wales!' She pulled away a corner of his covering. They were at the end of a small car park across the bay from the dock, where the ship that had conveyed them safely, if not comfortably, across the sea, was now bathed in light as trucks unloaded and cleaners went about their unpleasant duties. The slim finger of a breakwater stretched into the darkness, a small light blinking at its end. A westerly wind blew straight at them, making his eyes stream with tears. The tears were of relief as well. Here were his feet, planted back on British soil; he had escaped!

'The sign back there said A40 to Have-a-something or this way for Fishguard town centre,' Tara pointed towards a brightly lit roundabout near the car park's entrance.

'Brilliant!' he said. 'You can't go wrong with the A40, at least not until you reach Marylebone Station at the other end.'

'Marylebone Station?' She looked at him excitedly.

'Yes. Know it?'

'I've been there!'

'Oh?'

'Yes, every time I've ever played Monopoly. It's a twenty-five pound fine.'

'Rent.'

'What?'

'It's rent,' he insisted. 'The money you pay when you land on someone else's property is rent, not a fine. Fines are in the Chance and Community Chest cards.'

'What exactly is a Community Chest?'

'Well, there was a girl in my year at university who was widely known as the community chest.'

'Oh, very funny. So, are we going there?'

'Where?'

'Marylebone Station!'

'No, not to London; just to Vereham, see what's left of my house. But the A40 will be perfect for the time being. How are we off for petrol?'

'We'll be fine for an hour or so.'

Martin looked at Tara. She was staring out to sea, her long hair streaming back in the wind. He wanted to tell her how he felt about her but bit his tongue. Although gushing words of love were welling up inside him, he feared that he would only ruin everything. She must have had many men falling for her, plenty closer to her age and doubtless more desirable than this awkward, elongated, lovesick tramp. The moment she knew of his infatuation, she would run a mile; as long as he kept himself in rein, he could prolong the joy of just being with her.

'Look, you don't have to worry about me,' he said, lying. 'I'd be a lot happier if you made your way home. I've put you to so much trouble already and I'm concerned about Harry.'

'Hush! You're wasting your time.' They climbed into the pick-up, Martin glad to travel on a proper seat again. They turned away from the sea and headed east towards the first faint signs of a pink dawn.

~

The traffic travelling in both directions was dominated by trucks, the odd interloper from continental Europe mixing it with the British and Irish ones. Tara seemed at ease just drifting along with the flow, a rate of progress that suited him well. They passed various signs pointing down unclassified roads towards attractions such as beaches, antiquities, woollen mills, dressed crabs, B&Bs, art galleries and more; he would quite like to explore were it not for the fact that he had more pressing things on his agenda. The road signs were less intriguing, flashing past in a haze of English and Welsh, the latter involving a great many Ds, Ls and Ws, usually without any vowels to ease the pronunciation.

'Hwlffordd,' Martin offered.

'I beg your pardon?'

'Actually, I think it's something like Hoowoolforth. This is the way to Hoowoolforth.'

'Uh?'

'Hoowoolforth. We're heading for Hoowoolforth. H W L F F O R D D. Hoowoolforth.'

'I don't think I've seen a sign for that.'

'It's Haverfordwest in Welsh. I reckon it's just done to confuse English tourists,' he continued.

'Oh, you mean the way they use French in France.'

'Exactly!'

'I've always been a great admirer of English tolerance; it's what earns your country respect all over the world.'

He looked across her, pleased to see her smiling but aware that the chiding was genuine.

'Those bits of the world that we never conquered you mean. Sorry! You're absolutely right,' he retreated. 'I think that you Irish are magnificent in the face of your awful, trespassing, arrogant, boorish, hooligan neighbours. Your whiskey is wonderful, your Guinness pure genius, your music marvellous, your novelists nonpareil, your poets perfect, your, your...'

'You're obsessed with nationalities!'

'No I'm not. Anyway, let's talk about the Welsh; look at these place names.' They passed another big road sign. 'Why do they have places that require you to cover the inside of the windscreen with phlegm when you say them out loud? Hghrrghglth!'

'Stop it Martin, you're making these up!' She was laughing again but it had been a close thing. She must think of him as a narrow-minded, xenophobic plonker. He had a mountain to climb, if he was ever to impress her.

'Can I buy you breakfast?' Shit! How sleazy can you get? Impress her? Might as well leap out now; try one's luck in the ditch. On the other hand, it's not as though the question was posed the night before, in true slime-ball fashion. Of course, she's got all the money, so it was an invitation for her to buy the breakfast. Not good, but not as bad as asking her to go to bed.

'Okay.'

They drove on for a few more miles.

'Here we are; gwasanaethau, or however you say it! Pull in here.'

She did as instructed and steered into a large lay-by, parking the pick-up between a milk tanker and a Welsh water engineer's van.

'And to think that I was expecting a nice little tearoom at least,' she complained. She pointed to the little trailer from which sustenance was being dispensed to weary looking men. 'I'd heard that your British catering standards could do with a little lift, but I didn't expect this.'

'Now who's being insular?' he retaliated.

'I never said I wasn't; I merely pointed out that you were. Anyway, there's probably some old Brit somewhere in my blood – it just popped out to say "hello!". Look at that.' She had stepped out and was looking at the sky. 'It's going to be nice day after all.'

They bought bacon sandwiches and tea, the latter delivered in half-pint mugs, and settled at a wooden table on a small grassy area. A Dutch florist's van shielded them from the road and they enjoyed an uninterrupted view in the other direction. Daylight had revealed a sky now much more blue than grey, and a ground-hugging mist lent mystery to the valley that lay six or seven hundred feet below. The sandwiches were generous – thick hunks of bread, lots of melting butter, the bacon just turning crispy.

'An English middle-class upbringing denies millions of people like me this culinary experience,' said Martin in his best attempt at exquisite Queen's English. 'It just melts in one's mythe don't y'know.'

'And the English could never get it right. Thank god we're in Wales.'

'Amen to that, love.' The Welsh water engineer raised his mug in Tara's direction on his way to the trailer for a refill.

'What's the time?' Martin asked Tara.

'Just about seven.'

'I don't know what to do.'

'I know. I don't know what you should do either. You're the only witness to what's happened. I don't see that there's much you can do, except go back to your normal life – well, as normal as you can make it – and, if Monan comes back into the picture, then call the police. Maybe you could get a restraining order or something.'

'It's scary, isn't it? That you can be abducted, have your house trashed, be beaten up, bumped off for god's sake, and no one bloody knows. Nor cares!'

'Let's just get to your house and see what the damage is, then we can see your solicitor, the police and anyone else who's interested. Then, if they do come back, at least you'll be prepared with the law on your side.'

'What if he's dead?'

'Evans? What if he is? In any case, he isn't.'

'I wish I shared your confidence.'

'Listen, I've hit people over the head before, and with bigger things than frying pans, I'm telling you. None of them's dead as far as I know. I've seen your Evans; he's a monster. It would take more than a frying pan to put him in his grave.'

'It was a wok. A big one. With onions and garlic.'

'Whatever, it wasn't a proper big casserole pan, was it? There were no potatoes. You'd need potatoes. You're not a killer. I can tell.'

'Thanks. I think.' She was making good sense.

'Martin, you really must try not to worry. You got away from them; that means you've won this round. You're ahead right now. I know it must have been scary, but it's over now that you're away from them. They had their chance and you outfoxed them. Okay?'

'Okay. I appreciate your support, Tara; I just hope that your optimism doesn't prove to be ill-founded.'

They set off once more, in heavier traffic now that caravanners and other Sunday drivers were beginning to take to the road. He directed her to follow the signs for the M4 and they were soon part of a mixed clump of vehicles travelling east at a lazy sixty to seventy mph past the steel works and long-dead mines towards the twin bridges over the Severn estuary and into England. They had stopped to fill the tank with petrol and were now content to see the miles disappearing beneath them. A wire coat hanger performed surprisingly well as a radio aerial, providing an agreeable soundtrack to the scenes rushing past.

'My plan of action is this,' Martin announced after a quarter-hour of deep thought. 'The time is now nine. We should be able to get to Lockkeeper's Cottage by about ten-thirty. We can see what the damage is – well, subsequent damage of course – then have lunch at the G and D, tell every...'

'G and D?' Tara interrupted.

'The George and Dragon, in Shimbley; it's my local pub, well, local to the office, run by friends. They've been brilliant to me and you can stay there; there's always a spare room. Anyway, we can tell them all about it. Kevin helped me clear up my office after Essex's first visit. He'll believe my story. And, with you backing me up, I might be able to get the police to take an interest in my protection. Unless Essex and co have got to them first.'

'What, to the George and Dragon?'

'No, I mean the police. I might be a wanted man.'

'Well, I haven't noticed too many roadblocks. There haven't been loads of news flashes on the radio, warning the public not to approach a particularly tall man with a lethal frying pan.'

'Wok.'

~

The view from the Severn crossing was stunning, the clear air allowing them a glimpse of the Mendip Hills and Exmoor beyond. Many of the fields bordering the motorway were full of rich yellow rape flowers, their pungent aroma easily making its way into the pickup. They turned off onto a main road with roots going back beyond the Roman occupation and meandered between stone walls, passing houses of honey coloured stone, basking in the first proper warmth of the summer.

Martin toyed with the idea of going straight to Shimbley police station, but he wanted to inspect his house and see what remained of his belongings before doing anything else. What if Evans had tidied everything up before setting off for Liverpool? No; it would have taken an army of skilled labourers to achieve anything remotely resembling tidiness. And what about Alfredo? Would he still be there, faithfully awaiting the return of his master? Remembering that the front door had been hanging off its hinges when he last saw it, he realised that he would be lucky if no one had trespassed and helped themselves to whatever they fancied. He thought about what items he might particularly miss: photographs, CDs, books, some presumably irreplaceable old vinyl LPs, his favourite cooking utensils. Oh hell! A couple of old watercolour landscapes; not priceless, perhaps, but very special to him. The burglars would have also enjoyed the fact that everything had been packed in boxes, ready to take away. He continued to give Tara directions to the Verehams and, the nearer they came, the harder his heart beat.

'Well, that's it, up there on the left and I can't see any strange cars around.'

'I don't see how they could have made it here before us anyway.'

'Well, get ready to shoot off, just in case.'

They rolled slowly towards the house, Martin straining as if to detect intruders through the thick hedges. Drawing level with the gap in the hedge, Martin experienced huge relief to see Alfredo, standing exactly where he had left him and apparently intact.

CHAPTER 7: Sunday morning

'Your car?' Tara asked.

'Yes. Looks like we're alone, doesn't it?'

Tara turned off the engine and they climbed out. The cottage's front door appeared to have been mended, as it was properly closed and didn't look as though it had been broken down just two days earlier.

'It's pretty isolated, isn't it? No good shouting for the neighbours when the heavies turn up.'

'You're right there. I think I'll just have a little look around the side, make sure no one else is here. It's just that the door looks okay and it was practically off its hinges on Friday morning. Maybe someone's been in.'

'No; it was probably your Evans. I mean, he wouldn't want to leave the place looking like that, not when a passer-by could raise the alarm, and you in the boot of his car.'

'Hmm. I'm not convinced that Evans possesses that much thought.'

'Not anymore.'

'Don't remind me.'

They peered in through the broken windows. All of Martin's boxes were still placed in the middle of the sitting room floor. As they carried on towards the back of the house, the ground beneath their feet grew muddier.

'This is like an Irish bog. You must have had some of our rain.'

'No, I'm afraid it's coming from a broken cistern upstairs. What Evans couldn't wreck, the water probably has. Good job I'm not on a meter; could've filled an olympic-sized swimming pool by now.'

The back door was still locked so they completed a full circuit and Martin pushed gently on the front door, which groaned briefly, before crashing back onto the hall floor.

'Welcome to my humble home, Tara,' he said, politely standing to one side and gesturing for her to enter. 'Do try not to damage anything.'

'My God, I'll do my best not to,' she replied, picking her way carefully over bits of splintered wood and wet carpet. 'Where's the stopcock?'

'I never got a chance to find out.'

Tara led on into the kitchen and looked into the floor-standing cupboards one by one. A steady flow of water dribbled down the wall in the corner. Finding nothing, she unbolted the back door and went into the garden. She lifted a slate covering a hole in the ground against the outside of the kitchen wall.

'Found it!' After a minute, the flow stopped, creating a surprising silence.

'You've done that before,' observed Martin with some admiration. He had never been practically minded.

'Once or twice.' She stood back from the house and gazed up at the smashed bathroom window, then back at the ground floor, and finally at the quagmire in which she was standing. 'You're going to need a builder. Is anything missing?'

'Not that I can see. I was afraid I would lose all sorts of stuff of sentimental value but it looks as if my luck held. Even the car looks unmolested. And I can change into some of my own clothes – not that I'm ungrateful for the loan of these, you understand, but I do feel rather self-conscious.' Tara laughed. 'You wouldn't believe it, would you?' he continued. 'You leave a place wide open for three days and it's untouched, yet if you pop down to the shops for a paper and forget to lock the door, you have kittens.'

'Not where I come from. No one would dare enter a traveller's 'van, for fear of the dogs, let alone a good hiding. What now?'

'Well, I'm feeling rather peckish again. Let's gather up my stuff and take it back to Shimbley. I can't really leave it here anymore and a locksmith won't be available until tomorrow.'

'Locksmith! You need a carpenter, a plumber and a glazier at the very least. And a long, hot summer to dry everything out.'

They went back into the sitting room and picked up a box each. Fortunately for Martin, the water hadn't found a way into that room, and the only damp had been caused by rain blowing in through broken windows. Placing his box on Alfredo's roof, Martin instinctively felt in his trouser pocket for the key. Damn!

Had he left it at Monan's house? Or at Essex's flat, along with his watch? Suddenly inspired, he bent down and looked into the car; sure enough, dangling in the ignition was a bunch of keys, which included the new keys to his office. Once more he counted his blessings. It took just ten minutes for the two of them to load his belongings back into his car, and a further five to coax some life out of the temperamental little engine. With the front door placed back in its aperture and looking secure, at least from the road, they set off towards Shimbley, Martin leading and still glancing around anxiously, half expecting to be challenged either by murderous thugs or by police, curious to know what had been going on at this cottage in the middle of nowhere.

It wasn't quite noon when they pulled through the narrow cobbled archway that led into the George and Dragon's car park. Horse-drawn coaches had crossed the same threshold more than three hundred years earlier. John Richards emerged from the kitchen carrying a big, green plastic rubbish sack that he tossed into an industrial wheelie bin on the opposite side of the yard. He gave Martin a cheery wave and returned to his kitchen. Martin rummaged through a box on the seat beside him and selected various items of clothing and his washbag. He scooped them up under one arm and climbed from the car. Tara joined him.

'I see chef's working,' she nodded towards the kitchen door.

'Yes, that's John, the licensee. He's also the chef. Does roasts with all the usual trimmings on Sundays.'

'I'm certainly up for that.'

Martin led Tara into the lobby and through to the lounge. Kevin was standing behind the bar, slicing lemons.

'Bloody hell! If it isn't Worzel Gummidge! We don't let in just anybody, you know.'

'Good morning, barman. We'd like a prominent table for two for a nothing-stinted lunch.'

'Prominent?' Kevin looked Martin up and down. 'No chance! Have you been DIY-ing at Minchin Manor?'

'Kev, I'd like you to meet Tara Keogh.'

'Enchanted,' said Kevin, extending a hand. Martin shuffled between them, suddenly uncomfortable about Tara being gawped at by another man, even if that man was unquestionably honourable and loyal.

'Kev, I have a tale to tell which is so strange, I think you will scarcely believe it. First, however, I have a huge favour to ask: is there any chance of us using a bathroom each for twenty minutes?'

'No problem. Four's still empty and you can use ours.'

'You will be rewarded in heaven.'

'I want to be rewarded in here, mate. That's going to be at least a pint. Two pints.'

They were interrupted by peals of laughter behind them. Martin swung round to see Susan pointing at his trousers, her other hand covering her mouth but failing to disguise her mirth.

'What do you think you look like?' she asked, between giggles.

'This, I'll have you know, is the very best Irish corduroy,' he said with as much dignity as he could manage, 'and this is my friend Tara. Tara, Susan, Kevin's boss.'

'Martin,' Susan continued, 'you look as though you've been sleeping rough. For a fortnight. And you appear to have been in a fight. Are you alright?'

'Not entirely. It's a very long story with which I shall regale you over an aperitif. Kevin kindly offered us a couple of bathrooms; we've had a rather long journey.'

'Right. Well, you know your way to number four. Tara, you come with me.' Susan led Tara out of the room.

'Here you go.' Kevin pushed a freshly poured pint towards Martin.

'Kev, the only money I've got is, er...' Martin patted his pockets sheepishly.

'On the house, mate. Take it with you.'

'You're a star, Kev.' Martin picked up the drink and went in search of a much needed wash.

~

By twelve-thirty, Martin was back in the lounge, perching on a bar stool and contemplating the bottom of his empty glass. An elderly couple had entered and ordered sweet sherries. Not persuaded by Kevin that the beef on offer was the best on the planet, they ordered chicken and sat at a table in one of the window bays. Having delivered instructions to the kitchen, Kevin returned to Martin's end of the bar, looked around furtively and turned to Martin.

'Come on then, who's this Tara? Where did you find her? Are you and her, you know? She's a cracker, Martin!'

'She certainly is. She's from Ireland.'

'Well, bugger me sideways. You div, I didn't think she was from Wolverhampton!'

'Sorry. She's just a friend, a new friend.'

'Nothing more?' Kevin frowned, as though not fully believing it.

'Don't be daft, Kev! She's young enough to be my daughter. Nearly. Well, perhaps not, really. Anyway, I don't think there's much about me to excite her.'

'Except your exciting story, you mean?' His cross-examination was interrupted by the entry of Susan and Tara. Tara was wearing her jeans as before, but with a clean, bright green tee-shirt that complemented her captivating eyes.

'Susan's been very kind, Martin,' she said, as Martin leapt to his feet, 'and you're looking a lot better! I've never seen him in his own clothes', she added for the benefit of their hosts.

'You sly dog!' Kevin muttered.

'Right,' said Susan. 'It's story time. Kevin, Tara would like a cider – a pint. Martin obviously needs another beer and I'll have a large G and T.'

'Is that all, dear?'

'No. We want a full bowl of cashews and some of that tasty cheddar.'

'Jawohl, Frau Überkevin!'

Tara and Susan sat on bar stools and Martin stood and delivered his tale to an enraptured, almost incredulous audience. As more customers arrived, Kevin kept breaking away to serve drinks and take orders, obliging Martin to go over some parts again. The wokking of Evans was the bit that Kevin and Susan had the most difficulty with.

'You mean you knocked him out cold? With a wok? *You?*'

'I tell you, you'd have done the same. These guys mean business. They'd already assaulted me two or three times.'

'It's the truth,' Tara confirmed. 'Monan's a really unpleasant piece of work. He pushes people around and gets what he wants. You see his trucks going back and forth, with no telling what's inside them. He thinks he owns the whole place, and his heavies make sure his word is law. The trouble is, there's no one ready to stand up to his kind. You keep your head down, you might avoid a beating.'

'But he's got to be deranged if he thinks he can make a fortune out of a non-existent spring. I mean, a bit of robbery, a bit of smuggling, a bit of fraud: that you can understand. After all, the mafia and that sort have been making a decent living for decades. But lordships and your silly well? It's the Godfather goes Monty Python.'

Martin acknowledged Susan's succinct summary of Monan's quest for Lockkeeper's Cottage, but pointed out that it was really happening; not on television or in the cinema, but in real life, to him. He and Tara had taken seats at a table by a fireplace and tucked into roast lamb. Meanwhile, Susan and Kevin took turns to join them to pore over certain details again and speculate about possible ulterior motives. The consensus was that the spring and Lord of the Manor bits were red herrings, absolute hogwash to put Martin off the scent of their genuine intentions, whatever they were. Kevin suggested that Beverley had put them up to it, to punish Martin for something or other, like existing. Martin wasn't so sure. If Beverley had had anything to do with it, she would have boasted about it. She didn't do things without taking full credit for them. Monan had seemed so sincere about his plans, plausible even, if one overlooked the lack of a spring. But this didn't rule out the possibility that he was barking mad.

Having been assured that they could have rooms for as long as they needed, and after Tara had succeeded in contacting Harry to let him know of her whereabouts, she and Martin strolled down the High Street, along the river bank for a while, and into the modern police station adjacent to the supermarket on the outskirts of the town. They found themselves in a lobby with an abandoned enquiry counter at the far end. Martin leaned over it and looked around the room on the other side.

'Business must be a bit slow on Sundays,' he said, banging a bell. This eliciting no immediate response, he wandered around the lobby, looking at various posters about home security, drugs, suspect packages and free shop-your-neighbour phone lines. Eventually, a policewoman materialised and addressed him.

'It's Mr Minchin, isn't it? WPC Brown; I attended the break-in at your office.'

'Yes, I remember. Hello.' He stretched out his right hand, then sensed that this might not be a hand-shaking moment and hesitantly withdrew it.

'Do you have more information on it?'

'No. Er, yes. Actually, I want to report something else.'

'To do with your break-in?'

'Yes, well, sort of.'

'I'll start a new crime sheet, then,' WPC Brown cocked a slightly quizzical eyebrow at him and started to write at the top of a pre-printed piece of paper. 'Assuming you're here to report a crime?'

'Oh, right. Yes, I mean. I'd like to report a breaking and entering.'

WPC Brown put down her pen. 'The one at your office?'

'No, a new one.'

'Oh, I see. Now whe...'

'And some criminal damage, I think it's called.'

'At the same place?'

'Yes.'

'Right. Whe...'

'And an assault.'

WPC Brown put her pen down again and looked at Martin. 'I'm all ears, if you'd like to start at the beginning, Mr Minchin.'

'And an abduction, another assault, smuggling, false imprisonment, extortion, death threats and another assault.'

'Another assault?' Tara chipped in. 'What other assault?'

'Well, I think I ought to make a clean breast of it, you know: Evans.'

'I don't think that one will be in the jurisdiction of your people here somehow.'

'Could I have a word?' WPC Brown held a forefinger in the air and smiled patiently at her customers. 'I need to take some details, then see whether it's something CID should know about.'

Once more Martin related his story, WPC Brown taking down every detail in laboured longhand. Occasionally she sucked through her teeth or tut-tutted. Martin felt that he was now under suspicion of having had one too many drinks with his lunch. Indeed, at one stage the constable enquired as to where he had parked. She looked disappointed when told that they had walked.

'So you, Miss Keogh, smuggled Mr Minchin here into the UK, yes?'

'Yes.'

'So you're here under false pretences, Mr Minchin?'

'Of course I'm not! I'm a UK citizen, and the only reason I had to be smuggled into this country is that I'd been smuggled out of it in the first place. Against my will.'

'Right. So you're here under false pretences, Miss Keogh?'

'I don't think so. I wasn't smuggled anywhere. As an EU citizen I believe I'm entitled to come and go.'

'Right.' WPC Brown looked increasingly dubious about something.

'We're here to report crimes against me,' Martin reminded her, 'and my property. I haven't committed any crimes, as far as I know and neither has Miss Keogh.'

'What about this chap you struck with a frying pan?'

'Wok.'

WPC Brown flicked back through a few pages of her notes, as if to check the veracity of Martin's stated choice of weapon. 'Mmm, yes, wok. He may want to press charges.'

'Well, if you find him, you can ask him. Then, while you have the opportunity, you can arrest him for the crimes I've spent the last half-hour reporting to you.' Martin was beginning to wonder what the purpose of the police was.

'Yes. If you'd like to take a seat, Mr Minchin, I'll be back as soon as I can find somebody in CID.' She walked away into an inner sanctum, re-reading her notes and shaking her head slowly from side to side.

'I get the feeling I'm about to be arrested,' said Martin as they sat down on a bench.

'You and me both, Martin. They must be the same the world over. But I guess you have to go through the motions.'

'Yes, and Kevin said that the insurers won't pay up unless there's an official police crime number.'

'Well, you should have about ten of them before we're through.'

'Look, I'm sorry it's taking up so much time. You must be bored stiff.'

'I wasn't planning on going anywhere. Anyway, I want to see if your CID is going to do anything about these people. Perhaps Monan's out of their reach but the other guys might have records already.'

'True, but "Thidney Ethicth of Liverpool" and "Evans the Wokked of Wales" aren't much to go on.' He folded his arms protectively across his chest and yawned with a shudder. 'Sitting here makes me feel very wobbly; I can't help thinking I've done something wrong. I suppose it's because I'm still worrying about Evans. Did you see the way she looked at me when I got to the wok?'

'You've nothing to worry about.' Tara squeezed his arm reassuringly. 'Even the police can see there's nothing dangerous about you.'

'Thanks.'

'I meant it in the nicest possible way.'

'Was your dad really okay about you being here?'

'Absolutely delighted he was. It gives him the freedom to have the boys round for cards. And he said that if anything happened to me he'd tear you limb from limb with his bare hands.' She laughed and playfully slapped his leg as he tensed at her words.

A door beside the counter opened and a young man wearing a crumpled dark blue suit entered the lobby.

'Mr Minchin? You're not having much of a weekend, are you?' He tapped the papers prepared by WPC Brown. 'I'm Detective Constable Dee. Now, if what you've told WPC Brown is correct, there are some villains out there that we'd like to talk to. Trouble is, we don't know where they are. There's no Sidney Essex on national police records and Evans without a first name is too big a mountain to climb. A Snowdon, if you will.' He snorted at his joke. 'Are you sure you can't give me some address details for this Liverpool flat? Road? District?'

'As I explained to Constable Brown, I was taken there in the boot of a car; a Rover 600, if that's any help. As I've never, I mean had never been to Liverpool before in my life, I haven't a clue where it was, or even if it was actually in Liverpool. That's my assumption. For all I know it could have been Birkenhead, Bootle or wherever.'

'Oh, so you know those places?'

'No! I know of them. I don't know Merseyside from Adam.'

'Right. But you were taken from your property in West Vereham, after being assaulted?'

'Yes.'

'Of what nature was the assault?'

'I was knocked out cold by some sort of blow on the head.'

'And it was this Evans?'

'He was the only other person in the room, as far as I know.'

'How tall are you, Mr Minchin?'

'What's that got to do with it?'

'Oh, nothing. No, I like to estimate people's statistics; you know, height, weight. I reckon you're a metre ninety-five and, ooh, ninety odd kilos. How am I doing?'

'I can't tell you. I'm six-six and around fourteen stone, if that's any good to you.'

'Not bad. That's lofty, that is.' Detective Constable Dee chewed on the end of a pencil, his brow furrowed in thought. Finally he looked up at Martin. 'Could I take a look?'

'At what?' Did he want to inspect his body? Double-check his weight?

'Your house.' He looked again at his notes. 'Lockkeeper's Cottage. My treat, if you call a standard issue police Astra a treat.'

'Well, it's fine by me. How about you, Tara? Do you want to go back to the G and D – this might be a bit boring.'

'No way. I want to see the detective detect something!'

The three of them walked out into a courtyard. Dee looked around at the few cars parked there.

'Where are you parked, then, Mr Minchin?'

'At the George and Dragon.'

'Ah yes.' Dee strode purposefully towards a maroon Vauxhall Astra with plain, black-painted wheels and a couple of extra aerials. 'Just as well, sir. I believe you might have had a drink or two.'

'So, why did you assume I was breaking the law?'

'I didn't.'

'Could've fooled me,' Martin mumbled to Tara.

'Told you: they're all the same,' she replied.

'What?' asked Dee.

'Insurance companies,' said Martin. 'All the same. They want all the details so they can wriggle out of it.'

'Oh.' The ride in DC Dee's 'company' Astra promised to be unsettling. Tara volunteered to sit in the back, while Martin was ushered into the front passenger seat; he would have preferred to snuggle up with Tara. Dee purposefully pushed his seat belt buckle into its dock between the seats, adjusted the rear-view mirror and announced, as much to himself as to his passengers, 'I'm an advanced driver; did the course at Hendon.' A moment's silence followed.

'Gosh,' said Martin eventually, not intending to sound sarcastic.

'It's a bloody tough course, actually, excusing my language, Miss.' He caught Tara's eye in the rear view mirror.

'For some,' she mumbled.

'It's only a ten minute journey.' Martin anticipated Dee's enthusiasm. 'At a modest thirty or so.'

'No problem,' said Dee, squeaking the front tyres a little as he accelerated in the direction of the Verehams. 'Isn't it your wife, drives that Beemer?' He turned to look at Martin as he asked the question.

'Where?' Martin looked about, unsure of whether Beverley's presence was worse than the risk of a serious car crash.

'Nowhere. I mean I've seen her around. Good looking woman, your wife, if you don't mind me saying so, Mr Minchin.'

'Not in the least. She's divorcing me, so you're most welcome.'

'Oh, I'm quite sure she's too rich for me, sir.'

'Quite so.'

'Sorry, sir?'

'You've no need to apologise.' A snigger from the rear seat was barely stifled. 'Bless you, Tara', Martin added.

DC Dee decided that listening, rather than contributing, to the conversation was the best option. Martin found his right foot reaching for an imaginary brake pedal as the Astra sped along, the road leading to Lockkeeper's Cottage just wide enough to allow two cars to pass each other, as long as both drivers put their nearside wheels onto the grass verge. The problem with Dee's driving style, as far as Martin could see, was that he didn't expect anything to be coming in the opposite direction; and, if he did, he wouldn't see it anyway, because his head was turned every way except for the road ahead. Tara saw the tractor before her fellow travellers, but Martin was the first to say anything.

'Shit!'

The tractor bounced wildly as it traversed ruts and culverts hidden in the long grass and giant hogweed beside the road. Dee's reaction to its presence wasn't to turn the steering wheel or stamp on the brakes; he pressed a chubby thumb on the horn button on the steering wheel and shouted at the hapless tractor driver, 'Stupid dickhead!' Bits of spit and other things, perhaps salt and vinegar crisps, splattered against his window. 'Shit!' He scowled at the mess. 'Sorry. But did you see that driving? What a plonker! Bloody farmer. Mr Mangelwurzel, eh? I'll bloody have him.' He snatched a tissue from a box on the shelf under the dashboard and rubbed halfheartedly at his side window, creating a large smear. 'Good job I've been on that course or you two might have been under his wheels. Took you by surprise too, didn't he Mr Minchin?'

With considerable relief Martin saw Lockkeeper's Cottage. 'Here, on the right,' he said. Dee braked to an unnecessarily sharp stop and the three of them climbed out. Once more, Martin allowed the front door to fall in with a loud crash and led the way over it into the hallway. Dee whistled through his teeth as he took in the mess.

'I hope you've got an account at Do-It-All, because you're going to be spending a lot of money down there,' he said.

'Sadly, constable, I'm not much of a hand at DIY. Painting a wall and putting up the odd shelf is about my limit. Very odd shelf, probably.'

Martin gave Dee a guided tour, pointing out the less obvious bits of damage. Upstairs, Dee carefully removed the axe from where it was still embedded in the wardrobe door and placed it in a large plastic bag. 'You never know, your Welshman or the other one might have left some prints.' In the sitting room, Dee coerced Martin into re-enacting Evans's assault. In the garden he picked up and inspected the lump of bathroom basin and put that in a separate bag. A voice, distorted and competing with static, made an unintelligible announcement from Dee's radio. He walked away from Martin and Tara, the radio pressed against an ear, and muttered a reply into it.

'Sorry, folks,' he said, returning to them. 'A sudden death at the wrinklies' home. Got to go and do my bit, though how anything can happen suddenly in there is beyond me.'

'Maybe it's another drowning.' Martin's suggestion clearly enthused the detective.

'Hey! You never know with them old folk, do you? Give you a lift back, then?'

'No!' Martin and Tara were unanimous. 'We'll make our own way, thanks.'

'Right. I'll fill out a report and make some enquiries. You can pick up a crime sheet from the station tomorrow, say, after eleven.' Dee walked out to where he had left his car in the road.

'I wouldn't lay odds on him detecting anything,' said Tara. Martin shook his head in agreement. 'Never mind,' she continued. 'Let's have a wish.' She tossed a coin into the well. It bounced on the chicken wire before falling through into the darkness. 'Let's wish that some good comes out of all this.'

'Amen,' added Martin, 'but I wouldn't bank on that monstrosity granting any wishes.'

'It is a bit over the top for a garden ornament, isn't it? Are you quite sure that there isn't a water source down there?'

'I think the previous owners and the estate agents would have made something of it. Come on; I better make a list of the repairs I'm going to need. Make some tradesman's day.' They tiptoed their way through the mud to the back door.

~

As they progressed from room to room, making notes of glass, window frames, kitchen and bathroom ware, doors and floor coverings, Martin was surprised by Tara's knowledge of technical terms and methodologies; where he would have struggled to explain a requirement to a builders' merchant, her input would lend an air of professional authority. By the time they had finished, there were several pages of measurements and descriptions in his notebook.

'This is going to cost a small fortune. The trouble with being an accountant is that people assume you're made of money, as if accountants can't possibly experience the sort of money shortages which other people do.'

'I suppose, when I think about it, I imagine accountants to be pretty well off.'

'It's the old theory that if your business is dealing with money, some of it always sticks. I wish.'

'What about insurance?'

'Ah, well, that does pay, if you're good at it.'

'I mean this damage; are you insured?'

'Oh, sorry. Yes. Well, I don't really know. They might say that I have to take a civil action against the perpetrators, rather than putting a claim into them. I really haven't a clue. I mean, the small print lets them out of acts of God or terrorists, doesn't it?'

'I wouldn't know. What's the time?'

'Don't know. Essex still has my watch. It must be getting on for seven or so. I suppose we ought to think about getting back to Shimbley. Are you hungry?'

'Good God no! Not after that lunch. I wouldn't mind a drink though.'

'A drink!' Martin suddenly remembered Petey P-T's bottle of malt. 'Look what I have here.' He conjured the whisky from its hiding place in the fireplace. 'Fancy a drop of Scotch?'

'That's some trick!'

'My solicitor gave it to me as a housewarming present. Evans deprived me of a chance to get into it. Oh bugger!'

'What?'

'No glasses. Or cups, or anything.'

'Don't be a wuss! Just pass the bottle!'

They sat on the concrete floor, leaning against a wall, and passed the bottle back and forth. He savoured the peaty, smoky flavour that reminded him of Christmas and log fires. He wondered whether he would ever enjoy a Christmas in this room and realised with a growing feeling of self-pity and anger that he probably couldn't. He actually now hated the place and, the more he hated it, the more resentment he felt towards Evans and Essex and Monan and insurers and the police.

'I hate this place, Tara.'

'You're upset.'

'No. I really, really hate it. I'm going to have to sell it. You know, I thought that this was my little piece of paradise, a place where I could grow old in peace and tranquillity. So much for that dream. From that poxy stove to that poxy well out there, I've had it. I'll get it done up and flog it. Should've flogged it to Essex in the first place. You never know, I might make a profit. On the other hand, I'll probably lose a bundle, as is my wont. And people put so much faith in my fiscal acumen.'

'You'll feel differently when it's back in a decent state.'

'I have my doubts. I reckon I'm destined to live in towns; my rural solitude has rather lost its attraction, more's the pity.'

'Rural solitude? Hell, you're barely ten minutes from the town here. Back home, rural solitude would be a three day hike from the nearest road. This isn't so bad.' Tara looked Martin in the eye. 'Pretty good, I'd say, for an English place.' She smiled.

'Better than Irish places, eh?' Martin perked up.

'Don't push it.' They both laughed and surveyed the ruined room once more. As far as Martin was concerned, he could sit here for weeks with Tara, drinking in her beauty, her wisdom, her wit, this single malt; he wasn't going to be the one to break up the party. She told him how she had worked alongside Harry, renovating her little house and learning all sorts of building skills. He suggested that he could hire her to see to Lockkeeper's Cottage and was astonished when she responded that she wouldn't mind. She asked him about Beverley and he told her about the rocky foundation of his marriage and how his lack of a sizeable inheritance had proved to be the main problem. He found it unusually easy to talk to Tara, feeling no self-consciousness about revealing personal things. The alcohol helped, of course, and the sinking sun had bathed the room in a warm orange glow, which complemented the inner glow that Martin felt just being in her company. She noticed the light too and said that it was the sort of light she had tried to capture in pictures, with varying degrees of success.

'Do you have a hobby?' she asked. Martin considered the question and was embarrassed to realise that he didn't really, apart from the usual books and music, which everyone has to some degree or other.

'Must have. Got to think about it,' he stalled, feeling deficient. 'Excuse me, I need to, er...' Martin stood up, feeling a little unsteady as he rose to his full height. 'I must just go outside.' He walked towards the broken French window and was surprised to feel light-headed. 'I think I might be a little bit inbri... ininbri... inebri... pished,' he exaggerated. 'Shan't be long.' He pushed the door open and stumbled into the garden, surprised by the step down onto the grass where he had planned to install a patio. After taking a few deep breaths, he crossed the lawn, ducked under an overgrown buddleia and emptied his bladder into the hedge. He wondered briefly why he was feeling squiffy, before reasoning that action-packed days and nights, on top of very little sleep, are bound to exact their revenge. He should have been getting his head down while he had the opportunity; instead, he was trying to enjoy for as long as possible the company of a woman with whom he had fallen in love, but in front of whom he had merely succeeded in overindulging. He shook his head vigorously and inhaled some more fresh air. They must return to Shimbley and catch up on sleep; a lot of sleep. He strolled back to the house slowly, looking around and wondering why he now saw little to excite him where once he had loved the place. What a difference some days of unpleasantness can make. On the other hand, if it hadn't been for his new enemies he would never have met Tara. And that certainly didn't bare thinking about. Maybe he should look out Evans and Essex to thank them. Maybe not. He laughed aloud as he stepped back into the sitting room.

'Laugh at this,' said Evans as he landed a right hook on Martin's left ear.

CHAPTER 8: Sunday night

Martin sat on the floor staring at Evans's cowboy boots, waiting for his head to clear but suspecting that it wasn't going to do so for a while longer.

'Sorry, Martin.' Tara's voice startled him. He looked across the room and saw her kneeling on the floor. Essex was standing behind her, holding a rope that was coiled around her neck, not so tight as to prevent her from speaking, but sufficiently constricting to subdue her.

'You bastard!' Martin shouted and made a lunge towards them but was felled by a punch to the back of his head.

'I'll fucking kill you boyo. You should've finished me when you had the chance.'

'It would take an elephant gun to put you away, you moron.' Tara's spirit clearly wasn't dampened by her predicament.

'And what would you know, you filthy gyppo. Maybe you could do with a bit of prime Welsh pork.'

'Pork would be right!' Tara retaliated. 'I'll cut it off and keep it in a thimble, you fat eunuch!'

'Thut up!' Essex tried to regain control.

'Eunuch is it? I'll tear her fucking Irish...'

'Thut the fuck up!'

Martin managed to haul himself up to a sitting position once more and leant back against the wall, his breath heaving. Evans was standing over him, rubbing his right fist with his huge left hand. Martin looked him in the eye and Evans lifted a foot, as if preparing to deliver a kick.

'Evanth!' warned Essex. Martin looked at Essex, who retained a grip on the rope, as though holding a dangerous dog, rather than a scared young woman.

'What are you going to do now?' Martin directed the question at Essex. 'You want this house? Take the bloody thing. I assume you've got a big lorry out there? One of that madman Monan's fleet? You can take every fucking brick. You can even take the bloody well; see if that lunatic can squeeze any water out of it. Go on, what are you waiting for? Get this idiot to earn his bananas.'

He nodded towards Evans. 'He's built like a dumper truck. Now get that rope off her neck, you bastard.'

'You're a dead man,' whispered Evans towards Martin.

'Give it a rest, you big fairy.' Martin was astonished at his own impertinence, then he remembered that he was less than sober and shrugged his shoulders. 'Why don't you and I rustle up something for supper, eh?' Evans looked ready to explode.

'Enough!' shouted Essex. 'If you know wotth good for thith young lady,' he pulled on the rope, making Tara choke, 'you'll thtop mucking uth around. Evanth, do try to get him over here without getting hit by a frying pan.'

'It was a wok!' Evans corrected, beating Martin to it.

'Don't lay a finger on her.' Martin looked pleadingly at Essex. 'I'll do what you say. Just let her go, please.'

'I think heeth rather fond of her, don't you, Evanth?'

'Like a bit of rough do you boyo?' Evans grabbed Martin's upper arm and hauled him to his feet. Martin sneered at him.

'Come on, mith,' Essex coaxed Tara to her feet by pulling up on the rope. 'Letth even out the height differenth a bit. Thtand on thith.' He led her to the fireplace and made her stand on the thick, slate-topped hearth, which was seven or eight inches higher than the floor. 'Come on now, Martin. Give the girl a nithe hug.' Martin put his arms gently around Tara. 'And you, mith.' Tara's arms circled Martin's waist. Essex removed the rope from Tara's neck and used it to tie Martin's wrists tightly together. Behind Martin, Evans pulled Tara's hands together, forcing her to press tightly against Martin. They looked at each other apologetically, their eyes almost at the same level. Evans busied himself binding them together, first around their chests, then at their waists, and finally their thighs.

'You make a lovely couple,' said Essex. 'Now then, Mithter Monan, or thood I thay "Lord Vereham", ith on hith way here. Tomorrow, Martin, you and he are going to vithit a tholithitor and agree to the thale of thith pigthty at a prythe of Mithter Monanth choothing. Evanth and I will thtay here, and entertain your lovely companion, while you do thith. Providing you cooperate, little more harm will come to you or her. Indeed, Evanth may even forgive your vithus athault on the back of hith fortuituthly thick thkull.' Turning his head awkwardly towards Essex, Martin prepared to interrupt, but Essex held a forefinger to his mouth. 'Thh. If you thow any thine, whatthoever, of unwillingneth, churlithneth, dithobedienth: I will inthtruct Evanth to thow your girlfriend thum unplethantneth. Do you underthtand?'

'If that rock ape comes anywhere near me, I'll bite his bloated nose clean off his face.'

'Not if you've got no teeth left, you bitch.' Evans looked as though he could use his fists on Tara just as readily as he did on Martin, but the click-clack of Beverley's heels in the hall caused everyone to freeze.

'Martin?' She entered the room with her head held haughtily high and an expression of great distaste on her face. 'Good God, Martin, what do you think you're...' she was cut short by Evans who, in a moment of rare deftness, had stepped behind her, swept one of her arms into a half-nelson and clamped a hand over her mouth. As she tried to splutter indignant complaints, Essex turned towards Martin.

'Who ith thith woman?' he asked with remarkable composure.

'It's my wife,' Martin replied without thinking, immediately wondering whether he should have added the ex- prefix or the word 'estranged'.

'What'll I do with her?' asked Evans, shrugging off Beverley's spirited but futile kicking and wriggling. Essex went over to them and peered closely at Beverley.

'Did you come here in a car, Mithith Minchin?' Beverley stared back at him, wide eyed as though she took him to be a lunatic. In her experience, people visiting remote houses without the assistance of the internal combustion engine were inclined to wear mud-caked hiking boots and unbecoming plastic outer garments. Did she look as though she had walked? Extraterrestrial visitors would be more acceptable to her than hikers, particularly if they arrived in a craft bearing the right, preferably German, badge. Evans tightened his grip on her arm and removed his hand from her mouth.

'Of course I came here in a car! What the hell do you...' Essex slapped her face hard, the shock and the pain rendering her speechless.

'Hey!' Martin and Tara protested in unison. Martin's current dislike of his erstwhile love did nothing to lessen his sense of outrage.

'Keeth,' Essex stared Beverley in the eye and held out his hand, palm upwards.

'Keith? Who's Keith?' Beverley's voice betrayed justifiable fear.

'Give me your car keeth, now!' Essex closed his hand into a fist as Beverley hesitated.

'In my bag.' Essex pulled her small Gucci handbag, which was still attached to her shoulder by a long gold chain, towards him and rummaged inside it. 'Bring her,' he said to Evans and headed out towards the front door.

'So that's the wife, then,' Tara observed.

'Yes.' Martin felt himself shaking and didn't know what to say.

'That was a nasty slap he gave her there. What do you think they're doing with her?'

'I've no idea, but she won't take kindly to it.' He nodded towards the floor where a solitary high-heeled shoe had been abandoned. 'That's probably a hundred quid's worth. We've got to get out of this...'

'Ssh!' Tara silenced him as Essex and Evans returned to the room.

'Fythety woman, your wife.' Essex laughed. 'I'll bet theeth amaithin in the thack. Whatever did thee thee in you, Martin?'

'What have you done with her?'

'Do you care?'

'Of course I care! It's pretty shabby of you to assault a defenceless woman. Fortunately we've been to the police and told them everything. In fact Detective Constable Dee from Shimbley station is due back here any minute.'

'You're lying,' said Evans.

'How do you think we got here, you idiot? If you check upstairs, you'll find that he's taken your axe away for forensic tests. You can use the phone up there to call the station and check.'

'Martin, you're mithtaking me for thumwun who givth a thit. I don't care if you've told the Deputy Commithoner of the Met; I don't think they're coming back here for you. The poleeth are known for a lot of thingth, but running a minicab thervith thertainly ithn't one of them.'

'What about my axe?' Evans sounded worried.

'Well you thoodn't have left it here. Will it have your printth on it?'

'I don't know.'

'Have the poleeth ever taken your printth?'

'No.'

'Then why are you waithting my time? Jutht thtay out of their way, yeth?'

'I'm going to be missed,' Tara suggested. 'If I don't turn up in Bristol by midnight they'll report it.'

'Brithtol? *Brithtol?* Where did you pluck that one from?' Essex voiced a question that had also occurred to Martin. 'You know what I think, mith? I think nobody ecthept Martin here even knowth you're in thith country. The only people who'll be mithing you are the other gypthith, and a poleeth thtathon ith about the lartht plaith they'll go. Anyway, a thpirited young lady like you? I bet you're alwayth taking off.' He placed a couple of fingers under her chin and lifted it, tilting her head back. He looked from her to Martin. 'Proud, ithn't thee? And quite pretty, too. You have a curiuth ability to gather good looking girlth around you, don't you Martin? God knowth how.' A mobile phone chirruped from somewhere inside his jacket. He walked to the French window as he retrieved and answered it. It was dark now and Martin could feel the chill of the night. Essex listened to the caller and occasionally grunted in response.

'What's up?' asked Evans.

'Immigrathunth giving him grief.' Essex flapped a hand at Evans as he concentrated on what the caller was saying. 'Thit!' He silenced the phone and returned it to his pocket. 'I have to go to the airport for him.'

'What about these two? And her?' Evans tilted his head and rolled his eyes in the direction of the road outside.

'I'll do the airport run; you take the wife and get thot of her thumwhere. But I don't want theeth two tagging along.'

'I know what to do with them.' Evans steered Essex into the garden and a hushed conversation ensued, followed by the sound of them struggling with something metallic.

'Tara, I'm so sorry,' said Martin.

'It's not your fault.' Her breath, right under his nose, bore the distinctive scent of single malt whisky. 'They must be completely insane. I really don't see how they can pull this off.'

'It's the insanity that scares me. Monan might prefer to kill us and buy from the bank, as he threatened to when I was back at his place. I should never have let you come this far.'

'You'd have had a job getting here without me.'

Essex and Evans returned from the garden.

'Lord Vereham hath landed, tho you'd better get ready to deal,' Essex said. 'We'll be back before you've even begun to mith uth.'

'It's a long way to Gatwick,' ventured Martin, certain that Evans was incapable of ignoring the bait.

'Well it's Birmingham, boyo, so stuff that up your know-all arse.'

'Thank you Evans.' Martin sniggered.

'Jutht fetch them, will you, Evanth!' Essex's tone betrayed impatience. Evans approached Martin and Tara, looked them up and down, removed his jacket and rolled up the sleeves of his black shirt. Essex opened the other half of the French window. Evans took some deep breaths and stretched his arms, his joints making light cracking sounds.

'Time to go swimming, boys and girls,' he said, squatting down and putting his vast arms around the upper thighs of the trussed-up couple. He took another deep breath, voiced a committed hwulp! and stood to attention with Martin and Tara balanced horizontally and precariously on his broad shoulder. He walked unsteadily into the garden, his prisoners hardly daring to move, lest he fall, taking them with him. To Martin's mounting horror as he saw the house receding, they appeared to be heading for the well, and he saw that the chicken wire covering had been thrown onto the lawn to one side. Evans turned towards the house and started to shift his load until Martin and Tara were staring straight at the gaping hole.

'You'll kill us,' shouted Martin, convinced that he and Tara were about to be dropped headfirst into the void.

'Evanth!' shouted Essex. 'Letth keep them alive a little longer, yeth?'

Evans grunted and turned through one hundred and eighty degrees. Bending forwards and letting go, he let them slide down his barrel chest, straight into the well.

'Dear God,' Tara appealed softly.

'Ohh.', said Martin.

It seemed to last an eternity, but the fall could not have been more than ten feet. Martin hit the bottom first and Tara's forehead smacked him in the jaw. Their knees buckled simultaneously and they tipped sideways into the wall, bruising their shoulders. The surface underfoot felt like some sort of primeval goo as they struggled to regain their balance and stand upright.

'Are you alright?' he asked in a panic. He was hurting in several places and was terrified that she might be injured.

'Yeah, I'm fine, I think. But I must have nutted you. Are you okay?'

'Yes. Absolutely. You stupid bastards!' He had tilted his head back and was staring up at two dark heads silhouetted against the grey night sky. 'You could have killed us! How did you know it wasn't deeper than this? Eh?'

'I didn't, boyo, believe me.' Evans laughed.

'Hey! Essex?' Martin saw an opportunity to bring Monan's lunatic quest to a swift end. 'So much for the well, eh? Where's the water, then? Where's the source of Monan's bloody millions now? There's no bloody spring down here!'

'Thave your breath, Martin.' Essex sounded calm and in control once more. 'We'll thee you in the morning, yeth? Don't do anything I wouldn't do.'

'I don't believe it; I've spent the entire weekend trying to avoid selling this damn well, and now I'm stuck down the bloody thing.'

'The company's not so bad though?'

'Oh God, Tara, the company's wonderful. I mean, I just wish you weren't here.'

'Well thanks a million!'

'No! I mean... oh, what have I done?'

'Ssh!' They listened as two cars started and drove away. They remained quiet for what seemed like an hour but was probably more like a minute. There were no other sounds.

'I'm afraid I drank too much. It's my stupid fault.'

'Nonsense! Tell you the truth, I think I was a little off my face too. But there's nothing like this to sober you up, so there isn't. How deep do you reckon this is?'

'I really don't know. Ten, twelve feet?'

'We seem to be sinking.'

He was already aware that he had descended to ankle level in the slush and that his descent hadn't yet stopped. He leant back against the wall of the well and lifted her up a little. The fall had done nothing to slacken the ropes and they remained intimately tied together. To his surprise and intense embarrassment, he could feel a hard-on approaching, something that she couldn't fail to notice.

'Try feeling around for something solid,' he suggested. Idiot! Stuck down a bloody well with the planet's loveliest woman, out pops a lewd double-entendre. Uninvited, one has to emphasise. Could be sued for aggressive behaviour with mouth and member. Puns and pecker in bad-taste double-act; Dick Dilly-Dallied As Damsel Drowned in Dirt. Trial by tabloid. Think – not of sex! Shit. Got to concentrate on boring things before drilling right through Tara into the wall the other side. Doh! Pit, yes, pit. Er, Armpit. Bottom. Chest. Damn! Best start in the middle, well away from Bosom. Mud. Nipples. Tara's firm breasts now really digging into one's chest, her soapy-scented hair up one's nostrils. Oozing. Pumping. Quivering. Rumpy-pumpy. 'Shit!'

'What's the matter?' she asked, startled.

'Nothing! Er, can you feel anything?' He was sweating. It was more than a slight swelling now; his prick was straining against the front of his jeans, pushing into her crotch. It was the most intense erection he had experienced for years; the sort of erection he had looked forward to enjoying again, but not in these circumstances.

'I rather think I can.'

'Wha...?'

'I can't feel anything down there. Under our feet, I mean. Martin, I don't mean to worry you, but we're still sinking.' She was right. The mud was now up to mid-calf.

'I don't understand it. This is an ornamental well, not a real one.'

'Hmm.'

'It must be all the water from the cistern. That's been pumping away for three days; enough to make anything a bit soggy.'

'A bit soggy? If we don't get our act together soon we're going to be eating mud.'

'Okay. Let's be methodical. You feel around first, then me.'

With their thighs bound together, it was a struggle for either of them to probe for solid surfaces with their feet. With each passing minute they sank an inch further. It was now pitch black. Martin, emboldened by their jeopardy, gave her a squeeze and rested his head tentatively against hers.

'If I had to be tied up with anyone in the world, it would be you,' he said, fully prepared to be knocked back. 'I can't hide my feelings Tara; I can't help it. I've fallen in love with you.'

'And I thought that was a gun in your pocket.'

'Oh God, I'm sorry.'

'I might be flattered.'

'Might you? Really?' He had picked his head up from her shoulder.

'Well, you certainly don't make a dull date.' As she spoke he could feel her breath on his face and he sensed that she was looking him in the eye, or thereabouts. He carefully leant forwards until he felt the bridge of her nose with his lips. He kissed it. 'My mouth's down here,' she whispered. Slowly at first, their tongues explored each other, becoming more urgent as their mouths sucked, teeth occasionally clashing, she nibbling his lips one by one. Shivers of excitement ran down his spine, the back of his neck tingling; he was hugging her tightly, never wanting to let go, even if he could.

'Oh Tara!' he said at last, giving their lips a brief rest. He couldn't think of anything else useful to say, so felt his way towards another kiss, already missing the deliciousness of her mouth, the most wonderful mouth on the world's most beautiful face. This time, it was she who surfaced first.

'Jesus!' she exclaimed. Something dislodged itself from the wall and slipped into the mud.

'What was that?' he had visions of disturbed rats' nests.

'It's a big stone, fallen right out of the wall here. Please, God, don't say the whole thing's collapsing around us.'

'No, of course it isn't.' He tried his best to sound reassuring. There was a grating sound, then something else plopped into the mire. 'What the hell was that? Another stone?'

'I don't think so. Whatever it is, I can feel it. Hold on, I'm standing on it. It feels like a rock. No, I think it's a box of some sort.'

'I don't like this; we've got to get out of here. If those idiots have really gone to Birmingham it gives us – what? Two more hours?'

'Ow!'

'Sorry! God, what did I do?'

'You didn't do anything; I just hurt my ankle on something. There's something sharp... hang on! Do you reckon we can squat down here? This might be our ticket out.' Bracing herself against him, Tara lifted her feet back; he tentatively bent his knees and they slowly and rather unsteadily descended into the mud. His knee struck something and he yelped in pain.

'What's wrong?' she asked.

'Funny bone in the knee. Felt like the corner of something. Oh, is this your box?'

'It must be, but can you feel this now?' She was leaning to her right and pulling down. He relaxed and allowed her to guide him until he felt his arm press against something protruding from the wall of the well. They managed to shift round so that he was able to feel the thing with his hands. It felt like an iron bar, rusting and jagged along its edges.

'It's something metal,' he said. 'I'll try and cut the rope.' He vigorously rubbed the rope binding his wrists. Despite sometimes scraping his skin painfully, he quickly broke free. 'Yes!' He fumbled for the knots that clamped their chests together and loosened them, realising that he might never again have the opportunity to press up against her delightful breasts. Next he freed their waists, then thighs. All that remained was the rope tying her hands together behind his back. 'I'm not sure I want to free you from this one.'

'Free me now and I'll hug you later. Promise.'

'Deal. How do we do this?'

'Well, I don't think you're going to be able to step out, so, if you duck and raise your arms, I'll try over the top.'

Martin did as she suggested and buried his face in her chest as she lifted her bound hands over his head and uplifted arms. He wondered whether having lascivious thoughts, given the circumstances, made him a pervert, then decided that he didn't care anyway. He felt for the knots in the darkness and tried to prise them apart; the mud had covered everything with slime, which made it difficult for him to get a proper grip, and the cold that numbed his fingers hindered him further. After several minutes of fumbling, he succeeded in releasing her. He hugged her and realised that they were both cold and wet.

'You're freezing! Come on; are there any decent footholds up here?'

'We could turn this box on end.' They felt around for the edges of the box under the mud, but it was too small to be of much assistance. 'Maybe it's buried treasure.'

'You wouldn't get much treasure in that, by the feel of it.' He was, nevertheless, intrigued by their find. 'I think we're best off if you climb up me and try to reach the top.' He squatted down again and felt for her lower leg. 'Here, a leg-up.' He clasped her foot in cupped hands and lifted; she placed her hands on his head, then braced herself against the wall as she brought her other foot up his chest and hoisted herself until she was standing on his shoulders.

'I'm out!' First one foot lifted, then the other, as she scrambled up, over the top. He pulled each of his feet in turn out of the gloop that was threatening to suck him further down and put one on the box.

'How are we going to get you out?' she called down.

'I don't know. What if I throw some of this rope up? Maybe you could tie it to those roof struts or something.'

'Okay.'

'Here it comes!' He tossed up a coiled length of the rope, as vertically as he could.

'Nope.'

It landed on his head. He tried again.

'Got it! Hold on while I tie it to this thing. It feels pretty firm.'

While he waited, he pulled the box up out of the mud. It had handles on two sides and felt as though it was made of wood, with metal edges and a curved top.

'Feels like a tool box or something,' he shouted.

'What does?'

'This box thing. The buried treasure.'

'Bombs away!' Once more his head was hit by a length of sodden, mud-covered rope. He found the end of it and tied it around the handle on one end of the box.

'Here's the box; pull it out!' It banged and scraped on the wall as she dragged it to the top.

'Okay. Now you.' The rope came back down. He tugged on it, gradually increasing the load until he was reasonably confident that it would support his weight. The slippery mud coating his shoes and the rope made his ascent difficult, but the cavity left in the wall by the box was well placed. He was gripping so hard that, by the time he hauled himself over the top, he barely had any strength left in his hands. He lay on his back on the lawn, panting. Tara sat beside him, clearly visible beneath the overcast night sky after the pitch black of the well. Her hair and clothes were covered in mud, as was the hand that tenderly stroked his face.

'So, what are your hobbies?' she asked.

'Apart from bondage and mud wrestling? Collecting tool boxes. Let's take a look.' He stood up, picked up the box and led her back into the sitting room. 'All the lights are shot in here. Let's go upstairs.' They climbed the stairs and he flicked light switches on and off until, in the smallest bedroom, they were bathed in the harsh light of a single bare bulb. 'So that's the secret behind your wonderful complexion,' he laughed, pointing at her mud-splattered face.

'You're no oil painting either.' She looked at the box. 'Dear God Martin, that looks old!' He followed her gaze. It was a small casket, wooden with a framework of intricately decorated metal. Underneath its fresh coating of mud it was blackened from years spent underground.

'Maybe it's one of those time capsules, put down there by whichever twit built the bloody well. I bet it's been there no longer than twenty years. What's it going to contain? A Philips 2000 format video of an early episode of Minder, an original cassette of Never Mind the Bollocks, a photograph of the last Labour cabinet...'

'Well, let's see if you're right.' She fiddled with the catch, which obliged her by breaking away at its hinges. 'Oops. Oh.' There was a note of disappointment in her voice. 'No pieces of eight this time.' She pulled some folded paper from the box and held it up. 'That's all folks!'

Martin took it from her and carefully opened it up. There were three brittle sheets, which he carefully laid out on the floor.

'Mary McConnelly!' he exclaimed. 'Bugger me if Monan wasn't right.'

'What is it?'

'It's some sort of deed, a – bloody hell!'

'What?' Tara knelt alongside him and peered at the papers. She slid the bottom one out to one side so that she could see it. 'Martin!'

'Yes?'

'This is dated 1795.'

'I know; that's what I was saying. That date's here too.'

'Yeah, but the address given is As from the office of the Prime Minister of the Government of His Royal Highness King George III, the Palace of Westminster. It's only signed by William Pitt!'

'What?'

'That'll be the younger one. Jesus, Martin, you've only got a museum-piece document of some sort. What's it about?'

'Er,' he scanned the paper frantically, 'okay, Mary McConnelly, as Freeholder blah blah of Loch Cuiphur House and its lands in the Barony of Vereham blah blah blah or her Heir or Whosoever being the Rightful Holder of the Deeds thereto blah blah blah is granted Demesne – what the hell is Demesne? – of Loch Cuiphur Castle, the Great Well of Cuiphur and all Lands and Minerals appertaining in the County of Inverness.' He picked up the second sheet. 'This Instrument presented to the Lord Clerk Register in Edinburgh before the expiry of two hundred years after the date set hereunder shall grant said Freeholder Demesne blah blah. In the event of Title not – there's some of this I can't make out – before the expiry of two hundred years after the date set hereunder said Title reverts to the Government of His Royal Highness King George III or that of his lawful Successor blah blah blah in respect of both Properties known as Loch Cuiphur House on the Manor of Vereham in the County of Wiltshire, England and Loch Cuiphur Castle in the County of Inverness, Scotland. What does that one say again?' He looked at Tara who was holding up the last page.

'There's a load of mumbo-jumbo and By the Hand and Seal of the Prime Minister of the Government of His Royal, etcetera, etcetera, William Pitt. Martin?'

'Yes?'

'You know you were wondering why this place was called Lockkeeper's Cottage, when there wasn't any lock or river or canal?'

'Yes?'

'It's because it isn't Lockkeeper, it's Loch Cuiphur!'

'It's named after a bloody loch!'

'And, unless I'm mistaken, this document suggests that you own not just this place, but something called Loch Cuiphur Castle too. And,' she checked something on one of the sheets, 'the Great Well of Cuiphur. So, there is a well, but it isn't here; it's in Scotland!'

'Holy shit!' Martin's eyes roved wildly over the papers again, then he sat back, stunned. 'No wonder Monan wanted the place.'

'Of course! He must have known about this.'

'It would be in his manorial papers, presumably.'

'When does this thing expire?' As she asked the question, she began to count on her fingers. They arrived at the answer simultaneously.

'Tuesday!'

'Come on,' he continued, carefully folding the papers and tucking them into a pocket, 'We've got to get moving again. We must get to Shimbley and see my solicitor; he's probably old enough to understand this stuff.'

'And probably in bed with his cocoa, or his mistress. Have you any idea what time it is?'

'Haven't a clue. It could be anything between ten and midnight. Hey, I could phone Shimbley police, call in that nice Mr Dee again, get him to set a trap. And pick us up.'

'God, do we have to travel with him again?'

'Fancy a walk?'

'What do you think?'

'Right, I'll see if the phone's still working.' He walked through into the mess that was the master bedroom, and looked around. He was certain that he could remember placing the phone on the floor, near the window, but it wasn't there now. He peered at the floor, as if a second look would suddenly reveal it, in this room devoid of furniture. He stared for a while at the empty socket on the wall until he was quite sure that there was no phone connected to it. 'Phone's gone,' he said, returning to Tara.

'Gone?'

'Yeah, strange. Maybe Evans took it, thought it might make a good car phone. We're going to have to walk after all.'

'How long do you suppose it will be before Monan and his bastards return?'

'I suppose if everything goes smoothly for them they could be back in another hour or so. God! I wonder what they've done with Beverley. All I need is her shouting at me on top of all this.'

'Let's hope she's still able to shout. Look, I don't imagine it will take them long to find us in Shimbley.'

'We'll see if John's got room in a garage for our cars. And we can always hide out in the police station. They're hardly going to come after us there.' Martin ushered her from the room and turned off the lights.

'Why not leave those on?' she suggested. 'It may slow them down a bit if they think that someone's in here.'

'Good idea.' They descended the stairs and stepped into the garden. Martin retrieved the front door from its habitual resting place in the hall and propped it up in its frame. His thoughts of sanctuary at the police station were dashed by the return of pessimism. 'The problem remains that Monan and co haven't committed a crime, as far as Dee is concerned. He's seen the result of some vandalism and heard a pretty far-fetched story. If Evans's axe doesn't yield any incriminating fingerprints, we're stuffed. In fact, there's no reason why Essex couldn't try to turn the tables, make out we've done something to them: assault, robbery, whatever. After all, Dee couldn't find any form.'

'What about Beverley? There's a clear case of abduction.'

'Only if she's around to make a complaint. In the meantime, we don't even know if she's being missed by anyone.'

'What do you think she was doing here?' They looked up and down the road, then set off, hand in hand, in the direction of Shimbley.

'Almost certainly a combination of snooping and demanding the collection of the rest of my stuff from our house. Her house.'

'Won't her other half be there? Couldn't we tell him?'

'I shouldn't think so; she specialises in the wealthy, already married types now. I imagine they need discreet hotel rooms around the world to consummate things.'

'I can't imagine you being married to her.'

'Nor can I now. Just the thought of it makes me shudder. I must have been out of my mind.'

'Still, I hope they don't do her any harm.'

He chuckled. 'You know, if it wasn't so serious, the thought of her coming face to face with those two amuses me. I don't think she's ever met the like of them; they may as well be from another galaxy. I'm not sure who should be the most frightened, her, Essex or Evans.'

'Maybe she'll try to woo you back, now that you've got that Scottish castle she was after.'

'Oh, no! A self-fulfilling prophesy. Oh, God, I do hope she doesn't.'

'Me too.' Tara snuggled up to him and he put his arm around her, hugging her tightly.

'She's got no chance,' he said.

'Why's that?'

'Because I'm hopelessly in love with you.'

Their walk to Shimbley was interrupted only twice by passing cars, the couple crouching in the deep ditch on both occasions, just in case it was Monan and his cronies. The dark sky was clear and, although there was little wind, the air was cold and neither of them had dried since their occupation of the well. They were both shivering when they reached the High Street and the clock on top of the Town Hall indicated twelve-fifteen.

Martin, aware that John, Kevin and Susan would probably be in bed by now, entertained the idea of eking out the remainder of the night at his office. When he realised that his office was likely to be one of the first places searched on the discovery of his escape from the well, he considered the police station. That idea also failed to comfort him; the police were as likely to put him in a cell as to take seriously his latest allegations. In any case, if the supposedly ancient papers in his pocket were genuine and there was substance to their contents, as far as he could understand them, he didn't need to waste time in the hands of Shimbley's finest; he needed to reach the Lord Clerk Register, if such a person still existed, within the next two days. In the meantime both he and Tara were once again desperately in need of soap and sleep. He wondered whether he would be able to identify Kevin and Susan's window and accurately lob pebbles at it. Probably get the bedroom of a nervous paying guest instead, and be carted away to the police station anyway. He was startled out of his thoughts by the sound of a cheery and familiar voice.

'There's only one person I know who has to duck under the shop signs!' Molly had drawn alongside in her weathered Range Rover.

'Molly! Hello. What are you doing here?'

'I might ask you the same. Why aren't you tucked up in your new home?'

'It's a long story.' He looked at Molly, who looked back at him impassively. After a long pause, she raised her eyebrows at him.

'Aren't you going to introduce us?'

'Oh, sorry! This is Tara. Tara, this is Molly, Susan's sister.' They exchanged greetings. 'Molly?' continued Martin.

'Yes.'

'Have you just come up? I mean, are you on your way to the pub?'

'Yes. Running late; they'd closed the bloody motorway at Taunton. It's taken hours. You look awful. Have you been in the river? What on earth are you doing? You're not drunk are you?'

'Not any more. Look, do you think you could let us in? To the pub I mean. We're actually supposed to be staying there but something happened and, well, here we are. I'll explain everything.'

'I wouldn't miss it for the world.' Molly pulled away slowly and drove through the archway fifty yards ahead, into the George and Dragon's yard. A minute later Martin and Tara joined her.

'Hi,' said Martin. 'I know this is going to sound funny, but do you think there's garage space for Alfredo and Tara's pick-up. We have to hide them.'

'What? Have you robbed a bank or something?'

'There are some people after us. No, not the police. It's quite bizarre, actually, but right now things are pressing. I'll explain but – garage?'

'Blimey. Okay.' Molly crossed the yard to a large wooden barn, opened a small door in its side and disappeared through it. A moment later one of the big doors at the end was creaking open. Martin ran over and helped her with the second. 'I reckon there's room in here', she said. 'Do you think you can start your heap without waking the entire town?'

'As long as the keys are still in him. Heap indeed. Do you have your keys, Tara?'

'Right here.' She pulled them from her jeans pocket.

Five minutes later, the two cars were safely shut in the barn. Martin grabbed the road atlas from Alfredo's floor, handed it to Tara and helped Molly in with her suitcase. They settled around the kitchen table with a large pot of tea and a packet of biscuits.

'Nothing,' said Tara, looking up from the index in the back of the atlas. 'No Cuiphur, no Loch Cuiphur, no Lockkeeper, no Loch Keeper and nothing looking remotely like those names anywhere around Inverness.'

'Oh. That doesn't bode too well then.' Martin was disappointed. 'Perhaps the whole thing's an elaborate hoax.'

'What are you two talking about?' Molly demanded.

Martin related his tale to a stunned Molly, while Tara contributed lurid descriptions of Monan's behaviour back home in Ireland.

'You are joking!' Molly exclaimed when they told of their plummet into the well. 'They must be crazy.'

'Not entirely,' Martin continued, 'because it's down the well that we found out what it was all about. Or rather, what we think it might be all about.' He brought out the three shabby sheets of paper. 'Take a look at this.'

Molly gasped, picking up the top sheet and studying it closely. Martin and Tara watched her as she carefully read all three pieces in silence. She read them twice, replaced them on the table and leaned back in her chair, looking at the ceiling.

'Well I'll be.' she said finally. 'You own a sodding castle, Martin. It came true after all!'

'You think this is genuine?' As Molly was a historian, Martin figured that her opinion was as good as he was likely to hear. 'Why isn't the place in the atlas?'

'In answer to the first question, I don't see why this isn't genuine. These instruments were fairly common things. They were a way of bestowing rewards, or of repaying favours, or of dealing with politically difficult situations. From this, I would guess that Mary McConnelly was the mistress of someone in the government; if she was a Scottish Catholic, for example, he would have had to keep it quiet. This could have been the price of her silence and loyalty. It may be that Baron Vereham was in the cabinet and got the Prime Minister's signature to safeguard Mary's wellbeing. Maybe Mary had the Baron's bastard child. If Loch Cuiphur Castle was a prize from some toff's adventures north of the border, then it would have been quite within Pitt's gift to sign it away to whomever he saw fit. In this case, apparently, our wee Mary here.'

'But if she was Scottish, why would she have been given Lockkeeper's Cottage? What was she doing there?'

'She could have been a pawn in somebody's game. For instance, her father could have been a clan chief or held some influence over the clans around Inverness. If she was held a not unwilling hostage by our Baron Vereham, and there were promises to bestow certain properties on her or her descendents in due course, then that could have been reason enough for the McConnellys at least to keep their knives sheathed in their socks.'

'Dirks.'

'Alright, in their dirks.'

'But, according to my atlas, there's no such place as Loch Cuiphur.'

'Place names change.'

'Come on! In two hundred years?'

'You go back two hundred years and ask George III's cartographer-in-chief what he thinks of Welwyn Garden City. You'll be met with pretty blank looks.'

'Oh right. But go ahead two hundred years and they'll know exactly where you're talking about.'

'Like Gipewiz?'

'Like what?'

'Gipewiz.'

'What's sheepwidge?'

'Ipswich. Place in Suffolk. To be fair, that was more like nine hundred years ago, but it shows that place names do change.'

'Okay, you win. So, if this is genuine, is there any danger at all of it having any legal relevance now, two hundred years later?'

'Oh heavens, yes. My God, if stuff like this was made null and void, just because of the passing of the years, our Royal Family wouldn't have a pot to piss in, God bless Lilibet and all. No, unless there was a bill passed to overturn this specific instrument, it holds good. What still exists of Loch Cuiphur Castle remains to be seen however. You may be acquiring a liability rather than an asset. What we need to do is find out what records are held locally.'

'What? Where?'

'In Inverness, maybe in the Town Hall. Or a museum. In Edinburgh, the Scottish land register, I guess.'

'Bloody hell. It'll take a day to get there.'

'How far is it?' asked Tara.

'Ooh, four hundred miles to Edinburgh, maybe.' Martin tried to picture a map of Britain in his head. 'And another hundred and fifty, perhaps, to Inverness.'

'Didn't you say that your friend Donut Dave was in Inverness?' Molly was sounding increasingly excited.

'Um, I believe he's near Inverness.'

'Call him.'

'Are you mad? It's nearly two in the morning.'

'And you've got a castle to claim, for crying out loud. Call him.' Molly pointed to the telephone on the wall.

'I'll have to find my address book; I think it's in one of the boxes in Alfredo.' Martin capitulated and went out to the barn to fetch Dave's number. He returned with it and, with a heavy sense of guilt about the unsocial hour, gingerly tapped out the digits. After half a dozen rings, Dave's unmistakable southern drawl came back down the line in a recorded message: Ya through to David Dawson. Ah'm real sorry ah can' talk to ya right now, but if y'all leave a message after the tone, ah'll come back at ya real soon, or ya can try the cell which is 07...

Martin had cupped a hand over the mouthpiece. 'Answering machine,' he explained to Tara and Molly. 'Hello, Dave. Er, this is Martin, Martin Minchin. Er, I've got a request, a favour. It's a strange tale. Er, if you're around, I want you, er, I mean I would be grateful if you were able to...'

'To what, for Chrissake? Get a grip, Marty. Whassup?' Dave sounded wide awake and surprisingly happy to hear from his old friend, considering the hour.

'Where to start. God, sorry to have woken you at this time.'

'Woken me? Jeez, ah ain' gotten inta muh bed yet. Whass troublin' ya, Marty?'

'Does Loch Cuiphur Castle mean anything to you?'

'Nope. That it?'

'What about Loch Cuiphur?'

'Ya got me beat there, man.'

'Is there any chance you could get over to Inverness tomorrow – today, I mean? I need some historical records looking up and I need to know how and where to reach the Lord Clerk Register, if such a person still exists.'

'Hell, Marty, ya must be movin' with the A-list now. Next ya'll be wantin' me to call at Balmoral. All that countin' other folks' green finally turned ya wacko?'

'No, I'm fine. Well I'm okay, considering there are people intent on threatening my life and robbing me of all my property. I haven't got time to explain it all now but, if you come up with the answers I'm half expecting, I'm going to be seeing you before the end of play tomorrow. Have you got a pen? Right.' Martin dictated the pertinent bits from the old papers and promised to call again on the hour, every hour, from wherever he was on the journey north. He replaced the receiver and sat down, yawning.

'Come on,' said Molly, standing up, 'we all need to get some sleep if we're going to be in Scotland for our supper.'

'We?' asked Martin.

'I'm not missing out on this. Anyway, I hardly think your precious Alfredo's the car to take you that distance; we can go in my Rangey. You don't mind, do you?'

'No, of course not; if that's what you want, I'd be delighted. Oh...' He glanced at Tara, suddenly aware that he was taking her for granted.

'It's a great idea,' said Tara. 'We'll have our own historian on hand and Essex won't be looking out for Molly's car.'

'That's agreed, then.' Molly made for the door and turned off the lights, leaving the place bathed in the soft glow of the battery-powered emergency lighting. 'Are you both sorted out for rooms?'

'Yes, thank you,' replied Tara, swiftly. 'We are.'

'Night-night then.' Molly threw Martin a knowing grin and walked towards the private stairs that led to the family's quarters. Martin took Tara's hand and led her quietly up the main staircase.

'Are you sure...,' he began.

'Yes.'

Having softly closed and locked the door to the room, he turned towards her.

'A bit muddy', he said. 'Shouldn't we, er?' he gestured towards the bathroom door.

'After we've slept. Do you have a toothbrush in there?'

'Yes. Help yourself.'

'I won't be a minute.' She walked into the bathroom and closed the door behind her. He sat on the bed, not sure whether he should remove his clothes. He got up again and walked to the other side of the room to peer at himself in a mirror. It had been a long time since he had been in a position of impending intimacy, if he didn't count the time that they had spent in the well. It made him simultaneously excited and nervous. He sat on the bed again and picked up the clock-radio. He wanted to set it to come on at a sensible time in the morning and fiddled in vain with the various buttons. Flummoxed, he admitted defeat and replaced it on the bedside table, now displaying 07:04 in a flashing green glow.

'Are you getting your kit off or what?' Tara's question startled him, but not as much as the sight of her. She walked across the room stark naked, her glossy black hair cascading around her shoulders, each firm young breast tipped by an exquisite nipple standing erect in a dark, perfectly round areola. Between her legs was the neatest little triangle of black hair. She slid under the duvet and expelled a satisfied sigh.

'Oh my God, you're absolutely beautiful,' Martin gushed, 'I think I must be in heaven. Don't move.' He sped into the bathroom, undressed and sank onto the lavatory. His stomach told him that he needed to empty his bowels, but they seemed reluctant to cooperate. He decided that he was trying too hard and tried to relax by sitting back and thinking of Tara. What a time to be stranded on the pan; the Gods had delivered an angel to him and now they were having a laugh. To make matters worse, the eventual successful evacuation was preceded by a fart of spectacular length and loudness. He wondered if Tara had heard it and identified what it was. Of course she had; she was neither deaf nor stupid. He brushed his teeth with a growing distrust of what his body might do to him next. No doubt he was about to suffer the ultimate humiliation, a willy that wouldn't. She'll jump to the conclusion that he's gay. After all, what other conclusion could there be? The opportunity to get seriously sticky with the planet's most ravishing woman, and matey won't come up to play. Those breasts. That mane of hair. Oh, those perfect breasts. He felt something stirring below. Thank you, oh, thank you, God. I will try to get to church really soon. He dried his face, bared his teeth briefly in the mirror, then opened the door. Tara was lying on her back, one arm thrown back on the pillow beside her head and a faint smile playing on her lips. From which came the sound of the gentlest, sweetest, most utterly feminine snore.

CHAPTER 9: Monday morning

Martin woke with a start.

'Hey, slowly.' Tara gently pushed his head back onto the pillow and stroked his hair. She was sitting on the edge of the bed, a towel wrapped around her. 'I've made some tea. It's only UHT milk I'm afraid. You don't take sugar, do you?'

'No. Uh, thanks.'

'I've had a really great bath: hot as hell, full to the brim and loaded with bubbles. I left it in but I'll run you a fresh one if you want. I think I was gone from the moment my head hit the pillow, eh? Sorry.'

'God, don't apologise. You needed the sleep. I was exactly the same.' Martin lied. In fact he had enjoyed probably an hour just lying next to her, one arm resting lightly across her tummy, rising and falling with her musical breathing, before he too drifted away. Now he desperately wanted to kiss her good morning. They hadn't kissed since they had been in the well many hours earlier, but he was wary of breaking the spell. He rather wanted her to make the moves, although he recognised the unfairness of that, particularly given the age gap. But then, girls were known for maturing well in advance of boys; ah, but he was hardly a boy any more, and she was certainly all woman. Perhaps she had only kissed him because of the drink and the unusual circumstances; now that they were supposedly safe, she might not feel the same way.

'Aren't you going to give me a good morning kiss?' She was looking at him with soppy, puppy-dog eyes. He didn't need asking twice; he pulled her down onto the bed, their mouths locked together in mutual exploration. Eventually she struggled free, laughing.

'Come on you! Get in that bath; we've stuff to do, a castle to find.'

'Sorry; I think I must be a bit gorilla's.'

'I beg your pardon?'

Martin stuck his tongue out, pulling a gargoyle face.

'Gorilla's armpit. Certainly tastes like it from here.'

'Well thanks.'

'Not you! Me. I'm going.' He leapt out of the bed and headed into the bathroom, worried that the very early stages of an erection might be showing. Once in the bathroom, he looked at the slight engorgement dangling between his legs and thought that perhaps he should have shown it off like that, passed it off as his normal flaccid state. What if she had seen it and correctly diagnosed the vestigial hard-on? She would be asking herself why he ran away from her, strangely reluctant to encourage further naughtiness. He sank into the still steaming water and stared dreamily at the ceiling. He could barely believe what was happening. All thoughts of houses, Monan, Essex, Evans, deeds and ancient instruments had departed, leaving his mind to be occupied only by visions of Tara. Every few seconds he felt a faint, strange nagging in his head, as though his brain was trying to remind him of something: what's that? Ah, Tara.

'You forgot your tea. Is the bath okay?' She placed the cup in a soap holder and disappeared before Martin had a chance to look at her.

'It's absolute bliss. I love you,' he called out. He drank the tea, convinced that he could detect her sweet perfume on the cup, in the drink itself. 'Oh my, oh my, oh my, how I love you Tara; please, never leave me,' he added in a whisper. Suddenly aware that he didn't know whether it was six in the morning or closer to noon he dunked his head and gave his hair a thorough shampoo. Determined not to be more of a slob than was absolutely necessary, he grabbed his razor from the basin and sat back in the bath, shaving blindly. The trickle of blood running off his chest and dispersing in the grubby water served as a warning that it was time to leave the tub and use a mirror. By the time he re-entered the bedroom, his modesty protected by a towel, Tara had made herself scarce; she clearly wasn't a woman who needed three hours of preparation before meeting her public, and Martin approved. He donned some fresh clothes and felt a pang of guilt about Tara's lack of anything clothing-wise, other than what she stood up in. The clock-radio on the bedside table indicated 14:22. He performed a quick mental calculation and estimated that it was well past nine. They needed to get a move on; it was a safe bet that his and Tara's absence from the well had already been discovered. He patted his pocket and was startled not to feel the reassuring scraps of paper, his passport to Loch Cuiphur Castle. Tara or Molly must have put them somewhere safe.

John was in the kitchen, performing a stock-take on the contents of the refrigerators. He responded to Martin's cheery greeting by straightening up, hands on hips, and looking him slowly up and down.

'What in God's name are you up to, Martin my lad? The boys and girls bring me strange tales, enough nearly to send me back to my sickbed.'

'John, I am so sorry about all this. I'll pay for all the lodgings and everything, of course. I really don't know whether I'm coming or going. It's been something of a nightmare.'

'Don't you worry Martin. I'll pour you a nice big coffee and fetch the three gentlemen through from the lounge, yeah?' Martin froze, his stomach suddenly in one huge knot, his mouth open but not able to utter a word because his brain was still trying to come to terms with the fact that his nemesis was in the next room. 'Ha! Always a sucker for it! Oh, God, I'm sorry Martin. Jesus, you look like you've seen a ghost. Oh dear.' John was quelling his guffaws with some difficulty; he plucked a tissue from a box on the sideboard, wiped away a tear and blew his nose.

'You bastard! I could have had a baby.'

'You look like you did, dear boy.' John was still laughing. 'I'm sorry, I couldn't resist it. You're serious about these blokes, hey?'

'Of course I'm bloody serious; I've been assaulted, kidnapped, assaulted again, left to drown and I'm now on the run. If it wasn't for the fact that I've got urgent business in Scotland I'd be down at the police station right now, demanding justice.'

'Yes.'

'And reparation.'

'Quite.'

'And where's Tara?'

'I think you're not telling everything about you and Tara.'

'Do you? Have you any idea as to her whereabouts?'

'Yup.'

'Well, would you please let me in on it?'

'You know the rules, Martin: give.'

'I have nothing to say on the matter.'

'I thought so. Look, you don't mind me asking, do you, but – she's a lovely girl alright, a raving bloody beauty in fact, but – Martin, isn't she just a little bit too, well, you know, young?'

'Too young for what, John? She's an adult. She's mature woman. She's her own boss, a free spirit. She's,' he paused.

'Yeah?'

'Bloody hell, John, she's wonderful.'

'Wow, you've got it bad, haven't you?'

'When Beverley kicked me out I really didn't imagine ever finding anyone else again, let alone someone like Tara. I'm in love with her and I think she might feel the same.'

'Look, my boy, you're a bit like family here; we're all very fond of you, so just take care. We don't want to see you hurt again.'

'I know. Thanks.' Martin casually lifted a saucepan down from a hook above him and suddenly made as if to assail John with it. 'Now, where the hell is she?'

'Whoa! She and Molly went shopping; women's stuff probably. Please put that down. And you're to contact no one except somebody called doughboy Dave and...'

'Donut.'

'Pardon?'

'Donut; Donut Dave.'

'Oh, right. Where was I? Ah! And you've got to have some breakfast as it might be your last meal.'

'Uh?'

'For a while. Bacon butty?'

'Brilliant. Thanks.' Martin returned the pan to its overhead home.

John busied himself with preparing another breakfast. 'It seems that Molly's intent on participating in your adventure,' he said, without taking his eyes off the stove.

'Yes.' Martin sensed the unease. 'Look, I really didn't intend it. In fact, she should stay out of it. They're really quite dangerous people; well, crazy people, nutters, desperate. You see, I think there's more at stake than what at first appeared. Maybe you could talk to her. It's my problem and she shouldn't be involved.'

'Martin! We're talking about Molly here. You try talking to her. On second thoughts, don't waste your breath. But for God's sake, and this goes for all of you, if there's the slightest risk of harm to anyone – but most of all to Molly – *run!* Alright?'

'Understood.'

'You're the oldest. And the tallest. And it's your fault.'

'Yes.'

'Look after them!'

'Of course.' The telephone hanging on the wall began to ring.

'Get that will you?' John was levering a mountain of bacon in between two doorsteps of bread.

'Good morning, George and Dragon,' Martin said into the receiver in his best maître d's voice.

'You missed your calling, Martin.'

'Oh hi Molly. Where are you?'

'I'm in your solicitor's office, with Tara.'

'What? At Petey P-T's? I don't suppose he's in circulation yet. What are you doing there?'

'Ha ha,' Molly's stagy chortle was followed by a loud aside: 'He says you won't be up yet, Petey P-T. Why does he call you that?'

'Molly!' Martin's hoarse whisper was no more subtle. It was met with Molly's genuine laughter.

'It's okay. He's photocopying stuff to do with your house purchase.'

'Does he know what a photocopier is?'

'He wonders if you know what a copier is.' Another aside.

'Molly, stop it!'

'Did you miss your historical papers?'

'Of course I did.'

'Don't worry; I've got them safe and sound and we're copying them too. We should come away from here with enough to show to the Scottish land people. And we've kitted Tara out with some fresh clothes.'

'Oh God, what about money?'

'No, we just grabbed a load of knickers and bras and legged it.'

'What?'

'My flexible friend. Don't worry about it.'

'My hole-in-the-wall card is in my office. I'll collect it and extract a decent float.'

'Forget it.'

'Why?'

'Because Tara has already pointed out your poor victim, Evans, to me. He's got a huge lump on the back of his head.'

'What? You're kidding! Has he?' He didn't recall noticing any injuries last night.

'Maybe it's just his ponytail.'

'Molly, be serious, please. Are they really here?'

'Of course they're here. You didn't think they were going to pack up and go home after all that's happened, did you? The stakes are obviously way too high. Which is why we've got to plan things quite carefully.'

'Molly, I don't think you should get involved anymore.'

'Ha ha, say hi to Dad for me, will you? You're not keeping me away, Martin. In any case, you need my historical expertise. And Tara needs someone closer to her own age to talk to.'

'Very funny, you cow.' Martin looked at John, who was studying him with a frown, and decided that lobbing insults at Molly while under the stern gaze of her knife-wielding father would be less than smart. 'By which I mean of course that you're, er, cowmpletely wonderful!' He looked over at John who was shaking his head sadly from side to side as he placed the sandwich on a plate and pointed at it with his knife. Martin nodded and gave him a thumbs-up before returning to the phone conversation. 'Money!'

'What?'

'I've got an idea. Mehmet's got a key to my office. You could get my card and some cash.'

'But they're bound to be watching your office. And we don't want to lead them straight back to the pub.'

'Petey P-T – he can do it! They wouldn't suspect him of being up to anything. In fact solicitors are often responsible for property, aren't they?'

'It's worth a try I suppose; we're going to need our own oil well to get us up to your new pile. Here he is, I'll hand you over. It's Martin, P-, Mr Parver-Thrupp.'

Martin explained his predicament as briefly as he could and described Monan, Essex and Evans. Petey P-T took it all in his stride, somewhat enthusiastically in fact. Martin gave him precise details of the whereabouts of his card, the PIN, the amount he wanted to withdraw – he settled on £600, which was enough to see him and his fellow travellers through the next couple of days but not enough to risk the request being rejected – and the instructions to speak to no one other than Mehmet. Eventually Molly came back on the line.

'We'll wait here for Mr Parver-Thrupp to return with the money, then we'll get out over the back wall. We should be back shortly after ten, alright? Don't forget to phone Mr Donuts at ten.'

'Right.'

'And don't stand by any windows.'

'No, ma'am.'

'Ciao. Wait! Tara wants a word.'

He waited, his pulse quickening. All that came down the line was a long, slow kissing noise, then she hung up before he had a chance to respond.

'The game's afoot,' he said, before taking a big bite into his breakfast.

'Well, let's not close up any walls with English dead, eh? What are they up to?'

'Apparently the baddies are back in town; Petey P-T's enjoying a clandestine mission to liberate my savings; Molly and Tara have been shopping and intend to take the cat burglars' route back here. I think that about covers it.'

'And you reckon there's no point in just handing it all over to the police now?'

'Can't risk it. If there's really a chance of lucking into some free property – and Monan clearly thinks it's worth sticking his neck out for – I've got to go for it. There's no time to get into a Shimbley CID investigation, especially since I might be the one winding up on a charge. No, if I can stake my claim to whatever it is by the deadline, and beat Monan to it, then we've all the time in the world to chase the bastard back into the Irish Sea and put Essex and Evans in the dock. If I haven't achieved part one by the end of play tomorrow, then we're all stuffed, me and Monan that is. I just hope they don't do anything stupid with Beverley.'

'Beverley? What's she got to do with it?'

Martin realised that John had been spared details of the most recent abduction; of course, if there was talk of women being kidnapped by ruthless criminals, John would use every kitchen implement available to him to prevent Molly from becoming involved.

'Er, they threatened to drag her into this to make me cooperate, but I think I convinced them that Beverley and I hated each other with a passion. I shouldn't think they'll go near her. I hope not, as I say.'

'Hmm.' John sounded unconvinced. 'Okay,' he said at last. 'When you've finished that, go and get your things from your room. I'll find you a suitcase and fetch anything you need from your car – it would be a damn shame if they caught sight of you now. You and Tara will have to lie low until you're well clear of Shimbley. Do these guys know where your castle is?'

'I've no idea. Certainly Monan knew about Mary McConnelly before I did.'

'But do they know how you're to lay claim to it?'

'Your guess is as good as mine. It depends what details there are in Monan's manorial papers.'

'Well, I see no reason why manorial papers should contain the fine detail; that's the job of your instrument thing. My guess is that he doesn't know that he's within hours of seeing the title revert to the state.'

'I'd better call Dave; it's just gone ten.'

'Go ahead.' John nodded towards the phone.

Martin once more encountered Dave's answering machine, this time making a note of the mobile number, which he dialled next.

'Dawson.' Dave was shouting above a noise reminiscent of rolling thunder and howling wind.

'It's Martin,' Martin shouted back. 'How're you doing?'

'Hey, Marty. On muh way, man. Take us twenny minutes more. Y'all started yet?'

'Shortly. I'll call you at eleven, right?'

'You do that.'

'What a terrible signal.' Martin replaced the receiver. 'Still, I suppose I'm lucky to get through at all to a mobile up there. It sounded like awful weather.'

'Strange. I could have sworn the weather woman said Scotland was going to be basking in sunshine today. I was going to remind Molly to take something for the midges. Right, what do you want from your car? And you'd better leave the keys with me. I never thought I would hear myself saying this, but I really wish that at least one of you had had the foresight to equip yourself with a mobile 'phone.'

~

Shortly after ten thirty, the George and Dragon's kitchen hosted a small assembly. Molly and Tara had returned from Petey P-T's office via a circuitous route, giggling like excited schoolgirls and armed with Martin's cash and some bags of shopping. Kevin, Susan and Art were all present, determined to make the most of this unusual start to the week. Susan was strongly of the opinion that, if there was any truth in Martin and Tara's tale, the whole matter should be handed over to the police forthwith. Kevin, on the other hand, between elbowing Martin and muttering 'lucky dog' and similar expressions, was full of the spirit of derring-do, encouraging Martin and the women in their heroic quest, much to the obvious irritation of his wife. John occupied a position somewhere between his elder daughter and his son-in-law, concerned for Molly but also intrigued by Mary McConnelly's legacy. Art was simply overjoyed to be in the presence of so many noisy people and gushed his own incoherent contributions to the debate, along with plenty of saliva.

'Shop!' A gruff Irish voice called out from the lobby. Martin froze and Tara grasped his arm with both of her hands. Molly gesticulated to them to hide under the big table in the centre of the room, a large lump of furniture that would only have provided cover if it were wearing a Victorian-style, floor-length tablecloth. Kevin stood with his mouth hanging open, while John reached instinctively for a meat cleaver. Art gurgled, a big grin playing across his rosy face. Susan looked around at the assembled group, sighed deeply and strode out.

'Can I help you?' Her voice, decidedly chilly, carried back into the kitchen. John placed a finger on his lips and indicated that it was time for Martin and Tara to make for Molly's Range Rover, now packed with various suitcases and bags and parked immediately outside the back door. Molly went out first, checked that no one was snooping around in the yard, opened a rear passenger door and signalled the all clear. Martin and Tara dived onto the back seat, pulling a tartan rug over themselves. The doors slammed shut and Molly started the engine. John kissed Molly and told her to be careful.

'You let any harm come to her, Martin my boy,' he addressed the rug, 'and I'll come after you with a cleaver, understood?'

'Understood,' Martin replied.

'Good. Well, good luck all of you. And don't forget to call.' With that, the car rumbled over the cobbles under the arch and accelerated down the High Street. Martin clutched Tara and kissed the top of her head. Tara kissed his chest and let out a laugh.

'Hey!' Molly feigned disapproval. 'You two behave back there. I don't want my upholstery soiled.'

'That's disgusting!' Tara sounded shocked at the suggestion.

'That's exactly what I feared,' Molly countered. 'Tell him to put it away.'

'Talking of disgusting,' Martin joined in, 'where exactly has this rug been?'

'Ah, sorry about that; I meant to warn you about it. It's best that you don't ask.'

Cautiously, Martin and Tara both sniffed their cover with new interest.

'Wet dog?' Tara muttered the question quietly to Martin.

'No. It's worse than wet dog; could be Art fart.'

'Martin!' Tara stabbed at his ribs with a couple of fingers, causing him to yelp.

'Play nice you two. Carry on like that and everyone in Shimbley will know I'm not alone in here. Oh, wow!'

'What?'

'Taffy the ponytail appears to be staking out your office. Oops. Hey, I think he smiled at me. I could've pulled.' They motored on for a few minutes before Molly spoke again.

'I spy with my little eye something beginning with, er, E F G.'

'What the hell are we supposed to spy under this?' asked Tara.

'It's best to play along with her,' Martin advised. 'Extremely frightening Glamorgan-man.'

'Not even warm.' Molly had the confident air of someone who knew that she wasn't going to lose.

'Exceptionally floppy geranium,' guessed Martin.

'Oh, I get it!' said Tara. 'Elephants frolicking gaily.'

'Homosexual elephants, eh?' observed Martin.

'Why not?'

'No wonder they're becoming extinct, then. I mean, if they're all gay, what chance elephant puppies? Or cubs?'

'Dumbos.'

'You calling elephants stupid as well as gay?'

'No! The babies; they should be called dumbos, after the film.'

'Oh. I think I missed that.'

'Nobody missed Dumbo!'

'Excuse me,' Molly interrupted the debate, 'it's nothing to do with elephants, homo or hetero, okay?'

The suggestions now came thick and fast: eggs fried greasy, edible Flemish gymnast, every feller's Goldilocks, even frogmen gobble, existentialists favour gin, exterminate frigid greengrocers.

'Exterminate frigid greengrocers?' cried Molly in despair. 'What do you mean, "exterminate frigid greengrocers", for God's sake? How the hell am I spying exterminate frigid greengrocers? I mean, sure, I could spy the extermination of frigid frigging greengrocers, but...'

'No!' It was Martin's turn to interrupt. 'That would be something beginning with T E O F F G.'

'What?'

'Yeah, Martin's right.'

'Stay out of this, Tara, you obviously don't know how to play.'

'I think I've got the hang of it actually. And I don't think it's very honourable to start cheating in round one.'

'Cheating! Who's bloody cheating? Here I am, spying something perfectly normal and, and spyable, and you lot go off on some bloody surreal journey of your own. Are you sure it was that Evans chap who got the wok over the head and not you two?'

'No one likes a bad loser,' said Martin, giving Tara a playful hug.

'Loser!' Molly was ranting quite loudly now. 'What do you mean, loser? I'm still in the chair, with a perfectly reasonable, not made up, on this planet spy thing, and all I get is a bunch of utter, utter, utter crap. Do you give up?'

They didn't answer.

'*Do you give up?*' screamed Molly.

'Yes!'

'Empty fuel gauge.' She delivered the solution quite matter-of-factly.

'Oh boring,' said Tara.

'Oh shit,' said Martin, 'time to get into my savings. We can put in our next call to Dave at the same time.'

'I still say she's a cheat,' continued Tara.

'Why?' asked Molly and Martin at the same time.

'You can't have an empty fuel gauge, can you? You can have an empty fuel tank, but the inside of the gauge has all sorts of stuff in it, yeah? Needle thing, that writing and other stuff. Maybe a warning light.'

'What do you do for Irish jokes over there then?' Molly asked.

'We go to Kerry.'

'Oh, right.'

'Or England.'

'Oops. Here we are.' As Molly spoke, the car turned sharp left. 'Stay hidden; we're still too close to home. Show us your wad, Martin!'

'Ooh, don't, missus.'

'You want anything else? Newspaper? Chocolate? Sweeties?'

'Neither thanks, sweetie.' Tara answered for both of them.

Molly laughed and slammed her door shut behind her. Within a few seconds they could hear the petrol glugging into the tank beneath them.

'Molly's a good sport, isn't she?' Tara ventured.

'No kidding,' he agreed.

'The two of you never...'

'No.'

'Just good friends, eh?'

'Yes, good friends. But not as good friends as I want you and me to be.'

'Don't wriggle! Someone might notice an animated rug. How long do you think it will take us to get to Scotland?'

'Certainly until mid-afternoon; it depends where we aim for.'

'Do you think Monan will be after us?'

'I think we've got to assume that they're after the same thing, so yes. But he might not realise that we've discovered the secret of Lockkeeper's Cottage, so he shouldn't be aware that we're heading north.'

'Do you think there's anything in this? I mean, a castle?'

'And a mineral water spring. No; I think it's a load of bollocks. But it's like the pools, isn't it, or the lottery: you've got to check, just in.'

'Justin?'

'Just in case.' He cuddled her and they lay quietly under the aromatic rug, Martin's mind floating all over the place, from Shimbley to Liverpool to Ireland to Wales, back to Shimbley and now to Scotland. The more that he recollected the activities of the last few days, the more absurd they seemed to him and the more convinced he became that he would soon wake from it. The door opened and shut again. Molly broke the silence.

'Mr Donuts is a bit of a southern man, isn't he? Does he wear a stetson and ride a wild mustang? Does he wear chaps and twirl a lasso?'

'He's a landscape gardener, not a cowpoke. So, what did he have to say?'

'He says that he's at Inverness Town Hall. Now it just remains to be seen whether he can find anything to confirm the details of your instrument and whether it can be transformed into some wonderful title deeds. He sounds a bit of a hunk, I must say. I can't remember if you said he was attached.'

'Nor can I.'

'Hmm. I reckon we can get to the Lakes before we need to stop again. We'll be off these roads and on the motorway in fifteen minutes, wouldn't you reckon?'

'Yes, no problem.'

'It'll probably be safe for you to come up for air then, eh? If you want to, that is.'

'We want to,' Tara said with feeling.

'Oh,' said Martin.

~

When Martin and Tara did emerge, Molly's Range Rover was thrusting its way north, towards Birmingham, at a steady eighty miles per hour. Occasionally she was forced to slow behind a carelessly driven company car, before a flash of lights and some less than ladylike gesticulations moved it out of the way.

'Why are you blokes so useless?' she asked semi-rhetorically.

'Don't like women. Threatened. Little woman in big car: bad. Woman at stove: good. Woman no drive. Woman good for two things: cook and get beers in. No other point. Woman and M5: bad. Woman and Range Rover and M5: baddest. Ow! Sorry.' Tara had elbowed him again.

'Woman go in front, man stay in back. Less conspicuous to have eejit in boot. So, behave yourself, Martin Minchin!'

Tara clambered between the seats into the front, while Martin pulled his seat belt around him and stretched his legs out along the rear bench. Tara turned and blew him a kiss before fastening her own seat belt and admiring her surroundings.

'You don't use a horsebox then, Molly?'

'What?'

'You just have him ride in here with you?'

'Ha bloody ha. Look, I know it's a bit shitty in here, but I'm a working girl; there's no time to clean out the detritus of a modern, active life.'

'Hose,' said Martin.

'What?' Molly looked at him in the rear view mirror.

'Hose it out. These things were designed to be practical workhorses; you could just remove the mats and hose out all the manure and stuff. The seats were upholstered in plastic and there was no wood or leather or shag-pile carpet, until the hoorays discovered the need for four-by-fours in Chelsea.'

'You're not coming anywhere near this with a hose; try it and you're dead meat, matey. Even if it isn't exactly showroom fresh.'

'Well, I think it's great,' said Tara. 'I'll not fancy taking my old truck more than a few miles after this luxury. Birmingham,' she pointed to an overhead sign, 'is that good?'

'Birmingham good?' Molly considered the question for a few seconds. 'Martin, name something good that's come out of Birmingham.'

'Kevin?'

'Okay, besides Kevin. Anything else?'

'I meant,' Tara interrupted, 'are we making good time? I don't know where Birmingham is.'

'It's over there.' Molly pointed ahead, slightly to the right.

'You're a laugh, aren't you? It's a wonder I've not seen you on TV.'

'You have TV in Ireland?' Molly sounded incredulous.

'Do you know,' Martin stepped in with a change of subject, 'that Birmingham boasts more canals than Venice?'

'That cannot be true!' Tara protested.

'Just saying. Anyway, what do you reckon, girls, another three hundred miles or so to Edinburgh?'

'If you say so,' Molly answered. 'Maybe another four, four and a half hours, then. What do you want to do for food?'

'We don't really want to stop, do we?' said Martin. 'Get some sandwiches at the next fuel stop?'

'Well, it's going to be quite a while.'

'Suits me,' said Tara. 'I'm looking forward to seeing Scotland.'

'Okay,' said Molly, 'let's just get this bastard out of the way.' She leant on the horn, rather aggressively to Martin's mind. 'There we go! He's another... oh, it's a woman. On the 'phone! You're letting the side down, you silly tart!'

'Martin?' Tara turned back to face him.

'Yes?'

'Please don't you ever let me get on the wrong side of this woman.'

'Tough one.' He stroked his chin, considering the request. 'She sure is.'

~

The Range Rover made good progress up to and beyond the English heartland. Martin pointed out places of interest to Tara as though she had paid for a guided tour: over there, to the west, Worcester, home of Lea & Perrins Worcestershire Sauce; to the right, Bournville, now home to the Cadbury chocolate visitor attraction; beyond that, Longbridge, where Austin cars were built – strikes allowing – before the brand was put out of its misery and replaced by Rover.

The motorway provided little in the way of great views as they sped past successive conurbations, but the frequency of the numbered junctions gave the impression that they were taking huge strides. During a period of silence Martin reviewed to himself his recent commentary and began to worry that he had unintentionally pontificated about uniquely English enterprises; surely he had already given Tara sufficient reasons to suspect him of xenophobia without this travelogue.

'Ooh, there goes Crewe,' Martin observed, as they approached another overhead sign. 'That's where Rolls Royce, the world's greatest motor car, is built.' Oh, Fuck Git Huge Idiot Jerk Knob Loser Moron! 'Er, no better of course than Mercedes-Benz or, or, er, Cadillac, or whatever.'

'Or Land Rover,' suggested Molly.

As green hills appeared on the horizon, the cars and vans and bikes thinned out, retreating at the same pace as the urban scenery. The users of the three winding lanes of tarmac, gently rising and descending as the natural landscape once more took charge, acquired a predictability: one articulated truck after another used the first two lanes to perform their slow, carefully considered ballet of passing manoeuvres, complete with shows of flashing headlights and orange indicators; the occasional large saloon, usually German, swept its highly paid driver towards his next deal, or his next bawling out; the rented vans defeated headwinds as they battled up the right-hand lane, diesel engines rattling hopelessly against rev limiters, the drivers happy in the knowledge that they would never have to pay for anything other than the slippery stuff that was being consumed by the gallon and belched out in their wake in opaque, carcinogenic, oily, brown clouds.

Martin was feeling surprisingly at peace; his fear of Essex, Monan and Evans was diminishing and, for a southerner, he found it strangely comforting to shake off the English midlands. His paternal grandfather was half-Scottish, so he assumed that his sense of returning home was an ancestral throwback.

'I spy with my little eye something beginning with T A C W M C I W F M.' He waited, but Tara and Molly seemed uninterested in his challenge.

'I said I spy with my li...'

'I give up,' said Molly. 'Do you give up?'

'I give up,' agreed Tara.

'You're not even going to have a guess?'

'No.'

'No?'

'No!'

'I'll have to tell you.' He waited for a reaction. 'And then it'll be my go again.' Silence. 'Last chance.' A longer silence ensued.

'Martin,' Tara turned again to look at him, 'Are you going to tell us, or are you sulking?'

'No I'm not; sulking that is.'

'So tell, talk to us!'

'I can't.'

'What do you mean, you can't?'

'I can't remember what I spied.'

'What?'

'I can't remember what I spied.'

'Oh boy.'

'I remember,' Molly chipped in, 'it was T A C something C W M.'

'Okay, I think I've got it: I spy the auld country where...'

'Old? You said "T *A* C"!' Molly's recollection for detail was working well.

'Auld. Starts with A.'

'What?' It was Tara's turn to be argumentative.

'Auld; the auld country. It's Scottish, isn't it? It's spelt with an A – A U L D, as in Auld Lang Syne. Anyway: the auld country where Mary's castle is waiting for Martin. See?'

'You spy the auld country?' Molly protested. 'We've not even reached Liverpool yet; hardly half way to Scotland, my bonny wee lad.'

'Can't you sniff the heather, the peat smoke? Hark – the mating call of the wild haggis!'

'Aargh! Tara, give me music.' Molly switched on the radio and instructed Tara to keep searching the airwaves until she had found something more entertaining than Martin's schmaltz.

Martin sat back contentedly, vaguely watching the passing traffic, the hills, clouds scudding across a light blue sky. He looked forward to reaching the higher ground of the north of England: the romance of moors, of mountains, of rocky outcrops, howling winds, deeply drifting snow, dry stone walls, sheepdogs, doughty veterinaries tending their clients' livestock in yards barely changed since the last century. Most of his visions had been influenced, if not created, by television, as well as by road trips enjoyed during the years when youthful exuberance regularly waved two fingers at common sense and self-preservation, and somehow got away with it. He gazed idly at another young businessman thrashing his Ford past them up the outside lane.

'Mondeo,' said Tara, 'what sort of name is that?'

'Made-up name, like Vectra,' Molly replied. 'I couldn't have a car with a made-up name. Cars should have proper names. Like Rover.'

'Yes, brilliant, naming your car after your dog,' Martin suggested. 'Ford Fido. Peugeot Patch. Toyota Tyson.'

'I'm not sure I'd want a Toyota Tyson breathing down my neck.' Molly peered nervously in the mirror.

'They used to like using place names. Austin and Morris used to make Cambridges, Oxfords, Herefords and Somersets. Then Ford decided to go exotic and did the Capri and Cortina. Rolls followed suit with Camargue and Corniche – although corniche is just a cliff-side road, but it's French so sounds like an exotic place – anyway, before long all the great names were taken so Ford claimed the whole planet with Mondeo.' Martin's brief history of car names was met with silence from the front seats, so he continued: 'Wind's popular.'

'What are you talking about?' Tara twisted around in her seat again.

'Wind. Maserati did wind: Ghibli, Mistral, Bora, Khamsin, they're all winds. And Volkswagen did the Scirocco.'

'Your car sounds like it's got wind,' said Molly.

'That's the taut rasp of a competition-bred, high performance motor,' protested Martin, 'in a car with a noble and sporting pedigree.'

'Sud; that's an odd name for a car, isn't it?' Molly was in the mood to wind him up. 'What's that all about? Soap suds? Or did someone take the P out of spud?'

'Calling 'Fredo a spud will make him very unhappy. It's not wise to cross him you know – he has friends in southern Italy, you know what I'm sayin'?'

'Oh God, I'm going to wake up next to Henry's head.'

'I hate that film,' said Tara. 'As if Hollywood knows what real menace is; they haven't been down Main Road in Ballymadrone after chucking out time on market day.'

Martin drifted into further reverie. Tara possessed such an arsenal of alluring qualities: wit, grace, self-confidence, naughtiness, femininity, kindness. He had always looked upon women like Beverley as ultimate women, empowered women, women who demonstrated their attained status simply by the way they dressed for breakfast. But all of Beverley's haute couture and high-proof, high-cost scent couldn't begin to compete with Tara. Beverley, he realised, had a veneer of human being, but where was the fun? Where was the personality? Where was the unique human spirit, the ability to look adversity in the eye and not be cowed. Tara, he knew, could emerge even from a pub brawl like an angel. She was flawless. She had entered into Martin's messy escapade with a cheerful fascination that their latest encounter with Essex and Evans had failed to dent. He could see her now, cooking supper in her caravan, giggling over a beer on the ferry, guiding her pick-up through the British countryside to Shimbley, waiting patiently in the police station, maintaining a stiff upper lip down on the shifting bottom of the well from hell, gliding towards the bed in room four at the G and D. Always completely naked, just as she had been last night. What on earth did she see in him?

~

'Martin!'

Somebody was pulling at his hand. It was Tara.

'Where are we?' He sat up and rolled his head around, the days of varied and unconventional travel now taking their toll as his neck cracked and wheezed. He held onto Tara's fingers and wished that he had a strong peppermint to suck on before allowing anything else to escape the fetid confines of his mouth.

'Fuel and phone stop,' said Molly. They were pulling up in the fuel section of a motorway service area.

'Crikey. I must have been asleep for a bit.'

'For a bit of snoring, yes. You didn't tell me that you snored.' Tara adopted a tut-tutting tone.

'You can talk,' Martin replied, immediately wishing that he hadn't.

'What?' Tara shrieked.

'Now now, children.' The instinctive teacher in Molly stepped verbally between them. 'Who's filling and who's phoning?'

'I'll fill.' Tara opened her door and jumped down.

'And I'll phone and pay.' Martin climbed down from the back seat and took back the roll of cash from Molly. There were some telephones alongside the pay booth. Martin pulled a new phonecard from its cellophane wrapper and pushed it into the slot. He punched out the numbers for Dave's mobile and listened.

'Dawson.'

'Dave! It's Martin.'

'Hey, Marty! Where ya'at?'

'Services on the M6. Somewhere near the Lakes. Where are you?'

'Jus' sittin' in muh car at Inverness Castle, in the Sheriff's Clerk's space.'

'What the hell are you doing at Inverness Castle?'

'Lookin' for the Sheriff's Court. It's jus' like bein' back home.'

'Oh, right.'

'Nah, not really.'

'So what do we want with the Sheriff's Court?'

'Well, ya wanna claim ya castle, dontcha?'

'You've found something?' Martin could scarcely believe his ears. His heart was pounding almost as much as it had when he had been making his escape from Monan's house.

'I ain' the dude who found it, man. If ya got what ya said ya got, ya gotta ticket into the Scottish landed gentry. Ah'll be bowin' an' walkin' backward away from ya, man.'

'Okay, okay. Why are you there? What about the Lord Clerk Register?'

'Ain' no such dude these days. The Town Hall guys sent me here, an' the guys here, the Sheriff's deputies, say ya gotta go see the Registrar of Land in Scotland an' show him ya credentials.

'Where do we find him?'

'Edinburgh.'

'Oh.'

'So, ah guess we gotta meet down there, ol' buddy. They copied me some stuff that goes with what ya got. We'll show it all to the Edinburgh dudes an' see what they gotta say.'

'Did the Sheriff's deputies say anything else? Good grief, you've got me at it now.'

'Yup. They said if what ya got's the real McCoy, it's another lump o' Scotland landing in the hands of a Sassenach at the behest of the bastards in London. Or words pretty much like that.'

'Blimey.'

'Blimey indeed, Marty boy. Hope ya read the thing right, or it's a whole lotta gas ya wastin'.'

'Truer than you think. Where do we meet and when, then?'

'Ya'll got a little less than four hours to get to Edinburgh, man, a place in Dundee Walk.'

'Okay, see you around five, five-thirty, all being well. Where? And will you be wearing a carnation and carrying a copy of the Financial Times?'

'Yeah, man, ah'm the one in the rattler skin boots. Look, ya might get to this Land House before they go home. Ah reckon ah can get there about that time. Either way, we'll do some sweet talkin', get 'em to wait for Sir Marty's papers, eh? Look for Dundee

Walk, off Princes Street. Head straight for the middla town an' ya'll find Princes Street, okay? See ya later, man.'

'Okay. Look, thanks Dave. God, you've already put yourself out for me on this one. I must be keeping you from your paying customers.'

'Ya mean ya ain' payin'? Sheeit – guess ah'm workin' for royalty now, jus' doin' it for the honour. Gee, jus' wait 'til I tell the folks back home.'

'You're a star, Dave.'

'Ain' that the truth. See y'all in Edinburgh then. Y'all take care now!'

Martin replaced the receiver and looked over to Tara.

'Nearly there,' she shouted. 'How's Dave doing?'

'I think he's losing touch with reality.'

'Done!' She tapped the hose nozzle against the filler and replaced it on the pump. 'Holy mother!' she added, looking at the price read-out. 'I hope this isn't a wild goose chase.'

Martin walked into the little shop and selected a variety of rolls, sandwiches, cartons and bottles of fruit drinks and mineral water and little boxes of peppermints, putting them on the counter to add a tiny increment to an alarming fuel bill. Having paid, he felt guilty for depriving his fellow travellers of a proper meal in this quest for his lucky jackpot. They were both outside the car, Molly stretching and laughing.

'I've got some stuff to eat and drink here. Maybe we should have a break before carrying on.'

'Bollocks to that, I want to get into the glens where the boys have no knickers under their skirts.' Molly was sounding quite skittish. 'What's the next stop?'

'Edinburgh – we're going straight into Edinburgh and hopefully meeting Dave at a place called Land House off Princes Street. He reckons we might all be able to get there before they shut up shop.'

'Let's go then,' said Molly cheerfully, 'What's the deadline?'

'Five-ish.'

'You want to get to Edinburgh by five-ish? You do it.'

'You want me to drive?' Martin stared at Molly. He had never driven a Range Rover and, although he realised that this one wasn't exactly a pristine example, he knew that it was the closest non-human thing to Molly's heart, after Henry.

'Can't handle it?' Tara taunted. 'C'mon, give the poor girl a rest.'

'Okay. Keys?'

~

The lofty vantage-point helped Martin to familiarise himself with the large car. He would have preferred a hip-hugging seat in something low-slung and Italian but, considering the potential of the journey, to have trusted something like Alfredo would have been imprudent. At a comfortable cruising speed, between eighty and ninety miles per hour, he relished the difference in road manners between the traffic here and that back in the south, where to give way to any other road users is apparently regarded as a sign of inadequacy. Here there were fewer cars and more trucks; fewer drivers therefore displaying impatience, aggression and selfishness. Of course some of it may have had something to do with the fact that he was now behind the wheel of a powerful heavyweight, a vehicle that was probably capable of punting a stray parcel van right off the road. Certainly he couldn't remember fellow road users being quite so chummy whenever he pointed Alfredo's nose at a gap. He realised why drivers of large four-wheel-drive cars invariably looked so smug and was thankful that the front of Molly's didn't wear a bull-bar, the automotive bovver boot so beloved of suburban 'off-road' drivers.

To his left the Cumbrian mountains rose alluringly, promising a scenic reward for a detour. His ears popped as the road continued to climb towards its zenith at Shap. Here he marvelled at the feeling of great altitude, the sense of big sky, the romanticism of long-haul road journeys. The word Palermo written in large letters on the back of a grubby trailer made his own journey look a little tame, the cab of the Sicilian truck festooned with souvenir stickers. What must it be like, he thought, to have to cover such heroic distances, with only your own thoughts and some music to keep you company? What must these visitors think of us? With our potholed roads and crappy roadside catering? And rude road manners? He made an extra effort to demonstrate to these transcontinental heroes that not all Brits were ignorant. He backed off and flashed his headlights to allow lumbering lorries to pull out and complete four-mile overtaking manoeuvres; he flashed his headlights to let them know when it was safe to pull back in front of him, once safely past. He all but drove onto the hard shoulder in his willingness to help these leviathans on their way.

'Martin, we're going backwards here!' Tara's comment from the front passenger seat startled him. He had assumed that both of his passengers had been asleep.

'What? Are you okay Tara?'

'I'm fine but you're not – just look at the speed we're going.' He looked; it was a shade under fifty. 'You're so busy being polite to these truckers that we're not going to make it to Edinburgh until a week next Thursday.'

'Sorry.' He felt a bit ashamed.

'No, please don't be sorry. You're tired – hell, we all are. I wasn't really criticising. I was worried that you might have been asleep.'

'I think I must have been. But I tell you what, I'm wide awake now.' And he genuinely felt it, suddenly imbued with a second wind, clear headed and raring to go. 'Right. Now we're motoring.' He floored the accelerator, indicated right and pulled into the centre lane.

'I didn't mean for you to go crazy, you know.' She was apprehensive.

'Not crazy. No, you woke me up. Thanks. What does this thing do flat out, Molly?'

'She's asleep and I think this is fast enough. We're going from one extreme to another.'

'Oh. I didn't really mean speed; I meant miles to the gallon. I could swear I just saw the famously visible contents of the petrol gauge drop.' He indicated right again and pulled into the outside lane. The speedometer needle jerked backwards and forwards around the ninety-five mark. They bore down on a much slower moving estate car; he flashed the headlights but there was no reaction.

'Poor chap,' he said, 'probably as knackered as we are.'

'Poor nothing. Get the eejit out of the way!'

He applied a longer dose of full-beam, which prompted its driver to move slowly to the left, thrusting a middle finger out of his window as he did so. 'Must be a southerner,' Martin commented.

CHAPTER 10: Monday afternoon

As they swept swiftly up the motorway towards Carlisle, Martin considered taking the opportunity, while Molly was asleep, to discuss with Tara where their relationship might be going. It struck him as bizarre that, although they hadn't consummated it, they had enjoyed some serious kissing within twenty-four hours of meeting, not to mention sleeping naked together. For him, this easily represented a record. She hadn't struck him as a promiscuous type, but he was unconvinced that she could find him attractive. Nice enough, maybe, but attractive? But, if you didn't fancy someone, surely you wouldn't stick your tongue in their mouth and exchange saliva. What if he questioned her about her feelings and she said she didn't want to get serious? That would burst his bubble. He decided to keep quiet and wait to see how things developed.

'Hey! Let's get married!' Tara's suggestion startled him and he lifted off the accelerator and looked open mouthed at her.

'What?'

'Look – Gretna Green two miles. Isn't that where everyone elopes to?'

'Yes.' Realising that it was a joke sparked by her observation, he felt deflated again. 'I very much regret that I'm still married to Beverley. Otherwise I would marry you like a shot.'

'Would you really?' She didn't sound as though she was teasing.

'I think so.'

'Yeah. That could be good.' She turned away from him to look out of her window. 'So, this is Scotland.'

'Yup. And look at those mountains rising in the distance. I love the feeling I get coming up here; it makes me go sort of shivery.'

'Would that be the cold?'

'Probably!' He laughed. Again, the moment for conversation about them had passed and left him not much clearer about where he stood with her. But he had no reason to doubt her sincerity and he felt uplifted and happy. 'I think you'll like Scotland.'

'I think you're right.'

Tara rummaged in the glove box and extracted some cassette tapes. She chose a blues compilation, the gentle guitars and harmonicas providing a mellow atmosphere and adding to the poignancy as they passed Lockerbie where so many people had perished just a few years earlier. Motorway gave way to dual carriageway that in turn gave way to two-way road as they speared northeast for the final leg to Edinburgh. Molly awoke and found a plan of the centre of Edinburgh in an atlas. It didn't show much detail but at least gave them something to aim for. A sign indicated eighteen miles; Martin performed some rough calculations in his head.

'You know, I reckon it's going to be damn near on five when we hit the Edinburgh rush hour. I wonder if Dave's beaten us to it.'

'It looks like a hell of a way from Inverness,' said Molly, still poring over her atlas in the back seat.

'Yes, but you haven't seen the way Dave drives.'

'Well, if I was this Lord Clerk Register, or whatever it is now, I'd want to hang around and see what it's all about.'

'That's because you're a historian. These people might just be pen-pushers, anxious to get home to a bit of poached salmon.'

'Martin! Just because they're not English, it doesn't mean they're thieves. I'll bet they go to the supermarket just the same as you and me.'

'Well actually, Tara, I was referring to the method of cooking: simmered gently in some water, white wine, lemon juice, a sprig of thyme.'

'He's sweet when he rises to the bait, isn't he?' Tara laughed.

'Oh, we shouldn't tease him,' Molly replied, 'It's way too easy. God, I hope they'll see us. I'm on edge. How's the petrol?'

'Getting low so we'll need to fill up before we leave Edinburgh.'

The traffic soon thickened as they crossed the ring road and headed through the suburbs, following signs to City Centre. The castle jutted into the sky in front of them, dark grey and brooding. On the pavements, as on the roads, people went urgently about their business. There was a vibrancy about the place and a flavour, Martin thought, of continental Europe.

'What the hell did you do that for?' Molly alternately barked directions and recriminations.

'It was sign-posted Princes Street.'

'It was sign-posted pedestrian access to Princes Street. Why don't you try listening to me? Now where the bloody hell are we? Ah! Go right.'

'Can't.' Martin turned left.

'God almighty Martin, do you want this sodding castle or not? Okay, take the next right you can and then another.'

'What, any right?'

'Just bloody do it!'

Martin turned right, across the bows of a taxi coming the other way with its horn blaring. He pulled up between a couple of parked cars, a low wall preventing him from driving any further. Molly looked up again from her map.

'Why have we stopped?'

'Wall.'

'Where is this?'

'Don't know.'

'I think,' said Tara, 'that this is a private car park. Oh yes! There's the sign. It only belongs to a law firm. So that's alright.'

'Who's this?' Martin lowered his window to listen to an elderly man wearing a porter's cap who had marched purposely towards them from a ground-floor office.

'Can I help you, sir?'

'No. Well, maybe', Martin replied. 'We're lost, as you may have guessed. We're looking for Land House which I understand is in...'

'Dundee Walk.'

'Yes!'

'Off Princes Street.'

'I wonder, could you kindly tell me which is the quickest way to get there?'

'In this?' The old man nodded at the car.

'Yes.'

'Now?'

'Yes.'

'Best not go now; the streets are all full of traffic for the next hour and you'll not find parking.'

'I don't mind getting a ticket. Which way?'

'Well, you see those offices through there?' The man pointed beyond his employer's elegant building, through a gap in a wall, to a taller, rather austere terrace.

'Yes.'

'Land House, it's one of those.'

'Brilliant! How do we get there?'

The man scratched his chin, took a couple of paces back from the car and gazed at it, shaking his head slowly.

'In this?'

'In this.'

'You'll never get this in their car park. They're most particular at Land House. You're best on foot.'

'Yes, thank you, but we still need somewhere to put the car. How much is it to park here for thirty minutes?'

'Ten pounds.'

'Here's a fiver. You needn't tell the partners and I won't bust you to the Revenue.'

'You're too kind, sir.'

'Not at all. Come on, gang, let's see if this Registrar's still on duty.'

The three of them climbed out of the car, Martin checking the presence of Mary McConnelly's instrument in his inside pocket at least every ten seconds. The clock in the car had read five-twenty. They ran from the little car park and crossed a side street before turning into the narrow, canyon-like Dundee Walk. A large brass plaque identified Land House and they ran up the steps to confront a huge, imposing front door, immaculately finished in dark blue gloss paint and very shut.

'Damn.' Martin looked around for a bell, a knocker, anything that would give them a chance of gaining entry. There wasn't even a letterbox to peep through.

'There's got to be a tradesmen's entrance,' said Molly. 'I can't believe they've all gone home.'

'Can I help you?' The woman's voice seemed to come from nowhere; Martin, Tara and Molly all swung in different directions to try to identify the source. 'Here. Down here.' Martin leant over the stone balustrade and saw a middle-aged woman standing at a basement door. 'Can I help you?' she asked again.

'We've come to see the Registrar of Land,' Martin explained. 'We are expected.'

'You're rather late. Is it important?' The woman looked up at Martin with a friendly smile, her hand shielding her eyes from the bright sky.

'I think it is, yes. You see we've got an important historical document here that the Registrar must have this afternoon. Race against time you see.'

'Would you be the party expected to join Professor Dawson?'

'Professor who? Oh, Professor Dawson, yes!'

'Well, you'd better come this way.' They went back down to the pavement and she ushered them down some further steps and in through a door beneath the grand main entrance. 'It must be something of great importance to keep them all behind like this, with an American professor too.' Her manner was inquisitive and Martin didn't like to disappoint her, since she had so far shown every willingness to help.

'It's a two hundred year old document which has come to light. Its importance is of academic rather than material interest,' he lied. 'Thus the professor's interest.'

'That's funny; and I heard it was to do with valuable property, mineral rights, a castle and all sorts. Still, I suppose you know your business.'

She led them through a bewildering maze of corridors, up two flights of stairs and onto a grand landing, sparsely furnished with benches upholstered in dark red leather.

'Would you wait here please and I'll see if I can find Dr Kennedy.' She disappeared through a swing door.

'Professor Dawson?' Molly was looking at Martin with her eyebrows raised.

'Yes, ha ha. He always did have a bit of neck. Looks as though he might have pulled it off for us though – keeping them here. Dr Kennedy must be the Registrar bloke.' Martin looked out through a massive sash window onto a pretty little courtyard garden; just a few yards from the city's main thoroughfare, yet a haven of peace. Everything was coming to a head now. He was about to find out whether Mary McConnelly had left him something of value or just a pain in the arse named Monan.

'Hey, Marty!'

Martin spun around to see his old friend Dave advancing towards him, arms outstretched. Dave had hardly changed; there was a little bit of spread around his middle, his hair, long and unkempt as ever, was receding at the temples and had a few wisps of grey, while his face looked as though he hadn't shaved for a couple of days. He was wearing faded and frayed blue jeans, a plain black sweatshirt and a black, sheepskin-lined motorcycle jacket. His right hand clasped Martin's and his other arm enveloped his friend in a warm, tight hug. 'Look at me, ma, ah'm huggin' a dook! How ya doin' man?'

'Very, well thanks. It's really great to see you.' Martin extricated himself and made introductions. Dave took his time to appraise his new acquaintances, holding their hands for longer than Martin thought was necessary and looking them up and down in a manner that could have been offensive were it not for his exuberantly charming personality, which was shining right now from his every orifice. Same old Dave, thought Martin.

'Marty, this is Doc Kennedy, Deputy Registrar of Land. That right, Doc?' Dave stood aside and Martin extended his hand towards the woman who had led Dave into the hall. Grey haired and aged around sixty, she was short and plump, with thick-lensed spectacles dominating her face. An all-brown, frumpy ensemble of cardigan, skirt, woolly tights and sensible shoes gave her the appearance of a spinster who had never needed fashion. She looked up at Martin and beamed.

'Well, Mr Minchin, I am extremely pleased to meet you, but I fear that you're going to have to sit down if we're to have a successful conversation.' She looked him up and down, as though double-checking his height. 'Come! Let's sit over here and see what you've got. I'm most excited!' Martin followed her to the benches closest to the windows with the garden view. He detected a twinkle behind her glasses, bright blue eyes taking everything in. He wondered if the dowdiness was partly affected, to hide a powerful intellect, to disguise an ability to ambush the unwary in the same way that clever, unassuming looking defence counsel tend to wrong-foot prosecution witnesses in courtroom dramas. He pulled Mary McConnelly's papers from his pocket and smoothed them out on his knee before handing them to the agitated Deputy Registrar. She studied them carefully, reading each one in full, occasionally muttering extracts aloud to herself. Eventually she rested them on her lap, removed her spectacles and stared at the ceiling high above them. Martin looked from her to Dave. Dave shrugged his shoulders and looked at Molly. Molly looked like a young child on Christmas morning, standing on tiptoes from the excitement, eyes wide open and one hand held to her mouth. Tara was clinging on to Molly's arm, looking ashen, as though she had just received some shocking news. The room was silent.

'Oh my word,' said Dr Kennedy at last. 'Oh Mr Minchin. Oh my.'

'Is it the real McCoy, Doc?' Dave decided to lead the cross-examination.

'One could say that it's the real McConnelly!' she replied, to a chorus of gasps. 'But...'

'What?' Martin regained the power of speech. 'But what?'

'I didn't want to say anything earlier, before I had seen the Instrument myself. There is another condition to be met: there's another deed which has to be produced for you to gain full title to the property and to the rights thereof.'

'What deed?' It was Martin's turn to be agitated. 'There's nothing about another deed there.'

'There's a reference here to the Great Well of Cuiphur and the right to extract minerals. Do you know anything about this place, Loch Cuiphur Castle and its Great Well?'

'No, nothing,' said Martin. 'What is it?'

'Oh, I don't know myself, Mr Minchin, but I believe your friend, the *Professor* here, has been doing his homework.' Her emphasis left no doubt that she was unimpressed by the spurious title that Dave had assumed in order to gain an audience. Martin looked at Dave who unfolded a large scale Ordnance Survey map and spread it out on the polished wooden floor.

'Gather round, folks. This here's what y'all be lookin' for.' He stabbed a finger at a marshy area apparently in the middle of nowhere to the south of Inverness. 'This is the last known location of the only Loch Cuiphur and the only Loch Cuiphur Castle recorded in Scottish history, accordin' to the guys at Inverness library. So ya Great Well of Cuiphur's gonna be here too if it's gonna be anyplace. But there ain' no evidence of it existin' for a hunnerd years or more. No mention since, man.'

'The problem is, Mr Minchin, that the state will regain the mineral rights by this time tomorrow unless you can produce the deed for the well itself.'

'So? What minerals? Why should I be bothered about mineral rights?'

'Because, if there are minerals of value beneath your castle, you can, as it were, say "goodbye" to your castle. The state's ownership of the minerals would render your castle and its land valueless, if they're not that already. Indeed, they might become a liability. The state's right to mineral extraction will outweigh everything else.'

'But what minerals? I mean, if it's a well, we're just talking water here, aren't we? Not oil! Not oil?'

'No, no, certainly not oil. This would be about water and the government would straight away put the rights to the water up for auction, sell them to the utility company with the fattest wallet, perhaps even a foreign one.'

'English, huh? Tch tch.' Dave's Scottish loyalties were clear.

'So, bringing these papers here has been somewhat pointless?'

'Oh not at all, Mr Minchin, not at all. With this Instrument, you assume title to Loch Cuiphur Castle and its lands, as described in the Land Register and identified by your friend here, with the help of Inverness library.'

'Yes!' Martin punched the air and looked from one person to the next with a triumphant grin on his face.

'Hey, man, listen up. What the doc here says about the title to the Great Well is kinda important. So, hear her out.'

'Thank you, Professor. Yes, Mr Minchin, there is nothing I would like more than to see an Instrument such as this actually deliver a property to someone other than the government of the day, particularly after such a period. Nearly two centuries!'

'So what's the problem?'

'The problem, Mr Minchin, is that you really must try to find the deed in respect of the Great Well of Cuiphur. Without that, I very much fear that your lucky find might be entirely worthless to you.'

'Where's this deed likely to be?'

'Perhaps where you found the Instrument?'

'Oh no, not back down there.' Martin's head sank to rest on his folded arms. Visions of his dilapidated property swam before his eyes and he imagined the ghastly well full to its brim with thick, slimy mud.

'It was down the well at Lockkeeper's – I mean Loch Cuiphur – Cottage,' Tara explained, 'about four hundred miles and most of a day's drive from here.'

'Oh dear,' said Dr Kennedy, frowning.

'Has anyone seen this Loch Cuiphur Castle?' Molly sounded as though she wished to inject a note of calm, rational thinking. 'I mean, I don't know anything about eighteenth century property law, but I do know enough about the past to recognise a very simple pattern. If the Instrument connecting the cottage to the castle was down the cottage's well – God, maybe that's why the well was dug there in the first place – then why can't the deed to the Great Well be down the Great Well itself, at the castle. If there is a castle, of course. And if there is a Great Well.'

'The young lady has a very good point, Mr Minchin.' Dr Kennedy brightened again. 'Are you quite certain that there was nothing else down the well at your cottage?'

'No, not at all sure, but they wouldn't have buried the things in separate caskets down the same well, would they?'

'I would say it's highly unlikely.'

'That's settled for me then. What's the verdict, people? We go and look for my castle first thing tomorrow?'

His suggestion was met with unanimous enthusiasm and a burst of unexpected clapping from Dr Kennedy.

'It's so nice that you're surrounded by friends and family who can help you to claim Mary McConnelly's legacy,' she said.

'No family, I'm afraid. Just this bunch of gold-diggers.'

'And your geologist cousin; he's going to prove invaluable tomorrow, isn't he?'

'What geologist cousin?' Martin was floored, embarrassed that he was unaware not only of assistance being offered by a relative but also of the very existence of that relative. A geologist? He flicked through a mental kaleidoscope of faces and names, failing to find a match for Dr Kennedy's description.

'Oh.' Dr Kennedy looked equally bewildered. 'What was his name? He was so pleasant and courteous, it obviously runs in the family. Sidney! That was it, your cousin Sidney, on your mother's side he said. Anyway, you'll have time to catch up this evening, I'm sure.'

Martin felt as though he had just received another blow to the balls or stomach or both simultaneously.

'Essex!' Tara voiced his thoughts.

'Yes!' exclaimed Dr Kennedy happily. 'Essex. Sidney Essex. Such a polite man.'

'Has he been here?'

'Oh no. He telephoned but he said that he was on his way to meet you.'

'Exactly what did you tell him?' Martin's panicky interrogation had Dr Kennedy leaning away from him, a worried expression replacing her ready smile.

'Why, er, just that you were due here to stake your claim to the castle and the well. He said he wants to help you. He *is* your cousin?'

'No.'

'Oh dear. But he is a friend?'

'No. He wants to kill me.'

'Oh no! This will never do. What a horrid turn. He wants to *kill* you, you say?'

'I suspect so, by now.'

'Are the authorities aware of this?'

'Yes, in a manner of speaking.' Martin watched concern and confusion fighting for position on Dr Kennedy's face. 'The police have been told, but they aren't terribly interested until they have tangible evidence that a crime has been committed.'

'A crime? Surely you don't mean your death?'

'Yes, that should do it.'

'Oh Mr Minchin, I'm so sorry. Are you quite sure that we're talking about the same Sidney Essex?'

'A lithp?'

'Oh goodness gracious. An assassin you say? It's, it's, it's...'

'It's easy for you to say, Doctor!' Tara butted in. 'He wants to kill me too. In fact he's already tried.'

'Oh no!' Dr Kennedy's discomfort was growing by the second.

'Let's see what the score is, eh?' Molly took charge. Dave raised appreciative eyebrows at her and patted his bench, inviting her to join him on it. 'Thanks, Dave,' she grinned at him and sat down. 'Now, what's Essex going to do? Dr Kennedy?'

'Yes?'

'Does Essex know of the existence of Loch Cuiphur, or Loch Cuiphur Castle or the Great Well of Cuiphur?'

'I think so, yes.'

'Shi-, damn.'

'I rather think, now that I recall, that I mentioned them. Sorry.'

'Alright. Does he know that the deed to the Great Well has yet to be found?'

'Oh dear. Yes.'

'Does he understand the potential value of this deed?'

'I'm so sorry. He said he was your cousin, Mr Minchin. He sounded so supportive.'

'Has he any idea where Loch Cuiphur is?'

'Ah, no. That he doesn't.' Dr Kennedy relaxed for a moment. 'Oh bother!'

'What?' Martin tried to sound as gentle as possible; he was beginning to feel rather sorry for the woman.

'I might have suggested that he try the library.'

'Might ya've suggested Inverness library Doc?' Dave voiced the question that concerned them all. There was no need for Dr Kennedy to answer; she stared miserably at the floor, her mouth downcast. 'Well, no point in gettin' heavy, but looks like we got ourselves a fight. Shame ah ain' got muh great grampappy's six-guns. Feel like quittin', Marty boy?'

'No he doesn't!' Tara displayed some fighting spirit. 'We can go up there tonight and start looking at daybreak. Essex won't get into the library until... until when, Dave?'

'Ten, ah guess.'

'See?' She continued. 'It's a cinch. We could be back here with the deed before he's even got the sleep out of his eyes.'

'Maybe she's right, Marty,' added Dave, brightening. 'They gotta find us first. An' until they've gotten this stuff,' he held up his map and the bits of paper he had gathered during the morning, 'they're right up sh-, the creek, ya know what I'm sayin'?'

'Shit creek, Professor. Quite so.' Dr Kennedy's readiness to complete the phrase was surprising, coming from one so demure. 'It seems that I've been indiscreet, for which I offer you all my sincerest apologies. I am also bound to warn you that whoever presents the correct deed here before the expiry of your Instrument, in other words by this time tomorrow, will win the rights to the mineral extraction. And, in the event of no one doing so, your government in London will reap the benefit.' She paused to make sure that everyone was listening. 'And that would never do.'

'Little bit of politics there,' Molly affected a stage whisper.

'Well, Mr Minchin, I do wish you the very best of luck. I sincerely hope that our Mr Essex, if he is indeed up to mischief, doesn't upset the apple cart. And I hope to see you here tomorrow, preferably before five. Allow me to show you all out.'

Back on the pavement in Dundee Walk, Dave addressed the gathering. 'Okay, listen up! Tonight we're gonna sleep at mine an' get a good, early start in the mornin'. It's two an' a half hours, M90, then A9 all the way. Ah know a good eaterie on the way, near Kingussie. Ah'm gonna fetch a coupla things in the store here, so why don' we all meet at the restaurant, yeah?'

'Sounds good to me,' said Martin. 'What's it called?'

'Ya got me there, man.' Dave scratched his head. 'It's a purdy lil place, kinda ol' farmhouse hotel, close by the highway, lotsa flowers in the garden, rhododendrons, that kinda thing. Ya know what rhodos look like?'

'Of course.'

'Sweet! Where ya parked?'

'In a lawyer's place over there.' Martin pointed. 'What about you?'

'In a vet's. Macduff's muh ticket.'

'Macduff?'

'The houn' dawg.'

'Ah. Right, then, shall we go? I'm getting rather peckish. See you later then.'

Dave gave them a wave and sauntered away down the pavement. The others went in the opposite direction, back to where they had left the car. There was no sign of the old man and, although there was a sturdy, lockable gate to the car park, it hadn't been closed. Martin volunteered to continue with his driving stint and Molly climbed into the back. Martin had a look at the atlas and tried to get his bearings. In practice, one way streets provided few options, but they eventually picked up signs showing the way out to the M90.

'I like Donut Dave', said Molly.

'Yes, he's good fun. Nice bloke too.'

'Professor Dawson,' Molly continued, 'He's a cheeky chap, isn't he? Married?'

'Gosh, not to my knowledge. I don't know if he has a partner. Obviously has a dog. There was no other name on the Christmas card as far as I remember.'

'Hmm.'

'I think she's smitten,' observed Tara.

'I imagine a girl could do a lot worse.' Molly wasn't denying it. 'And I just lurve that accent and proper old-fashioned, southern courtesy.'

'I wonder if I should warn him,' said Martin, only to be rewarded with a hard punch in the back of his seat.

'Dr Kennedy was a bit of a giggle, wasn't she?' Tara said. 'The poor woman looked mortified when we told her about Essex.'

'Yes, we could have done without her help in that department. Anyway,' Martin's dreams were fast disappearing, 'there's not much hope of finding this deed, is there? I mean, no one had actually ever heard of Loch Cuiphur, let alone a castle. Dave's map just showed a load of old bog, if he's got the correct place of course. How are you supposed to find a deed that's been sitting in a bog for two hundred years?'

'Don't be such a pessimist. At least we can enjoy an early morning walk in the wilds. I should have brought my sketchbook.'

They stopped for another tankful of petrol before joining the M90 and charging north towards Perth. There was little in the way of traffic and Martin rarely had to slow. Even after the motorway had ended and they were back on two-way road, he was able to maintain a high speed. The surface was perfect, unlike the potholed horrors in the south, and it was wide. They could see ahead for miles at a time as the road gently rose and fell, swept left and right in long, fast bends. It was the sort of road that Martin loved to drive on, with stunning scenery all around them. It was a little after seven-thirty when they approached Kingussie.

'There, on the left!' Tara exclaimed. They had come over a brow and she was pointing to an attractive roadside hotel. Sure enough, it had a beautifully tended and colourful garden, with some tables scattered on a close-cropped lawn. Indicating left, Martin braked hard and pulled into the gravelled car park.

'The Clansman Hotel,' Molly read the sign aloud. 'Haute Cuisine Française – 7pm to 10pm – No Coaches. Charming. Any sign of Dave?'

'I don't know what he's driving these days,' said Martin, looking around the car park, 'I didn't think to ask. If he's not inside, we can always have a drink out here and look out for him. This must be the place he meant.'

Ten minutes later, having confirmed that Dave wasn't inside the hotel and having reserved a table in the dining room, the three settled with their drinks on a bench on the lawn, looking out across the road to the peaks of the Cairngorms. Molly had insisted that she would take over the driving again, allowing Martin and Tara to indulge themselves with thirst quenching pints of ice-cold lager. The sun was beginning its descent behind them, casting a rich, golden glow over the view.

'What a gorgeous setting,' said Molly. 'I could get used to this.' She suddenly looked at the sky, from horizon to horizon. 'That can't be thunder...'

CHAPTER 11: Monday evening

'What in God's name is that?' Tara was also unsettled. Preceded by a deep roar, a large, very fast-moving car exploded into view over the brow of the road from Perth, shards of evening sunlight bouncing off brightly polished paint. It was deep metallic red with two broad white stripes running from beneath the gaping air intake at the front, up over the bonnet and back down its sloping roof. The ground vibrated as the car thundered past, the shock wave setting off the alarm of one of the cars in the hotel's car park. Sitting behind the wheel, on the left hand side, window open and his elbow resting casually on the top of the door, was Dave, his eyes hidden behind dark glasses. Just behind his left shoulder, its head poking out into the airstream with hair and ears flowing back in the wind, was a big grey dog. They had already travelled nearly one hundred yards beyond the hotel's entrance when the brake lights lit up, their redness outshining even that of the paintwork. The nose of the car plunged towards the ground and a plume of light blue smoke billowed up on each side as the front tyres shrieked in protest, depositing two wide black lines along the tarmac. Suddenly the rear wheels started spinning, launching more smoke into the air as the car pirouetted through a one hundred and eighty degree spin turn. It came back up the road more calmly, turned into the car park and idled towards a space on the far side, a deep, uneven rumble emanating from two drainpipe sized exhausts.

'That,' answered Martin, 'is a Ford Mustang. Do we pretend not to know him?'

'It might be wise,' said Molly. 'So that was a doughnut?'

'Half a doughnut.'

'I'd hate to come by him when I'm out with Henry on an early morning ride.'

'I would think he's more circumspect on lanes,' said Martin, not entirely sure that Dave deserved this character reference.

'Hey, Marty, this ain' the place!' Dave followed his bouncing dog onto the lawn. Macduff had the look of a wolfhound but wasn't quite large enough, and he obviously possessed one or two other bits of mixed ancestry. 'Easy, Mac! Ah meant a place closer to Kingussie, maybe the other side. Hell, it don' matter, this'll do just fine. If ya lordship's payin', I ain' fussin'. Looks kinda rich mind. Anyone drinkin'?'

'It's my round,' said Martin, standing.

'Ah'm comin' in too; need the john. Stay there, boy.' Dave followed Martin into the hotel and dived into the men's room.

Martin was still waiting to be served at the bar when Dave re-emerged.

'Yeah, this is cool,' he said, looking around appreciatively.

'We'll be lucky not to be shown off the premises; that was a little over the top.'

'Over the top? Whass over the top?'

'The entrance of the bloody Queen of Sheba. The hooligan of the A9. Hell, Dave, an old lady out there nearly gave birth.'

'Yeah, it was kinda gross, ah guess. Ah just saw y'all there in the garden an' kinda overreacted. Still, no harm done, huh?'

'You set off all the car alarms!'

'Hell, man, thass always happenin'. Any little vibe, they all start yammerin'.'

'Little vibe? That was an earthquake.'

'Yeah.' Dave laughed. 'Wakes 'em up, don' it?' He opted for a large glass of iced Coke. Martin paid the barman and made a move to rejoin the others in the garden.

'Whoa, not so fast, man,' said Dave. 'Who are these women? Jeez, it ain' so long since ah saw ya walkin' away from the altar with ol' Ginger. Whaddya got, huh? Surely not the ol' long-body-mean-mighty-pecker crap?'

'What makes you think it's crap?'

'Yeah, yeah. Come on, man, who are they? We're talkin' babes here.'

'Well, I met Tara in Ireland the day before yesterday.'

'What in hell were ya doin' in Ireland the day before yesterday? Man, ya got one weird situation here.'

'We'll tell you all about it over dinner; it's a pretty amazing story. Shall we join them?'

'Hold up. What about this Molly?'

'What about her?'

'She sure has a cute ass, ya know what ah'm sayin'? Where does she fit in? Ya not, er?'

'No, never. Do you remember the George and Dragon, the old coaching inn in the middle of Shimbley?'

'Yeah, guess so.'

'Molly's the landlord's youngest daughter.'

'Okay. So, the Irish babe, yeah?'

'Yes. No. I mean, it's a little confused. We need time. Isn't she wonderful?'

'Like ah said, man, she's kinda cute. But Molly, now... any partner on the scene? She, like, single?'

'No. She has a love. Called Henry.'

'Jeez, no kiddin'? Shit! So, where's Henry?' He gave the name a sarcastic, snooty, English emphasis.

'Knowing him, he's getting his oats from someone else while she's away.'

'*No way!* He's gotta be some kinda dumb asshole.'

'Neigh.'

'Pardon?'

'Nothing. Come on, they'll be wondering what we're up to.' They walked back out into the garden, Martin grabbing a couple of menus as they passed the dining room.

The sun was now an enormous orange ball, about to touch the horizon. The lightest of breezes carried a touch of chill, but not enough to make them want to go indoors before they were ready to dine. A jovial woman came out to take their order and fussed over a happy Macduff. She promised to produce some scraps from the kitchen for him.

'Would that be your car over there, sir?' she asked, looking directly at Dave. Martin concentrated hard on a woodlouse crossing the table as he waited for the inevitable ticking off – maybe expulsion from the premises.

'The Mustang? Yes, ma'am. Beauty, ain' she?'

'Sounded good. Sixty-seven?'

'Sixty-eight. Three-ninety cubes, three-twenty horses an' gas mileage to almost make me wanna be back home.'

'I wouldn't be surprised either, the way you were going. It's given half of our diners indigestion from leaping up thinking world war three had broken out.' She laughed and walked away around the side of the building.

'God, I thought she was going to give you a bollocking then.'

'Marty, there's somethin' ya gotta know: everyone loves a real automobile. You, me, her, everyone.'

'What's a real automobile, then, cowboy?' Tara asked.

'One that makes the earth move, darlin'.' He grinned at Molly.

'Dear Lord!' Tara grabbed Martin's hand. 'You weren't like this when you were a schoolboy, were you, Martin?'

'Heavens no. Not until I was about twenty-three.'

'Yeah,' Dave added. 'He just ain' a V8 kinda guy.'

'I've got a V8,' said Molly enthusiastically.

'Well, ah'll be.' Dave looked at her lasciviously. 'A beautiful lil lady with the right stuff, huh? Ah'm gonna bet it's in that Range Rover right over there.'

'Martin told you!'

'No I didn't!'

'Actually, ah'm blessed with the gift. Ah just know.'

'How?'

'Well,' Dave took a deep breath, 'ya was born under the sign of Capricorn an', possessin' the mountain goat's yearnin' for adventure, ya needed to be able to go places nobody went before. Realisin' ya high-heeled sneakers didn't cut it, ya took 'em back to the store an' swapped 'em for an SUV. How'm ah doin'?'

'You're doing shitty, Mr Donuts. I'm a Leo.'

'Hell, ah knew that! Whoa! Donuts? Ya heard about the donut woman?'

'Yes.'

'If this duplicitous bastard told ya ah was hot for the donut woman, he's lyin' through his sorry ass. She was the grossest...'

'She was my late Auntie Betty.' Molly's expression was downcast and hurt.

Dave's jaw dropped and the blood drained from his face. He looked at Martin who stared back impassively. Tara stared at the ground, absent-mindedly tickling Macduff behind the ear. Even Macduff looked solemn. Eventually, Dave regained the power of speech.

'Oh man, tell me ya kiddin'.'

'Okay, I'm kidding.' Molly gave him a cheerful smile and Tara gave up her battle to stifle laughter.

'Hell, ya an evil woman!' Spluttered Dave. 'Sheeit! An' ah thought ah'd found me a soulmate, goddammit!' He turned his attention to Martin.

'Nothing to do with me, Dave. Hey, I think we're being called in. What are you going to do with Macduff?'

'Macduff can go make big eyes at the kitchen staff. He's real good at that. It's cool,' he added, sensing disapproval of his abandonment of Macduff in the hotel grounds while they went in to sate their appetites. 'He won' go anyplace. As trustworthy as the day is long. Plus he's lost his cojones. Kinda dents the spirit of adventure, ya know? Ya should consider it, Marty boy.'

They rose, picked up their empty glasses and entered the dining room. Martin was surprised by the size of it, and by its formality compared with the pubs that he was more used to frequenting. The majority of the men present wore jackets and ties, while Tara and Molly appeared to be the only women wearing trousers. A waiter showed them to a table tucked away in a corner, as far from the windows as it was possible to get without actually leaving the room. A pillar shielded them from most of their fellow diners.

'Hey, excuse me, buddy.' Dave beckoned to the waiter and treated him to a deadpan Georgia godfather routine. 'Ya got nuthin' more discreet here? Muh colleagues an' ah are kinda shy. We don' wanna be seen by jus' anybody, ya know what I mean? Specially the cops.'

'I'm afraid we're very busy tonight sir,' the waiter replied, nervously casting his eyes around the room. He was probably still in his teens and clearly didn't know whether or not to take Dave seriously. 'Did you have a reservation sir? I can have a word with the manager.'

'We're fine, thanks.' Martin intervened to curtail Dave's performance. 'Could we have some mineral water and a wine list please. Dave, I want you to promise me something.'

'Sure thing.'

'When a waiter or waitress comes to the table and says, "Who's are the frogs' legs?", please do not, under any circumstances, look under the table or say, "It's the way he walks". Okay?'

'Jeez, man; ah only get to say these things once in a decade, an' that's if ah'm real lucky.'

'I want to enjoy this meal, without pissed-off people standing over me, waiting for us to leave.'

'As if...'

'Every time, Dave. It's not big and it's not clever. It's one of the reasons I'm very glad that you live in the Highlands and I don't.'

'An' this guy's supposed to be muh good buddy!' Dave appealed to the women. 'Calls me up outta the blue, in the middla the night, demands all kindsa help an' then don' let me have muh fun. Hey, but he's an accountant, so who's surprised? Not many, ah guess.'

'I gather you're a landscape gardener.' Molly changed the subject. 'It must be a great way of life.'

'Right now, with summer comin'? Yes, ma'am, there's none better.' He speared a coil of butter from a dish in the centre of the table. It fell off the end of his knife and he wrestled it back to his plate, leaving pale yellow smears on the table cloth and on the edges of the cruets. 'But when it rains up here, ah tell ya, it *rains*. An' when the wind starts blowin', ya kinda think Alaska's gotta be better than this. Hey, ya know there's more people on Prozac in Scotland than in the rest of Europe put together.'

'Don't exaggerate. Anyway, why stay here? Don't you miss Texas?'

'Hell, no, ah don' miss Texas.'

'He's from Georgia,' Martin explained.

'Same sort of thing. So, you don't miss Georgia?'

'Whass there to miss? Better climate? Better health? Better prospects? Better welfare? Better wealth? An' gas a dollar a gallon! Who needs all that shit? Sorry, ah'm just goofin' aroun'. We might have the best vehicles over there, an' the best roads to run 'em on, but do we? Do we hell! Drive above the double-nickel in mos' states an' a sanctimonious trooper's gonna bust yo ass. Either that or ya get ya head blown clean off by some redneck jerk in a pick-up truck with a six-pack in his belly an' jello for brains. Now, take that road out there. Ya can *drive* that road, an' thousands like it all over this country. An' thass Scotland ah'm talkin' about, honey, which is why ah'm here.'

'Oh come on! There must be more to it than that.'

'Nope.' He shoved a big lump of buttered bread into his mouth. Molly looked at Martin, in search of corroboration of Dave's explanation.

'It's true,' said Martin, 'it's the roads. He's barking.'

'But it's such a beautiful country,' Tara protested. 'No one's mad who wants to live with this scenery.'

'You're right,' Martin agreed. 'Of course, you're absolutely right. The trouble is, he doesn't see it that way. If they had roads like this around Slough, he would live in Slough. He's blind to the natural charms of this place.'

'Henry would love it here,' said Molly.

'Henry's into Franco-Highland cuisine, huh?' Mention of the name made Dave bristle. 'So why ain' Henry here?' He shot a glance at Martin, who had to turn towards the kitchen door to conceal a quivering smile.

'I didn't mean he'd like this restaurant; I was alluding to the countryside,' Molly responded with a somewhat hollow laugh, while pulling a quizzical face in Martin's direction.

'Some sorta eco-weenie then?' Dave muttered.

'Does he have a problem with horses?' Molly demanded of Martin, nodding her head in Dave's direction.

'No, he loves them, particularly with roast potatoes and Yorkshire pudding.'

'What friggin' horses?' Dave was suddenly confused. He turned to Tara, flapping his hands in the direction of Martin and

Molly, as though fending off their incomprehensible utterances. 'Tara, honey, please tell me: whass with these flakes? What horses? Who's eatin' horses?'

'Nobody's eating Henry,' Molly asserted, frowning.

'Who said anythin' about eatin' Henry?' Dave's voice had reached a pitch that attracted the attention of a stern looking, elderly couple at the nearest table. 'Whass this Henry gotta do with eatin' horses? Jeez! Is he French, huh?'

'Certainly not! Henry's a true-blue, English vegetarian. Can't have him getting ESE.'

'ESE?' asked Tara.

'Equine Spongiform thingy,' said Molly. 'Comes from cannibalism, so I understand. Ugh.'

Dave leaned back in his chair, eyes shut tight. He lost his balance and the chair went over backwards, his feet kicking the underside of the table as his head thumped onto the fortuitously thick carpet. Martin's hand shot out to prevent the bottle of water flying over, while the cutlery performed a clattering, unsynchronised jump. There might have been a serious mess had the meal already been served.

'Shame,' said Molly.

'What?' asked Martin, gasping for breath between convulsions of laughter.

'Well, I thought old Donuts here was alright, but he's obviously completely off his trolley.'

'Me?' Dave picked himself and his chair up. He brushed himself down, carried out a cursory check on the solidity of his chair, gave the occupants of the neighbouring table a dazzling white grin and resumed his place, to the obvious relief of the restaurant manager. '*Yer* the kooky one here, lady. What in heck's name does this Henry guy see in ya?'

'I give him his oats and his exercise.'

'Duh!' Dave was stunned by Molly's openness, but recovered his composure. 'Not the only one, way ah hear it.'

'Eh?'

'Well, it sounds like he monkeys aroun', ya know? Plays dirty.'

'And that's why I muck him out every morning.' Molly cocked an eyebrow at Dave. 'Henry is my horse, Dave,' she explained, the truth dawning on her that Dave might be envisaging some other type of being.

'Huh?'

'He's a horse. My horse. You know, a gee-gee. A hunter. Tall, dark and handsome. Big soppy eyes. Not unlike you as it happens. Well, the soppy eyes, anyway. What did you think he was?'

Dave was looking across the table at Martin with a murderous expression on his face.

'Martin, what have you been saying to him? About Henry? Martin?' It was no good; Martin was incapable of speech. A prim, slightly effeminate waiter approached them.

'Who will be having the frogs' legs?' he asked nervously.

'Go ahead an' lop 'em off the bastard before he quits laughin',' Dave instructed, 'an' make sure every person in this room gets to have a bit, ya understan'?'

The waiter stood patiently and silently, allowing the diners time to compose themselves.

'I bet you love it when funny people come in,' Tara suggested.

'I wouldn't know, Miss.'

~

The next ninety minutes sped by in noisy conviviality, conversation and spontaneous laughter flowing in equal amounts, enhanced by good food and unhurried service. Even the precious waiter warmed to them, perhaps realising that there was greater job satisfaction, not to mention gratuities, to be had from this disparate quartet than from the starchier and disapproving occupants of some of the neighbouring tables, who ate and departed in haste and near silence. The jovial lady who had earlier taken their order in the garden, and who was evidently the manageress or someone of similar authority, conducted a poll of the remaining diners and secured a majority in favour of admitting Macduff. The lepers' table in the corner was by now the centre of attention. Or rather, it was whenever Macduff stopped at it.

'Fort Dawson is about forty minutes up the road,' announced Dave, after losing an argument with Martin about splitting the bill.

'Anyone gonna ride with me an' Macduff?' He looked hopefully at Molly.

'I'm driving, I'm afraid,' said Molly, a note of genuine disappointment in her voice.

'We're sticking with Team Molly tonight.' Holding Martin's arm with both hands, Tara quickly staked their claim in the Range Rover.

'It's jus' me an' Mac as usual then. Ah'll go real slow so y'all can follow us.'

'Yes please, I like it real slow!' Molly's response was thrown out lightly but loaded with innuendo nevertheless.

'Oh ah'll not let ya down there, honey.'

'Whoo,' Tara whispered into Martin's ear. 'Did you ever witness chemistry quite like that? I can almost see sparks!'

'Come on folks,' said Molly, climbing into her car. 'Let's go.'

Dave gave them a wave and followed his happy dog across the gravel to his revered piece of Americana. Less than a minute later the two cars left the hotel's car park and headed north in convoy, Martin rather enjoying the deep rumble of the Mustang ahead. He wondered if he should question Molly about the flirting that had broken out between her and Dave but concluded that she was sufficiently mature to know what she was doing, notwithstanding the undertaking he had given her father to look after her. He reasoned that his duty was to keep her from physical danger, not from voluntarily participating in some friendly hanky-panky.

The road was now almost empty and the clear air and moonless sky enabled them to enjoy a sparkling, crowded display of stars. The miles disappeared rapidly beneath their wheels, with Martin and his companions taking turns to point out grand, floodlit houses and count off the diminishing distance to Inverness on roadside markers. Martin pondered the likelihood of lucking into estate ownership. He was concerned that the whole adventure was coming to an end and, with it, presumably, his relationship with Tara. The vision of Essex also haunted his thoughts.

'Did you call John back there?' He asked Molly.

'Yes,' she replied.

'Did you tell him about Essex?'

'Yes, duh! Of course I didn't tell him. No point in the old chap having kittens.'

'Hmm. I'm not very happy about this. As long as there was no threat of them following us, it was pretty cool. Thanks to the good Dr Kennedy, I feel I'm leading everyone into the lion's den. And I really don't think it's on. For either of you I mean.'

'Martin, that's nonsense. Apart from the fact that we're well ahead of them.'

'We don't know that.'

'Twenty four hours from now, it'll all be over. Essex and his chums will have to bog off with their tails between their legs.'

Tara introduced her own note of caution: 'Molly, I know these people and they don't just play around you know. But I agree that we've likely got a lead over them. We just need to be careful, yeah? Stay on our toes.'

'Maybe we should turn the tables on them,' suggested Molly.

'How?' chorused Martin and Tara.

'Hide up near Cuiphur, let them do the searching, mug them if they find anything.'

'I am not going up against Evans again with anything less than a Chieftain tank,' Martin said with feeling.

'You beat him with a wok before.'

'And he subsequently chucked me down a well.'

'*And me!*' Tara protested.

'All square then.'

'I hardly think so.'

They were interrupted by the sight of Dave's Mustang slowing and indicating left. It led them along a single track road for several miles, the gurgling exhaust note lazily rising and falling with the driver's right foot. Dave maintained what seemed to Martin to be an injudicious speed, nonchalantly brushing past dozy sheep on either side with inches to spare. A splash of white paint on a menhir-like gatepost marked the entrance to Dave's home and now he used caution, picking his way left and right around the deep ruts in his drive with practised delicacy. Molly had no such qualms following him. They parked side by side on a wide grassy area in front of a small, whitewashed cottage that looked as though it had grown out of the land many hundreds of years ago.

'Welcome to Rancho Dawson,' Dave shouted, slamming his car door shut. He opened the boot and hauled out two handfuls of well-packed carrier bags. Macduff leapt around happily from person to person. Tara sidled up to Martin and squeezed his arm. 'Hold up while I get the lights.' Dave fumbled at his front door for a few seconds, then his guests were surprised to find themselves bathed in the bright white glow from a halogen floodlight mounted high in a tree.

'I'd like to see what he does at Christmas,' Tara whispered. She helped Martin pull assorted bags from the back of Molly's car while Dave progressed through the cottage, switching on lights and giving the place a welcoming glow.

'For chrissake sake mind ya head, Marty!' he shouted from the inner recesses. 'This place ain't designed for modern man. Or you!' He returned outside. 'Hey, Molly! Let me take that thing for ya.'

Martin entered the house and began to explore. A wide, stone-flagged hallway provided sufficient dumping space for bags and coats, alongside Dave's collection of macs, waxed jackets, boots rugged, wellington and cowboy, galoshes, flip-flops and slippers, the latter either very high-mileage or Macduff's favourite toys. The accommodation was compact: there was a room either side of the hallway, one with a bed and some cupboards in it, the other with an assortment of sagging armchairs, matched by sagging shelves of books, records, CDs and sundry bits of hi-fi and TV hardware, all plugged into over-occupied power points. At the back of the house was a galley kitchen, complete with an ancient, chipped enamel sink and a wooden draining board that might have harboured some interesting life forms. A bathroom, in which an open fireplace stood out as the overriding design feature, led off one end. It was the first time that Martin had seen a bag of Coalite and bundles of kindling occupying the space beneath a bath. A steep and extremely narrow staircase rose along one side of the hallway into the roof space where he assumed Dave slept. He decided that he had better not ascend unless invited to.

'Okay,' shouted Dave, 'ladies use the bathroom through there; you men, Macduff an' Martin please take note, pee outside since we got company. For those who wanna bathe, there is hot water. Nightcaps will be served in the ballroom in approximately two minutes: very best Bourbon or ya local single malt. Sleepin' arrangements: well, puttin' aside any obvious aspirations, is it gonna be a boys' room an' a girls' room?'

'Where does that leave Macduff, as he's got no, you know?'

'Please don' be shy, honey; balls is the word. If ya wanna take a big Mac to bed, ya most welcome, but ah gotta warn ya he blows off aroun' four in the mornin'. Marty, would ya please pour some booze while ah make sure the maid's done her work. Ya'll find it on the shelf right through there.'

'Thanks, Dave, you're a star.' First Martin went to the kitchen and selected four clean glasses of varying sizes and styles, together with a small jug, which he filled with cold water at the sink. Unable to find a tray, he placed everything in a rusty old roasting tin and took it into the sitting room. There was an array of bottles on the mantelpiece. 'Okay, Tara, Molly, let's see what we've got. Aha! Would you like a wee drop of Glenmorangie or a Jack Daniel's?' After accepting drinks and declining water, Molly and Tara excused themselves, leaving Martin on his own. He scrutinised the contents of the bowed shelves, which neatly summarised their owner's principal interests: an elderly guide to British motor sport venues; biographies of Jimi Hendrix and Mario Andretti; a tuner's guide to Dearborn V8s; an encyclopaedia of shrubs; a video entitled Rolling Thunder at Road Atlanta; a surprisingly eclectic range of CDs, and a number of vinyl LPs, which immediately brought back memories of university and earlier days, mostly fond.

Martin coaxed a doomy looking black and white album sleeve from its resting place and studied it: The Parkerilla by Graham Parker and the Rumour. He remembered seeing this band perform live and realised that now, as then, Dave was still the only person he had ever come across who possessed any of their work. He wondered whether the sound of it now, in the presence of younger, more sophisticated listeners, would be embarrassing or still impress. The smoked perspex lid over the turntable hadn't seen a duster for months and probably hadn't been lifted for even longer. A prod at a large button set some LED lights of various hues twinkling and the record began revolving as soon as he lifted the arm. With the needle settled on the edge, there was still no sound coming from the speakers. He turned a knob from CD to PHONO and settled down in a squashy armchair on the opposite side of the room, clasping his glass warmly to his chest. Parker's trademark line, 'HEY LORD, DON'T ASK ME QUESTIONS!' was delivered shatteringly loudly; a panic-stricken Macduff leapt from his beanbag and shot out into the hallway as though a rocket engine had been installed somewhere in the vacant region between his hind legs. An equally alarmed Martin dived across the room and turned the volume control from 9 to 2, as Molly entered again.

'Are you intent on waking *everyone* in Glasgow?' She frowned at Martin in her best schoolmarm manner and sipped her whisky.

'We're nowhere near Glasgow,' Martin protested, a little smugly.

'Quite.' She rolled her eyes in despair. 'Listen, just so's you know, Tara's bagged Dave's room in the roof.' Martin was confused. 'For you and her, okay?' Martin's mouth was open, but he wasn't responding. Did she just say that Tara had reserved a room for him? And her? Did Tara intend that they should sleep together again? 'Good grief, love's young dream, or what?' Molly laughed. 'You're on a promise, you idiot!'

'Oh. I mean I knew that. Well, not exactly knew, but, er, you know.'

'Yes.'

'What about you?'

'Yes, I knew too.'

'I mean, where does it leave you?'

'Well, Martin, I'm disappointed, of course. Upset, even,' she wiped an imaginary tear from her cheek, 'but a girl must realise when she's lost to another, and,' she sobbed a little, 'I've just got to accept it and move on, you bastard! You knew how much I wanted your babies!'

'About as much as you wanted herpes?'

'Oh God no, not that much!' Molly brightened miraculously. 'I'm going to be in there.' She pointed in the direction of the hallway and the bedroom beyond.

'And Dave?' A cleaver-wielding John suddenly loomed large again in Martin's imagination. What if Dave slides his smooth southern manner into maximum output? He had seen it before: girls could simply melt, as though hit full-on by a sleaze-ray. By the look of the cottage, Dave hadn't enjoyed much female company for a while. Not even a retainer with a bucket of soapy water and a scrubbing brush.

'Dave? He'll be there.' She pointed to the sofa. 'Never bonk on the first date. That's his rule, anyway, and he's sticking to it. I'll get over it. What's this?' She nodded towards the mess of hi-fi components. 'It's not bad.'

'Graham Parker and the Rumour.'

'Oh.' Molly looked blank. 'You excited?'

'Bloody terrified.'

'I'm sure she'll be gentle.'

'What?'

'Tara. She's self-assured, but you shouldn't fear her.'

'Molly, behave! I'm talking about tomorrow: Cuiphur Castle, Essex and all that.'

'I know, I know. Listen, you.' Molly put her glass on top of a speaker and gave him a friendly hug. 'Let's get your head sorted out, shall we? Do you love her?'

'Tara?'

'No, Mrs Bever-bloody-ley Minchin; of course Tara!'

'I think that's a, er, it's...' Martin knew that the answer was 'yes', but he wasn't ready to own up to it, in case it revealed laughably naive daydreaming on his part. He was, after all, a reasonably well respected professional person in their hometown; he didn't want to return to be the central joke of the place, the muttering fool at the end of the lounge bar. Don't mind him, he's Walter Mitty-Minchin, the accountant who married a beautiful Irish princess and lived in an imaginary castle, ha ha ha. Buy him a Scotch and you'll hear the funniest story you've ever been told with a straight face.

'Martin!' Molly was shaking him.

'Yes?' He looked down at Molly's happily smiling face.

'For God's sake, let it happen. I'm so fond of you, I don't want to see you waste this chance. And, for what it's worth, I think Tara's the dog's bollocks!'

'Don't tell Dave, or he'll have her super-glued to Macduff's undersides before you can say, er...'

'Yes?'

'Dave!'

'How y'all doin'?' Dave strolled into the room, took the glass proffered by Martin and added some water to the Jack Daniel's.

'I understand I'm turfing you out of your room.'

'It's cool.'

'Are you sure? I mean, I don't mind.'

'Marty, muh friend, just take it easy an' enjoy some good ol' southern hospitality up here in the frozen north.'

'Well, I appreciate it, really. Thanks.'

'Sure. Now then,' he changed the subject, 'whass the plan?'

Tara entered almost silently and settled lightly on Martin's lap. She draped her arm around his neck and snuggled up against him. He wondered if the exquisite trembling within his ribcage was visible to the others.

'I don't think I've got a plan really,' he replied.

'Okay,' said Dave, 'Ah like that. That's cool.' He rubbed his chin while his guests looked at each other through heavily lidded eyes. 'Ah gotta lil tractor an' tools an' stuff, in case there's the usual overgrown crap. Let me think, ah gotta map. Ah got some food for breakfast an' some more to take with us. An', unless you guys got any better ideas, ah think that's about it. If we hit the road at, say, seven? We'll have gotten two hours searchin' done before those jerks get to Inverness. That's a head start ol' Butch an' Sundance woulda killed for. Who wants the tub? Ah've lit the bathroom fire so someone can go wallow.' He gazed around the room. 'C'mon! Ah don' turn the heatin' on for jus' any folk ya know!'

'Well, if there are no other takers,' Tara sat up and looked at Dave and Molly in turn, 'I wouldn't say no.'

'As long as I can have a wee first,' said Molly, rising.

'Ah'll get it runnin'.' Dave rose as well. 'Ah mean the tub, okay?'

Tara leant close to Martin's ear and whispered, 'Dave's given us his bed.'

'I know.'

'He's put clean linen on it.'

'That's a comfort.'

'So, we should make sure we're clean. Fancy sharing my bath?'

The hairs on the back of Martin's neck bristled and he felt the first stirrings of something interesting in his underpants. Tara certainly had a way with his most private parts.

'Oh yes, yes please,' he murmured, cupping the back of her head in his hand and drawing her gently towards him. Their lips met, softly at first, caressing each other as though for the first time again. He could taste the smoky whisky on her breath, a scent not normally recognised as an aphrodisiac but, in these so appropriate circumstances and to this romantic, would-be Scottish laird, as seductive as the most exclusive concoctions ever distilled by Chanel. Their tongues performed a twisting, straining, aching dance. Her teasing fingernails on his earlobe made him shiver again and he hugged her even more tightly, thrilling at the feel of her breasts pressing into his ribs with every breath she took. Her hip pressed into his crotch and his hard-on pushed more insistently against his jeans. As the kissing, hugging and rubbing increased in intensity, worry barged its way into his head; what if the others came back in now? And shouldn't he hold back, keep his juices in harness until sufficient love making had been completed in the cosy confines of Dave's roof space? He needed something to distract him, something to run in parallel, mentally, with the sexually charged experience continuing apace in this armchair. The last thing he or Tara needed right now was a pair of St Michael briefs full of semen. His pair, that is; he wasn't sure whether M&S had stores in Ireland. Ah, but she had stocked up on knickers and suchlike in Shimbley. There was certainly no M&S in Shimbley. Ann Summers? There's a thought, oops, rather too erotic. No Ann Summers there, either. Ann Summers, BHS, C&A, Debenhams – he couldn't recall doing shops before – where? C&A, Dixons. Ha! He could just imagine a vision like Tara flooring a young Dixons salesman with a request to see their frillies. Er, Debenhams, Etam, Fortnum & Mason, blimey. Gateway, Harrods. He was on a roll. I, er Ib, Ibby, Iccy, Idiot? Tara lifted her face a few inches away from his and brushed a stray hair back.

'What are you thinking?' she asked.

'Can you think of a retailer beginning with I?'

'Pardon?' She sat up and pushed him on the shoulder with the palm of her hand. 'What in God's name are you talking about?' While she paused, waiting for an explanation, Dave walked back in.

'Hey, guys, ya need anythin'?'

'He needs a retailer, beginning with I.'

'Ironmonger. Tub's runnin'.'

'Yeah, thanks, Dave,' said Tara, still staring at Martin with a quizzical expression on her face. 'Does ironmonger solve your problem here? Or do you want to take a stroll around the estate, to think, while I have our bath?'

'Ironmonger's fine, thanks. I'm sorry; brain not functioning correctly. Lack of oxygen.' He caught a reproachful look. 'But no complaints, none whatsoever! Shall we?' He invited her to rise from his lap. Arsehole, Bozo, Cretin, Dickhead.

'Eejit! Come on.' She held out her hand and he uncoiled himself from the depths of the chair.

'Here's to Robert E. Lee an' William Wallace.' Dave sloshed another measure of whisky into Martin's glass. 'Don't ya let the bugs bite. See y'all tomorrow.' He ushered them from his temporary bedroom and closed the door.

Tara led Martin by the hand, down the hallway, through the kitchen and into the bathroom, in which steam had already coated the walls and window with running condensation, reflecting both the electric light and that thrown by the flames licking around a spitting log in the hearth. She tugged on the string dangling by the door, extinguishing the harsh glow of the bare overhead bulb and leaving them bathed in shimmering orange. She pushed the door closed and wrapped the string around the latch as a makeshift protection from intruders. Martin placed his glass on the window-ledge on the far side of the bath and turned the taps off. He dipped his hand into the water, finding the temperature to be just right, and turned back towards Tara. He put his arms around her, resting the side of his face on the top of her head.

'This is idyllic. I mean, all the other times I might have said "This is idyllic" in my life, like maybe watching a sunset or Alfredo starting at the first attempt or just having a pint in a nice pub garden with people I like or... well, it's nothing compared to this. You know, I really thought it would be impossible for you to be any more beautiful than you already are but, like this, with you all orange, you're just, just...'

'Suffering from jaundice?'

'No! I mean the orange light, from the fire.'

'I know what you mean, Martin, and I love you saying it.'

'I'm not very good at saying the right things. My vocabulary packs up and buggers off and while I'm groping around, looking for the simplest words of endearment, the moment passes and I've cocked it up, so to speak.'

'You do fine.' She leant forward and softly kissed his chest. 'I want to be with you. I wish you could relax and accept it. No I don't, actually; your modesty is charming. All the same, you've no need to get so anxious, okay?'

'I'm sorry. Thank you, I mean. It's just that, I've never regarded myself as much of a catch, as such. Tall, yes, reasonably bright, bit of a laugh sometimes, but, a beautiful, talented girl like you: you could have any man on the face of this earth, I swear it. What on earth would you see in someone like me?'

'Listen now.' She lowered the lavatory lid and sat on it; Martin lowered himself onto the edge of the bath. 'I liked you the moment I saw you. Don't ask me why, I just did. So did Dad. We weren't wrong; you're a nice man, one in a million. In the short time that I've known you, we've barely been separated, yet you've never taken me for granted, you've always put my welfare before your own, you've been the most perfect gentleman I've ever met. I'm getting to know your friends and they all love you, because you're a nice, generous, thoughtful person. You've every reason to be pleased with yourself but I've not seen you show it. I like your attitude, your manners, your altruism, your bravery and your sensitivity. I'm intrigued by your physical dimensions and immensely attracted to the idea that you might be Lord of an enormous estate. Now, will you undress and get in that bath before it turns to ice?' She hauled her jumper over her head.

'Iceland!' Martin was up and running again, thanks to her inadvertent contribution.

'What?'

'I imagine this room's like Iceland in the winter.'

'Hot pools of bubbling mud? Come on, you.' She tugged on his jumper. 'I think I need the toilet.'

'Oh, right. I need one too.' He felt awkward, sure that the courteous thing was to make himself scarce. Apart from which, he really did need to relieve himself, and he was pretty certain that urinating in front of the one you love wasn't the best strategy when trying to romance her. 'I'll pop out.' He moved towards the door, but she grabbed his arm.

'No you don't!'

'What?'

'You can't have forgotten the last time you popped out? I got throttled and thrown down a well.'

'Oh.' Now he didn't know what to do or say.

'You stay right here. I tell you what; if you're squeamish about this, look the other way. I'll be really quick.'

'Yes, right.' He fixed his gaze on the plastic switch on the ceiling from which the light's string dangled. Iceland – brilliant! Beverley would never have contemplated having him witness her toilet, or *toilette*, as she would have insisted. He found it extraordinarily frank, something that knocked mere sexual intercourse into touch as far as openness was concerned. Good grief, this is why the English are so mocked. If the simple act of having a pee is regarded as unspeakably awful, it's little wonder that we're all as screwed up as they say. He began to feel brave and modern about it. That puts old Bev in her place, ha! Here's new man Minchin, doing what comes naturally with a world-class babe no less. Shit! Poor old Bev – what the hell have they done with her? She's going to go absolutely ape. If she can, that is. Jesus. Jewson, Kebabbaburger, Londis, Moss Bros, NatWest. Hardly a retailer any more, of course. The first of the big banks to shut up shop in Shimbley. And to think that his own profession sat bang in the middle of this hated financial services sector. Nationwide, ah, that'll do nicely. Beverley will have raised the alarm, no doubt. Get it into Detective Constable Dee's thick skull that the villains spoken of really do exist and are running amok throughout the British Isles. Probably pointed the finger at Martin himself, have him topping Interpol's list of most wanted. Does Interpol still exist? Old Bill... Oddbins! Prontaprint, Queensway, Radio Rentals.

'Martin!'

He spun round to see Tara lowering herself gingerly into the bath. Shit. Arse, Bollocks, Crap, Doh! Thank God for retail multiple, non-sexual thoughts, apart from that brief excursion into Anne Summers of course; at least he was going to be able to piss into the pan without standing on his head. Coyness returned as the new man ran and hid. He stood right over the lavatory, guarding his modesty like a schoolboy trying to prevent his neighbour from copying his answers. Good grief, there was steam rising from the bowl, as though he was emptying a freshly boiled kettle. It sounded like the Niagara Falls, and it went on and on. He didn't remember drinking the entire contents of the Firth of Forth when he drove over it earlier in the day. At least he looked quite well endowed; it wasn't an erection, but it wasn't entirely flaccid either, not the sorry looking specimen that lurked in a corner of his underpants most of the time. At last the stream turned into a trickle and he took care to keep his wrapping-up sequence well below the fart-risk level of effort.

'I needed that,' he said on autopilot, before waking up to the fact that a commentary wasn't required. 'How's the bath? Okay?'

'Empty.'

'I wouldn't say that.'

'Are you coming in?'

'Yes!' He started to pull off his clothes in what he hoped was the correct order. When he had been starting out on his working career, a trainee minnow in what had seemed like a huge pond, he had once found himself on the fringe of a coffee-machine convention of young female colleagues, half eavesdropping, half participating. They were comparing notes on how their partners dressed; socks first was clearly risible, followed closely by shirt first. The only acceptable way was underpants first and, conversely for undressing, underpants last. Any other sequence deserved mockery at the very least, if not a consultation with lawyers. He had once raised the subject with Beverley, asked her for confirmation of the U and non-U methods of disrobing. She said it really didn't matter because she had absolutely no interest in watching him either dress or undress. He must have been mad!

He now found himself topless, but still with shoes on. Was this an awful faux pas? No, not unless he tried to take his jeans off before removing the footwear. He reversed down onto the lavatory, only to realise, to his dismay, that he had not only left the lid up, but the seat as well. There are few stranger seats to have under one's buttocks than the naked enamel of the pan. He sprang back up, accidentally allowing the heavy wooden seat and lid to slam down with a bang that would doubtless be heard throughout the house. Very quietly, he sat back down and concentrated on removing his shoes. Tara was giggling and he briefly returned her amused gaze with a weak smile of embarrassment. Here he was, in the middle of the most erotic moment in his entire life, and he was turning it into slapstick comedy; Pussy Galore awaits James Bond and in stumbles Benny Hill. He discarded his shoes and socks, then removed the jeans and briefs as one.

'Man overboard!' he said in a hoarse whisper, carefully stepping either side of Tara's legs and lowering himself into the piping hot water, allowing his feet to resurface either side of her head as his bottom sank lower. 'Eureka! That's what I call displacement.' The level came within a worrying inch from the top, before the overflow outlet began to redress the balance. Martin stared at Tara. The water was clear, providing tantalising glimpses, in this flickering light, of her neatly trimmed black pubic hair, her slender waist, her big, smooth nipples. Nipples were odd. His own were small, scrunched up and had motley hairs protruding from them. He recalled that Beverley's had appeared to age rather more swiftly than their owner. In fact, he reckoned, the best place to view nice nipples, untouched, unchewed nipples, was in art galleries, adorning virgins fashioned by Renaissance artists. Until now, of course. Tara's nipples were real, moving, perfect, uncreased, bulging, alluring, mesmerising.

'Hello.' She stroked her hot, watery hands over his chest and shoulders, which towered above the water. 'All of you,' she added, looking in turn at his ankles either side of her.' He allowed a sybaritic smile to stretch his lips, folded his hands behind his head and leant back.

'Aaarrgh!' The combination of an icy tap on one side of his spine and a searingly hot one on the other inspired a sub-aqua commotion which nearly dragged Tara under the surface. 'Shit, sorry! Hot tap. And cold. I don't normally sit this end.'

'You're not really designed for conventional baths, are you?'

'It can be trying. Swimming pools are better, but you need a lot of bubble bath.'

'Did you and Beverley share baths?'

'You've got to be joking. The bathroom was her private domain. If I didn't scrub it all spotless after me she wouldn't say a civil word for a week. Quite good, really.'

'Why did you marry her?'

'Brain fade. I was kind of swept along into it. No, that's not true – I absolutely worshipped her.'

'Why?'

'Insanity. Just another case of a cow giving a man the mad disease.'

'Hey, we shouldn't really be slagging her off, eh? At the moment, you know?'

'No better time. Come here.' He puckered up and leant forward. She responded and they put their arms around each other as they kissed. He brought one hand back and hesitantly traced the edge of her breast with his fingers. He shivered as she slid a nail down his side and felt between his thighs until she held his swelling dick. He gently rolled one of her nipples between thumb and forefinger, feeling its subtle response. He wondered whether he should open his eyes or not. Their mouths were still locked together and he wasn't sure of the finer points of snogging etiquette – it had been a while. On top of these worries he was almost bent double, his feet hanging behind her, over the end of the tub, and the small of his back being tickled by the chain attached to the plug. Spinal pain wasn't supposed to get in the way of heavy petting. Cautiously, he opened one eye. All that he could see in the dim light was an out of focus close-up of ear and hair. A bead of salty sweat rolled lazily into his open eye and began to sting. He closed it again, tightly. His hands were roaming her back, and occasionally bits of her front, and he marvelled at the feel of her skin; there were no flaws, no spare bits. It was smooth, taut, moist and sexy. Skin had never turned him on, as far as he could remember, but Tara's was sensational. Its perfection was making him aware of the tiniest scars in his own finger tips. She pulled her head back to give their mouths a rest. Martin opened his eyes and cupped her face in his hands. Through the stinging perspiration he admired her glowing face – so that's what they meant by women glowing. He recalled a chat-up line which had been espoused on the radio by a keen young clubber from Tyneside, and started giggling.

'What's funny,' she asked.

'You don't sweat much, for a fat lass,' he responded.

'I've heard it before and it's not very nice.'

'But it is very funny.'

'And very mean.'

'And very inappropriate in this company.'

'You mean I don't sweat?'

'Well, not much for – I mean you're glowing, darling!' He could have bitten his tongue; the last thing he wanted was to be too forward.

'What's the matter?' It was her turn to look concerned.

'I'm sorry. I was worried that, I thought maybe, I called you, you know, "Darling". It slipped out. I don't want you thinking I'm being over familiar.'

'Darling?'

'Yes.'

'I can live with that.'

'You don't mind?'

'Silly! We're sharing a bath, both as naked as the day we were born, and doing rather intimate things. You know, I don't do this with every man I meet. Of course I don't mind. I love it.' She smiled at him and slid down into the bath, her ankles clasping his waist. Her hands found his dick again and quickly provoked it into the hardest, most painfully swollen erection Martin had ever experienced.

'Swap ends,' she said, standing up, her feet either side of his legs and her crutch exactly at his eye level. She steadied herself by placing her hands on his head. He couldn't resist the allure of what lay behind the little triangular patch and planted a kiss on the hair. She pulled his head firmly towards her and he felt his way into her with the tip of his tongue. He placed his hands on her buttocks and marvelled at their firmness, smoothness and perfect roundness. Her hips were gyrating slowly, rhythmically and she was muttering words of encouragement. He weighed up the pros and cons of continuing until dead from suffocation or saving himself. Valour lost and he retreated surreptitiously to grab some air and dispose of a couple of loose hairs from his mouth.

'Mmm.' She stroked his head. 'Can you get up the other end?'

'Huh?'

'Of the bath?'

'Oh, I'll try.' He folded his legs up tightly to his chest and struggled to turn around until he faced the taps. He leant back, preparing to perform a limbo in reverse through the arch of her legs, but he was too large and Tara nearly toppled out over the back. Laughing, she clumsily climbed over him, allowing him to steal another personal kiss en route. Now he was lying back at the more comfortable end, his feet jammed against the wall, high above the taps. He found himself staring at his hard-on right in its one eye.

Tara lowered herself, sliding her body up and down his, kissing his lips, neck and chest, her breasts slithering over him, her gliding stomach maintaining his erection until she positioned herself on its end and slowly surrounded him in a tight embrace. She seemed so small and he had never felt so enormous. He was also stuck, his prone position rendering him unable to contribute much more to their lovemaking than his dick. Tara was rocking up and down, creating in the bath the same effect that occurs in swimming baths when they turn on the wave machine. Water was cascading over the edge in every direction. He was ready to come, only, what, forty seconds in? Oh God please no. He stared at the ceiling, the firelight performing its flickering dance, the dusty, grey light bulb swaying just a little. Thanks be that Tara had the presence of mind to wrap that string around the door latch. Had it moved? Had someone tried the door? No, of course not. Ha! That little worry bought some much needed time. Don't want her thinking she's landed a complete plonker – Premature Ejaculationist of the Universe. Ejaculation! Jesus, he hadn't even begun to think about precautions. Talk about unsafe sex. No, that sounded as though it maligned her. What he meant was unwise from the accidental babies perspective. She was pretty relaxed about it; she must have her own arrangements. She's a good Irish girl! Uh oh. He'll have to do the honourable thing, probably after receiving a sound beating from her dad. Brilliant! That means he'll have to spend the rest of his life with her. And her kids were bound to be perfect.

'Are you alright?' she whispered, panting slightly and squeezing new energy into his dick with skilfully deployed muscles.

'Oh yes. God I love you. You're the most amazing person I've ever met. Look...'

'Yup?'

'Oh hell – er, precautions. Not exactly prepared.'

'It's okay.'

'Oh?'

'I trust you.' She nibbled his chin.

'Mmm.' Trusted him; what the hell did that mean? Did that mean he would be expected to pull out with exquisite timing? What if he failed? He was in no position to pull out or in or any which way. She certainly wasn't behaving like someone with half a mind on the rules of coitus interruptus. Or was she? He hadn't a clue. Good grief, he wasn't going to be able to hold out much longer. Her voracious little fanny was sucking him into a vortex of overwhelming sensations. He was completely unprepared for his orgasm, the huge moment subsiding as quickly as it had arrived, leaving him shuddering, breathless and startled. And worried.

'Sorry,' he croaked.

'Thank you!' Tara lay on him, humming softly and happily as he slid from her, utterly spent. 'You're a lovely man.'

'And you're a lovely woman.' His worry disappeared, to be replaced by bliss. 'I love you, my darling. I love you so much. Thank you.' He hugged her. 'That was rather explosive – probably included some cobwebs.'

'That was just fine.' She rested her head on his chest and they lay still, their breathing gradually subsiding to normal levels. Five or more minutes passed with just their beating hearts and the softly fizzing fire disturbing the extraordinary peace. He couldn't recall feeling happier. And so much in love – he had always thought that he had loved Beverley, but now he wondered whether that could have been the case. He certainly couldn't remember feeling quite like this, so overcome with emotion, so utterly occupied with his feelings for this wonderful, beautiful, clever, sexy, thoughtful person now stirring on top of him.

'Hey, let's get this finished.' She sat up, rotating so that she now had her back to Martin, leaning against him and allowing him to envelop her in his arms. She picked up the drink from the window-ledge, took a sip and pushed the glass into his hand.

'It's probably shipped a bit of water,' he said, surveying the pools of water surrounding them. The level in the bath had certainly gone down several inches since they first climbed in.

'Oh God!' She put a hand to her mouth and gasped as she realised the extent of the mess. 'I'm surprised we didn't put the fire out.'

'That's the first time I've ever had a bath in front of an open fire.'

'Not for me.'

'And it's the first time I've had sex in the bath.'

'Ah yes, I'm with you on that one.'

'We must do it again.'

'What, now?'

'Well, much as I'd love to, I'm not sure I have it in me right now.'

'Nor do I, more's the pity.' She giggled

They snuggled together, warm in their easy familiarity, their friendship, their survival together and, now, their sexual intimacy. Oh, requited love – how marvellous it felt; like a fantastic dream from which there is no danger of waking because you know it's real, but which is punctuated by little spasms of the past, bits of happiness experienced along the way, bits of What's that? Oh, it's cool, it's happiness, it's lovely. It's love.

CHAPTER 12: Tuesday morning

'Is his dookship ready to rumble?' Dave's cheerful call up the stairs only just managed to precede a bouncy, slobbery greeting from Macduff, trailing the detritus of a dawn rummage in the wilds of his back yard. 'Breakfast in ten! Do y'all want tea up there?'

Discourteously, Martin managed to push the happy dog onto Tara and peered towards the open door.

'It's okay, Dave. I'll be down in a minute, thanks. Do you want your soggy doggy back?'

'Nah, ah'm good.'

'Darling,' Martin managed to wrestle his face in between those of Tara and the dog. He kissed the end of her nose. 'Urgh!'

'What?' Tara drew away from him and frowned.

'Dog got there first. Ready for a cuppa?'

'Mmm. Come here.' She pulled him down onto her and planted a loving kiss on his mouth. Not wanting to be left out, Macduff climbed onto Martin's back and planted loving kisses wherever he could.

'Come on,' said Martin, rising from the bed and reaching for his clothes. 'There's an Essex gaining on us. Would you like your tea up here?'

'No, I'll be down. Oh my!' She took a towel from the airing rack in the corner. 'It'll be fully three months before these dry out.'

'We'll say we used them to dry Macduff.' He struggled to pull on his jeans while stooping under the low, sloping ceiling.

'They're not covered in mud.'

'We'll say they were dry until he came up this morning and dribbled all over them.'

'Be off with you!'

'Okay. Bye.' He blew her a kiss and made for the door. Half way down the stairs he turned and repeated the gesture. She shooed him away.

Dave was in the kitchen, a vision of multi-disciplinary enthusiasm; on the cooker top various pans were deployed, vying for the chef's attention with a grill, a toaster, a kettle and a radio issuing farming news and weather reports. Martin stumbled over a dish on the floor, sending Macduff's drinking water flying over the floor tiles.

'Oops, sorry. I'll clear that up. Where's a…'

'No worries, man. Ain' nothin' compared to the swamp through there.' Dave nodded towards the bathroom door.

'Oh shit, we thought we'd mopped it all up. I'm sorry.'

'Ha, gotcha!' Dave laughed. 'So y'all made splashdown last night, huh?'

'What? I mean, er.' Martin was embarrassed and didn't wish to be indiscreet, even with his dear old friend.

'Hey, Marty, ah'm just guessin', man. Whaddya fancy?' He pointed with a fish slice at the various menu constituents where they sizzled. 'Apart from the babe descendant of the ol' kings of Tara, that is.'

'First and foremost, Princess Tara needs a cup of tea.'

'Pot's over there, milk's in the jug on the side, sugar's in that cupboard. Shit!' An exuberant flourish with his all-purpose prodding utensil had sent a portion of hash browns in a gentle arc which was intercepted by the remarkably alert Macduff, who swallowed the hot morsel in a gulp, with no visible signs of discomfort. 'The jaws of no return,' observed his master.

'Is Molly up?'

'Up an' outta here. She's gatherin' fungus.'

'I'm not sure I like the sound of that.'

'Should do. Ah learned a lotta things about fungus. Ya get it right, ya gotta feast for free.'

'And if you get it wrong?'

'Well, then it don' matter none. Nah, to be fair it's Mother Nature out there, man, not Sister Borgia. It ain' too dangerous.'

'Until you die.'

'Die, nah. Bad trip, maybe, but dyin's unlikely. Unless ya got no brains at all.'

'Or you're too adventurous.'

'Ya listened to yar ol' mom too hard. Ah bet she said never t' eat anythin' ya scraped up off the road.'

'Of course she did. The bladder bursts on impact and the urine infects all the meat and makes it all very dodgy.'

'Tasty.'

'What?'

'The word is tasty, man. Gandhi drank his, ya know?'

'I know.'

'An' wossname. Actress.'

'I know.'

'Invigoratin' was the word ah heard.'

'If you say so.'

'Talkin' of which,' Dave turned towards the door, 'Whass Fungus the bogeywoman gotten for us?'

Molly came in and emptied the contents of a plastic bag onto the sideboard. She had collected quite a diverse range of fungi, from snow-white puff-balls to very dark brown, sinister-looking things with pimples and frilly bonnets. Dave swiftly picked his way through them, dividing them into two groups.

'Good, very good, could be good given lotsa slow cookin', not good, good, good, blegh – unwise.'

'Give you the collywobbles, eh?' Molly asked.

'Well, if ya ate that, ya'd be callin' for Huey for a week, an' ah ain' talkin' choppers here unless it's the air ambulance. Hmm, good, good, not good, too soft.' He swept the rejects up in his hands and threw them into a large plastic bucket containing other discarded organic matter destined for his compost heap. 'That's a darn fine harvest for a rookie,' he said to Molly. 'Ya can stay an' do this again. Ya wanna peel off? The skins?'

Martin poured tea for everyone and took his turn in the bathroom for some quick ablutions. The fire, which had illuminated his passionate dip with Tara just a few hours before was now reduced to ash, a few lumps of clinker the only solid witnesses remaining in the hearth. Light from the rising sun was pouring in through the window and he made a mental note that he too would strive to possess a bathroom facing east. What better way to lift the gloom from the start of the average working day? Average working day! The very thought of an average working day had assumed the sort of greyness usually associated with his chosen profession by so-called comedians. He couldn't hide from the fact that his average working day was spent in lonely, sedentary toil. Was this newly born suspicion of the pointlessness of what he did for a living simply a side effect of a few days of wildly abnormal experiences, or were they rooted deeper than that, a creeping frustration, a changing of perspective allied to approaching middle-age? He certainly didn't want to spend the rest of his life being stimulated by the likes of Monan and his hangers-on but, as an involuntary passenger on this current crazy roller-coaster, he had enjoyed moments of great friendship and high eroticism, together with the little business of falling arse-over-tit in love. Could he really return to his regular, unremarkable life after this? It was stupid even to ponder it because, just like everyone else, he had no option; food had to be earned, mortgage paid, death anticipated. But he must never return to that loneliness. He hadn't felt lonely, as such. Self-sufficient, that's what he had reckoned. He'd had his books, music, TV, the pub – everything a man needs. Now, more than ever, he knew the value of companionship. After all, he'd have been nowhere in all of this mess without his friends. Lovely, sympathetic Molly; funny, generous Dave; and Tara: good God, she made him feel ecstatic and frightened at the same time. Ecstatic because she was the most perfect woman on the planet and, unlikely as it was, he was the one sharing a bed with her; and frightened because the romance could be so fragile, so one-way, so fleeting, so attached to this adventure which was about to be resolved one way or another. He was resigned to a disappointing conclusion regarding property acquisition. Indeed he would be very happy just to get stuck in to renovating Lockkeeper's Cottage – or Loch Cuiphur Cottage as he would have to rename it – and making the monthly loan repayments, without having to bear responsibility for a patch of Highland bog. In fact, he must have lost a considerable number of his marbles to have chased the silly dream this far. He stared at his reflection in the mirror and saw his familiar companion, Martin Minchin, accountant, with bags under slightly bloodshot eyes and a part-sad, part-anxious demeanour. Hell, he had made love with an angel! His face broke into a lunatic grin and, ready to face the next round, he opened the door and walked back into the kitchen.

'Hi.' Tara put her mug down and draped her arms around Martin's neck. She kissed him and looked him in the eyes, smiling. He smiled back, otherwise paralysed by his extraordinary good fortune. Before he snapped out of his trance, she had withdrawn and disappeared into the bathroom, leaving his senses overwhelmed by her sweet, feminine scent.

'Isn't it heartwarming?' Molly asked of no one in particular.

'Weird,' suggested Dave.

'Don't be so unkind. It's great to watch love work its magic right in front of your eyes.'

'Thank you.' Martin threw a reproachful look at his host. 'Is it a bit obvious, then?'

'Look at yourself!' Molly laughed. 'Talk about puppy-dog eyes.' Seeing his furrowing brow, she quickly made to reassure him. 'It's reciprocated,' she whispered up towards his ear.

'How can you tell?' he whispered back.

'The good old WI.'

'Huh, the *WI?*' Disturbing thoughts swam around his head of middle-aged women, discussing his private life over cups of tea and knitting.

'Not the Women's Institute, you twit: women's intuition. Besides, being a woman means I know how we work.'

'Oh.' Martin felt, on balance, a little bit reassured. He realised that he should be contributing more to the breakfast preparations. 'Can I lay a table or something?'

'Sure,' Dave replied. 'If ya can find one. Likely we'll be slummin' it on our knees, if that ain' too low down for the Dook of Cuiphur.'

'Peripatetic,' said Molly.

'Whassat, honey?'

'I thought it was a Scottish tradition to breakfast peripatetically, scoff your porridge on the move.' She saw the puzzlement on the faces of the men and continued. 'Though there's some disagreement about the reason for it. The boring people maintain that it's simply a health and fitness thing, that you eat and burn it off simultaneously. A more interesting notion is that you stay on your feet in case your neighbour decides it's time to kebab you, Celts being rather excitable and untrustworthy you see.'

'I heard that!' Tara's disembodied voice floated through the bathroom door.

'With many and notable exceptions,' Molly quickly and loudly endeavoured to extricate herself from potential conflict.

'Ah like the sounda that.' Dave stared at the ceiling, lost in thought. 'Jus' strollin' aroun' with ya chow. It don' have to be porridge, right?'

'Not as far as I know.'

'Cool. Would ya care to peripatake with me while we eat, ma'am?'

'Why ah'd be honoured, kind sir,' said Molly with an approximation of a southern drawl.

Martin watched the exchange and reckoned that his two friends would happily do together what he and Tara did last night. Now that his own life seemed so complete he wanted others to enjoy the same satisfaction; he wanted to tell them to throw caution to the wind, to stop wasting time and go for it. His natural reticence held him back and he told himself that it was really not his business anyway to encourage them or to interfere. They were old enough and experienced enough to work it out for themselves, and neither of them was what he would call shy in any case.

'Come on now, folks, don' be shy. Ah ain' cooked this up jus' for the good of muh health. Molly, honey, whaddya fancy? To eat? For ya breakfast, ah mean.'

Martin took his turn, scooping bacon, sausages, eggs, mushrooms, tomatoes, hash browns and buttered toast onto his plate. Three cafetières provided sufficient coffee to wake the dead. He followed Molly through the back door into Dave's 'garden'. It was no such thing, being rough grazing land populated by scrawny sheep and liberally strewn with big chunks of stone. The view was outstanding, barely a building to be seen; just undulating land in greens and browns as far as the horizon. A pew, at least eight feet long, was gathering moss under the kitchen window and provided the ideal spot for alfresco breakfasting. Although fine and sunny, it was distinctly chilly; the heavy, almost frosty dew on the ground reminded him that he was several hundred miles north of home. He balanced his plate on his lap and attacked its contents with enthusiasm.

Fifteen minutes later, fortified and wide awake, he was at the front of the cottage, helping Dave to manoeuvre a trailer and attach it to the tow bar on the back of the Mustang. In the trailer was a sturdy looking garden tractor, a chainsaw, various spades, forks and scythes, an aluminium stepladder, some coils of rope and a bulky tool-box.

'That's gotta be everythin' we're gonna need,' said Dave. 'D'ya wanna ride in a proper automobile?'

'Looks quite improper to me. Yes, okay. I don't suppose you're likely to do anything too frightening with this thing attached. How big did you say the engine is?'

'Just an iddy-biddy lil six-fifty twin. It's Japanese.'

'Not the bloody tractor, the car!'

'Ah, the car. Three-ninety cubes. Six-point-four Euro litres, sir.'

'Blimey.' Martin studied its shamelessly macho lines. Its vast, flat bonnet looked like the deck of an aircraft carrier, acres of space with the twin white stripes emphasising its length. From the top of the windscreen the roof maintained a briefly horizontal line before taking a long and lazy swoop to the high, cut-off tail; the slope was so gentle that the rear window, its pale turquoise tinted hue revealed clearly in the morning light, was more like a roof light. The big, black exhaust pipes, protruding ominously from beneath the rear end, exuded menace, like the big guns on a battleship.

~

It was a glorious morning for a drive through some of Britain's least spoilt land. The only other vehicles on the road were a post van and occasional Land Rovers and pick-ups; their drivers all flashed their headlights and waved familiar greetings to Dave, his car being somewhat unmistakable. Martin revelled in the deep, offbeat rumble produced by all those enormous cylinders in front of him. He loved thoroughbred Italian engine notes, particularly the shriek of a competition Ferrari V12, but there was something irresistibly macho about the basso profundo of a big old lump of

Detroit iron. Macduff paced the back seat from one side to the other, excitedly studying the passing scenery while, further back, Molly and Tara followed in Molly's Range Rover. Martin could watch their progress in his door mirror but, frustratingly, sitting in the right hand seat in this left hand drive car, his wonderful Tara was out of his sight for all but the briefest moments. He unfolded the map and studied the area where the castle was supposed to have been. Dave said that an old map he had been shown at the library indicated that there was a path or small road leading south off the one they were heading towards and that finding a trace of that was their best hope, not just to reach the site but to indicate that there had been something there at all.

They had turned into a narrow road, with no signpost to suggest where it led and no hint that it would peter out in the middle of nowhere, as shown on the map. First it descended between mossy banks under a canopy of trees, twisting through corners which required some care with the combination of trailer and large car. It ran alongside a stream for a few hundred yards before turning sharply, over a little bridge over the water, and climbing again towards higher, more open ground. They were fortunate not to encounter anything coming in the opposite direction because passing places were infrequent. Martin wondered whether anybody actually used the road at all, since it supposedly led nowhere. Now they were in wide open space, albeit still confined to the narrow road by formidable ditches on either side. A strip of grass, kept neatly trimmed by sheep, bisected what was now a surface of compacted stone.

'I reckon we start lookin' for clues now,' said Dave.

'Yes,' Martin agreed, trying to trace the route on the map. As far as he could tell, they were pretty much adjacent to the area which Dave had highlighted. 'That ditch is going to be something of an impediment.'

Dave was driving at about ten miles per hour, leaning out of his window and studying the verge closely. Macduff sensed the excitement and stepped up his exercise, panting happily. A few hundred yards ahead, on the left, a tree stood alone, windswept and crooked. It looked out of place.

'Now that's what I call interestin'.' Dave pointed at it.

'You reckon?'

'Sure do. There's always gotta be a reason for somethin' stickin' out like a cactus in the desert. Right on, man! Would you take a look at that!'

Sure enough, the tree marked a spot where this ditch ended and another started ten feet later; it was either nature's signpost or one created by man many years ago. Dave stopped the car and they studied the ground. It was all rough grassland, rocky here and there and occupied only by sheep. Towards the south it sloped gently away from them until falling out of sight. Martin thought that he could identify a subtle difference in colour, distinguishing an old track from the surrounding land, but he realised that it might be wishful thinking. If he wasn't on the lookout for it, he would never have given it a second glance.

'Weird, isn't it? Do you reckon that was a track?'

'Hell, man, ah ain' no injun scout, but that has gotta be the way.'

'Do you intend taking this over there?' Martin wasn't sure that the Mustang was a suitable mount for off-roading.

'Can't think of any good reason not to. Just keep a lookout for big holes. If we stay on the old track, we shouldn't get in no shit.' He twirled the steering wheel anticlockwise and prodded the throttle. Martin turned to look at the women through the narrow slit of the back window. Of course, Molly's car was in its element here, going where it had been designed to go – something of a novelty for the majority of such vehicles. Macduff's heightened state of excitement was now manifesting itself in an occasional whine, between huffs and puffs. Without stopping, Dave opened his door and braced it with his left foot.

'Do one Mac.'

'Are you mad?' Martin was concerned for the dog's safety.

'Nope. Happy trails!' With that, the excited hound struggled through the gap between the front seats, smacked Martin in the eye with his tail, bounded across Dave's lap and hit the ground running. Dave pulled the door shut. 'Hell, ah ain' got the energy to walk him proper.'

With Macduff bouncing happily along in the lead, they progressed carefully down the barely visible track, the ruts and humps not quite large enough to bother the car. Once they had dropped from sight of the road, the track became clearer. It was leading towards a copse, maybe quarter of a mile away.

'It rather looks as though there might be something there,' said Martin, not quite believing his eyes. Although he couldn't see anything that looked man-made, the trees and bushes were sufficiently dense to conceal a structure, perhaps even a small castle.

'Kinda remote, ain' it? Ah sure as hell wouldn' wanna try to get back up after rain. This'll be a one-way piste an' no mistake. Man, if this is it, ya'll sure be thankful for Molly's car.'

'You're not wrong. Oh, is that a bridge?' As they drew near, they could see that their path crossed a stream; a low, stone balustrade decorated either side of a little bridge which could have been ornamental were it not for the fact that the stream had quite steep banks and contained sizeable boulders. 'It's a bit narrow, isn't it?'

'Ooh boy.' Dave stopped the car and they both climbed out. 'Well, thass us fucked,' he added. The balustrades were about two feet high and the width between them no more than five feet. The copse was still a few hundred yards away and no normal car would be able to ford the stream, certainly not in the immediate vicinity. Macduff was splashing around in the fast flowing water, snuffling under the surface for things to eat or to play with or both. Molly had pulled up beside them.

'Are we getting warm?' she asked, jumping down. Tara walked round from her side and took Martin's arm.

'Well, we reckon there might be something there,' Martin said, pointing towards the trees. 'And this bridge lends credence to that. But it's the bridge that's the problem.'

'Why?'

'Cos it's a lil bit narrow, honey,' Dave butted in, talking slowly as though to a very dim child.

'Is it?' Molly continued, innocently. 'Are you sure?'

'It's jus' gotta be true,' said Dave. 'Women really cannot judge distances.'

'Huh! You know why that is?' asked Molly.

'Because men have always said that this is eight inches.' Martin held his thumb and forefinger about an inch apart.

'Oh, you've heard it then.'

'Well I hadn't,' said Tara, laughing. She tugged on Martin's arm so that she could whisper into his ear. 'If that's eight inches, you should be in the Guinness Book of Records.' He beamed.

'Can't see a damn thing except greenery. Could be somethin' in there.' Dave had taken a small pair of binoculars from his coat pocket and was training them on the copse. 'Ah'm gonna have to find another way in, from the south ah guess,' he said, spreading his map out on his car's hot bonnet. 'Whaddya reckon, Marty? Try from here?' He pointed to another minor road which led to a similar looking dead end.

'I can get over this,' said Molly, peering downstream. 'Down there it doesn't look so bad.' She was looking at a stretch where the banks weren't so steep, though the bed appeared to be uneven and strewn with big stones. 'How long will it take you to go round another way?'

'Shouldn' take more 'an a half hour.'

'Well, why don't we just throw some tools in the back of mine and all go in that?'

'No way.' Dave sounded absolutely firm. 'Ain' leavin' muh stuff here. Nah, we'll find a way, won' we Marty?' He headed for his car, leaving no opportunity for further discussion on the matter.

'Alright, have it your way. Tara and I'll go and get started.'

While Dave turned the Mustang, Martin and Tara stood arm in arm on the bridge and watched as Molly cautiously coaxed her car down into the water and scrambled up the other side. They snatched a hurried kiss and returned to their waiting seats. For a few seconds Macduff was undecided about which party he should travel with, before playing safe and choosing his master. Now aware that the track held no nasty surprises, Dave drove back to the road with rather more gusto than before. The rumbling exhausts were joined by the clattering of tools jumping around in the trailer. Back at the gnarled tree, Martin let the dog into the car and they tackled once more the sinuous return journey to the main road.

'Ah truly hope we gonna find another way,' said Dave, 'Or ya gonna have to work some on that bridge before takin' up residence in Castle Minchin.'

'Ha! Take up residence? What, in a clump of trees?'

'Maybe ya'll be allowed to build a new palace on the site. Minchin Towers.'

'With what? A lottery grant? I mean everyone loves an optimist, but we've got to be bonkers if we think we're going to find an ancient piece of paper in the middle of nowhere. Talk about the proverbial needle.'

'Makes a change though, don' it?' Dave seemed lost in thought as he casually guided the car with a couple of fingers, his left arm resting casually on the window.

'Dave?'

'Yeah?'

'Why didn't we go with Molly and Tara? What's the problem?'

'Ah, yeah. Ah wanna have a word.'

'Sounds ominous.' Martin braced himself for some well-meant, friendly, cautionary advice about the perils of falling headlong for someone who, quite frankly, could set her sights a great deal higher than him. Or maybe it would be a lecture on safe sex.

'Tell me everythin' about Molly.'

'Eh? Like what?'

'Hell, man, ah don' know. Maybe it's havin' you an' Tara climbin' all over one another, but ah'm gettin' that ol' stirrin' of the heart-strings, not to mention the loins.'

'Oh yes?'

'Over Molly, yeah? Ah know ah don' know her or nothin', but ah get the feelin' she might be on, ya know what ah mean? Ah mean, ah sure as hell am. She's a babe, man. Whaddya think?'

'A babe? Well, I think, er, under present circumstances, you know, I can't possibly comment. Though she is, of course, a babe,

I suppose. Not in the fancying way, mind. Well, not by me, as I told you before. I couldn't, certainly not now. We've always been good friends, nothing more. No, I don't think it's ever crossed my mind to, er, nor hers. No, just friends.'

'Jeez, Marty! Ah don' much care what ya think *yer* prospects are with her. Fuckin' zero ah should think; ah wanna know what ya think *mine* are. Christ, sheeit!'

'Sorry!' Martin instinctively felt protective towards Molly. His mind's eye saw her laughing face, open, innocent, generous, fun-loving, enjoying a joke, having a giggle, never being cruel, unsullied by hard knocks and let-downs. Her dad standing there, with a hefty lump of razor-sharp stainless steel in his fist. Hearing a laddish bloke, even a great friend like Dave, voicing lusty thoughts and intentions for her made him feel uncomfortable. Then he remembered her looking at Dave when she first saw him, licking her lips, a flash of lasciviousness lighting her face, exchanges of a potentially naughty nature firing between them in rapid succession. Molly needed a good fling. She had practically told him so over dinner the other night in Angelo's. God, it was like years ago. Anyway, it was her turn for a bit of a wild time, with a real man, a wild man, someone who could take her on and leave her breathless from laughter and sex, preferably at the same time. Hysterical sex. From the way she had described her colleagues and acquaintances at work, hysterical sex was simply not on the menu. In fact, heterosexual sex was a long shot. 'I think you should go for it. She likes you.'

'Now we're talkin'!' Dave perked up.

'You know she does.'

'Ah thought so, yeah. Ah jus' needed to hear it from an independent source. But ah need to know the best strategy too.'

'Oh come on! You've never needed to consult me, for God's sake. Since when have I been the bloody oracle?'

'Yeah, man, true enough. Ah always was kinda better at this. So, ya reckon I just go for it. Ooh man!'

'Yes, that's what I reckon.'

'Whoa! We got ourselves another way.' Dave applied the brakes, then swung into another narrow road, this one sporting a sign at its entrance promising the destination Archnuidh Only.

They clattered over a cattle grid and quickly climbed to a plateau, where the road ran more or less straight along the top of a ridge. Again, open grazing land stretched away on both sides. Martin tried to trace their progress on the map, but it was an inexact science and he came to the conclusion that they should strike off to the right at the first point where the ground to the north looked accessible and reasonably smooth. If they reached such a point, of course. He began to resent being dragged on this detour, just so that Dave could quiz him on his chances of getting sticky with Molly. And what about Molly and Tara? Were they alright? Bloody hell! What's the time? Is Essex on his way? He looked at the dashboard, on which two stationary hands recorded the death of the clock at eleven twenty-three at some point during the previous thirty years.

'What's the time? I think we should head back to the first place and join the others.'

'Chill, man. It's only jus' gone half eight. Hey! How about that?' Dave pointed to the ditch on Martin's side, where boulders, earth and hard-core had been deployed to provide a crude crossing onto the scrub. They could see that the road turned sharply to the left a little way ahead and started to descend quite steeply, so it was clear that it would carry them in the wrong direction from this point. There was no option except to take to the wilderness again. Dave coaxed the car gently onto the grass and steered in what seemed to be the general direction towards the copse.

'Who actually owns all this land?' Martin began to fear the consequences of trespass, assuming that not many Scottish farmers would stand for American Mustangs mingling with their livestock.

'National Park, mos' of it. Farmers pay peppercorn rents fer grazin' – so long as ya don' kill, steal, fuck or otherwise mess with their animals, they're pretty cool. Have to be, as the land belongs t'us taxpayers. Looka that.' He pointed at the ground ahead. 'This is a regular damn freeway.'

Several tyre tracks ran through the grass, dodging between clumps of heather and around large rocks.

'Do you think they're heading for our castle?'

'Search me, Marty. Ah guess we'll find out soon enough.'

'These look recent. Do you think anybody else is rummaging around for this thing?'

'Nah. It's gotta be a farmer bringin' feed up here. Time to let ol' Mac out again.' Dave repeated his trick with the door and, in a moment, the big hound was bounding ahead, diving right and left, not letting much of the ground remain unsniffed. Martin kept his eyes firmly on the unfolding view. There was the copse – it had to be – looking much the same from this side as it had from the other, but he couldn't make out the Range Rover, let alone a castle. The proportion of rocks to grass was now swinging heavily in favour of the former and Dave was finding it increasingly difficult to plot a navigable course. They came to a point where the ground sloped down into an area which looked potentially boggy, now only two or three hundred yards from the periphery of the thicket.

'Enda the ride, Marty. We can find a way in for the tractor if we need it.'

'You mean we leave the car here? And the trailer?'

'Way ah see it, we ain' gotta whole lotta options. Anyhow, who's gonna turn up here on the chance of boostin' a Mustang?'

'I'm not fussed about car thieves, you idiot. If Essex is within a hundred miles of here, this car's going to be shouting, "Spot me! Spot me!" at the top of its voice, isn't it? It's not exactly a shrinking violet. There's got to be a way down. How about over here?' Martin pointed away to his left, where the descent was gentler and the lower ground appeared to support less watery-looking plant life.

'Ah tell ya, we get stuck in there, ya doin' the pushin'.'

'Don't get stuck. Just follow me.' Martin got out, lifted a fork from the trailer and ran down the slope with Macduff skipping in circles around him, apparently mistaking the implement for a stick to be thrown and retrieved. As the ground levelled out, Martin used the fork to test its firmness and toss aside any larger stones which might present a threat to the underside of the car, which was following very slowly, voicing a low grumble. Occasionally they had to retrace their steps a little, to find an alternative way around the larger, immovable boulders half embedded in the earth.

Bit by bit, they neared the copse, which looked no less dense from here as it had from a greater distance – just larger.

'Tara!' Martin called out. 'Moll!' He looked around for a suitable place to hide the car. Vast bushes dangled floor-length branches, laden with polished green leaves and sweet smelling blossom, like a thick, soundproof curtain. Above, conifers fought for clear sky with beech and oak. Ivy struggled to suffocate everything it could cling to. Pulling some fronds to one side, he ducked into a glade which made a perfect garage; he used the fork to hold branches aloft as the car burbled through the trailing greenery, into its secret shelter. With the engine shut down and silence returned to the scene, Martin called out again.

'Here, Martin!' Tara's voice was faint, but Martin was enormously relieved to hear it.

'Here we go, then,' he said to Dave. 'Let's see what's here. I think they're in that direction.' They each took an armful of things from the trailer and set off across the thick, dry carpet of dead leaves, pine cones and bracken, occasionally lit by slender sun rays which had found chinks in the natural ceiling. Macduff had disappeared from sight but they could hear him crashing about in the undergrowth in search of playmates. They zigzagged deeper into the wood until a barrier of thistle, bramble and nettles stood between them and a glade bathed in light.

'Cover muh tail, buddy,' said Dave, brandishing a machete. 'Ah'm goin' in.' Between them, Dave slashing ruthlessly and Martin following up with a scythe, they fought their way into the open, emerging with a few minor scratches and various strands of cuttings clinging to their clothes and hair.

'Hi. What kept you?' Tara walked into view. 'My God, look at the sight of you! You boys haven't been fighting in the bushes now?' She laughed, then grabbed Martin's hand. 'You're not going to believe this, Lord Cuiphur.' She grinned.

'What?' The back of Martin's neck prickled with excitement. 'What's here?'

'Wait and see. Come on.' She led them through a narrow gap, taking care not to let leaves spring back into Martin's face. She squatted close to the ground to squeeze beneath the trunk of a tree which had fallen across the path. Martin scrambled over it.

'How about this?' She stood to one side, allowing Martin a clear view of the edifice hidden in the middle of the thicket.

In his imagination, Martin had pictured Loch Cuiphur Castle in various guises – all the way from a vast, sprawling stronghold with towers, battlements, curtain walls, keep, moat, dungeons and drawbridge, to a castellated folly barely large enough to garrison a single, tall person. What stood before him looked as though it had been designed by someone heavily influenced by illustrations in fairytale books; part château, part Schloss, part Disney, it was certainly more decorative than functional, built with romance in mind rather than war. Despite being built of stone of rather gloomy hues of dark grey, it had an indisputable charm. Its size was modest by castle standards, but generous for a family with not many live-in staff. The dominant feature was a square tower, three storeys high and topped by a small, circular room at each corner, two of these still wearing the remains of tall, conical slate roofs. A low stone balustrade, closely resembling the ones on the bridge, linked the corner rooms, which had been built jutting out from the corners of the tower, so that at least half of each was overhanging the ground. Martin could imagine Rapunzel draping her tresses from one of the little windows. Instead of hair, however, greenery sprouted from every orifice of this deteriorating monument to a bygone age. One of the corner rooms, missing any trace of roof structure, resembled nothing so much as a plant pot made on a heroic scale.

Abutting the big tower was the central part of the house, a simple, rectangular, two-storey building with large windows, the ground floor ones just gaping black holes while the foliage of healthy trees bulged from those above. There was no roof on this part, just treetops and a number of chimneys, surprisingly intact, poking forlornly skywards, like the waving fingers of a drowning person. Indeed, Loch Cuiphur Castle was losing its long battle with nature and, perhaps in another hundred years or so, it would be swallowed up, returned to its original organic state. From deep in his stomach, a powerful wave of emotion took Martin by surprise; he felt immense sadness at the sight of such grandness, such elegance decaying before his eyes, deserted by its creators and helpless against the forces which surrounded it.

'Isn't it beautiful?' Tara sighed wistfully and stared up towards the top of the tower. Martin followed her gaze, then looked back down, to his right, and then behind, impatient to take everything in as his focus adjusted and the man-made structures distinguished themselves bit by bit from the greenery – here was a little wall, there a short flight of stone steps, up there yet another conical roof, this one topped by a decorative sphere speared on a delicate spike. The stone balustrade made another appearance, this time defining the semicircular balcony which protruded from the tower in front of a fine first floor window which must have reached from floor level almost to the ceiling. Looking down, he realised that the ground they were standing on had once been terraced; perhaps it had been a genteel, landscaped garden. A narrow doorway led from the terrace into the nearest corner of the tower. Squinting against the sun to his right he calculated that this was the south side, the sunny side, the side in which the fortunate owners – the McConnellys? – had once enjoyed a life of considerable comfort. Yes, it was utterly beautiful.

'What kinda oddball put this up? Hey, Lurch McAddams, show yo ugly self!' Dave brought them down to earth. 'Okay, so where's the well?'

'Don't know. We've had a look around but there's a terrible lot that's buried deep under bushes and there's bits of fallen stuff all over the place. We're going to have to be a mite careful, else we'll be taking this place's secrets to our graves.'

'Where's that sweet Moll gotten to?' Dave shielded his eyes from the sun and looked around.

'She found a pony in the tower there. Someone's using the place as a stable. She went all soppy and took it for a trot around the estate.'

'You don't mean a wild pony – you mean somebody's pony?' Martin felt threatened by the possible presence of people other than his party, no matter who they might be.

'It's a funny sort of wild pony that ties itself up for the night with a bail of straw to nibble on. Of course it's somebody's pony. And it's left a calling card by the fireplace.'

'Terrific.' Of course, if people kept their animals here, it was hardly likely that anything of value would have lain undiscovered until now.

'It'll clean up!'

'I'm not worried about that. I mean, this place isn't exactly a secret, is it? How many hundreds of people do you think have tramped all over the place between Mary McConnelly's leaving party and our arrival?'

'There must be plenty of hidey-holes, my darling.' Tara gave him a hug. 'So let's get looking, eh? Would you like me to give you the guided tour?'

'Yes please, I'd like that.' He smiled at her eyes, then kissed them. 'This place is beautiful, you're beautiful. I'm a lucky, lucky man. Thank you.'

'You're beautiful too.' She smiled back. 'Don't ever change.' She took his hand and led him into the tower. He looked up. A little bit of daylight shone through a small hole in a stone and timber ceiling some sixty feet above, the only ceiling remaining; the intermediate floors were marked only by their fireplaces and the dark holes leading into a precipitous looking stairwell in the opposite corner. Big stone corbels, sufficiently engineered to support floors of considerable substance, protruded uselessly from the walls. The large window on the first floor was even more impressive from this perspective; Martin wondered if it had been the master bedroom. How decadent, to step from one's bed and stroll onto the balcony to gaze out upon one's rolling acres. Not that one would have much of a view with one's thick cloak of forest all around. Have to get to work with one's chainsaw; create enough fuel to keep one's fires burning for another hundred years. He looked down in time to avoid stepping in a souvenir of the pony's stay and noticed that ashes in the fireplace indicated relatively recent attempts by someone to take the chill off the place. The pony's owner providing some central heating for his or her pampered pet? Or maybe some hikers had decided to have a barbecue or a rave in ragged, stately splendour.

Tara tugged on his arm and they entered a long, narrow room which looked out onto the south terrace. Neither ceiling nor roof remained and a pair of gnarled trees climbed from the floor and groped for daylight through the first floor windows, as though someone had neglected to keep the indoor plants under control. The wall on the north side was interrupted by two symmetrically placed doorways which led into the main hall. This had once been a galleried showpiece. Grand twin flights of stone stairs, leading now to thin air, swept up either side of a lilac tree which was probably a later addition. Ivy climbed with them, like a rich green carpet. The western end of the room was dominated by a fireplace so large that it could probably accommodate the entire living room of the average modern house. Martin was amazed to be able to walk under its mantle without ducking and he gazed up the slightly crooked flue to the blue sky above. A doorway to the left of the fireplace led into the northeast corner of the tower. In the centre of the northern wall was the front door, half blocked by thistles and a tangled mess of wire and broken planks, installed at some time to deter trespassers. They went through a small doorway at the eastern end and did a whistle-stop tour of kitchen, pantry, stores, stairs and cubbyholes and an intimate little chapel with gothic mullioned windows. The more he saw of Loch Cuiphur Castle, the more Martin loved it and Tara's bubbling enthusiasm showed that she too had fallen under its spell. Everywhere were piles of rubble and broken slate, and enough indoor greenery to rival Kew Gardens' grander glasshouses. There were occasional traces of its original occupation: the carcass of a massive oak dresser which must have been purpose built for the main kitchen; a couple of bread ovens built into a wall, either side of another large fireplace; a low-roofed walk-in larder with a substantial stone slab, clearly the forerunner of the refrigerator.

Unlike the ruins of older castles, where it required some imagination and the artists' impressions in the guidebook to picture how people lived in them, here it was easy. Despite the extraordinary scale of nature's incursions onto the property, or rather her reclamation of it, it was tempting to believe that some simple DIY, the attentions of a glazier and some heavy duty hoovering were all that were needed to make the place half fit for human habitation. They made their way back to the main hall where Dave had laid out the tools which he and Martin had brought with them from the trailer.

'Come on,' Tara implored, dragging him into the tower. 'I've saved the best bit to last.' She was making for the frightening stairwell in the corner. Martin held back and stared up. The yawning holes which once led onto the first and second floors made him feel distinctly queasy; it looked about as safe as a derelict lift shaft. Some of his strongest feelings of vertigo had been experienced visiting the crumbling towers of semi-ruined, National Trust-owned castles, where even the presence of such modern safety features as sturdy railings and grilles didn't entirely allay a giddy fear of falling. Here there were no such sensible devices to protect clumsy sightseers from themselves.

'Oh no.' Martin shuddered. 'I am not going up there, deed or no deed.'

'It's alright, it's safe enough.'

'What!' He stared at her incredulously, scarcely wanting to think of her scaling this fragile, rotting pile. You didn't? You've not been up there? Please tell me you've not been up there!' Martin waggled a hand roughly in the direction of the ceiling high above them.

'It's okay – I spread my weight and I came back down by the slow route. And, I'm sorry, my darling, but you're going up there too.'

'Oh God, why?'

'To get closer to Him.' She laughed, then gave his arm a hug. 'Because it's magic, it's wonderful. You've just got to, okay?'

'Do you think it's up there?'

'Huh? Oh, er, well, with the rest of the place in such a mess, you know, I think it's an area we've got to search properly.'

'Bugger.'

'You're not frightened of a simple staircase, are you?'

'Scared bloody shitless, actually. It could all come tumbling down any second.' He gazed up. Two huge timbers and a few smaller cross beams remained in place right at the top, apparently the only support for the flat stone roof. He envisaged being rooted to the spot with timber and stone raining down on him, as in the worst nightmares.

'Come on! It's stood here for however many hundreds of years.'

'Only two.'

'Two hundred, then.'

'And a bit.'

'And a bit.' She said it through clenched teeth. 'So it's not going to come down today.'

'It might.'

'Come on!' She dragged him over to the corner and gingerly started climbing the narrow stairs which spiralled steeply clockwise into darkness. Martin followed, unable to take his eyes off her stupendously shapely bottom, tightly held in blue denim. He kept to the outside, where the steps were widest – they barely accommodated a toe where they coiled around the central pillar. With a wall to hold him in and no terrifying sight of the drop to terra firma, his fear was under control. He remained worried about what happened at the top, but he was reassured by the certain knowledge that Tara was an intelligent person, someone unlikely to take foolish risks, let alone lead a friend or loved one into danger. 'You alright?' she called down.

'Yes, no problem. Lead on.'

'I remember the last time I got this wobbly feeling in the tummy; it was when I tricked my friend Mary into doing a two-up bungee jump. That was a rare fright.'

Martin felt a sinking feeling come over him.

'I'm not sure whether it was the climb which was the worst bit,' she continued, 'or the fall.'

'Oh God.'

'What? Anyway, the fall was pretty bad, to tell the truth. But the climb – I remember it feeling like this. Uncertain, you know?'

'I thought you said you'd been up here.'

'I have. But I think that's what makes it worse the next time – knowing about some of the dodgy bits and not knowing about the others.'

'What others? What dodgy bits?'

'Oh, you know, loose stones mainly. And cracks. Like, was that crack there the last time? That sort of thing. On the jump, the rope made twanging noises as it stretched and tensed up. On the second jump you ask yourself, Is that twanging louder than before? First floor, building materials and thin air. Going up.'

Martin watched Tara, bathed in light, pass the open doorway and continue up the tower. As he neared the aperture he became uncomfortable. He had allayed his vertigo by sliding his back along the outer wall as he ascended; if he continued to do that, he would sail straight through the hole and plummet to the floor of the tower. He stared out, across to the opposite wall. Now it all seemed a great deal higher and more hostile than it had from the ground. Almost certain that he was going to be sucked out into the void, he turned towards the central pillar and gripped it with his right hand, while his left extended vertically and felt for something sturdy to hang onto. His fingers traced the edges of each step at its narrowest, smoothest, most worn point, detecting every groove and defect, as he forced his trembling legs to continue his ascent in an ungainly, crab-like fashion. Once a safe distance from the gap he resumed his previous style of semi-leaning on the outer wall as he trod carefully up, further and further, around and around. His calf and thigh muscles were aching and he was short of breath.

'It's hard work, isn't it?' He was aching because he was so tense. He wondered what damage he was doing to himself. Probably have a stroke up here; have to have a paramedic abseil him down the outside, tied to a stretcher, mumbling incoherently from a drooping mouth. No, probably just die. Heart say *Bugger this* out of abject terror. Cancel the paramedics, just lob me out through the next doorway. Second floor, cowards, sissies, unnecessary ballast, going down.

'You didn't strike me as being out of condition last night. Come on, just one more to go.'

Once more he performed his clumsy dance past a horribly inviting hole, this one even more scary than the last on account of it appearing to him to be three miles higher. He tried to reassure himself that he was really not at risk. Hell, people regularly fall off things as high as this and live to tell the tale. His nose was now hovering just above Tara's right, trainer-clad foot. Above them, some rotting wood and a few slates were all that remained of the stairwell's conical roof. So, this little corner room, right at the top of the big tower, was not a room at all – just a landing made to resemble the other three corners, which, presumably, contained proper rooms. His forearm dislodged a loose but heavy feeling object and he flinched as something large and dark fell out of the darkness towards Tara's legs. She casually caught it and pushed it back out of the way. Out of the corner of his eye he caught sight of some writing on it, large and in white: DANGER KEEP OFF. It had been daubed crudely onto some rough old timber. It resembled the battered remains of the top or bottom half of a stable door and bits of wire, some of it barbed, sprouted from its corners.

'Tara, darling?'

'Yes?'

'Have you seen that warning sign?'

'What warning sign?' She appeared to be preparing to crawl out onto the roof.

'That bloody sign! The one that says DANGER KEEP OFF.'

'Oh, yeah. That sign.' She started to crawl out, carefully testing the surface in front as she went.

'It says danger!' Martin grabbed her ankle.

'Ow! Hey, there's no need to shout. I know what it says.'

'Well, somebody's obviously put it there for a purpose.'

'Well obviously. Look, Martin, lovely darling, can we get on?'

'Well, I hate to state the bleeding obvious, but why do you think they put it there?'

'I put it there to get it out of the way, silly.'

'You did?'

'Who do you think did? Of course I did.'

'Well, where was it? I mean, out of the way of what?'

'Out of my way, of course. How do you think I got through here before? Slipped through solid matter like the ghost of my great uncle Conor?'

'Who's – no, forget it. I don't want you going out on that roof. Okay?'

'Remember, don't go out of reach of the edges, yeah? And don't stand up! If we spread ourselves out, it won't concentrate our weight in any particular spot.'

'Well that's fine, because I'm going to make sure our weight's distributed absolutely fairly and evenly on these bloody steps and not on that bloody roof.'

'Watch me, then follow.' Tara ignored his protestations. She slid slowly out through the doorway on her front, feeling ahead with her hands. Turning to her right, she clutched the perimeter balustrade with her right hand, while thumping the stone floor with her left. 'See? It's quite safe.' She edged her way along the side towards the best preserved corner room. 'And this view is going to be the best in the whole world, as soon as we've got those trees trimmed down to a reasonable size.'

Martin was sweating a little; he could feel odd drops running coldly down between his shoulder blades and wasn't sure whether they were the result of physical exertion or high anxiety. He was so used to his head scraping the clouds that Tara's prone method of exploration up here seemed to be born of admirable thought and common sense. What on earth could go wrong here? Just the little matter of the tragic, fatal plunge of two tons of stone, two rotting timbers, a slender Irish woman and a stretched accountant who evidently soiled his underpants before hitting the ground. He sank to his knees and started to haul his torso over the low ledge which separated the stairs from the roof garden. Following Tara's example he started to pummel the surface with his left fist, while wriggling towards the first corner room.

'Hey!' she shouted. 'I felt that! Take it easy on this floor or we'll be waiting up here for the mountain rescue helicopter.' She rolled over onto her back, propped her head up under an arm and stared dreamily around. 'This place is something else, isn't it? What do you think? Are these little turret things great, or what?'

'They look like something out of Grimms' Fairy Tales. What's the betting Rapunzel's still shacked up in that one?' He pointed to the room immediately beyond Tara.

'You reckon she's constipated?'

'Pardon?'

'Constipated.'

'Was that in the story? I don't recall anything about constipation.'

'It's the lavvy.'

'Uh?'

'The lavvy. The loo, Martin. Got a big old slab in there with a hole in it and a pipe leading down over the roses.'

'You're joking.'

'I'm not! They had to poo even then. And no risk of blocked drains here – the pipe's like, the pipe's big enough to deal with the worst, if you know what I mean. That's why they built these things with the towers dangling out beyond the walls – they didn't want it dribbling down the walls. Why am I telling you this? I'm sure you can work it out.'

'Molly's been up here too, hasn't she?'

'Umm.'

'Jesus, and I told John I'd take care of her.'

'She's been a very good guide, actually.'

'How's that?'

'Well, for starters, did you know that all these spiral staircases ascend clockwise?'

'Might have.'

'Want to know why?'

'Maybe.'

'Imagine you're attacking, right? You're climbing these stairs and Lord Cuiphur comes down to defend his lavvy and roof garden. Well, he can wave his sword about in his right hand, can't he? Cut and slash, loads of room. On the receiving end is poor little you. Well, not little. All you can do is flail around, blunting your steel on the stone on the inside – no room to swing it you see? And Lord Cuiphur's bearing down on you, ready to chop your head off.'

'What if we're left handed?'

'Eh?'

'Well, if Cuiphur's left handed, he's going to be coming down the stairs all over the shop, stabbing the central pillar and not a lot more. Meanwhile, I, deadly Left-hand-Lofty, can cut and slash my way up the stairs, shred his ankles. It's a little detail, sure, but one that the architects of the day overlooked.'

'You're not left handed, are you?'

'No.'

'In that case, shut up. They probably burnt left-handers at the stake, so it didn't matter.' She continued to crawl, past the well preserved privy towards the giant plant pot and stopped midway between the two. She sat up and beckoned Martin towards her. 'There we are.' She pointed out over the trees to the sky beyond. 'That will be your southerly view. You've just got to get the title deed and save this place. Just for this tower alone – it's quite the most fantastic place. I do believe there's magic here. I can sense something special. Can you?'

'All I can sense right now is my mortality.' He had reached the loo in the corner and braced himself in its doorway. He quite liked the idea of using it, if it wasn't for the fact that it would entail him hanging his bum out into practically open air a dizzying height from the ground. Having regained some composure and put most of his fear to one side he realised that there might be something in what she said. There was a specialness about the place, a benign feeling, rather than the feeling of treachery and death associated with many castles which had seen centuries of bloody dispute. Cuiphur felt as though it had absorbed the joy of laughter, not the misery of pain. Tara was absolutely right; this house deserved to survive and, with no one to claim title to it, it was surely going to submerge. Quite how he could tackle its rescue, in the unlikely event that he would be able to assume ownership, he had no idea. The only way would probably be to give it to the National Trust of Scotland, and hope that public sponsorship would meet the undoubtedly hefty fiscal requirements. Of course, the custodians of the public purse strings might regard it as beyond redemption.

'You're right, my darling. We've got to look properly for the deed. At least then we'll know we did everything we could. So, did you search up here?'

'Yes, we gave it a thorough look. It doesn't take much, you know? No loose stones, hidden nooks and crannies or anything like that.'

'Time to go back down, then.' Although uneasy about the prospect of retracing his steps down the spiral stairs, he would be relieved to feel solid ground under his feet again. He was about to start crawling towards the stairwell turret when he thought about what he would do when he reached it; going headfirst into it was a worrying prospect and the only solution was to crawl backwards to it, thus going feet first onto the steps; once safely standing on the steps, he could turn round and descend them normally. Going this way also enabled him to keep an eye on his love's progress, though he wasn't at all certain that this was a benefit. She had adopted a more cavalier attitude, standing, with both hands keeping a steadying hold on the balustrade, sliding her feet along, inch by inch. The sight of her, the precariousness of her position, brought out the worst symptoms of vertigo in him, a feeling of sickness in the pit of his stomach and an uncomfortable dizziness.

'Please, darling, be careful.'

'I'm fine.'

'You shouldn't be standing. Please get down – spread the load, remember?'

'It's already held you and you're twice the weight of me. Come on, shift along – you're holding us all up. I just love that lavvy. I wonder who the last person was to sit in there; Mary McConnelly, perhaps?'

'It was damn nearly me.' Martin reversed into the turret, feeling around with his feet and surprised to sense something moving. Instinctively he twisted around and reached out to steady himself on the doorframe but, inexplicably, he couldn't reach it – it shot away from him as he descended into the darkness of the stairwell. He looked down between his knees, not knowing what he expected to see; to his surprise, he saw some runic daubs. He nipped his tongue which was irritating, because it was such a childish, yet painful thing to do. His teeth were slamming together quite violently by the time he realised that the runes were upside-down and spelt out the now familiar message DANGER

KEEP OFF. So that's what the warning was all about: keep off the bloody stable door. Because it just bolted.

'Shiiit!' Brakes! He had to apply some brakes. Keep descending at this pace and ears will start to bleed. Or does that happen on the way up? No way could you get up these stairs at this speed, not without a rocket strapped on. Brakes? Inner wall on the left no good – just pillar and precipice. Right brake, could get right brake sorted. Bloody hell, barbed wire tearing into right calf, perhaps bring left foot over to – no! Damn near lost it there, over the back. Rather stay on vehicle, no helmet and all. Hard surface – best Scottish granite, or whatever the fuck these steps are made of. Radioactivity in granite, so they say, but that's not what makes it dangerous – oh no, the unyielding hardness of the stuff is what's dangerous. Stay aboard this board, don't munch on granite. Granite now making a nuisance at the old coccyx. You keep a knocking but you can't come in. Spine being compressed quite badly; going to be five foot nothing if we ever land. Pull that leg! Fucking barbed wire, should be illegal. Got torn jeans, bleeding leg, about to break sorry neck. Just stick right foot out now, gently, against outer wall, gradually increase pressure to decrease speed – don't want to lock up in case thigh bone forced up nostril. Must be going more than five hundred miles per hour now and still accelerating. Await sonic boom, another record for the Brits, hardy champions of all those pointless speed-chasing adventures in foreign deserts. Ha! Never mind your rocket fuel, your carbon fibre, your kevlar, your ceramic tiles and all your other space-age materials; be the first to cause the double-crack of success riding a bloody castle. So, Martin, you are the first person to go supersonic. How did that feel? Well, Parky, old chap, it was f-f-frankly painful, ha ha ha! Wonder if soles of shoes are up to working temperature, ready to deliver some serious decelerative Gs.

He was strangely detached from what was happening to him, as though having an out of body experience. The noise was extreme: cracks like gunfire as bits of wood beneath his buttocks fractured; deep, vibrating thuds as his shattering sled crashed down onto every second or third step; a terrifying screeching which at first he couldn't place but then realised was wire digging into stone at excessive speed. His peripheral vision was full of blurred stone, flailing wire, flying splinters, flashes of spark. The slow thud was his heart, the distant scream was Tara. The amazing thing about being in the centre of an accident is that you can casually watch it happening; it's as though the real world slows to your own speed, to give you just a fighting chance of getting away with it. He had been here before, the result of over-exuberance behind the wheel. The trouble was, this time he didn't have a wheel to hang onto. Never mind, he was beginning to feel pretty relaxed. The foot brake was going to work and, any moment now, his trip would be over. He extended his right foot towards the wall and grabbed bunches of wire in both fists to brace himself..

'Shiiit!' For the briefest moment the gaping hole which was the second floor doorway held him transfixed, silly bunny grinning inanely at ruthless headlights on full beam. Reverse foot, quick! Fuck it! Knee hit chin, teeth go bite, again. Gap passes by in a flash. Must be nanoseconds from death, can hear panting, heart going boff, b-b-b-boff, boffboffboffboffboff! Sweat getting worse, though blast of cold air was bracing as hazard passed without incurring penalty points. Could've been on the ground by now. Maybe not in one piece. Not much good being in a wheelchair – never see top of tower again. Not likely to in any case after application of dynamite. To tower, of course, not wheelchair. Once stable door removed from arse. Need dynamite for that too. Not going to try brakes again; next gap approaching fast. Have to lean to inside, not drift wide – wide drift means big drop. Jesus! Bum now getting badly pinched between loose planks. No doubt get bollocks impaled on two hundred year old rusty nail. I'm frightfully sorry, Mr Minchin, but you appear to have contracted a somewhat out of fashion strain of tetanus. Be sure to make a will. This ride is going to self-destruct before it ends. Wonder if anyone else ever took joy rides down here. Ms McConnelly's sprogs maybe. If she had any. No place for sprogs anyway. Look at the dangers! Falling masonry, voracious wildlife, deadly spiral slides. Death defying? Here's the first floor. *Aaarrrgh!*

It was quite neat, really: he had gone clean through the doorway without even brushing any part of it. Perfect points. The stable door was well and truly unlocked and he watched its remains gracefully part from each other as they shot towards the ground on a lower trajectory than his own. Than his own, Christ! Could he not have a second shot at this? He didn't mean to take that exit, just lost steering, helpless passenger, good afterble constanoon. Quite sober, yes. There's Dave! Hello Dave! Dave already running away, thankfully dragging his stepladder with him. Macduff also deciding to leave the catch of the century until after the first bounce. Bloody good job; probably squash the poor mutt, turn him into a hearth rug right there, in front of the fire. Save a trip to Carpet City. The garden fork which Dave had abandoned was still hovering almost vertically; Martin watched as the first remnant of his gate, carrying the vertically stacked letters A K O, sliced clean through its long handle, so shiny new that it still bore the stickers. He tried to remember everything that a Territorial Army-obsessed work colleague had repeated ad nauseum on Monday mornings following a weekend's exercises: feet together, allow knees to buckle, roll with it. The jolt took a moment to spread from his feet to his jaw when he hit the ground and he felt as though he was never going to stop tumbling. He estimated that his descent had lasted some twenty to thirty minutes, with a terminal velocity of Mach 2. He would need to hail a cab to return to the bottom of the stairs. Every part of him was hurting, but maybe that was a good sign, a sign that life still existed within his traumatised frame. He lay on his back and stared up at the roof onto which he had foolishly ventured such a long time and longer journey ago.

'Martin!' Tara was standing in the second floor gap, one hand held to her mouth. 'Oh my God, are you okay? Dave! Is he okay?'

'Of course I'm okay. Are you coming down or what?'

'Oh God.' She stared down for a moment longer before quickly descending out of sight. Martin had decided not to move, maybe not for a few weeks. He watched impassively as Tara shot past the first floor gap, happily not following his route to the ground. Macduff approached him cautiously, then plucked up the courage to climb onto his prone body and lick his face. A paw landing heavily on his balls caused Martin to scream and the dog, ears standing on end and a startled expression on his face, retreated into the fireplace.

'Holy shit, Marty, yer alive!' Dave was leaning over him. 'Stay still, man – ah think you gotta check things one at a time. Jeez, where do we start? Is there any pain, buddy?'

'None whatsoever.'

'Way to go! Ah thought ya'd checked out, man.'

'GET OFF! Of course I feel pain!'

'Okay, sarcasm, thass good. Where does it hurt?'

'It hurts bloody everywhere! I've just fallen eight thousand feet! Without a bloody parachute.'

'Martin, darling, oh God, oh no, are you okay?' Tara was approaching nervously, arms outstretched.

'*Don' touch him!*' Dave's urgent order shocked her. She froze, her face sheet-white. There was an awful pause.

'Why?' She finally asked.

'Well, he's jus' a lil bit cranky right now, darlin'. Hey, Marty, seriously now, d'ya need the paramedics?'

Tara pushed Dave to one side and knelt beside her grounded flyer, gently placing a hand on the side of his face.

'Are you hurting anywhere, darling?'

'Only when I laugh.'

'No one's laughing. Okay, can you wriggle your toes?' Bit by bit, Tara established that the ultimate helter-skelter ride had done no permanent damage, except to Dave's fork handle. Martin had escaped with grazes, cuts, bruises and a newly jaundiced view of Cuiphur's magic tower. With Tara's assistance he sat up, wincing at the pain in his buttocks. His jeans had sustained some tears at the bottom of his right leg and the blood smeared all around his ankle made the wounds caused by the barbed wire look more dramatic than they were. His heart was still hammering and he recognised the symptoms of the adrenalin rush, the thrill of getting away with something dangerous, against the odds. He wondered when the shock was likely to kick in. Post-traumatic stress disorder. God alone knew what this was going to do for his fear of heights; he would probably have to live the rest of his life in bungalows. Hell! He'd have to move his business too.

'So, did ya find anythin' up there?' Dave was inspecting the remains of his fork handle and shaking his head in disbelief.

'Just a loo.'

'Oh good. Ya lookin' like ya need one. Anyhow, ya'd best rest up while we do some more searchin'. Ah'm gonna give the ol' chimneys a look. Ah'm sure folk used to hide stuff up chimneys. Y'all take it easy, huh?'

'Yeah, Martin's not doing *anything.*' Tara's concern for Martin's condition was plain from both her tone and the still deeply worried expression on her face.

'I'm fine, darling, really. Just a bit sore.' To demonstrate his fitness, he gradually rose to his feet. 'But no more stairs today, please!'

'Well, if you're sure.'

'The well! Our best bet is to find the well. And it won't be up any stairs.'

'Yeah, right!' Dave snorted derisively. 'We got more chance o' strikin' gold. Hell, man, there's supposed to be a damn lake here too, an' we don' even got that.'

'Just you get climbing your chimneys, you pessimist. Come on Martin, darling, let's see if you're up to looking at the outhouses in the courtyard. I'll take on the kitchens and chapel.'

They followed Dave into the hall and helped him to brace the unfolded steps to provide a reliable platform from which to examine the first twenty feet or so of the capacious chimney. While Dave climbed up the steps, torch in hand, Martin selected the scythe, rake and chainsaw and headed towards the front door. He pushed past the rudimentary barrier which Tara and Molly had breached earlier and trotted down the steps from the porch. Looking back, he saw that it had once been an imposing front. One of the thick pillars supporting the portico had been fractured and pushed askew by the encroaching branch of a powerful tree. A notice nailed to the trunk of the tree instructed KEEP OUT.

The courtyard was square, with various lean-to structures clinging to the perimeter walls either side, while the two far corners were identified by large, circular huts which echoed the design of those topping the tower, right down to their weather-beaten conical roofs. Everywhere trees of varying ages conspired to make it look like an orchard, emphasised by windswept piles of blossom not yet converted to compost. He walked down the left side, looking into the remains of the sheds, stables and stores, probing the undergrowth with the rake. What was needed here were ruthless applications of defoliant; did the Americans still have stocks of Agent Orange? A modern air force has to find an income – allow some low level bombing practice in return for scrub-clearing chemicals. No, that would be antisocial. Probably wind up with three-headed sheep nibbling the grass on the terrace.

He reached the northwest corner and decided that the brambles defending that cornerpiece could wait. The gateway through which formal visitors would have entered the property, assuming that they could drive their carriages across the narrow bridge which had defeated twentieth century vehicles, was impassable thanks to more fallen chunks of masonry and a triumphantly sprawling clematis. Molly's car was parked outside and behind it more trees masked the property from the binoculars of the most committed castle hunter. Discarded on the ground was a faded, hand painted sign, warning: DANGEROUS STRUCTURE – DO NOT ENTER. Too bloody late for that!

They couldn't have asked for better weather; a lack of wind allowed the warmth of the sun to reach the ground and the only clouds in the sky were high, white and wispy. It looked, at least for the moment, as though the country's famous rain was taking a few days off. He approached the northeast hut, very much the more dilapidated of the two. Only a few slates remained on its roof and, instead of a door, there was a large hole, irregularly shaped because so many of its surrounding stones had been removed. He put the rake and chainsaw down and performed a few practice strokes with the scythe, before advancing on the tangled mess and slashing at its outer extremities.

Soon he had layer upon layer of plant trimmings lying around him, like discarded hair on the floor of a busy barbershop. He raked the loose bits to one side and set about the thicker parts of the stems, nearer to the ground. He remembered that Dave had been wearing sturdy looking gloves and wished that his own hands had similar protection. He looked down at his forearms, streaked with pink weals and spotted with blood, and imagined that he could be mistaken for a short-sighted junkie. At last he had created a passage to the entrance and, using the rake to push aside the straggling remains, he stepped inside the little room.

To his dismay it was utterly bare. A blossoming fruit tree outside the courtyard was doing its best to infiltrate through the narrow windows, the dense foliage blotting out any view. The man-made roof had long ago been replaced by one of brambles and thistles, intertwined and seemingly impenetrable. He prodded the stones in the wall, hoping that one might slip sideways to reveal a secret place, but in his heart he knew that this wasn't the place. The floor appeared to be solid rock, with no trap door concealing any Great Well. He jumped up and down a couple of times to emphasise the disappointing solidity of the ground and immediately regretted the pain it caused from his toes to the top of his head. What he needed now was a big mug of tea. It must be time for elevenses; a biscuit to dunk. He walked back into the courtyard, vaguely hoping to see one of the others, but he was on his own. There was no choice but to hack his way towards the hut in the other corner.

This one looked much the same as its twin, except that the natural barrier of thorny undergrowth was backed up by a sturdy timber door. The roof also appeared to be considerably more intact.

'Right, you bastard.' Martin took a couple of wild warning swings with the scythe. 'You want a fight?' He waded into battle, unconcerned now by the injuries which the defences were raining down on him; a few prickles were nothing compared to what the tower had tried to do to him. This time, he held the advantage. He slashed high, to take out the dive bombers, and he hacked repeatedly low, to destroy the enemy's base. Dave was obviously a serious artisan, because the scythe was scalpel sharp, slicing with ease through some very mature stems. By the time he reached the door he felt the weight of multi-pronged greenery clinging to the back of his shirt and realised that some regrouping would be a good idea before he went and kicked his way into the bunker. He stabbed the scythe into the door and used the rake to haul mounds of cuttings out of the way. A few minutes later just two strands of barbed plant life barred his way. He pulled the scythe from the door and cut through the remaining pieces.

'I take great pleasure in opening this hovel. God bless all who sail in it.' He rested the scythe in the V of two surviving branches of a wild rose, raked the final cuttings to one side, took a short run and kicked the door in what he thought might be the karate style. Once more an unyielding surface sent shock waves up his leg, this time leaving him in no doubt that he had just done something extraordinarily stupid. The door felt as though it was a trompe-l'oeil, a temptation cruelly masking a wall of solid concrete. The combination of surprise and pain sent him reeling backwards; he lost his balance and landed heavily on his bottom. He lay flat out and stared at the sky.

'Shit!' He had known that the search wasn't going to be easy, but why did it have to involve so much pain?

'Shit, is it?' A big, dark shape loomed over him, surreally inverted. Dave's chainsaw, held aloft, glinted in the sunshine. 'You and me have some unfinished business, boyo.'

CHAPTER 13: Tuesday late morning

Evans beamed. His eyes were nearly black, hooded by the matching, one-piece eyebrow. One eye seemed to open wider than the other and Martin wondered whether this was a result of the wok incident. Evans's grin was decidedly weird. Martin spun around rising to his knees, and looked up at Evans, thankfully now the right way up. He couldn't run because Evans blocked the only path; Evans-the-Massacre one way and the door from hell, the trompe-l'oeil, the other. Just have to reason with the man.

'About the wok,' Martin began.

Evans yanked on the saw's pull-start, the sudden blatter of its two-stroke motor obliterating all other sounds. He didn't look like a man in a hurry; he was laughing, throwing back his head, his pony tail swinging wildly and his tongue lapping around the surfaces of his gleaming teeth. He was saying – no, shouting – something, but Martin was too busy with his own unexpected paralysis to concentrate on lip-reading. Evans was blipping the saw's motor, revving it like a boy racer waiting for the traffic light to turn green. Martin wished that the noise would stop; if he was going to die to a din, he would prefer it to come from his own lungs than from those of the murder weapon. He could barely think, let alone warn Molly of the danger.

'Get away!' he yelled in desperation. Up there, on that bloody horse, Molly! Christ, it's only Molly. Where in hell did she come from? Great time to put in an appearance. For God's sake, read my lips! Jesus, she's cantering straight at a lunatic with a warmed-up chainsaw. Is she mental? Suicide not the best example to set to impressionable undergraduate minds. Shit! Evans had seen the mouthed warning; couldn't have heard it, surely? He was turning towards her. Oh bloody hell, don't want Molly to die. I'll miss her. As will her family. Uh oh – John will get his revenge of course: Minchinburger, served with sour cream. Susan cheerfully wading in with cooking instructions and a wicked chilli sauce. Once they've scraped up the key ingredients from around this courtyard. Molly now travelling at one hell of a lick; she's never going to be able to stop or turn at that speed. Why do fools rush in? One swipe of the weapon Evans is holding and she's going to be experiencing something close to the Godfather scene, but from a rather more dangerous perspective, considering she's sitting five feet above the ground. Five feet dangerous? Ha! Thirty thousand's dangerous; done that this morning. Evans counting on chainsaw stopping this pesky, trespassing pony. No problem! What's the pony going to do? Pull the pin from a handy grenade and lob the bomb into Evans's gaping gob? Doubt it. Surely Molly isn't intending to reason with this madman? No, not at full gallop and with that spear. *Spear?* No! Don't be daft, it's a walking stick. Big one, mind. Tree branch, really. Quite long. What the hell's she doing? Playing an unhinged baroness of Camelot? This bloke's going to kill us, Moll. *RUN!*

Molly, with a long, corkscrewed souvenir from the woods tucked up under her right arm, thundered towards the astonished men with an intent which would have had the Apocalypse Four drawing up contracts to expand into a quintet. The pony looked as though it was laughing – this was the most fun it had seen in its life. Small stones and bits of earth flew up from its dancing hooves. There was no saddle; a length of rope served as reins, while Molly's legs, slender but strong, tightly clenched the animal's bare flanks. Martin watched the next few milliseconds of action fascinated, while Evans watched aghast: the end of the makeshift lance dipped and, with the fail-safe accuracy of a laser-guided missile, struck him exactly where his immaculate black shirt stretched over his belly-button. Martin was glad to find himself back on his feet, not only because it made it easier for him to see Evans's stomach implode, but also because it meant that he might avoid being squashed in the process. Although he was now falling to one side, inevitably into a barbed bed, he was able to watch Evans's cheeks puff up like those of a cartoon character attempting to inflate an unfeasibly large balloon. Molly had released her grip on the big stick just before the moment of impact and was now fully occupied reining her charger to a halt, half in the bushes opposite the spot into which Martin was crashing.

Initially Evans held onto the chainsaw with both hands, as though it was the last toy in the shop on Christmas Eve. Shortly after the spinning teeth passed their apogee over the back of his head, and began a descent towards his lower spine, he accepted that it now represented a danger to himself and released his grip. He let out a guttural cry as it whizzed between his buttocks and gnawed into the ground between his outstretched feet, its motor now quietly idling. He landed heavily on his bottom and, with Molly's piece of tree now sailing off in another direction, continued to roll backwards over his shoulders. Martin winced as he heard a crack – was that Evans's neck breaking? Oh God! Maybe he'll be paralysed; wouldn't like to be a stretcher bearer. With a loud, hollow bang, a pair of ornate cowboy boots struck the hut's door in perfect unison. The wood shattered, barely slowing Evans's head-over-heels tumble into the gloomy interior. A deep, furious, defiant roar erupted from his mouth before his head banged onto the floor on the far side of the room. The last sounds were of his legs clattering to the ground among broken pieces of wood. He was unconscious once more. Or dead.

Martin peered through the doorway, too wary to move closer to the slumped remains of his tiresome foe. He couldn't remember extricating himself from the brambles, but his bleeding forearms looked even worse than they had before. He whirled around, suddenly worried about Molly. She had led the pony away from the hut and tied it to a bush. She whispered into its ear and stroked its mane before approaching Martin cautiously. As she walked, she pointed at the turret and mouthed questions.

'It's alright,' he reassured her. 'I think he's out cold.' He thought better of voicing the possibility of a broken neck or skull or both – Molly didn't need to worry about that sort of complication. 'I think you saved my life there. It was quite magnificent. Thank you. You were so brave. You were so stupid! You might have been killed. What were you thinking? A chainsaw beats a bit of old wood in the game, you know? Stone beats scissors, scissors beat paper, paper beats stone, chainsaw beats bit of old wood.' He finished blathering.

'Bit of old wood beats chainsaw actually.' She picked up Dave's rake, its wooden handle now in two pieces. 'And big tub of lard beats rake.'

'Oh thank God for that.' Relief washed over him.

'What?'

'I thought I heard his neck snapping, but it must have been that.'

'Oh, right.' She dropped the rake, grabbed Martin's arm and looked in at the recumbent Evans. 'Yikes. To be honest, I didn't really take in that it was a chainsaw; I just recognised the chap and thought I'd better deal with him. He's a bit slow, isn't he?'

'He is now.'

'Oh God! You don't think I've killed him, do you?'

'No, of course not. It takes more than that to finish him off. He's just having a rest. Shit!'

Molly jumped, her fingertips sinking into the flesh of Martin's biceps, to add to the other discomforts he had suffered in his quest. 'What?'

'Essex!' Martin delivered the name in a hoarse whisper. 'He must be here. Oh God. Where are the others? I think we should run. Come on – back into the house.' He grabbed the chainsaw from its resting place. 'They're not having that either.'

They were met on the porch by Tara and Dave who had either heard or sensed some commotion. Feeling too surrounded by hiding places and opportunities for eavesdropping, they gathered in a circle in the centre of the front courtyard, Martin in particular keeping an eye on Evans's hut, just in case the Welshman pulled off another Lazarus-like recovery. Apart from the pony, waiting patiently for some more exercise, there was no sign of uninvited life. Nevertheless, Martin sensed the tension in the air. Molly had the look of someone who hadn't yet come down from the terrifying high of being in a violent battle, a joust, a battle for life no less. Tara, who had the benefit, if that's what it was, of knowing this enemy, was quiet and frightened. Only Dave was exercising the down-to-earth bravado of one who had never crossed swords with genuinely dangerous villains.

'Okay now,' he said. 'Ah know that y'all be feelin' a mite nervous, but ya gotta face facts: the big guy in the hut there ain' goin' no place. Is Essex with him? No, he ain'. They'lla stopped at the exac' same bridge we did. Essex willa stayed with the car an' sent this butthead over the river to take a look-see. It's gonna be a ten minute walk to here an' Essex is gonna allow this lummox some time to look aroun'. Remember, Essex don' know whass here. He don' even know if it's the place, right? An' he don' know that we're here cos he don' see us an' he don' see our cars. Cool. What we now gotta do is slow this guy down, big time, okay?'

They approached the little corner building slowly and silently. Despite now having seen Evans felled more than once, Martin still felt scared, as though he was approaching a dragon's lair. After all, anyone who would happily slice you down the middle with a chainsaw demanded a certain amount of respect. Dave had no such worries; he practically swaggered up to the broken door.

'How y'all doin' in there, ya big Welsh gal?' he bellowed, walking in. 'Sheeit!' Evans's outstretched hands nearly reached Dave's neck, but Dave recoiled in time. Martin had armed himself with the longest piece of the rake handle and now he waved the jagged end towards Evans, not at all confident that it was sufficient to fend off the lunatic. To his surprise, however, Evans disappeared.

More accurately, one of Evans's legs had miraculously shortened, all the way up to a chubby thigh, and his head was now three feet nearer to the ground. For a nightmarish moment Martin assumed that the chainsaw was following its own agenda, chopping limbs off willy-nilly – until the silence was broken by a distant splash. Evans looked at the broken slabs beneath his substantial bulk and braced himself.

'*Help!*' he cried. 'The fucking floor's falling in!' As though to underline the statement, another piece of stone slid away and fell from sight, followed, after an eerie pause, by another splosh.

Evans had adopted a keeled-over position; one boot strained against the wall while the other dangled helplessly somewhere down the dark hole. With hands on outer edges of the floor, and arms stiffly braced, he tried to keep his considerable weight off the crumbling centre. There was no mistaking the fear in his eyes; Martin actually felt sorry for him and his instinct was to help him, before he plummeted to whatever fate lay below.

'Jeez, this dude ain' no oil paintin'. Ya got hit by the ugly stick, boy?' Dave was warming to his role as redneck tormentor. 'Hey,' he said, turning to the others, 'How long do y'all give him with the ol' congers down there? Hey, asshole! Anythin' chewin' on yo sorry lil feet yet?'

'I'll fucking chew on you, you... *please!*' His countenance morphed from anger to fear.

'Ah got no time fer yeller folk.' Dave took Martin's weapon, asking: 'This muh rake?'

'Er, yes.'

'First ya break muh bran' new fork, now muh goddam rake!' He looked accusingly at Martin.

'I didn't break the rake,' said Martin rather petulantly. 'He did,' he added, pointing at Evans.

'No shit?' Dave turned to the struggling Welshman. 'Did ya break muh goddam rake, asshole?' He leant forward and jabbed Evans gently in the crotch.

'Don't! Please, help me out!' Evans was increasingly desperate.

'Ya gotta be jokin', man – the conger eels are callin' for ya. Ya swim, fatso, or jus' bob up an' down?' He prodded Evans's belly.

With sad futility, Evans thrashed out with one arm, only unsettling another piece of stone.

'Please, Martin, Mr Minchin. Stop him. Please don't let me fall.'

'Oh, he wants our mercy now, is it?' Tara had displaced Martin in the doorway and was taking the opportunity to vent her justifiable anger at Evans. 'Not so brave without your keeper here, are you? Did you say there were conger eels down there, Dave?'

'Sure did, honey. Big 'uns. Big hungry congers.'

'Well, why don't we just make the fat eejit bleed some, then let him go?'

'Let him go?'

'Yeah, down the hole.'

While Dave and Tara filled the doorway, taking turns to terrify their captive, Molly dragged Martin back, tugging urgently on his arm.

'This is it!'

'What?'

'This is it!'

'This is what? Evans?'

'No, I mean yes, of course it's Evans, but that's not my point you idiot! The *well!*' Grabbing his hair, she pulled Martin's ear down to her mouth. 'This has got to be the Great Well of Cuiphur.

That big jerk is about to descend, God knows how far, into your, or rather Mary McConnelly's, inheritance. We've got to get him out of our way, urgently!'

'Jesus, Moll, you're right. Dave!'

'Yo!'

'Come here – now!'

Dave handed the rake handle to Tara and instructed her to push it up Evans's nose if he so much as twitched a muscle. Keeping his eyes on the doorway, he walked cautiously backwards towards Martin and Molly.

'Tara, darling,' Martin called out. 'Don't let him move, okay?'

'Oh, can't I just make him move a little bit?'

'No!'

Molly had already won Dave's attention, rather obviously Martin thought, by grabbing both of his ears and pulling his face into hers until their noses touched.

'That, in there, is the well,' she whispered, while Martin hovered impatiently beside them. 'We've got to get lardy-boy out of there so that we can search for the deed.'

'Okay, thass cool.' Dave pursed his lips and scratched his head.

'What about Essex and Monan? What if they turn up?' Martin couldn't envisage them standing by while he found the deed and delivered it back to Dr Kennedy in Edinburgh.

'If you guys can deal with Evans and take a look down the well, Dobbin and I can deal with the others.'

'Dobbin?'

'My little pony.'

'How the hell do you propose dealing with Essex? With Dobbin?'

'Yeah,' Dave shared Martin's scepticism.

'Have you not heard my Scots?' she replied, in her best attempt at a gentle highland lilt. 'I'll go see if I can be of assistance to whichever gentlemen are out there; point them in the right direction, if you follow.'

'Oh good grief.' Visions of John's cleaver swam in front of Martin's eyes. 'You can't just go and front up to Essex. He's dangerous!'

'And he's no reason to disbelieve a wee lass out for a ride. I'll tell him that there's nothing but trees here and that I've not seen anybody. If he asks.'

'Ya know, Marty boy, thass likely the best plan we got. An' ah'll tell ya somethin': thass a rare friend ya got here.' Dave nodded towards Molly. 'That gal's gonna deserve a big ol' drink if she buys us a bitta time.'

'Thank you, Dave. I'm not just a gorgeous face, you see.'

'No, ma'am. Thass a damn fine ass ya got too.'

'Well, thank you again.'

'Please, give it a rest.' Martin silenced the mutual admiration society. 'Let's just get on with it. How do we shift Evans?'

'Let me get Dobbin fired up, then I'll pull him out. Just attach a rope to the big dope and give him a helping kick or three.' Molly walked towards the pony. 'But make sure you keep the bugger down.'

'Right.' Martin returned to the doorway where Tara was using the stick to goad Evans, as though she had paid her sixpence to get a rise out of the inmates at Bedlam. He hugged her while putting a restraining hand on her arm. He addressed Evans in his best authoritative, no-nonsense manner.

'Do you want to fall into the ravenous jaws of the conger eels or get out of here in one piece? Try to give me an answer in, say, the next ten seconds.' He took the rake remnant from Tara and thumped its end down on the edge of a broken piece of stone. To his satisfaction, a chunk broke away and fell into the black void. Evans was on the verge of panic.

'Please!' He held out a hand towards Martin. 'I'll not hurt you! I mean, I'll leave you alone. Get me out of here. Please!'

'Who's with you, Evans?'

'Huh?'

'Who's with you? Essex? Monan? Don Corleone?'

'Who?'

'Yes, who?'

'What?'

'Evans! If you don't answer the bloody question now, I'll send you to the eels. Without your bloody ponytail! Where's that scythe?'

'He'll kill me, Mr Minchin.'

'Who will?'

'I can't say.'

'Oh for heaven's sake!'

'But he will. He's said so before. He'll kill me.'

'No he won't.'

'He will!'

'No he won't. Do you know why he won't?'

'No. Why?'

'Because the bloody conger eels will have eaten you. For the last time, who's with you?'

'Ess... Mr Essex.'

'Who else?'

'Nobody else. Look, *help!*'

'Where's Monan?'

'I don't know. Honest, Mr Minchin, I swear on my mother's grave.'

'Evans?'

'Yes?'

'We're not going to feed you to the conger eels. To lose something so unique would be a crime.

'Oh?'

'But you're going to behave yourself. Okay?' Martin turned to Molly. She had fashioned a harness around the front quarters of the pony from which stretched two lengths of rope.

'Help me tie loops in these,' she said, passing one end to Martin and fiddling with the other. 'Get him to put them under his arms or around his neck or whatever, and be prepared to give Dobbin here a helping hand.'

Evans's list was now more pronounced than ever. He was looking anxiously from side to side, as though trying to predict which piece of the floor was going to give way next.

'It's like watchin' the Titanic goin' down,' said Dave. 'Look at all them fleas an' stuff queuin' for the lifeboats. Gettin' that sinkin' feelin', asshole?'

'Jesus Christ, get me out!'

Martin passed the ropes to Evans one at a time and watched him pull the loops over his head and under his right arm, his left being occupied with preventing a fall. The big man was sweating profusely now and appeared to be mouthing silent messages to an unseen deity. The hole through which his leg was dangling was increasing in size and he was keeping as much of his weight as possible off the diminishing floor.

'Ready?' Asked Martin.

'Hurry for God's sake!' Evans replied.

'Okay Moll!'

Molly coaxed the pony into action and Martin, Tara and Dave all pulled on the ropes. Evans bumped and crashed towards the door as more lumps of stone and earth fell down the well. Both of his legs were now swinging over the void and only his hands, scrabbling for a grip on the surface, provided assistance to the people and the pony pulling on the ropes. Behind Evans a big hole had opened up and there was a constant background noise of earth and stones slipping and splashing into water deep below. Martin, having checked that Dave, Tara and the pony had a good hold on the ropes, went forward and pulled on Evans's outstretched arm. A few seconds later, their weighty catch lay panting on firm ground. Molly unfastened the rope from the pony, gave the assembled company a wave and trotted out of the courtyard.

Martin and Dave stood side by side, staring at their enemy and wondering what on earth they should do next. Evans shook his head and propped himself up on his elbows. Tara, the trusty rake handle back in her hand, had crept around behind him and was weighing up bits of broken door for auxiliary protection. Martin had a flash of inspiration to buy time and measure the mood of the fast recovering man at his feet.

'How many fingers am I holding up?' He waved a V-sign slowly from side to side in front of Evans's face.

'Are you winding me up, boyo?'

'No, of course not. I'm worried you might be concussed.'

'Yeah, man,' Dave agreed. 'A knock like that can do bad stuff to folk.'

'I've taken worse than that. Haven't I, Minchin?' He was beginning to exude menace again. Martin struggled not to look at Tara who, in the background, had retrieved a sturdy plank and was taking a practice swing.

'So you don't mind it when your head collides heavily with blunt instruments?'

'It doesn't worry me, boyo.' He grinned and lumbered to his knees, brushing bits of dirt from his trousers and jacket sleeves.

'Good. Hit him, Tara.'

Holding the plank in both hands, she swept it through a horizontal arc and caught him a perfect blow just behind his right ear. For a moment he knelt there, not moving, his upper body upright and his head lolling over his left shoulder. Then he crumpled, like a collapsing house of cards, his head falling into the dirt between Martin and Dave's feet.

'Homer!' shouted Dave. 'Awright!'

'Quick!' Tara said, dropping the plank. 'Tie the bastard up – he's got a nasty habit of recovering.'

'We're going to have to hide him too,' said Martin. 'Somewhere he can't be seen or heard. Do you reckon we can cart him into one of those huts up the side there? Come on, Dave – grab his other arm.' With an arm apiece the men hauled on the inert body, moving it about a foot with Evans's rotund stomach dragging along the ground.

'Holy shit, he's a big boy, ain' he?' Dave rested.

'I'll take his legs, ease the weight a bit.' Tara clasped an ankle tightly under each arm and leant back. After ten minutes of clumsy manoeuvring, they reached the shallow threshold of the shed.

'Okay,' said Martin, panting. 'This is the final hurdle. Ready?' He and Dave heaved on the arms; Tara strained to lift the legs higher. Martin looked at her across their burden. 'Okay?' he asked.

'No sweat – oh!' She shot backwards, a shocked expression on her face and an empty cowboy boot tucked under each arm. Evans's feet hit the ground as Martin and Dave stumbled back into the hut. Tara was rolling in the yard, laughing hysterically. She recovered her composure and studied the footwear dangling from her hands. 'Brilliant! He'll not be hurrying anywhere with just his socks on his feet. We can lose these down the well. Perhaps congers like cheesy snacks.'

'Congers, my foot. Where on earth did that idea spring from?' Martin didn't know a great deal about fish, but he was pretty sure that conger eels lived in the sea.

'Sure got him heated, didn' it?' Dave grinned, then heaved again on Evans's arm.

Five minutes later, Evans was ensconced inside, curled up and tied hand and foot as securely as they could manage. Martin would have preferred to see him held by chains and maybe a concrete overcoat, but the one rope had to suffice, as they would need the other to investigate the well. They finished off the rudimentary prison by piling some of Martin's more prickly undergrowth cuttings in the doorway, both to hamper Evans's escape and to hide him from prying eyes.

'Tara, honey, did Molly leave her car keys?'

'Yeah, I've got them here.'

'What do you want with Molly's car?' Martin was perplexed; searching the well was his priority.

'Okay, jus' how deep do ya figure this is?' They were back at the corner hut and Dave pointed at the remains of the floor inside.

'I don't know. It sounded as though it might be quite deep.'

'Quite deep, okay. So, we're gonna need more than an ol' bush to swing from.'

'What are you suggesting?'

'We tie the rope to the car. Should hold me. Tara, hun, would ya be so kind as to put the car jus' the other side o' the wall there, an' fasten this to it. Tight as ya can.'

Tara took the rope and ran off through the gateway. Martin and Dave knelt cautiously by the hole in the turret floor, prising loose the most wobbly bits of stone in silence. Martin tried to recall Dave's exact words.

'Dave?'

'Yo.'

'You said something about – I think...'

'Still listenin', buddy.'

'Holding you. The rope holding you.'

'Sure did. When ah go down this hole.'

'You're not going down this hole.'

'Ah'm not?'

'I know my way around these wells now,' Martin staked his claim. 'And you are a little, how should I put this? Overweight?'

'Overweight? Don' bullshit me, man! Ah'm in peak physical condition. There's never been anyone more sleek. So help me, ah'm goin' down the damn hole.'

'But you don't know what to look for or where to look for it, whereas I do, having found the first one. And, being slimmer, I'll be able to manoeuvre better down there.'

'Yeah, right. An' I guess ya'll be wantin' me an' Tara to hol' yo sorry ass up outta the water?'

'Tara's not holding anyone's arse but her own up out of the water.' They turned to see that she was already fastening the rope around her waist. 'Who's the lightest? Me. Who's the slimmest? Me. Who's got just as much experience down these wells as any other here present?' She cocked an eyebrow at Martin, daring him to disagree. 'Me.' She pulled the rope over the wall until it was taut. 'Now, do you boys want something else to take the strain as well as your tender hands?'

'That tree.' Dave capitulated immediately, indicating a crab apple by the wall. 'C'mon, Marty, sometimes there ain' no arguin' with 'em.' They tossed the rope over the tree on the third attempt and yanked it down to ground level. 'Still wanna go, honey?'

'No question. Sit down over there and please hold on tight.' She picked up the torch and approached the hut. Martin sat with his feet straddling the doorway. Tara stepped carefully between his legs and kissed the top of his head. She put the torch down by one of his feet and lowered herself backwards through the hole. 'I'm relying on you,' she said. 'Hold me, won't you?' She took the torch in her right hand, gripping the rope with her left. Martin leant back, taking the strain on the rope, as she descended out of his sight.

'You okay, Marty?'

'Yes. So far so good. We're going to need some more rope though.'

'You got it.' Dave fed some slack rope to the tree, enabling Martin to feed it, inch by inch, to Tara.

'Tara darling, can you hear me? Are you alright?'

'I'm fine. I need some more length.' Her words sounded as though they had bubbled up from beneath the water's surface, an effect of her voice spiralling up the well's narrow funnel.

'Hey, Marty, ain' that what ol' ginger...'

'Shut it Dave! Just shut it and do as she says.' As Dave fed more rope around the tree, Martin passed it through his hands into the void in the turret.

'Whoa!' Tara's shriek had Martin pulling urgently on the rope. 'Sorry! The water's cold. Hold still.'

Martin braced himself once more.

'Right,' she continued, 'There's no sign of anything yet – no shelves, no hidden panels. I'm going to have to go into the water. Give me another metre.'

'Are you sure you're alright, darling.'

'Yeah. Just a bit. H-h-holy m-mother! Cold. A bit more.'

Martin fed a few more inches through his fingers and turned back towards Dave.

'Ah got three feet, then ya got no more,' Dave said. 'Sounds like Tara's chillin' down there.'

'You're not kidding.'

'Okay, buddy, hol' on real tight, cos ah'm out.' He pulled on the remaining slack until the last few feet lay between the tree and Martin's hands, then got up, sauntered over to the doorway, stepping over Martin's legs, and looked down into the well.

'Is she okay?' Martin asked.

'Damned if ah can see, man, but ah think her head's still above water. How ya doin', honey?'

'Fine, thanks.' Her voice sounded so distant to Martin. His hands hurt, as did his legs; an all-over aching as though he was in for a bout of serious influenza. All you need. Straining to suspend the love of your life above icy waters and killer fish and along comes the big germ, trying to weaken your grip, sap your strength. You're not getting me, you bastard. Would tighten grip if possible. Fingers too numb. Blood from scratches on arms has rendered trousers useless for all but gardening. Thighs desperately need exercise. Just like when you've been sitting at your desk for too long with your legs folded stupidly around the base of your chair; the pain suddenly presents itself, Helloo, how are you today? You have to leap up and perform a frantic war-dance around the office, tripping over phone wires and bringing things crashing to the floor. Same if cramp gets you in the night – scream house down. If the cramp doesn't get you, the stubbed toe will. Leap up now and splosh goes Tara. And her lovely nipples, and clever fingers and tight, hard-working, miraculous fanny. Oh God this hurts. Might have to let go. Hell of a way to dump a girl.

'Chill, man.' Dave was squatting at his side. 'Yer haulin' on that like there's an elephant on the end. None too flatterin', Marty.'

Martin looked down at his hands; through the rusty, sticky trails of blood he could see clenched white knuckles. Sweat was pouring from all around the top of his head, dripping off his chin and running down his back. He realised that a fraction of the effort he was investing would be perfectly adequate. There was no need for pain or for deep reserves of great strength. He had succeeded in wearing himself out, completely unnecessarily. He relaxed; Tara didn't fall to her doom and his aches vanished. It helped that Dave had taken up part of the load.

'Go take a look, buddy. Ah've gotten hold here.'

Martin rose slowly to his feet, relieved to feel his blood start to circulate normally again.

'Don' go too close to the edge now.'

He absorbed Dave's cautionary advice and lay down on his front, wriggling forwards until his upper body was through the door and he could hang his head over the opening in the floor.

Light from the torch was bouncing and flickering, reflecting off each ripple in the water and each damp facet in the stone wall.

'Hello darling,' he said softly into the gloom. The beam met his eyes for a bright second, before returning to its examination of the well's interior.

'Hi. Come on in – the water's lovely.'

'Really?'

'It's f-f-f...'

'Freezing, yes. Come on out – let me have a go.'

'No way! Now, can you remember what you were feeling about for when you found that casket?'

'Yes.'

'What?'

'You.'

'Think! I remember you saying that you felt something.'

'Wasn't that the gun in my pocket?'

'Behave!'

'Sorry. I hurt my leg on a bit of jutting metal. And the box slid out of the wall. A stone fell! Then the box. I don't think the metal spike had anything to do with it.'

'Right.'

'So what do you reckon?'

'I reckon there are no loose stones above the surface. How much more rope is there?'

'Can we give her a bit more, Dave?'

'Comin' up.'

'I don't think you're going to be able to see anything under the water, are you?' Martin was speaking down the well again.

'I'm just trying to feel for things, you know? Something out of place, something loose, whatever. A bit lower?'

From Martin's vantage point it was difficult to judge her progress, to see exactly how deeply she had descended into the water. The sudden sound of her spluttering and spitting was a better indication.

'Pull up, Dave! She's drowning! Tara darling, are you alright?'

'I'm fine.' She was panting, regaining her breath. 'Phew! Hey, your water here doesn't taste at all bad. Oh my God!'

'What?' Martin envisaged a ferocious freshwater conger. More spluttering sounds rose to the top. 'Tara? Darling? Speak to me!' The reassuring light from the torch had been extinguished and he felt a rising sense of panic.

'Ugh, sorry.' Martin breathed again at the sound of her voice. 'There's a hole down there. God, it's cold. I'm afraid Dave's torch isn't waterproof. Wherever it is now. Damn, I was hoping to see into this. It feels like a shelf. I can get my feet in there a little. Can you lower me a bit more?'

'More?' Martin turned towards Dave.

'No can do, man. She's got the lot.'

'There's no more, darling. I think we've had it.'

'No way! I'll turn turtle. If you don't hear me in sixty seconds, start pulling.'

'Wait!' It was too late; the noise of splashing suggested that Tara had gone in head first to investigate her shelf. Martin stared as wide-eyed as he could into the gloom, but he was unable to make out a thing. He could barely imagine what it was like down there, in the cold, black water. 'Come on, Dave, let's pull her out.'

'Cool it, man. Give the gal a fightin' chance. Another few seconds.'

Martin gazed down. He could see nothing and there was now an eerie silence.

'Now!'

'No, man!'

'Are you bonkers?' Martin started to grapple with the rope, ineffectually thanks to his prone position.

'Hey, cut that out you guys!' Tara spat some water out of her mouth. 'I think I've got something, but I need more rope. Can't you give me a little more?'

'Absolutely not,' said Martin smugly, pleased that she couldn't risk her life any further.

'Okay then, make sure you hold it exactly where it is, so I know where to find it.'

'What do you mean, "know where to find it"?' Martin didn't really need to ask the question, as the rope twitched from some activity at Tara's end of it. 'Do not remove that rope!' His tone, one that he recognised, nevertheless took him by surprise; he had just turned into his father.

'Well you can spank me later.' Tara must have caught a sense of it too. 'I'm perfectly safe, as long as I know that the rope's here, okay?'

'I'm not sure.' A plopping noise suggested that she had gone beneath the surface again and that further protestation was pointless. What if she didn't come back up? They couldn't haul her out – one of them would have to go down and try to retrieve her. How would Harry take it? Sorry, my friend and saviour, all I wanted was a lift to the ferry and I've somehow gone and got your daughter drowned down a well in Scotland. Never mind, eh? And I wanted to marry her too! That's two of us pissed off then. Ha ha. No, Harry will go berserk. Have to stay on the run, like a supergrass. Tricky thing to disguise unusual proportions; maybe get corrective surgery done, like a foot out of each leg, six inches below the knee, six above. Wind up looking like a bad impression of Toulouse-Lautrec: too much torso and slippers worn on the knees. Might as well go down there myself. He sleeps with the eels, they would say with a knowing and reverential nod.

'Aargh! Blegh!' Tara startled him. 'I think I've got something.'

'What? I mean, you must come up now – it's too dangerous. And not worth it.'

'Not worth it? What do you mean not worth it? Of course it's worth it you eejit!'

'Not worth your life, my darling.'

'Well I grant you, there's nothing worth that. But I think I've found Mary's hidey-hole.'

'You're joking.'

'I am not. There's some big loose stones in there, put there I reckon. I've shifted two; just got to be careful not to send anything important to the bottom. Another couple of dives. Just get my breath.'

'Are you...'

'I'm fine.' The sound of a blown kiss floated up to him and he returned one.

Once more Martin heard the sound of his beautiful Tara submerge. What a girl, a heroine, an absolute babe. Aquababe, hee hee, Buoyant, Clever, Diving, Eel-busting, Feminine, Gondola. Gondola? Wrong location. Going to have to kick this silly habit. It's a compulsion, a semi-superstition, like saluting magpies. Angst inducing. Will we ever reach Z? Do pigs fly?

'Got it!' Tara gasped fresh air into her lungs. 'Hold on, just got to tie it...'

'What? What is it?' Martin was hanging dangerously over the edge.

'It's a box, another box. Wait a sec.' Her words were punctuated with sounds of panting and splashing. 'Okay now, pull it up. Carefully! It's not too secure there, and I don't want it coming back down to put a dent in my head.'

Martin slithered backwards out of the turret and rose to his knees. He grabbed the rope to slow Dave's enthusiastic retrieval of whatever Tara had attached to it. It suddenly dawned on him that Tara was still in the water, with nothing to help her stay afloat; they were removing her only means of escape.

'Stop, Dave!' He craned forward again towards the hole. 'Tara? Darling? Are you alright? Do you need the rope?'

'I'm okay. But please get a move on.'

'Right. Come on Dave. She needs the rope back.' He began hauling with renewed urgency.

'Fast, slow, stop, go. We got some mushroom management goin' on here.' Dave's muttering was interrupted by a thunk, the sound of something solid snagging on the jagged edge of the hole. A couple of small pieces of stone were dislodged and fell into the void.

'Hey! Watch it up there!'

'Oh God! Did it hit you?'

'Just get the box!'

Martin eased the box out from where it was trapped and pulled it away from the edge of the hole. He quickly untied the rope and threw it back down.

'Rope!' he shouted a warning, before turning to Dave. 'You ready to pull her out?'

'No sweat, Marty. Why dontcha get the box open, huh?'

As far as he remembered the appearance of the first casket, this one was very similar, but it was heavier – very heavy for its size. He assumed that it was full of water and shook it, placing an ear against it. There was no sound. A small padlock, which he tugged at ineffectually, secured the contents. He grabbed a stone and struck it, succeeding only in skinning two of his knuckles.

'Hell, Marty, hit the goddam thing where it's gonna hurt some. That's only rotten ol' wood there.' Dave continued to pull the rope up, hand over hand.

'Right.' Martin turned the box over, revealing what he hoped was its soft underbelly. He picked up a larger, sharper edged stone and brought it crashing down onto the flat, dark, wet wood. 'Shit!' Fully expecting the box to cave in, he was surprised to find the stone bouncing off it with a dull thud, barely making an impression.

'Send a boy to do a man's work,' Dave grumbled. 'Here buddy, pull ya gal outta this hole. I gotta key for that thing.' He and Martin completed a clumsy waltz in which the burden of holding Tara changed hands once more. Martin wondered what the key might be as Dave carried the box away to the clearer ground of the yard behind him.

'Is it the deed?' Tara reminded Martin of her presence.

'Don't know. Can't get it open.'

'Well, keep pulling, because I won't be finding anything else down here except pneumonia.'

'I'm pulling!' Martin heaved more determinedly on the rope. Even if ownership of Loch Cuiphur Castle fell into the hands of the state, nothing could take away his small place in its history. What was more, he was no longer coasting, as he had been. Now he had a purpose: he must ensure that he and Tara stay together, that they find mutually agreeable objectives and pursue them. They could go anywhere, do anything. Whatever she wanted. To hell with accountancy. He continued to pull until a small, very white hand appeared over the edge, followed by another and then Tara's head, framed by shining, crinkly ribbons of black hair, dripping with water. He pulled harder and she braced her arms, carefully levering the rest of her body up onto firm, dry ground. She lay still on one side, regaining her breath as she untied the rope from around her midriff. He was about to suggest that a rug might slow the approach of hypothermia when the calm was shattered by the shrill noise of Dave's chainsaw.

'Oh shit,' said Martin, swivelling around in time to see his friend approaching the box with the steely confidence of a well-equipped and ruthless interrogator on the scent of something big. '*No!*' he shouted uselessly, convinced that the contents of the box were about to be destroyed. The whirring teeth slowly closed in on the lid. Martin and Tara both scrambled to their feet and ran towards the treasure which had proved so challenging to locate. The narrow, rounded end of the saw glanced off the surface in a shower of yellow sparks. Dave took a step back and placed the idling machine on the ground. Martin selflessly placed his body between Dave and the box and inspected the damage. The saw had gouged a strip in the wood to reveal a metallic layer beneath.

'It's lined with metal.'

'Lemme see.' Dave knelt beside Martin and looked closely at his work. 'That's lead, man. It's lead-lined – waterproof, see? Thass why the lil thing's so goddam heavy.'

'We've got to break this padlock off. Won't your saw do that?'

'Sure. Stand back.' Dave picked up the saw and revved the motor. 'This is gonna reduce its value some.'

'I don't care – I'm only interested in what's inside it.'

'Ah'm talkin' about muh saw.'

'In for a penny, eh? Get on with it.'

'Okay.' Carefully, he pushed the end against the lock's curved hook. There was another shower of sparks and a brief screech of tortured metal as the lock flew apart. Dave killed the motor and put the chainsaw back on the ground. 'Ya'd best open the box, Marty.'

A feeling of great anxiety had come over Martin. It was as though everything was about to turn to dust, that it was downhill from here. The first two numbers revealed in the lottery were his but the rest were going to disappoint; his coupon had six of the eight score-draws; using the NO envelope to enter the Reader's

Digest contest had been the wrong strategy. He looked up. Tara was stunning, her wet clothes clinging to her slender frame, nipples pointing provocatively at him through her T-shirt. What if the damn thing was empty? He felt ashamed that she had undergone such an ordeal in order to find this box just for him. And it would prove to be a wild goose chase, of course.

'Thank you, darling,' he said sincerely, looking up at her with what he realised must be a fairly soppy expression.

'I didn't do it for you, you eejit – I want to know what's in the box.' She looked down at him with her eyebrows arched, an expectant and encouraging smile on her lips. After a second or two of inactivity, her expression changed into the slightest of frowns. 'So open it!'

Martin jerked back into life and pulled the lid open. Nestling in the deceptively small confines of the casket's cosily protected interior was a roll of yellowing paper tied with a narrow black ribbon. He slid the ribbon off one end and carefully unfurled the sheets.

'Thif Deed,' he read. 'YES!' He jumped up and punched the air. Tara wrapped her soaking arms around him and he buried a kiss in the cold, tangled wetness of her hair.

'An' here comes the cavalry,' said Dave.

Molly trotted up to the group and jumped lightly down from the pony.

'Have you got it?'

'We have.' Martin beamed.

'Oh my God, Tara, look at you!'

'There's water in his well.'

'You don't say. Where's the big chap?'

Tara tossed her head in the general direction of the wall behind her. Molly misinterpreted the signal and the colour drained from her face. She placed a hand over her mouth, looked towards the well and stared from Tara to Martin and then to Dave, who read her thoughts and hastened to reassure her.

'He's trussed up good in that ol' hut over there,' he said, to Molly's obvious relief. Evans chose the moment to regain consciousness and make his presence known with one of his guttural roars.

'Oh my God!' Molly jumped.

'Curious, ain' it?' Dave looked puzzled.

'What?'

'Welsh. Curious language. An' how did ya get on with the other one, darlin'?' He turned his attention to Molly.

'Oh Christ! Yes, we've got to move – quickish.'

'Who did you see?' asked Martin. 'Was it just Essex? Any sign of Monan?'

'Just Essex. He's alone, but I think he was talking to someone on his mobile. Has this chap got one? A phone?'

'Hey y'all, relax!' Dave interjected. 'There's no goddam signal in these parts – the dude's gonna have to find a phone booth to talk to anybody and thass gonna be a long drive in any direction.'

'All the more reason he's going to be sniffing around here any minute then, looking for his mate. Now, he thinks I'm a local lass and he doesn't know Dave, so I reckon we ought to go in my car and delay him. Martin, you and Tara can take the deed in Dave's car and just head for Edinburgh. Essex isn't going to see you going out that back way.' She looked around. 'What do you reckon?'

'Alright Dave?' Martin looked at his friend.

'Sounds cool.' He pulled his keys from his pocket and lobbed them to Martin. 'Not a scratch, man.'

'Would I?'

'The brakes kinda need a firm foot, okay?' Dave motioned with his right leg.

'No problem.'

'She plows in the slow corners.'

'Slow corners. Ploughs. Okay, I think you mean understeers.'

'Steerin's more assisted than ya'll be expectin'.'

'Deep respect.'

'Well come on!' Molly tried to inject some urgency into the meeting.

Martin looked at Tara, sure that he noticed her shiver.

'Are you going to...'

'I'm going to Edinburgh. Come on.'

'Dave! What about your stuff?' Martin pointed at the chainsaw.

'Ya've broke most of it, man. Later!'

~

Martin took Tara's hand and they ran towards the house. He pushed the papers from the casket into his back pocket and patted it every few seconds to check that they were still there, as though the castle's grounds were overrun by invisible and highly skilled pickpockets. They skidded through the big hall, under the grand staircase and out onto the rear terrace. He tried to remember the direction from which he and Dave had originally approached the building. Tara took charge and crashed through a rhododendron, dragging him in her wake. They zigzagged through the undergrowth, Martin squeezing Dave's car keys painfully hard, certain that they would fall into a bottomless pit if he so much as thought about relaxing his grip on them. He patted his back pocket again. In front of him Tara ducked under a low branch; he followed suit, but not deeply enough, a fierce bang on the top of his head adding to the catalogue of injuries this place had rained down upon him. Perhaps it was jinxed, a hex upon all those who enter. I been hoodood. Abracadabra, Bewitch, Chaos, Darkness, Evil.

'Where's the car?'

'Eh?'

'Where's the bloody car?' Tara was shaking him. 'You look like a zombie.'

Brilliant! Short-cut straight from Abracadabra to Zombie. This woman can cut it! Where *is* the bloody car? Good question.

'Hid it.' He looked around in a panic. 'There!' A glint of loud paint gave away the Mustang's rudimentary shelter. They ran to it and stripped away the camouflage. 'Come on!' He wrenched open the door and dived into the seat he had occupied earlier. Where's the bloody hole for this key? Where's the bloody steering wheel? Tara flopped into the seat on his left and slammed the door.

'Let's go!' She grabbed the steering wheel. 'Shit!' She looked over at Martin, who was stabbing the air in front of him with the ignition key. 'I've got this. Gimme that!'

'We better swap.'

'*Gimme that!*' She grabbed Martin's wrist and prised the keys from his fingers. 'Let's just go, yeah?'

'Yeah. Good.' He pulled his seatbelt on, realising that Tara was no more likely than he was to damage Dave's precious pony car. 'Put your belt on.'

'Yeah, okay. Macduff!' The dog's face had appeared at Tara's window, a look of bemusement creeping into his normal expression of perpetual happiness. 'Better get in,' she said, opening her door. Macduff bounced across her lap and wriggled his way between the seats into the back. Tara turned the key and prodded the accelerator pedal. The V8 rumbled into life at a volume which Martin was sure would be heard by everyone in Scotland – felt too, probably, pulsating through the soles of their feet. Macduff gave an excited yelp. Martin stared through the windscreen, worrying that he might not recall the route across the scrub to the twisty little lane that led to the main road. He picked the map up from where he had left it on the floor and looked across at Tara. She was waving her hands in the air while staring down at her feet.

'Shall we go, then?' Martin asked.

'Only two pedals.' At first Tara spoke calmly and slowly. 'Where's the clutch?'

'No clutch. Automatic.' Martin leant over and gently touched her knees, right then left. 'Go and stop with this, as usual, and this one does nothing.'

'Gears?'

Martin pointed at the lever sprouting from the console between their seats.

'Put it in D.'

Tara yanked the selector back and released the handbrake. The car lurched forwards.

'Hey, this is easy! Where do we go?'

The grass was still flattened from Martin and Dave's arrival a few hours earlier and, as Martin tried to point out potential hazards, Tara twirled the steering wheel from hand to hand, retracing the tracks. Their style of departure from Loch Cuiphur Castle was considerably more urgent than the cautious approach which Martin and Dave had adopted; once clear of the longer grass and on the higher, firmer ground, Tara drove quickly and confidently, belying her brief experience of such an unfamiliar car. Martin felt pleased to be a passenger – he knew that he would have been a good deal more tense had he taken the wheel.

'Holy Mother of God, what's that behind us?' She was throwing panicky glances in the rear-view mirror. Martin's heart was suddenly racing. Could Evans have freed himself? Had Essex managed to get his car over the stream and around the castle? He turned awkwardly in his seat, only to have his view blocked by Macduff's happy face. Macduff licked his nose. He pushed the dog to one side and peered through the sloping glass, only to see the top of Dave's tractor bouncing around.

'I can only see the tractor.'

'That's what it is. It's in the trailer, is it?'

'Yes.' Martin wondered where else she might think it was. 'Was there something else?'

'No, that was it.' She steered a course around the large rocks and followed the tracks towards the road. 'Shall we get rid of it?'

'What?'

'The trailer. It's going to be a bit of a bummer dragging that thing all the way to Edinburgh.'

'We can't just leave it. That tractor's got to be worth a few hundred quid. It's Dave's workhorse – he'd kill me.'

'Okay.' They reached the road. 'It's your choice. Left or right?'

'What? Oh, left. Is it a problem? I mean, towing it. I can drive.'

'Me too. I've towed bigger things than that you know. I once pulled a seven-metre caravan right over the Wicklow mountains.'

'Wow. Well, I bow to your superior skills.'

'It's not what Dad said, I'll tell you.'

'Why?'

'The damn thing slipped its collar on a steep bend. There was I, thinking I'd got a bit of extra power from somewhere while over a tonne of caravan's careering backwards down the mountainside, shedding bits of itself all over the county.'

'And it was your dad's caravan?'

'Hell no! It was mine.'

'So why was he upset?'

'He was in it, sleeping off a lunchtime session. It was his worst ever hangover.'

'Was he alright?'

'Oh yeah, he was thrown clear – he managed to swim to the shore, but most of it sank.'

'Swim? Sank?'

'Oh, I didn't say? There was a lake in this valley. It was really nice; picturesque. Well, perhaps not with bits of white caravan bobbing about all over the surface. I felt I was a bit of a vandal.'

'Quite the litterbug.'

'I'll try not to lose this one then.'

'Yes, that would be for the best.' Martin studied the map. The route was pretty simple: once out of this little lane they had to follow a twisting B-road for a dozen miles before joining the main road south to Edinburgh, some way north of where they had enjoyed dinner the previous night. He wondered whether Molly and Dave would be ahead of them or behind. Essex was probably still wandering around, searching for Evans. Evans was certainly going to receive the rough end of Essex's lisping tongue. Mind you, Essex had been deceived by Molly. Monan was going to give them both a pasting. Wherever Monan was. They pulled up at the T junction and Martin pointed right. Tara pushed the accelerator pedal down into the rubber matting and the rear tyres yelped before she lifted off again, to apply a more prudent amount of power.

'I like this car,' she said.

'So does Dave.'

'It's fast.'

'Yes.'

'It's a shame we've got to haul that thing around.' She jerked a thumb over her shoulder and Martin assumed that she was referring to the trailer, rather than Dave's beloved pet.'

'There's no hurry. I mean, what's the time?'

'Just gone two-thirty.'

'Oh. Well, that's still plenty for us to get to Doctor Kennedy by closing time. How are we off for petrol?'

'I have no idea. Wait, is that it?' She pointed at a gauge. 'Half. Is half enough?'

Martin didn't know. He pushed a finger under his bottom to feel, again, the precious paper in his back pocket. Next he probed a front pocket and pinched a wad of notes. If they passed a petrol station he could bung twenty or thirty quid's worth in. What would it take? Being a sixties machine it would presumably want all the lead it could get. On the other hand, being American, it might well have been converted to run on the emasculated pump gas that all yank-tanks had been compelled to drink. No, he couldn't imagine Dave reaching for the green hose – full-fat LRP it would have to be. He looked across at Tara. She was relaxed, in her element, guiding this powerful behemoth through the corners with the lightest of touches on the steering wheel. She threw him a wink and a blown kiss, only taking her eyes off the road for the briefest of moments.

Perhaps he needed a bigger car – enough of this accountant's professional stinginess. What use is a measly thirteen hundred cubic centimetres when you can have real American inches? Alfa? Ha! American Motors, Buick, Cadillac, Dodge, Edsel, Ford. Edsel Ford! What a name to be saddled with. What was Henry thinking? Edsel! What a monument to have to one's name. Now, if there was to be Minchin progeny, there would be no such silly names. But, to follow the alliteration route or not? That is the question. Whether 'tis nobler to be, er, Martin Minchin Junior? No. Malcolm. Malc. Double-no. A girl! Loads of opportunity here, surely. Melanie, that's nice. Melody. Hmm. Mary. Uh oh, quite contrary. Tara will want to honour her dad. Hell, I'll want to honour her dad. Harry Minchin. Harriet Minchin. Wonder how Tara feels about kids. Could ask her. Better not. Want this relationship to last longer than a week. Ask her on our anniversary;

anniversary of meeting. Saturday. Blimey, that's a long way off. She's adorable. Adorable, Beautiful, Cute, Déesse, Exquisite, Fwooor. Perhaps that didn't count.

'Martin, my darling?'

'Yes?' Wow – darling. Yes!

'Oh God.' The car shuddered. Martin sensed that something was wrong with the car. Perhaps it was running out of petrol.

'What's wrong?' he asked, placing a calming hand on her shoulder.

'That car back there.' She looked in the mirror. 'It's Essex.'

'No!' Martin snorted, partly in derision, partly in awful fear. He turned to look through the rear window again. Even Macduff was unsettled, ears back, tongue inside his mouth for once. A dark blue BMW was weaving from one side of the road to the other, close behind the trailer.

'He bloody hit us! Did you not feel it?' She was clearly frightened. Their speed had increased and she was now attacking the corners with some aggression, the exhaust note rising and falling rapidly as she danced on and off the accelerator. Martin looked from her to the blurred vehicle beyond Dave's following tractor. If it wasn't Essex, it was a pretty pushy way of driving. The trailer took another knock. It must be Essex.

'Okay,' said Martin, thinking on the run and fingering his back pocket again. 'It's this deed he's after, not us. No need to panic.'

'He's going to kill us to get the deed.' Tara spoke slowly, loudly and clearly, as though addressing a very elderly relative. 'I think there's every need to panic.' There was a tremor in her voice.

'Yes, I do see your point.' Martin allowed a strategy to develop in his head. 'Best keep him behind us.'

'You keep him behind us! What do you think I'm doing? Looking for a nice spot for a picnic?' The trailer drifted wide on the exit of a bend, pulling the Mustang's tail out of line with it. Tara turned the wheel into the slide and floored the accelerator, successfully keeping the whole tyre-squealing show on the road, albeit on the wrong side of it. The BMW's nose sniffed its way up the left side of the trailer before Tara rudely slammed the door on it. 'Shit, Martin – we've got to lose this bloody trailer, else we're never going to be in Edinburgh before this bastard.'

Martin was bracing himself, with his right hand gripping a vinyl-upholstered grab-handle on his door and his left around the back of Tara's backrest. He peered through his window at the door-mounted mirror and tried to focus on the following car. He imagined for a moment that Essex was wielding some sort of shotgun, but then the mirror disappeared and he realised that he must have been mistaken. Oh bugger!

CHAPTER 14: Tuesday afternoon

'Go, Tara, go!' He turned to look once more through the rear window. It was a shotgun; double-barrelled, over and under, just like one which had once left his upper body black and blue after an afternoon's clay pigeon shooting. Essex was alone, steering with his left hand, shooting with his right, hanging out of the window like a Hollywood stuntman. Hanging out of the window of Beverley's car.

'That's my car!'

'What?'

'It's my car. He's in my car. Beverley's car. *It's my bloody car!*'

Strictly speaking, it wasn't Martin's car of course, but then strictly speaking, Beverley's car shouldn't be carrying a murderous outlaw who is apparently intent on assassinating the car's moral owner.

But this wasn't Hollywood; Martin and Tara were in serious danger. With the pride of Dave's gardening kit hanging off the back of the Mustang there was no chance of them outrunning a determinedly driven BMW. Bet it does thousands to the gallon too, unleaded as far as he could remember. It's got air conditioning, fresh air filtration – could use some of that, the way Macduff's responding to the peril – even got a multi-CD job in the boot, but no Beatles CDs. It's got airbags too, which the Mustang certainly doesn't. Those are the bastards that explode in the faces of unsuspecting accident victims; have a little contretemps with a hedge, next thing, you're concussed by a hundred cubic feet of PVC balloon. That's funny. Can't see out of the back window any more. Macduff's cowering on the floor behind Tara's seat. Glass has gone all shattered, just the way windscreens used to do when hit by the smallest of pebbles. Providing your speed was high enough.

'Martin!' Tara was yelling.

'I think I've got an idea.' He tried to sound in control, like Michael Caine at the end of The Italian Job.

'It better be a good one or we're toast.' She was wrestling with the wheel, competing against the trailer to see who or what had the most influence over the car's direction. 'Jesus, Martin, he's shot the back window!'

'I know,' Martin shouted. 'Don't worry.' He unfastened his seatbelt and clumsily squeezed his body between the front seats until he was in the back, giving the shivering Macduff a reassuring pat. He lay across the rear bench and looked up at the rear window, an opaque mess of crazed little shapes. He shielded his eyes with an arm and kicked up against the glass. It felt as though all of it fell in on him – it was hailing tiny pieces of pale turquoise. An area of about a quarter of the window had opened up. He kicked again and again, then used a road atlas to brush away remnants of glass from the bottom edge of the window's frame. Placing his hands on the top of the rear bench's backrest, he peeped out, in the manner of the old chad graffiti: Kilroy woz ere. The BMW had dropped back a few yards and Essex's attention was divided between watching where he was going and fiddling about on the passenger seat beside him, perhaps reloading the gun. Martin pulled out all the available length of his seatbelt and coiled it around his left ankle. He patted Macduff on the head and showed him an erect index finger.

'Stay,' he said. 'Good boy. Tara, darling?' He now had to shout above the increased road roar and the Mustang's thundering exhausts.

'Yeah?'

'Try to keep a steady speed, stay in the middle of the road. Don't let him past, or alongside. When I say 'go', step on it, okay?'

'Okay. Whatever are you doing?' She swung around, then back again just in time to tackle the next corner. Martin didn't need to wait for the next part of the conversation – it was now or never. Suddenly the lateral motion of the car appeared to him to be seriously energetic. He knelt on the rear bench, his knees far apart for stability. He looked back at Essex, who met his gaze with cold, expressionless eyes. He leant forward until his chest was flat against the backrest, his head now out in the airstream flowing down from the roof. He eased his torso out through the empty window frame, bringing his feet up onto the bench, the left one thankfully still tightly tethered. He tucked the fingers of his left hand under the base of the window and took a headlong dive over the car's boot towards the tarmac whizzing by below. Gravity took over and, for a second, he was certain that he was about to meet his maker under the combined wheels of the trailer and Beverley's car. The seatbelt and his tight grip on the window frame arrested the slide, but he was almost entirely outside the car now and feeling more vulnerable than ever. By raising his head he could glimpse Essex struggling to find a way past the swaying trailer. Judging by the way the white lines on the tarmac below were weaving from one side of the car to the other, and by the way he had to brace himself, Tara was defending her place like an unprincipled grand prix driver. He looked down at the union of trailer and car. The ball hitch was mounted on a sturdy steel plate, the electrical umbilical cord plugged in alongside. Pull the plug out first – no need for the bastard to receive too many signals of our intentions. Martin wrenched the plug from its socket and dropped it, letting it bounce along the road. He grinned at Essex. No brake lights now, ha! Try following that, you thad barthterd. The nose of the BMW nudged the trailer again; the Mustang wriggled, its tortured tyres howling. Hmm. Hasn't exactly fazed the man. Martin grasped the handle over the coupling and pulled furiously. Nothing budged; the trailer maintained a fierce grip on the tow bar. It was going to take a small nuclear explosion to separate these two. Must be some kind of fail-safe mechanism – as long as there is a pull on the coupling it can't be freed. But if there's slack?

'Come on, you wuss!' Martin bellowed at the following car. 'Call that driving?' He didn't think for a moment that Essex could hear him; he could barely hear himself. But all it needed was a nudge. 'What's the matter? You chicken?' He was yelling as loudly as his lungs allowed. The trademark chromed grille on the BMW's prow approached the back of the trailer, bobbing this way and that, like the feints of a nervous but fleet-footed boxer. Yes! Just a bit more, Mr Thtoopid. It fell back again. Damn. Come on, Essex, man or mouse? Quite suddenly, the car lunged and hit the trailer with a loud crunch. Martin heaved up on the handle with all of his strength. The BMW had fallen back twenty feet or so as Martin felt the handle, so heavy now, swaying at the end of his arm. Christ! He let go – it was as though somebody had fired the trailer backwards from a cannon. For a split second it kept travelling in a straight line before suddenly turning broadside and flipping over, tractor and all, in an explosion of noise and sparks, bits of wood, plastic and metal flying in every direction. Essex had nowhere to go but into it.

'Touché!' Martin enjoyed a brief glimpse of the shocked expression on Essex's face before it was obliterated by a colossal white balloon. As the road swept through a bend, the BMW, its front end crumpling every bit as progressively as the advertisements promised, continued straight on, pushing a pile of rolling, tumbling junk before it. This rapidly deteriorating train had barely slowed when it took off across the grass verge, smashed its way through the top portion of a five-bar gate and disappeared from view behind a tall hedge.

The relief provided by Essex's sudden departure was brief as Martin came to terms with the problem of returning to the inside of the car. Getting out had been relatively easy; now he had to fight gravity, backwards. His right hand was gripping the steel ball of the tow hitch but his arm was tiring and it would be all too easy simply to slide off the end, take one's chances on the tarmac at five hundred miles per hour. Motorcycle racers get away with it. But motorcycle racers wear protective clothing. And lots of them die anyway. He looked down at the black exhaust pipes, poking so wickedly from the back of the car, singing their deep, sonorous song. He could feel the heat rising from them. The rhythm slowed, the rushing tarmac became less blurred, the brake lights were shining red. Thank God – Tara's stopping.

'Martin, darling, are you alright?' She ran to the rear of the car and squatted down to be level with his head. 'You maniac. You could've been killed!' She tenderly held his head and kissed him. 'Are you sure you're okay now?'

'I wonder if you could just give me a hand here. No – in there. I've got my foot trapped in the seatbelt. It's beginning to hurt slightly.'

She opened her door and climbed into the back, letting the dog out. As she struggled to free the leg, Macduff jumped around excitedly at the back of the car, treating Martin's face to happy, congratulatory licks. As he felt the seatbelt relax its grip, Martin slid carefully down onto the road and wiped his damp face. Tara reappeared beside him.

'We got rid of the trailer then,' she said.

'We did.'

'And Essex.'

'Yup, and Essex.'

'Will Dave's tractor be okay? Do you think?' She looked at him as he slowly shook his head. 'Oh dear.'

'I think I may have killed Essex.' Martin couldn't extinguish the vision of Essex sailing into the field, his head deeply buried in airbag.

'Do you want to go back and check?'

'In case I need to finish the job?'

'No, you idiot!'

'I know.' He laughed. 'The trouble is, he's still got his gun.'

'That's true.'

'I mean, after what we've just been through, it would be a bit daft to just go and hand ourselves over to him.'

'You're right. We'll use a call-box, anonymously. Ambulance.'

'And an armed response unit.'

'Yes, and one of those. And Dave could report his trailer as stolen.'

'You're a devious one, aren't you?'

'Yeah, so watch it, mister.'

They retrieved Macduff from a damp and smelly ditch and climbed back into the car. As Tara started it up and set off, Martin looked around it; there was a carpet of tiny chunks of glass all over the back-seat and footwell and now Macduff had added a generous coating of dark, pungent mud, or worse. The rear window was open to the heavens and the right side door mirror had been decimated by lead shot. And then there was the little matter of the flagship of his landscaping fleet now scattered over half an acre, plus a dead trailer, a blunted chainsaw, broken fork, broken rake... it wasn't yet mid-afternoon and Martin had put his friend out of business.

'He's going to go ape.'

'Dave?' She raised her voice to overcome the wind noise and the exhaust now booming through the back window.

'Yes. Absolutely ballistic.'

'You don't think he'll understand?'

'Understand what? In a matter of hours we've destroyed him. Worse than that – we've destroyed his car.'

'Oh, this'll fix up.'

'Fix up?'

'Do you not think it will?'

'It's a sixties classic! You'd have to scour California just to find a replacement mirror. Where's he going to find an aquamarine rear window? Not in bloody Inverness he isn't!'

'It still goes nicely.' She gave an apologetic shrug of the shoulders and fed in some more power. 'Perhaps we could make him an offer for it.'

Martin checked again the presence of the deed in his pocket and sat back, staring at the sky which was rendered an extraordinarily vivid blue by the deep band of tint at the top of the windscreen. Thank God that he had witnesses to the events of today, otherwise there wasn't a person on earth who would believe the story. Give young Detective Constable Dee something to chew on. Vandalised cottage? You ain't seen nothing, matey. I'm on the run in a kick-ass motor having just left for dead a kingpin of the Merseyside underworld. Let's see: Beverley's BMW must have been worth twelve grand before meeting its maker, add in a grand for Dave's trailer and contents and what – two? three? – to put this machine back into the condition it had shown off this morning. All told, it was a fair amount of damages, and that wasn't including the cottage.

The car had rumbled over a cattle grid and was passing through a hamlet, little clumps of old houses passing by on either side. He spotted the petrol pumps at the same time that Tara saw the telephone box.

'Get the petrol first and then phone, yeah?' Tara looked across at him.

'Yes, phone and put as many miles as possible between us and this place. Here, give me the keys.' He stepped out and peered at the rear wing, hoping to see a filler cap. Nothing. He casually walked around the back, hoping that no one was witnessing his obvious unfamiliarity with the car. Nothing on the left flank either. Damn! He squinted at the rear end, then muttered through clenched teeth, through the gaping opening in the back. 'Can't find the bloody filler!'

'Isn't he the silly one, Duffy-baby?' Tara stepped out and gave each side of the car a quick inspection before flipping open a fat round badge in the centre of the rear panel to reveal the filler. 'There you go, my darling. Do you need a hand with the pump? It's that red tube thing over there.'

'Thank you, I'll be fine.' He fetched the nozzle, placed it in the hole and squeezed the trigger. It was an elderly pump and its delivery was arthritic. Instead of speeding around in a blur, the pennies were racking up at a leisurely rate that enabled him to take in his surroundings. A jovial looking, middle-aged woman walked onto the forecourt from a workshop alongside the little office.

'Good day,' she said, looking Martin up and down. 'It's a fine afternoon for being out.'

'Yes,' he agreed. 'Certainly is. Lovely!'

'From London?' Her eyes were lingering on Martin's torn, blood-stained clothing and his scarred forearms.

'Gosh, no!' He laughed. 'Wiltshire. Just up here inspecting undergrowth. You know, flora and fauna.' The woman looked at the car, her gaze now settling on the hole where the back window had been.

'This is Mick Dawson's car, isn't it?'

'Who?' He wasn't sure that he had heard her correctly.

'No, this is *Dave* Dawson's car.' Tara came to his rescue. 'I'm his cousin, Tara. From Ireland.' She demurely held out her hand and the woman shook it quickly, as though it was transmitting electric shocks. 'We're staying over for a bit.'

'Oh that's nice. Looking for wild life?'

'Yes.' Tara gave the woman her biggest smile. 'Macduff's showing us all the best spots,' she said, nodding towards the hound who was now standing with his front paws resting on the top of the rear seat back, his head enjoying the freedom afforded by the lack of glass.

'Och, get away!' She frowned as though not quite sure of how to take these strangers with the familiar car and dog.

Martin gave up pumping when just over thirty pounds' worth had been dispensed and replaced the nozzle in its holster. He pulled some change from his pocket and offered it to Tara.

'Why don't you call cousin David, darling, while I settle up here?'

'Okay.' She grinned again at the woman. 'It was so nice meeting you.' She turned and, as she walked towards the telephone on the opposite side of the road, the woman's eyes narrowed even further. She had just become aware that Tara was thoroughly damp.

'Couldn't resist a dip,' Martin explained, handing the woman some notes. 'Saw the loch and in she went.' The woman stared at Martin with her mouth open. 'Like a fish, she is; very keen swimmer. Born with gills, ha ha.' The woman inspected the money, shaking her head. Martin followed her into the office and selected some chocolate and a tin of travel sweets from the little display unit on the counter. The woman totted up the prices, occasionally throwing Martin a suspicious look.

'Shame she doesn't eat fish food really. Much cheaper than confectionary.' He offered her a weak smile. She slammed the till shut in what he thought was a rather pointed manner, so he thanked her politely and retreated to the car. As he was holding the keys and Tara was talking on the telephone, he decided that he might as well have a turn behind the wheel. He wriggled his long legs either side of the steering wheel and groped under the seat for an adjustment lever. Once satisfied with his position he fired up the engine and drove to the edge of the forecourt. The fuel gauge needle had climbed to a little over the three quarters full mark. Tara replaced the receiver and ran over to the car.

'Fancied a go, did you?' she asked, settling beside him.

'Yes, if that's okay. How did you get on?'

'I think I put the fear of God up the poor operator. They're probably sending in a helicopter gunship even now.'

'Yes, well I wouldn't be at all surprised if that woman puts the police on to us too.'

'Why?'

'I think she could smell something fishy.'

'Oh well, maybe we can get to Edinburgh before word gets out.'

Martin selected D and trod on the accelerator. The car sat back on its haunches and took off down the road with a yelp from the rear tyres. He stuck his left elbow through the open window and kept the lightest of touches on the wheel with the ends of his fingers. His right hand sought out Tara's left and held it, resting on her damp jeans. They could be cruising down the Pacific Coast Highway, Beach Boys on the radio, surf crashing on the shore. Or McQueen: he was McQueen, as Frank Bullitt, leaping off those San Francisco hills. Right car too; just need some funky wah-wah guitar and a big black Dodge to chase. With the right props one's straight into character. Move over De Niro; make way for Method Minchin. Quite a name. More alliteration, but he could live with that. Was Method a boy name or a girl name? Perhaps it didn't matter. Look at all those successful people who were blessed with alliterative monikers. Wow! This is a challenge: Arthur Askey, Benjamin Britten, Charlie Chaplin, Doris Day, Eddie the Eagle. Well, perhaps they weren't all brilliant successes. They approached a big roundabout; Edinburgh at three o' clock – decent road all the way now. He navigated cautiously around to the exit and waited until the car's snout was pointing straight down the outer lane of the southbound dual-carriageway before burying his right foot.

'Way to go!' shouted Tara, throwing her head back and laughing.

'Yeehaw!' Martin replied. The Mustang was gathering speed at a phenomenal rate, trailing its V8 cacophony behind it. There was the briefest pause, a slight dip in revs, as the automatic gearbox slid from intermediate to top. Martin looked at the speedometer; the needle was vacillating either side of eighty. In the rear view mirror he could see Macduff, still perched with front legs over the boot lid, watching the overtaken traffic vanish into the distance. Martin sent up a quick prayer that the dog wouldn't spot any rabbits. That would be the last straw. About Macduff, Dave; perhaps you better sit down. A sign flashed past, indicating that they were seventy miles from Perth, a bit over one hundred to go, then. They must have over ten gallons on board so, even at ten miles to the gallon, they were going to get pretty close to Dr Kennedy's office. And, if he kept to seventy-ish overall, it was less than an hour and a half away – a little before five, if they were lucky. It was going to be tight.

The Mustang was a mixed blessing: its fearsome presence in a rear-view mirror was sufficient to clear a path without recourse to headlight flashing and gesticulations; on the other hand, it was no shrinking violet – if the police were looking for it, they wouldn't need a magnifying glass. Add to that the outlaw look, thanks to the damage inflicted by Essex, and a soundtrack which, while tolerated in the deserted highlands, was going to turn more than a few heads in the genteel capital city: they might be better off taking the park-and-ride option.

Tara was doing a good job of feeding them both with energising chocolate while Martin wrestled with the arguments for and against running a gas guzzler. Every time he saw the fuel needle drop another fraction, he granted Alfredo a stay of execution. But then the seductive beat of all those cubic inches under his right foot yanked him back across the Atlantic.

'Alright, babe?' He couldn't help slipping into the vernacular.

'Just fine, honey,' she responded in character.

'Sorry. It's the car. Are you drying out yet? You'll be lucky not to get pneumonia.'

'What's a bit of wetness to a colleen from the Emerald Isle? I'm drying. Just a bit tired.'

Martin squeezed her hand and she snuggled into her seat. She was a remarkable woman – talk about calm under pressure. Surely most women would have crashed the car at the first bump, let alone under gunfire. Idiot! Most *people* would have crashed the car. He would have crashed the car. But he didn't, he made the other guy crash his car. Wonder what the Institute would make of that. Certified Accountants aren't encouraged to indulge in road-rage, let alone the sort of carnage he had wreaked. No, damn it, Essex wreaked it all by himself. If he was now lying in an ambulance, or on a slab, he had only himself to blame. He just picked on the wrong people. What does that mean? Is there an Institute of

Certified Tough Bastards? Oh yes, that'll be the Brotherhood of Receivers and Liquidators. Don't wish to join that, thank you very much; rather be an estate agent than one of those.

So, what does an accountant do with a Scottish estate? Monan reckons that a fortune is to be made from the water. A career spent perusing the books of successes and failures should give one a head start, shouldn't it? Say it costs, ooh, a quarter of a million to set up, a loan over ten years at thirty thousand a year and annual overheads at, say fifty thousand? Ha! More like a hundred thousand. So we need revenue of one hundred and fifty thousand a year to make it worthwhile. And the practice bills fifty in a good year. That's a lot of water to shift. Assuming that it fetches ten pence per litre at the factory gate, that's ten litres to achieve a pound. So we've got to sell ten times a hundred and fifty – one-and-a-half million one-litre bottles of water a year! Take just one thousand bottles out of that well and you'd be scraping the mud off its floor surely.

Maybe accountancy isn't so bad. Yes it is! Just try wandering up to a person like Tara – her a perfect, beautiful, artistic, free spirit and you an accountant from Shimbley, middle-England – say, hey babe, you and me, how about it? I'm an accountant. Hmm, have an idea what the response will be. Why do castles in Scotland always have to interfere in one's love life? Or cause one's love life? Bloody hell! Ah, but there is a difference, and a very important one: Tara didn't know about the castle. So what? She's going to want to move on. She's here because of the common enemy, Monan. Now that Monan's been thwarted, she can go home. Carry on painting. Oh God, to have the talent to do something like that. Some people paint, some make things, some can even play saxophone. How does mental arithmetic stand up in this company? Hey, babe, do you know the cube root of six dribblydwillion? No, mine's a small, sweet sherry, thank you. Gosh, I like that shade of beige.

Going to have to put some serious money into Lockkeeper's Cottage. How much is that going to cost? First job, have one of those big twirly-back cement mixer trucks in the garden, pump the bloody well full of concrete. Remove the farty old wall and roof, drill a hole in the centre of the solid surface and install a rotary clothes line. I say, Mr Minchin, why on earth do you have a concrete base for your washing line? Because I've got lead-lined knickers – much better sealing, don't you know, when one's had to shit oneself.

Only got a little money, scattered around sundry building societies and insurance companies; last of the carpetbaggers, one of the many thousands of junior shareholders in half a dozen of Britain's more recently floated enterprises. Liquidise the lot and be lucky to see ten grand. That includes the 'untouchable' rainy day practice fund. What practice? Be amazing still to have one after this absence. Clients queuing up along the pavement, catered for by Mehmet. You lookin' for the money-man? You got more chance seein' the Loch Ness bloody monster sailin' up the river 'ere. Burglars come, taken everythin', burnt down 'is 'ouse an' all. 'e's probly topped 'imself. Even 'is ol' wife gone missin'! Holy shit! Beverley! Don't want to see her for a while – couple of decades maybe. If she's survived. Would have put money on her outmanoeuvring Essex and Evans; should have had them for breakfast. Obviously didn't though. Christ – what did they do with her? Should have asked Evans before hauling him out of the well. Too late now. Wonder if he's extricated himself from that hut yet. Wonder if he ever gets headaches. Wonder where Dave and Moll are.

Martin couldn't remember what they had arranged, if anything, in the way of a rendezvous. Were they all to meet at Dr Kennedy's office? He felt the papers in his pocket again. No matter – he was going to go straight there anyway, assuming he could find it again. Shouldn't be too difficult. Tara was asleep. Even Macduff had deserted his look-out post in favour of sprawling across the rear bench. Martin had rolled his window up but there was still a late afternoon chill, exacerbated by the unwanted air conditioning. He played with the heater controls until a gentle warmth began to creep up from beneath the dashboard. The miles rolled on under the Mustang's fat tyres and he longed to flop once more into that soft bed, to entwine himself again with titillating Tara, his princess of impropriety. Will you marry me, Tara, my darling, please? Just as soon as I'm free to do so of course.

~

His eyes fell upon the sign quite by chance, high up on the dark granite wall: Dundee Walk. At last! He was thinking about losing his temper, getting so close to Princes Street before being pulled in the wrong direction, the city's one-way system working like a malevolent gravity field wrenching him from his chosen destination. As he had stumbled from street to street, slowly looking for clues from the forest of signs, cab drivers had hooted, pedestrians had stopped and gawped, buses had threatened to finish the job started earlier by Essex. Even the busker, in full tartan kilted regalia and accosting the ears of passers-by with the interstellar calling card of bagpipes, had looked down his nose at him and smirked. It was the car. How did Dave put up with it? Dave wouldn't notice. In any case, the last time Dave was behind the wheel, eight hours ago, he knew where he was going and his car was immaculate. People admire immaculate, smirk at gauche and gaudy. No entry, eh? It's only another bloody one-way street. What are the chances of finding Dundee Walk's in-door before nightfall? Zero. There goes patience: it got on its bike and was last seen pedalling furiously in the direction marked All Other Routes. Bang it into reverse – yeah, yeah, fuck you too, arsehole; remember Culloden! Oops, that's woken both passengers.

'What's happening?' Tara sat up and tried to regain her bearings. Macduff took up his vigil at the rear window.

'Macduff! Sorry, could you see if you could entice him away from the window? I want to reverse down here.'

'It's a no entry.'

'It's a short cut.'

'Okay.' She rattled a sweet wrapper and the always hungry beast deserted his post instantly. Martin, twisting around and trying hard to ignore the cramp in his neck, made a mental note that ergonomists must have been less highly rated than stylists in sixties America. The car weaved drunkenly backwards down the narrow street, veering from pavement to pavement. After two hundred yards, Martin had had enough. He slowed and eased towards the kerb on Tara's side. When the tyres squeaked against it, he stopped and turned the engine off.

'This is it, then.' He looked at Tara, a stupid smile on his face. He felt completely and utterly light-headed. It would appear that he had the necessary papers with which to claim ownership of Cuiphur Castle; on the other hand, it was such a surreal idea that he was unable to contemplate it with any gravity. Added to which, what the hell was he going to do with it?

'You're frightened, aren't you?' She took his hand.

'I think so.'

'Because you don't know what you'll do if this thing actually comes off?'

'Yes, I suppose so.'

'I guess you've just got to roll with it, see what happens.'

'But you, I mean you and me.' He waited.

'Yeah? What about you and me?'

'You know I love you.'

'Yes. And I love you too.'

'Jesus, do you really?' He didn't want to question it, but he simply couldn't stop himself. 'Why?'

'I heard you were coming into a bit of real estate in Scotland, so I decided to have your babies.'

Ohmigod babies! Babies? She pregnant? Already! Hey, babies! The Minchin twins, Harry and Method. Going to have to work on that second name.

'I'm going to hold you to that, Lady Cuiphur.' He leant over and they kissed, tongues lazily entangling, lips nibbling, teeth crunching – blimey, that's a new one. Where's she gone? That hurt. Lip's cut. She seems to be sucking the gear stick. Which is bleeding profusely. Odd. Something on nose. Hello, looks like gun barrels, side by side; old fashioned shotgun. Pressing painfully hard, actually, into one's nose.

'Suck on this, you lucky, lucky shit.' Monan looking quite manic, knuckles white, eyes staring wildly, slightly askew. He had Tara's door open and was half in the car. 'The deed.' He twisted the gun, pushing it until Martin could hear the sound of crunching gristle inside his head. He felt the cold, sharp metal cutting into his skin. Macduff's reaction startled Martin as much as it startled Monan. It started with a determined snarl, teeth bared, aiming for the gap between the front seats. Good boy! Monan tried to swing the gun barrel as Martin ducked; the weapon thudded against the head rest, unleashing an almighty bang – Armageddon in these confines. Macduff whimpered sadly as smoke and the smell of spent cartridge filled the car. Martin snatched the tin of sweets from the top of the dashboard and flicked it, like a frisbee, straight into Monan's right eye. The lid flew off and a shower of sweets and icing sugar was added to the interior decor. Sirens sounded in the distance, or was that just a ringing in the ears? Bugger this, get out of the car. Monan was struggling to pull the gun's barrels from between the seats; good thing he hadn't shortened them. He wants to empty the other one now.

Martin pushed his door open and threw himself onto the road as the car's windscreen exploded outwards. From his vantage point, lying on his back in the middle of the road, he watched the close-knit clump of black shot out-accelerating windscreen fragments against the bright blue sky. Sirens were getting louder and he woke up to the risk of being run over. Being run over by the Old Bill of Edinburgh. He felt his pocket – it's still there. Run! What, from the bastard who's just killed Tara? He peeped over the bonnet; Monan was standing on the pavement, fishing around in his jacket pocket for more ammunition. Martin looked up and down the disappointingly deserted street; the sirens were louder still, but there were no reassuring flashing blue lights. Got to stop him from hurting Tara any more.

'Hey, Monan – guess what I've got!' That got his attention. Better go for it.

It must have been a small stone, lodged in a crevice in the sole of his shoe, which gouged the deep, ten inch long valley in the much-lacquered paint on the car's bonnet, or hood as Dave called it. Martin had no time to inspect the damage as he skated over the glossy expanse of steel, because Monan was slamming the gun shut again. Martin half slipped, half fell past Monan, succeeding only in jogging his arm severely instead of flattening him. Typical! One's only chance to save what's left of one's skin and one misses. One should have played more rugby at school. At least the bastard's dropped his gun, clumsy idiot. Just a couple of strides now to the good Doctor's front steps. Fuck, that hurt. Shouldn't be kneeling here; got to get on. Why isn't that bloody leg working? Bloody's right! The stuff's everywhere. Tara? She can't have bled this far? Got it all over my jeans, soaking, sticky, wet. Shit! Left leg not willing to contribute in this moment of dire need. What's Monan up to? Can't make it out; bloody eyes failing now. He's shouting like crazy. Woozy with pain. A nice bit of kip is what's needed now. Doze it off. Sirens could wake the bloody dead. Touch pocket. Hey, yes! Fish it out, just deliver it to said address. Haul this distressed carcass along the pavement. There's the imposing dark blue front door. Why the steps? Bastard architect. Have to make it, deliver this precious parchment. Monan's not having it. No thanks, no signature required; just ensure that the Registrar knows who delivered it. It's Minchin. M for step one, I for step two, N for step three, C for step... shit, what was that? Shot whistling overhead, pinging off the door furniture and ripping shards of wood out of this once elegant portal. I do believe I've just been a little scalped. Good job I sugared his eyes. H for step... what step? Lost bloody count now. I, N, just raise oneself up against the freshly scarred gloss paint only to remember that there's no fucking letterbox. Bugger. Bang on damaged door with both fists, hard as possible. Blimey: seem to have pushed the whole thing in. Still clutching the prize. Oh, hello Doctor Kennedy, please excuse me if I don't get up. Have this thing. Doctor Kennedy floating upside-down, hands fluttering, brow furrowing. Oh my! blurting from her lips.

CHAPTER 15: Tuesday evening

The waiting room for Heaven Interviews was close, horribly stuffy with the indistinct murmuring of a thousand anxious interviewees. Martin didn't even want an interview; he had walked in, assuming it was the mended upholstery store, but it had been like the Tardis in reverse. The building which, on the outside, had looked like one of the biggest warehouses in the world, was only a small room. And Martin was concerned that he and his fellow hopefuls were encroaching on the space of the hip young couple dining in the corner. Martin tried to grab the waiter's arm but found that his own arms were restricted and the opportunity passed. Could have really used that water. Good grief, there must have been several hundred gallons in the bowser his BMW was towing. But shouldn't have shot him. Got to hide. Martin? Shit, they found me. Martin? Try not to breath. You with us, Martin? No! I deny it! Waiter!

'Ah think he wants water,' said Dave to someone.

'Dave?'

'Hi, Marty. How's tricks?'

Martin's dreamy other world reluctantly shuffled its way out of his head and his eyes slowly focused on reality. He was in bed. Dave was sitting close to him. It was a big room, a dormitory. No, a hospital ward. There were other people, other beds.

'Where are we?' He rubbed his mouth, immediately regretting it as his injured lips made their presence felt.

'Well, ya in bed.'

Martin's memory came rushing back, the horrific image of Tara, slumped and bleeding in the car, prodding him fully awake.

'Tara! Where's Tara?' He tried to sit up but Dave restrained him with a gentle hand on the shoulder.

'She's fine buddy. Tara's jus' fine. Ya the one gotten pumped fulla lead.'

'Uh?'

'Chill, man. They got mos' of it out.'

'How long have I been here? What's the time?'

'Don' ya go frettin' 'bout the time.' Dave looked over his shoulder. 'He's just woke up, Doc.' A young man in a white coat approached the bed and leant over Martin.

'Decided to rejoin us, Mr Minchin? How are you feeling?'

'Pretty bad, actually.'

'Headache?'

'Yes, and leg.'

'You're a very lucky man.'

'Lucky?' Memories were flooding back, of the noise and the stinging and the blood and the struggle to reach the registry door. 'I was shot!'

'Winged. There's a wee bit of damage; we had to remove a few pellets, but you probably won't even have a permanent scar to show for it. I want you to stay in overnight, make sure there's no infection, but I'm sure you'll be on your way by tomorrow lunchtime.'

'Where's Tara? Er, Miss...'

'Miss Keogh's fine. We're discharging her now and she's talking to the police. Do you feel up to seeing them? They're anxious to question you but I can keep them at bay until the morning if you prefer.'

'Hey, Marty, ah heard they got Monan in the slammer. Guess they won' be needin' any mo' evidence to keep him off the street – havin' a shootout in downtown Edinburgh kinda gets the cops pissed.'

'No, it's okay. I'm happy to speak to them. Get things clear, you know?' The doctor nodded and walked away. 'What about Essex, Dave?'

'What about Essex, man?'

'Any news?' In addition to wondering whether Essex had survived his 'accident', the awful reality about what had happened to Dave's property was coming back to him.

'Not that ah've bin told, man. Cops ain' said squat to me. Moll's with one of 'em now.'

'Are we in trouble do you think?'

'Ya havin' me on, Marty?' Dave laughed. 'Ya think ya done some kinda violation?'

'Dave, I'm afraid some of your stuff got damaged.'

'Yeah, ah'm willin' to wait until ya outta here before we talk 'bout that.'

'Oh, you've seen your car?'

'Yup. An' ah got a heads-up on muh lil tractor an' trailer from Tara.'

'Oh.'

'But ah'm gettin' comfort from hearin' Ginger's Bimmer got beat up too.'

They were interrupted by the arrival of two men, one middle-aged and the other in his thirties. Both wore suits.

'Good evening, Mr Minchin. How are you feeling?' The older man spoke and didn't wait for a reply. 'My name is Detective Sergeant Campbell and my colleague here is Detective Constable Kerr. Are you up to answering a few questions about today's events?'

'Hello. Yes, of course.'

'In private, if you don't mind, Mr Dawson?' He looked at Dave, who rose, winked at Martin and left. The younger man pulled the curtain closed around the bed and produced a notebook from an inside pocket.

Martin found the questioning disappointingly concentrated on Essex and Monan: who they were, where they were from, what his connection was with them, what had provoked Monan's attack. When Martin tried to embellish his replies with background information about his time in Liverpool and County Kilkenny, and about his encounters with Evans, Campbell brushed the details aside and dragged Martin back to today. Martin tried to explain his quest, the race to claim a castle under a two centuries old instrument, but the detectives showed no interest. He asked after Essex and was told that he had been severely concussed and had some minor injuries; he was being held under a police guard in a hospital in Inverness. They believed that Beverley's car would be an insurance write-off. Essex was likely to be charged initially with car theft and unlawful possession of a firearm.

'What about Monan?' asked Martin.

'Well, we've got unlawful possession of a firearm, attempted armed robbery and two counts of causing grievous bodily harm.'

'What about attempted murder?'

'We'd never make it stick, Mr Minchin. If he was trying to kill you, he's the most incompetent shot I've ever come across. The first barrel was at ten yards, the second one not much further than that. Most people could top a fly at that range – he could barely hit fresh air.'

'I don't believe this.' Martin was devastated. What if Monan or either of his cronies wanted revenge? The way this was going, they'd be bailed and loose on the streets by the time he was out of here. Detective Constable Kerr noticed his troubled face.

'Don't you worry, Mr Minchin. After hearing what your friends had to say we put in some calls to stations here and there. It appears that now we've got our hands on these characters there are a number of investigations they might be able to help with. Representatives of Merseyside CID are driving up in the morning to conduct interviews with the suspects and we've even got a gentleman flying in from Ireland in the morning. Unless they've got very clever lawyers, my guess is that they'll be going down.'

'What about Evans?'

'A man matching his description was picked up half an hour ago and charged with stealing a horse. He's in a cell in Inverness, apparently babbling something about conger eels.'

'Well that's a big relief. I didn't fancy bumping into him again.'

'There was one other thing Mr Minchin,' added DS Campbell.

'Oh?'

'A complaint has been made against you, implicating you in a kidnapping.'

'What?'

'It seems that your wife, er...'

'Wife? Oh God, Beverley!'

'Yes,' he glanced at his notebook. 'Mrs Beverley Minchin-Waverley.'

'She's alright then?'

'Apparently so, but she's said to be on the warpath.'

'What happened? I mean, it's not exactly my fault.'

'She was abducted in the boot of her own car.'

'Hmm,' Martin interjected. 'Not sure I would call it "her own car".' Campbell ignored him and continued.

'And she was abandoned in the middle of a field, with only one shoe.'

'Where was that? The field I mean.'

'In Cheshire, a couple of miles from the M6. She is extremely angry and demanding your arrest.'

'Hopping mad I would think!' Martin beamed at his own cleverness, briefly tolerating the pain in his lips. DC Kerr sniggered, but Campbell's expression remained deadpan. Martin quickly added: 'I think I know where her missing shoe is, which should help the Wiltshire force's clear-up rate.'

'Very good, Mr Minchin.'

'Still,' Martin stifled a giggle. 'Perhaps the experience will have made her a more well-rounded person.'

'Perhaps.'

'Better able to see the bigger picture.'

'Indeed.'

'And therefore less likely to lose her rag at minor inconveniences.'

'You may hope so, Mr Minchin. But there's an officer called Dee who intends to interview you when you return to – where is it? – Shimbley.'

'Oh, deep joy.'

'I shouldn't worry. She's bound to forgive you when she's over the shock and cognizant of the circumstances, isn't she?'

'Bound to, ha ha.'

'Anyway, I think we have all we need for now. We'll take full statements tomorrow of course, so please don't be off without calling me first.' Campbell placed a small business card on the bedside unit and tapped it with his forefinger. 'It may be as much in your interests to put these people away as it is in mine.'

Left alone, still surrounded by the curtain, Martin lay still, staring at the ceiling. He realised that he was famished. He wondered whether modern NHS trusts provided room service. Since his birth he had never been in a hospital other than as a visitor. Perhaps they allowed patients to phone out for curry or pizza. The very thought of a prawn madras and onion bhaji made him want to shout for service. The trouble was that he didn't know who was out there, in the ward; he didn't wish to wake anyone. He looked in vain for a button to push but couldn't see one. A chink opened in the curtain.

'Martin?'

'Tara! Oh Tara, are you alright?' She entered his little semi-private realm and approached him cautiously. Her bottom lip was cut, bruised and swollen and a lopsided, white bandage circled the top of her head. He noticed the large stain of rusty blood on her T-shirt. 'Oh my God!'

'I'm fine, you idiot! It's you who's properly injured – shot no less! My poor, darling Martin. I'm not going to come near your head and I'm not going to kiss you, okay?'

'Yes, that'll be fine. Come here.' He patted the bed.

'I don't want to sit on your wounded leg now.'

'It's the other one.' He nodded towards his left. 'Look at your bandage. I saw you bleeding. You looked like you were dead. What happened?'

'He slammed his bloody gun into the back of my head.' She pointed at her bandage. 'It's cut and it bled a lot but it didn't need stitches or anything. They cleaned it up. I'm going to have to lay off standing on my head for a while.'

'Me too. Grazed by shot.'

'Not much of a marksman, thank God. Shit!' She winced. 'My mouth feels as bad as yours looks. I'll not be kissing you again unless my back's to the wall. How's the leg?'

'Throbbing. The doctor doesn't seem too concerned. I get the impression it's easier to starve to death in here.'

'You're hungry, then? Feel up to a trip?'

'What trip?' He had visions of limping through the streets of Edinburgh in his hospital gown. Tara stood and drew back the curtain to reveal a wheelchair.

'Have wheels, will eat,' she said. 'I promised we'd be quiet,' she added in a conspiratorial whisper.

'Where are we going?'

'Family room. Dave's got takeaway, Molly's bought some wine and stuff.' She helped Martin from his bed. As he put a little weight onto his injured leg, he was grateful for the wheelchair. In addition to the insistent, throbbing pain in his damaged leg, all of his joints ached as though he had just completed a decathlon. Tara wrestled to guide him between the beds in the direction of the double doors at the end.

'Come back for me next, my dear,' called a man from a bed in the corner.

'You make sure you bring him back in one piece, now,' said a woman with a giggle.

The Family Support Room was a revelation. In the centre was a little galley, complete with microwave cooker and cupboard units. On one side of it was a sitting room area with sofas, armchairs, coffee tables and a TV. On the other was space to eat, with plenty of tables and chairs. Dave and Molly both occupied the galley, Dave examining the contents of various tinfoil cartons while Molly was struggling to pull the cork out of a bottle of wine. They were the only people in the room.

'Martin!' Molly abandoned the bottle and ran over to him. He raised his hands to encourage a gentle approach. 'You hero! Gunfight in Dundee Walk! Wow! How are you?'

'Never better.'

'I'll bet. And what about you,' she added turning her attention to Tara. 'Is the pain easing at all now?'

'Yeah, I'll live. This poor chap's crying with the hunger, though, aren't you, my big brave soldier?'

'What do y'all fancy, then?' Dave spread his arms towards the steaming packages, like the Pope blessing the congregation in St Peter's Square. 'Ah figured that John Wayne here deserved a choice, so ah got everythin': Chinese, Indian, pizza. Moll's on the bar.'

'Hold on,' said Molly. 'There's a special guest, someone who very much wanted to be here.'

Martin looked around. What was she talking about? Who was she talking about? Except for the four of them, the room was unoccupied.

'Right on time!' Molly said. The door opened a little and the owlish features of Doctor Kennedy peeped in.

'May I join you?' she asked.

'Yeah, come on in, Doc!' said Dave. 'His Lordship's awake an' the bad guys are in the slammer, so let's party, huh?'

'Oh good.' She entered, carrying a bulging carrier bag. 'I wonder, Professor, if you might kindly deal with these.' With a sly grin, she handed the bag to Dave, who pulled a bottle of champagne from it, then another. She turned her attention to Martin and fiddled with an envelope. 'Now then, Mr Minchin...'

'Please, call me Martin.'

'Yes. Martin.' She rifled through some sheets of paper, frowning. 'Yes. Quite so. Ah, here we are. This is your receipt.' She handed a sheet of paper to Martin with a flourish.

'Thank you,' he said, glancing at it. Receipt for what? He didn't recall paying for anything. Before he had time to read it the cork popped from the first bottle of champagne and slammed into the ceiling. Dave struggled to direct the fizzing stream into a tumbler.

'It's yours.' Doctor Kennedy stood in front of Martin, grinning down at him. 'You did it, Martin. Congratulations, Laird of Cuiphur. Your *very* good health.' She took the glass proffered by Dave, held it aloft, then drank.

Laird, eh? I've got the castle? The Great Well? I'm a bloody land owner. A bloody great castle owner! *Cheers!*

Epilogue

On the grounds that Lockkeeper's Cottage was vandalised before he had taken up residence, Martin graciously allowed the sympathetic and unusually accommodating vendor to undertake the entire cost of its repair and refurbishment. On the question of whether this was influenced at all by the considerable interest shown in his case by local and national media he had neither need nor wish to comment. With its name restored to Loch Cuiphur Cottage – no less baffling than its previous identity to those ignorant of its history – it would serve as Martin's base when in England.

Ah yes, because henceforth Martin would be living mainly at his castle, if not yet actually in it. The hapless victim of an array of violent crimes, he spent much of his compensation on a fleet of caravans which were installed in the courtyard. Venture capital from the Highland Industrial Development Agency saw the first truckloads of machinery entering the grounds before the end of the autumn – Cuiphur Spring Water would be in the shops within twelve months. A handsome grant from the Highland Historical Buildings Trust would meet the cost of restoring Cuiphur's tower. Scottish Telecom used a photo-opportunity to install digital communications with the outside world, enabling Minchin Associates to carry on its business from a laptop computer instead of from the rooms over Kebabbaburger.

Molly and Dave allowed their mutual lust to get the better of them on that Tuesday night, in a bed-and-breakfast establishment where the noise of their love making was matched only by that of their laughter. They were charged in full for the breakfast which they missed, and were asked not to return. Molly's letter of resignation to Exeter University was drafted soon afterwards.

Tara and Martin's baby is due in the early spring, just in time for it to gaze from the battlements upon its inheritance and skipping lambs and bareback pony riders and accountants with lucky stuff in their genes

And a small fortune bubbling merrily
From the fertile ground beneath
This magical pile called Cuiphur.

Unless you have just opened this book for the first time and turned straight to this page, I hope you have enjoyed Dirty Deeds as much as I enjoyed writing it. Overleaf are some notes. I'll endeavour to provide news and up-to-date information on my website:

www.jamie-buchanan.com

Many thanks for your support.

Jamie B

About the castle

The edifice depicted on the cover of this book is Buchanan Castle – no connection – photographed in 1989 by the author who happily admits that it gave him some inspiration. This rather lovely ruin, not far from the bonnie, bonnie banks of Loch Lomond, is not quite the ancient monument that you might expect. It was built in 1854 by the Duke of Montrose to replace Clan Buchanan's ancestral seat which had been destroyed by fire. Apparently the Duke and his family preferred life in London, so their 'castle' saw little use, except during World War II when, serving as a hospital, it played host to Rudolf Hess who had been injured parachuting into Scotland in a bid to negotiate a peace with the British government. Anyway, in order to avoid property tax, the owners had the roofs removed in 1954 and the picture reveals what then happens to an otherwise sound building. The photograph below was taken in 2014 by Ben Buchanan – the author's son – and shows the progress made by Mother Nature.

About the author

Another crumbling pile, Jamie Buchanan was born in Richmond, Surrey, on the southwest edge of London, in 1955. His first career was in the advertising agency business, which he pursued with varying degrees of success and failure for 25 formative years. Next came 16 years on the client side as marketer in a highly esoteric branch of the IT industry. From childhood however he had harboured an ambition to be a professional creative writer, not of advertising copy and marketing hyperbole but of entertaining and saleable novels. Now, with Dirty Deeds finally seeing daylight, it remains to be seen how successful he is in this endeavour. Jamie lives in a small hamlet in Buckinghamshire, England, near the top of a Chiltern hill.

In production at Fredbird Publishing

A new novel by Jamie Buchanan, due in 2016

A collection of poems by Archie Buchanan

A novel by Archie Buchanan

www.fredbird-publishing.com

Printed in Great Britain
by Amazon.co.uk, Ltd.,
Marston Gate.